WHAT SHADOWS MAY DREAM

JESSE'S LIBERATION

by

Andrew S. Banderas

The characters and events portrayed in this book are fictitious. Any similarity to real persons, living or dead, is coincidental and not intended by the author.

WHAT SHADOWS MAY DREAM: JESSE'S LIBERATION.

Paperback ISBN: 978-1-7362242-0-5

E-book ISBN: 978-1-7362242-1-2

Cover art & illustration by: Joey Akra – theakravision

Author photograph: Emily Van Gorder

www.shadowdreambook.com

Printed in the United States of America

For Hank,

Thank you for the minds you filled, the hearts you inspired, and the souls you saved with your passion for literature. Thank you for believing me and for putting your money where your mouth is. While the edition of *Writer's Market* you gave me is incredibly outdated now, it has remained on my shelf and always will. This first one's for you.

What Shadows May Dream

Jesse's Liberation

Jesse I
Me Llamaste

His father stood in the kitchen with one hand keeping the refrigerator door open, and the other holding a brown bottle of cervéza. Papá was a mountain, even more so in his wife-beater undershirt and boxers because his muscles, tattoos, and body hair seemed to burst from the seams. Jesse watched him stare into the open fridge and Jesse said hello, but Papá kept staring like he didn't hear him.

He ran to him, getting between his papá and the fridge, just wanting to be in his arms. The fridge was a building now, dark and gray with covered slits for windows. The clank of empty glass bottles on concrete echoed off invisible walls, and angry yelling followed it. Jesse just wanted to see his father's face at least, but he never got to; Papá was gone and Jesse was surrounded by darkness and strange voices.

The giant concrete building loomed behind him and he turned to face it. His lungs felt solid and his chest felt like exploding. He needed to get away from the gray and windowless edifice. Other voices called out to him as he attempted to run. They seemed familiar, but none stood out distinctly.

"You can't run."

"You need to be the man now, Jesse."

"Puta."

"You're fucked."

"...Got my back, hermano?"

"It's just business…"

"Mamá!"

"... day. And a new future!"

A gunshot rang out in the distance and echoed. As the shot reverberated off distant and unseen walls, it turned into a siren from afar. It wailed and became faster and closer. Metal doors opened and clanged shut behind Jesse.

He turned around and saw masked police in riot gear rushing out of trucks and vans. They charged past Jesse as if he weren't there. His eyes followed them and crowds of loud and anxious people cheered them on down a large street as they watched from the sidewalks. Jesse's view was blocked by the brigade of police, charging shoulder-to-shoulder in a straight line. All he could make out in the distance above people's heads were handmade signs and banners of various colors and designs, wavering umbrellas, and clouds of smoke.

The ongoing march of heavy boots on pavement seemed to skip a previously undetectable beat and a subtle rumble could be felt, like one of Jesse's cousins' had rolled up and was bumping music. But with this sensation, there was no particular tempo. Jesse thought it was thunder but it seemed so close. The tide of black uniforms began to vibrate with the rumbling.

Then they all blurred together. The excited and angry faces of the nearby crowds abruptly changed to wide-eyed surprise and fear as they all looked at Jesse. They vanished into dark mist that was a dense black.

This shadow grew like a stretched silhouette, shifting shapes of branches, tentacles, and wisps of cloth. Jesse could see other shadows reach out in the shapes of rifles, reaching arms, blades, ropes, and other things he couldn't completely recognize.

He began to hear faint but deep yells and screams float in and out of hearing, loosely strung together by whispered warnings and sharp words, all of which were in languages and dialects both familiar and foreign to Jesse. The shadow slowly cast itself upward, as if a prismed hologram that sucked in light instead of reflecting it. He saw faces, clothes, limbs, claws, eyes, hair, fur, weapons, scales, and more reflected in the shifting prisms of shadow as it swirled, recoiled, clouded, shaped, seeped, and crept closer to

Jesse. He was frozen in place but was able to see that more shadows were forming behind this horror. They began to move toward Jesse, then past him. They went on farther than he could see.

As the first one passed through, Jesse felt all of the fear, pain, anger, confusion, and despair of his worst nightmare, the same one he would have as a young boy every time he was sick with fever and he'd have to cry out to Mamá, too scared to go back to sleep. Then in the same instant, he felt and saw the same kinds of nightmares completely unfamiliar to him.

Jesse was still pissing himself when he woke up screaming at the top of his lungs. Sure enough, his abuelita rushed up and he heard his little sister crying.

"¡Ay, dios mío! ¿Mijo, what happened? Are you sick?" She came to the side of his mattress and wiped the sweat from his forehead and checked his temperature.

Marcy, Jesse's youngest sibling, scrambled across their bedroom, opened the bedroom door, and stood at the doorway. "Lita? What should I do?"

"What… what are you doing?" Jesse yelled out with anger, balled around a bit of relief.

"Jesús, mi nieto. Me llamaste. In your sleep, you called to me."

"I did?" Jesse asked, half-asleep still. He looked behind him on the bed and saw his younger brother Alfredo on the far side of the mattress, turned to the wall with his one pillow smashed over his head and ears. "I didn't even know I said anything."

Jesse didn't really sleep the rest of the morning. He tossed and turned on his bare and moist mattress, trying to fall back asleep. He got drowsy enough when his phone alarm went off, and he heavily fumbled to hit the snooze button. Finally, Lita came into the room, rapidly nagging at Jesse in Spanish as if she didn't need to breathe. She yanked his pillow out from under his head and threw it on the floor. She placed her phone on the dresser across the room and tapped a button. Ranchero music blared from her phone: accordions, horns, and all.

"Cuanto tiempo busque tu cariño," blared out of the phone. Then she walked out and left the door open, still mumbling and lecturing all the way into the kitchen. "Y anduve borracho, borracho perdido," cried an incredibly sad man. Jesse sat up and rubbed his eyes. "De tanto quererte, Yo me acuerdo que estaba chiquillo y no," the song trudged on. Today was his first day at his new school. He'd missed the first week because he was in Mexico with Lita, Marcy, and Alfredo. It had been his last chance for a long time to see Papá. "Iba a escuela porque ni aguantaba seis horas," the man bellowed from the phone.

"Shut up, Vicente. I fucking get it," Jesse mumbled toward the phone. About fifteen minutes later, Jesse sat down at the kitchen table with a plate of fried juevos topped with salsa, accompanied with refried beans, and a slice of Bimbo.

"Jesús, por qué -- why do you have nightmares?" Mrs. Ramirez commented to Jesse, shaking her head, and placed a glass of Tropico next to his plate.

"I don't," Jesse griped.

"Adios!" Dominique yelled out as she ushered Alfredo and Marcy out the front door as quickly as she could. Her own kids, Alexia and Antonio, would continue sleeping in their room until one of them woke up, and Lita would make them breakfast. Jesse wondered how much they had heard last night from sleeping next door to him. The front door closed shut, followed by the metal screen door outside a few seconds after.

"They're just dreams. You don't know what you're talking about," Jesse replied back coldly.

"¿Qué quieres decir? You think I don't know you're not sleeping? Todo esto con los gritos y el pipi en la cama. What is happening to you, Jesús?"

Jesse's face turned flush. "It was a fucking accident! Don't tell anyone I-- about the bed. And I sleep fine. You don't know anything."

"Jesús Ignacio Ramirez de Castillo, your brothers paid the price for you to be here. Hugo -- God watch over him -- is in jail, and Erik -- God rest his soul -- is…" her voice quivered before she regained herself again. "Enough, Jesús. Life is no party. You destroyed this family. *Mi* familia."

Now Jesse got really quiet. He had been waiting for this, actually. Lita finally said it out loud: he was to blame for his oldest brother being in jail. And his other brother, Erik, was dead because of his stupid actions. Now starting at a new school, she was right: this was it, his last chance. He'd messed up big time. He couldn't mess up again.

Mrs. Ramirez continued, "There is no one left to make tus problemas go away. You have to hold on and face what comes to you. Ponte los pantalones, por Dios."

"Put my own pants on? I fucking know these are my problems. I remember every day because you never let me forget with your goddamn prayers for Erik and Hugo and Papá. But none for me!" Jesse stood up from his chair and flipped his breakfast across the table. "Fuck this. I didn't tell Papá or Junior to stand up for me. They should have just left me alone for the cops. I probably would have been out of juvie by now, anyway."

Mrs. Ramirez stood leaning against the counter and didn't flinch when egg yolk oozed off the table's edge to the kitchen floor in front of her. She stood there calmly, looking past Jesse as he stormed out of the kitchen and slammed the front door on his way out of the apartment.

Jesse II
Welcome to Portola High School

"Fuckers."

Jesse Ramirez's stomach grumbled as the last of the cafeteria service windows closed shut just ahead of him. The workers inside pretended to ignore him.

By the time he had walked through the front of Portola High School around 8:00 a.m., the tardy bell had already rung and most students were in class. He was exhausted and felt the weight of his eyelids drag his entire body down. His first day at his new school was going as well as he could have imagined.

He then turned toward the 800 building. The crinkled print-out of his new schedule read for first period: *Spanish I - Padilla - Room 811.*

There were still a few stragglers scurrying to various classrooms when he entered the hallway of the old brick building.

Room 811 wasn't too hard to find as he quickly noticed all of the odd-numbered classes to his left. The hallway was mostly cleared out except for two guys leaning on the lockers across from 811. They both had earbuds in and bobbed their heads in different synchronizations.

The bigger of the two was fair-skinned with a fade haircut and wore a baggy white t-shirt with black sweatpants. He had all-white sneakers and a black Corsairs football cap with a silver pirate's skull on the front. The wide-framed, calmly intimidating young man flicked his fingers in front of him so they snapped as they flailed.

The smaller one was a squirrely-looking, dark Latino-mixed kid who wore a gray t-shirt with the words "Save the Trees" on the front over a graphic of a few marijuana leaves. A beat-up skateboard rested under his foot, rolling back and forth as he cussed. He slouched as if he was always ready to dodge something, his head and neck slightly twisting to catch any surprises.

As Jesse approached, their conversation trailed off with expressionless stares toward him. "What?" Jesse exclaimed, irritated.

"You look lost, homie. Are you lost?" the bigger Latino quickly asked with a cocked eyebrow.

Jesse snickered. "Psh. Nah. I'm right where I should be. What about you?" he asked, lifting his arm and pointing his index and middle fingers together directly toward the cholo's face, then the skater's. "You schoolies need some directions or some shit?"

The skater and the cholo looked at each other and laughed. They nodded and dapped, ignoring Jesse. The cholo said to his friend, "A'ight, Racha. Stay black." Then the cholo walked away, giving Jesse one last look and a chuckle as he passed him.

"Blunt or die, bitch." Racha watched the big cholo swagger down the hallway and open a classroom door, stick his head inside, and then continue trudging down the hall. A male teacher in 808 opened his door and poked his head out, staring down the hall at the cholo. "Hey! Anthony, is that you? Get back over here!"

But he walked on without flinching, lost in the deafening beats of his earbuds, all the way out of building 800.

"Damn that kid. And you two," he yelled, now glaring at Racha and Jesse. "Get to class! I'm calling security!" He then shut his door.

Both Racha and Jesse said "puta" in unison as his door shut closed. Then they looked at each other for a second, nodded, and grinned.

"So what's up with you?" Racha asked. "Never seen you before. Must be a newbie." Racha asked Jesse. "You slinging? Rolling?" He then tried to get stern and more serious, despite his smaller stature and youthful voice. "You in a squad?"

"Nah. I'm just… I'm trying to get through this shit, you know?" Jesse threw up his arms and gestured toward the walls surrounding them.

Racha nodded. "Alright, I feel you. These pendejos are trying to take my Moms to court again. Fuck that, you know what I'm saying? I feel you, I feel you."

"Yeah, fuck that." Jesse hesitated, then added. "Fuck the police."

Racha stared back at him with a slow nod.

Jesse went on. "And fuck this school, and fuck this Spanish class. I haven't even been to it yet and I already hate it."

"Oh, no shit? Right here with Padilla?" Racha asked, gesturing at 811. His back was slouched, and his arm bent lazily toward the door.

"Uh, I think. 811, right? I don't know this puto's name."

"Yeah, yeah, Padilla. Fucking boring. He's a joto, too. Fucking cocksucker and shit."

"Fuck."

"Yeah, I feel you. I feel you."

The two boys then stood in silence for a few seconds, nodding at each other. Jesse looked at the door and back at Racha. They both shrugged at each other and then walked in.

Mr. Padilla was leading the class through choral practice of irregular verbs and didn't skip a beat when he saw Racha and Jesse walk in. He continued on speaking with the class and simultaneously gestured at Jesse, waved with a smile, and pointed at a desk for him to sit in; and just as quickly and smoothly, he continued on with the class in their practice and gave Racha a stern look while pointing at his watch. Mr. Padilla was calling him out on being late again.

"Oh, it's 8:10, homie. If your watch is broken, get a new one, pendejo! Nyeehhhhh!" Racha howled, but was only half heard over the chorus of the classroom. Padilla shook his head with an eye roll and continued with leading the class in their practice.

The rest of Spanish class was a blur for Jesse. There certainly was some kind of lesson and discussion on diphthongs and acentos, but all Jesse paid attention to and remembered was Maria Fonseca.

From his seat in the back of the class, he tried to see her face completely as she sat unimpressed but still scribbled occasional notes in a lined notebook where she sat along the side wall near the front. Her honey-brown hair waved and curled at the tips like a fire stretching down and outward, flames licking at her tanned shoulders. The shape of her big eyes convinced Jesse that she could see things in the world he couldn't. She wore a white sleeveless top that was see-through enough for Jesse to notice the floral embroideries on her bra underneath. A delicate-looking gold watch was strapped to her left wrist, which she kept turning toward her to see the time slowly pass. She had squeezed into a bright blue skirt that was currently riding up to her bronzed mid-thighs, revealing the toned curves of her muscular legs.

Maria Fonseca felt eyes on her body and instinctively tugged her skirt out toward her knees and adjusted her blouse to make sure it was covering the side of her bra.

Jesse couldn't take his eyes off of her: there was something beyond her sexiness, something deeper. She seemed so innocent and beautiful in a way that he knew deep down and not so much saw with his eyes.

He knew this when Racha said something in response to Mr. Padilla's explanation of how a "small D" has to be used instead of a "big D" for a word. The class laughed and Maria turned her head to watch Racha be a fool. He could see the side of her gentle face now that she turned toward the class, but her flowing hair still covered part of it. There he still saw an effortless grin that dropped his stomach, and a twinkle in her gaze just before she rolled her eyes that made Jesse feel like the world had just ended and was created again in that twinkle.

Jesse convinced himself that in order for this girl to have this effect on him, she must have something or come from somewhere different than other girls he had come across.

"Damn, Newbie. You want to be her pet or what? You feel me?" Racha blurted out.

"'Ey, fuck off, puta." Jesse could feel his face getting hot and sweat breaking down his back. "It's not like that. I'd fuck her," he said, perhaps too carelessly.

Racha scoffed back, "Yeah, get in line."

"She taken?"

Racha shrugged.

"Don't be a bitch," Jesse said in a threatening whisper.

"I don't care about her. Why bother with what you can't have, Newbie?"

"So she has a boyfriend?" Jesse asked, and he almost showed his disappointment.

"¡No mames, guey!" Racha let out a screeching laugh. "Nyehhhh!"

Mr. Padilla stopped writing under the document camera and stared over the podium at Racha. "Señor Villalobos. ¡Por favor!"

Racha ignored him and continued on with Jesse. "Don't fuck around with Maria. That bitch is bad news. Trust."

Jesse thought for a moment as Mr. Padilla returned to his lesson, shaking his head in annoyance. Jesse turned again to Racha. "A'ight, then. Who is this guy? So, you know, I can swing at him first. If I got to."

Racha seemed to hesitate at first, then he seemed to make up his mind. "Oh, you'll know him when you see him, Newbie," he said with a slight grin. "He'll be the one with Maria sucking on his face. Nyehhhhhhh!"

Mr. Padilla reacted almost instantly this time. "Rogelio!"

"You can't call me that. Shut up," Racha replied loudly, but he looked at the floor when he said it, and directed the statement to no one and nowhere in particular.

Mr. Padilla straightened up and sighed. "Not this again, Mr. Villalobos. Do we need to write another referral or can we get along today?" Racha was silent, and Mr. Padilla turned his attention to a student nearby who was raising her hand. "Un momento, por favor, Sara." He then looked back at Racha. "Well?"

Racha didn't say anything and began tagging something on his desk. A few minutes went by. Then Racha got bored with etching something on his desk and got up. He started casually walking toward the door.

Mr. Padilla was crouching near the front, helping Sara with acentos on the whiteboard. He stood up quickly and sternly yelled out, "Villalobos! No one has been excused yet. Return to--"

Racha cut him off. "Bathroom. Emergency." He kept walking, raised his arm up to throw a peace sign behind him without looking, and shoved himself out the door.

"Rogelio! I'm calling security!" Mr. Padilla uselessly yelled from the front of the class. He looked at the class and put his hands on his hips. He shook his head and walked to his desk to pick up the phone. He dialed and put the receiver to his ear, waiting for the phone to ring on the other side, but instead he heard the bell ring. "Dammit," then he slammed the phone receiver back down. The classroom erupted into a cacophony of binders snapping and backpacks zipping, heavy chairs and desks grinding against linoleum flooring, students talking and shouting, all while Mr. Padilla was trying to yell over it and explain the night's homework.

But Jesse hardly noticed the entire altercation. He didn't want to be anywhere else at that moment, and he certainly didn't want to take his eyes off of Maria. He waited near the back of the classroom to see which direction Maria was heading out to class so he could talk to her; he needed her to know that he existed.

She gathered her things and walked toward the back. Jesse watched her turn and face his direction. She stepped with a confidence and grace that made Jesse think she was a natural at this school thing. Now that she was completely facing Jesse, he was awestruck at how beautiful she really was. Maria walked past him without ever looking up at him and he wanted to stop her, then he decided to follow her, and for the first time ever, he couldn't make an approach. The door clicked behind her as she left, and Mr. Padilla looked up at Jesse, now the last and only student in the class, as Mr. Padilla was shuffling papers at his desk.

"Ah, yes, Mr. Ramirez. I'm so glad you decided to stay after class and get acquainted with m--"

Jesse snapped out of his trance, let out an annoyed "Psh!" and then quickly left the classroom. Stepping through the doorway, Jesse found a renewed confidence to approach Maria since as far as he could tell, she had no idea who he was, or the kind of past he had for that matter.

He looked around for her in the busy hallway but didn't see any trace of her. He realized that he had another class to find and more teachers to be unimpressed by. There would be other girls, too, he reassured himself. Hot ones. But could any of them make him feel that same way Maria did, with just a look?

As the day dragged on, Jesse kept an eager eye out for Maria. Every time he was about to walk into a new classroom, he held his breath just before turning the doorknob and exhaled quietly as he pulled the door open and entered, subtly but carefully scanning the room for that fiery hair or her white top and blue skirt.

At lunchtime, Jesse didn't want to do anything else but get another glimpse at Maria, but wandering the campus and looking like a lost kid didn't seem too helpful or favorable in his mind. He found an unclaimed wall in the shade that he could put his back against as he ate dried out potato slices with watery ketchup and a spongy chicken patty suffocated by a pair of stale wheat buns. He tossed his condiment packets on the ground after each squeeze, noticing that the label read "Catsup" and below it in smaller print "Tomato Sauce."

"What the fuck?" he said to himself annoyedly. He shook his head and powered through the rest of his meal. The rest of the time his eyes scanned the passersby, looking for that fiery hair, those defined legs in that surprisingly loud blue skirt, the golden glisten of her fragile watch. But still, he felt like he needed more chances to interact with her.

By the end of his last class, sixth-period Reading and Writing Support, Jesse told himself that at least he had one class with her and that was so much better than nothing.

In the same moment as that realization, from out in the hallway Jesse heard the unmistakable, unlikeable, and unforgiving siren that was Racha's laugh: "Nyehhhhhhh!" He looked to the door, which had a window in it, and a few seconds later saw Racha pass by. For a split second, their eyes met, and then Racha was gone.

Jesse considered leaping out of his seat and running out so he could ask Racha more questions about Maria. Then Racha popped back into the frame of the window. He nodded his chin upward and grinned at Jesse, then followed up by flipping him off and smiling. Jesse smirked at him, made sure Mrs. Richardson wasn't paying attention, and then returned the favor. Racha motioned to Jesse to come out into the hall. Mrs. Richardson was still at her desk with a student and didn't have eyes on Jesse. He grabbed his backpack and calmly but quickly walked to the back door of the classroom where Racha was waiting outside.

He got about halfway when Mrs. Richardson stood up and exclaimed, "Excuse me, uh… Jesse! Jesse, where do you think you're--"

"Bathroom," Jesse interrupted confidently. "Emergency." From the hall as he walked out the door, the class heard a screeching "Nyehhhhhh!" followed by Jesse's laughter.

Aron I
The Tilson Plan

Aron shot up from his bed as soon as his eyes fluttered open. He could still feel the earth pound with thunderous footsteps from the beast that chased him on the Plane just a few seconds ago. Sitting at the edge of his bed, he rubbed his eyes with frustration.

Should I try to go back? He wondered to himself. He looked at the clock on his desk across the bedroom. *There's still time. But this guy is too strong for me,* he grudgingly confessed to himself. *Something's not right here.*

He pushed himself off the mattress and walked to his desk. He began shuffling through various documents, photos, notes, and graphs. He let out a long breath through his nose and hung his head down with his eyes closed.

Think, Aron, he commanded himself. *Why can't you get past this guy?* Aron sat down at his desk, resting his jaw on the palms of his hands. In his mind, he began to replay the confrontation he just had on the Plane. He recalled back to the beginning.

Before going to the Plane, Aron began in his subconscious, where all plebs and Readers begin. He was in his old backyard from childhood: in Georgia, at his Uncle Myron's house. He was standing in front of the big chicken-wire cage where his uncle kept his pet mongoose, Magoo. How his uncle had obtained that mongoose and managed to keep it for so long, Aron never knew.

He walked past the cage toward a rusted, iron hatch door that was slightly raised from the ground. Aron reached down and began turning the wheel that released the hatch door. With one last, long screech from the wheel, Aron pulled the hatch open and let it rest on its hinges, pointing straight up. There was nothing but pure darkness inside.

"Once more down the mongoose hole," he said as he looked over his shoulder to Magoo. Then he jumped in.

There was a quick flash of bright, purpled light and suddenly he landed. Aron was atop a hill that overlooked a small valley. On the opposite side of the valley stood a larger hill. He was standing exactly where he had left his sigil the night before on the Plane. It dissipated underneath him into a tiny cloud of purple dust.

In the violet darkness of the mimicked night, Aron peered around at the vast and mysterious topography of the Plane. He was amazed yet again with its layout. He thought about all of the weird, terrifying, and beautiful things he had seen so far during his years on the Plane. He also wondered about the citadels, people, and creatures that had been here before, and what things still remained and skulked from ancient years.

He began navigating down the hill and then started to think about what things he would leave on the Plane, if anything. *What things have I built that will last, after I'm gone?* Aron reflected.

He thought about the first autonomous golem he created when he was starting college. In his early years on the Plane, Aron had woven simple golems through the guidance of his mentor, Yusef. When Aron was ready to graduate to advanced independent golems and Yusef instructed him to go with a simple mud or stone one, Aron was too excited. He wanted more of a challenge and something really worth remembering as his first self-operating golem. He studied the biology of a carp to weave it with an elder tree sapling, a tree fabled to have protective powers against ancient evil.

The thought of those two contradictory organisms combined together to make a golem was amusing to Aron, and it was such an odd pairing that once he had thought it up, his curiosity wouldn't be satisfied until he actually made it and saw it come to life.

In fact, Aron had thought of a name for his golem before he had even made it. At the time, Yusef had recently taught him about Japanese Shinto gods, so he decided on naming his golem Ebisu, after the god of luck for fishermen and agriculture.

It fit perfectly, Aron had thought, for a golem that would undoubtedly accompany him on his travels through the Plane. He wondered what exactly it would look like and how it would function as a fish and a tree. Perhaps he should have thought it out more clearly.

Aron didn't like thinking about Ebisu. He had nightmares about it for years. And even his nightmares couldn't completely recall how gruesome and terrifying Ebisu had turned out to be. Its scaled bark and slimy tentacles reeked of decayed earth and sea. Ebisu's amber eyes fluttered with wild alertness. They had a depth matched only by Aron's regret and fear of his own imagination and curiosity.

A shiver ran through Aron as he thought about where Ebisu was lurking now, and what it had become after so many years if it had survived. He wondered about all of the other monstrosities he had created, by accident or with intent, and what other horrors other Readers had carelessly or maliciously woven on the Plane. *When it's my time to pass on, I hope I leave behind something more than just monsters,* he thought again.

Aron now refocused on the valley below him. Making his way around a small town, Aron headed for a particular street of houses that rested on the foothills. He was very close to finding the den of Bob Tilson after weeks of researching and mapping. Aron even spent a few nights managing to avoid wraiths, but he eventually ended up having to fight one off.

It wasn't uncommon to come across a wraith in areas where many people slept. The chances of someone having nightmares, and thus a wraith being present, were much higher in cities and dense suburban neighborhoods. The odds of their presence and their ferociousness increased even further where suffering occurred. Fear, anger, and sadness were the main elements that caused wraiths to form on the Plane.

Poor folks suffer greatly and have lots of problems, Aron knew. *But you don't really know how bad they are until you run into one of their wraiths,* he had thought.

That wasn't to say that there weren't wraiths out in the rural parts. Things were just so spread out that it was harder to actually run into one.

Then there was the putrisomn. Aron spent the next half hour carefully navigating through various hives of it as he made his way through the quiet mountain town. He came across the glossy form in blacks, browns, dark purples, grays, and greens. It grew thick like strong oaks and sagged like weeping willows. The putrisomn spread onto walls like veins and spread out on its own like vines. In other places, the proliferation formed pentagons, carapaces, and spirals.

However he found it, raw putrisomn always seemed to have a faint pulse, as if alive. Aron always felt uneasy, like the putrisomn had eyes, but it didn't watch what he did as much as it watched what he was feeling. But he had grown used to it by this point, and after all of the months of hard work he had dedicated to finding Bob Tilson's hideout on the Plane, he wasn't about to lose his cool over some overgrown putrisomn.

Of course, Aron knew where Bob Tilson officially was the entire time. Everyone in America did. He was the U.S. Congressman from Meridian, Idaho. When he was elected last year, he publicly stated that undocumented immigrants "are only good for one thing, and that's cleaning up after real Americans." The United States was already overpopulated, he reasoned. He wanted to change the law so that green cards were no longer given out and immigrants living in the States could not be naturalized into U.S. citizens.

"I know that brings up another big question," Congressman Tilson had said. "What do we do with the illegals that are here already?" Aron remembered watching Tilson on the television when he made this statement on the floor of Congress. Tilson gave an innocent shrug at this last question he raised. "Well, we can't hunt them down and exterminate them like animals, and deporting them takes too much time and money," he said with a grin. "A wall was a good idea. But it's expensive, slow, and can be circumvented."

Then he held up something small and white, pinched in between his thumb and his forefinger. "And we can't let them keep multiplying, either. So here's our answer." The camera zoomed in on his smiling face and the pill he held. "This little pill prevents the patient from having any children. It also contains nanochips that take an imprint of the patient's DNA, which registers with a government-issued identification number that will be used to electronically track the patient. The illegals that are here already can stay. But real, honest American jobs can't be taken by them anymore. They'll have special jobs. And they can't have kids anymore. That's the price to pay to live in America without being an American." By this point, Tilson's grin turned into a full smile. His arms went up in the air to welcome the applause from other congressional members.

Aron had thought that angry constituents would have dragged Tilson out of his office by the end of the day after giving that speech, but that never happened. In fact, Congress members from his party promoted it, calling it "the Tilson Plan." And of course, the President had endorsed it immediately. It wasn't his idea, but it might as well have been. Besides, anything more controversial to get the public's attention away from his own ongoing political gaffes and investigations he very much welcomed.

Tilson was becoming a lightning rod for public attention. Some people had even talked about having him run as vice president in the next election. Others were starting to suggest that he should run in place of the current President, who was deeply embattled with political opponents on both sides of the aisle amid impeachment charges and various scandals.

Aron had seen this story before: the charismatic man who makes many promises of solving the imaginary problems of his people, all the time convincing them of what and whom they should fear. It had many forms throughout history. He saw it in the patrician politicians from ancient Rome leading to the fall of the Republic. He saw it in revolutionaries who started with good intentions but brought horrific results to their own people, as did Robespierre, and Mao Zhedong. And he definitely saw it in leaders with the worst of intentions, like Hitler, Stalin, and Pol Pot. Aron wasn't about to wait around to see what Tilson's intentions -- or results -- were. He knew that this man wanted one thing and wanted it all for himself: power. And Tilson saw the power vacuum that lay ahead with the President's inevitable idiotic fall from grace. Tilson was willing to do anything to be the person to fill it when he was gone.

There weren't many people standing up to this man, and the few who did weren't heard or weren't saying the right things. So Aron recognized this moment like so many other crucial moments in human history. It was a moment when good people had to rise and take action. *I've had enough of the adults in my generation -- and the ones before -- who sat around watching the world fall apart, expecting someone else to fix it.* He knew he had to take a stand because no one else would.

Jesse III
Jack Your Shit

The pendejo narizone came around the corner and grabbed at his ribs. His brown face was dripping and his white t-shirt stuck to his body with sweat. The musulmán's messy, whitening hair was probably lighter without the sweat. But for now, it looked gray. Maybe that's why Jesse didn't think it'd be messed up to jack him.

This fool can still run, right? Jesse thought. The pendejo was old, but he couldn't be *that* old. However, the fact that Jesse could see the old man's watch glistening from his wrist was the biggest deciding factor.

"Your money or your life," Jesse said, as he pulled out his brother's switchblade and pointed it right at the man's throat.

The old man had stopped and bent over, leaning his hands on his knees. His chest pumped in and out repeatedly as he panted heavily. He didn't seem as concerned with Jesse holding a knife at his neck so much as he was concerned about breathing in the hot Southern California air.

"Gimme your watch, puta. Now." Jesse knew he had to push hard. They were watching him. He couldn't decide if it would be more impressive to get the guy's watch with as little effort as possible, or with a big beat down. He didn't really enjoy beat downs. Not like his older brothers, Junior and Erik. Well, used to. Jesse was still trying to refer to Erik in that way.

Jesse assumed that the pleasure of breaking someone's face would come in time with being a real man, with his chest hair, and really being with a woman. Or maybe it was a taste you start to like slowly, like the few sips of leftover beer he had snuck over the years, and still hated tasting. "Maybe I need to break your face first, then take your shit. Don't be a pendejo."

The old man opened his eyes, which had been tightly shut in pain or exhaustion. Or both. He turned his eyes toward Jesse, but didn't move anything else. He forced out a long exhale through his lips, then slowly stood up straight, still breathing heavily, but calmly. "That will not be necessary," the pendejo said, raising a hand of caution.

"Shut the fuck up. This blade's about to go into your neck, puta." Jesse straightened his arm and the blade inched closer to the old man's throat.

"What are you waiting for then?"

Jesse's eyes widened and his face flushed red in anger. He could feel eyes on him. He could already start imagining the shit they would be saying to him later if Jesse got shut down by an old raghead.

"Are you waiting for me to step into your thrust and disarm you while I armbar your elbow and break it, all before you realize you are on the floor and I am sitting on your back?"

Pinche puta! This viejo is crazy. Trying to play mind games. Now Jesse had to beat down the old man. And maybe he'd enjoy it this time: he wanted to.

"But it does not have to come to that. Especially with your friends watching." The old man thrust his chin in the direction down the street, behind Jesse, and the old man's eyes wandered across apartment windows, patios, stairs, lawns, and sidewalks. "I know I appear old, tired, and weak to you."

"Don't worry about my crew, pendejo. Worry about this blade." Jesse waved it at face level, inches from the old man.

"A perfect target," the old man went on, ignoring the empty threat. "You could not be more correct. But not for the right reason."

"What the shit are you talking about? You fuckin-- you towelhead!" Jesse thrust forward, knife-first and sliced the air where the old man had just been, but he stepped back a lot quicker than he had ever seen. Not even Junior was that fast.

"I will give you my watch right now. It is not worth much, but there is a catch."

What the hell is this pendejo's deal? Jesse thought. *Am I gonna have to chase this bitch? Can I even catch him? God dammit, Imma look so stupid.*

"Think about your happiest memory. You do not need to tell me, just think about it."

"Shut up, pendejo," Jesse quickly retorted back. "Watch. Now."

"Was it a gift you received some Christmas night? A day at the park with your father before he left?"

"I'm gonna cut you up and make you bleed, puta." Jesse said, genuinely angry now.

"Maybe a kiss with your first love? Or the first time you held your puppy?" The old man reached under his left wrist and began to unstrap his watch. It was an expensive-looking compact but heavy-duty diving watch. Jesse could hear howls and jeers coming from the neighborhood behind him. "I remember my first dog. Saeb." The old man had a distant look in his eyes, and he smiled. Jesse noticed that a lot of the lines and wrinkles in the old man's face lined up with his smile, which lit up his whole face.

"I don't care," Jesse said, trying to remain calm so he wouldn't embarrass himself trying to swing at the old man again and miss. The watch was off his wrist and he was holding it in his hand. It was almost over.

"Saeb Salam had protested against the British mandates in Palestine during World War II. He became prime minister of Lebanon six times. At that time, we lived in Kafr Qasim, a village on the West Bank in Palestine." Jesse's face turned blank. "In the Middle East," the old man clarified with a slight grin.

"Why are you still talking, pendejo? Gimme your shit." Jesse took a step forward, still brandishing the knife toward the old man's throat.

He grabbed the bottom of his own shirt and stretched it to wipe off the face of his watch. "Saeb -- my dog, not the prime minister -- loved that village. He was a stupid but happy black lab. My family had fled there after al-Nakba -- the '48 war. Saeb loved running through the olive groves. He was king!" The old man's smile faded and his face sunk. "He was a good friend. He deserved a better death."

"He won't have it as bad as you, puta," Jesse said, twisting the knife in front of the old man's face.

"I found him on a road one morning in October. 1956. It was my fourth birthday, and two days after the Israelis had murdered my uncle, cousin, and neighbors. My mighty Saeb had been shot through the gut, and his entrails had spilled out. He had been stabbed through his shoulder and again in his neck, and left to die. He was still wheezing for precious air when I ran to him. I did not notice his entrails at first because they looked like they were covered in mud, but they were actually covered in ants. His eyes were crusted shut from tears, and the incessant flies. I thought he was just sleeping and snoring in a tiny puddle of mud at first." The old man chuckled a little bit, then paused. "My joy of finding him made me so happy but it had turned into something so twisted, so quickly. I still remember all of the swipes in the dirt from his paws, as he probably tried in agony to get home. To his family -- to me. He must have been so alone and so scared: waiting for me to find him and help him. He could not open his eyes, but his tail wagged twice when he heard me crying, then lay still. My mighty Saeb."

Jesse's arm got really tired and he lowered it, but still held the blade threateningly. "That's fucked up."

"Indeed." The old man held up the watch to inspect it, but he didn't extend his hand to Jesse.

"But enough of that story for now. You still owe me a happy thought."

"Just give me the watch." Jesse said, trying to grab it with his off hand. The old man was too quick again, and Jesse felt his face get hot.

"Maybe it has not happened yet. Your wedding day? Buying a house for your mother? Watching your first child take his or her first steps?" The old man looked hard at Jesse now. Searching. Jesse shook his head. "Those things do not make you happy?" the old man asked with genuine concern.

"No!" Jesse said impatiently. "That's none of your business, bitch. Gimme that watch and go back to your camels, you-- sandnigger."

The old man smirked. "I think we are onto something here. I think under all of that toughness, there is a good man in there somewhere."

"Nah. Just a guy who's about to get paid."

"Well, I have got my breath back now. I think we have two choices. You can walk away with a watch in your hand and another happy memory to add to the one you are about to tell me, or do not: you will stare at me and this watch run off into the distance. Oh, and you have got quite an audience now, by the way."

Jesse quickly glanced over his own shoulder and saw a lot of familiar faces staring at him from the distance. He looked up at the balcony of his family's apartment and saw his neighborhood friends standing, watching. His little brother was there, too. Jesse turned back toward the old man and spat at the ground. He shifted his weight back and forth on his feet. He shook his arms and tilted his neck, cracking it loudly.

"You're not going to tell anyone, puta. Because I'll find you and fucking kill you. I swear on your mother's life."

The old man nodded slowly. "Of course."

"When I punked these Jordans from some puta at school. Best day ever. Now give me that shit."

The old man turned toward the sidewalk. "Have fun with your friends."

"Alright, alright, pendejo! Chill." Jesse spat again. "Don't punk me with this. I'll get all those fools back there to stomp your ass if you're shitting with me."

"I believe you. And I can tell the difference when not to. If you are not honest again, I am gone. And I have been a runner for a long time, my friend."

"You crazy or something?"

"I just think we would both feel better about this if it was an actual transaction. I give something, and you give something. No harm, no foul."

Jesse nodded his head. *I wonder if the cops can still roll up on me if we make a deal.*

"Alright, loco. Lemme think." The old man saw Jesse's eyes look toward the ground, at nothing. Sweat dripped down one of his sideburns. "There's this girl…"

The old man nodded. "Go on."

"She, uh… she's *fine*." Jesse looked at the old man and his face became stern. An eyebrow slowly began to rise into his sweaty brow. "I kinda…" Jesse looked around. No one was in earshot. "I like her. You know? I like her a lot," he said in a low voice, "for a few weeks now." He huddled a little closer. This now seemed easier. And Jesse realized that saying it out loud for the first time was starting to make him feel lighter, like he was carrying a heavy backpack for some time and just took it off. "Her name is Maria. I don't, like, talk to her a lot. But there's just… something about her. I, uh, feel weird when she's around. I like, forget who I am or some shit. I get weak -- in my legs. But at the same time, I feel like I could move mountains for her."

"So what makes you happy, exactly?" The old man asked.

"Psh, like you give a shit. I want that watch."

The old Arab calmly said, with a gentleness in his eyes, "You cannot have her. Is that right? You are trying to figure out how to reach her."

Jesse just stared at the Arab man. He didn't know if he should swing at him or confide in him. But he was serious, Jesse could tell that much. "I think she'd be like, perfect, you know?" Jesse looked right into the man's eyes, and they were focused on Jesse's eyes. He didn't feel threatened at all, and saying that out loud surprised even himself. "Sometimes I think about bringing Maria home after we start talking. And my abuelita is proud of me. For once. And I'll walk her home, and bring her through the hood, and everyone else will be like, 'Shit. Jesse's got it going on,' and she'll meet the crew, and maybe bring her friends around, too. Hugo will see when he gets out. And even mi hermano Erik will look down and be proud of me." Jesse realized he was holding the knife as his side now, and the pendejo was still holding the watch. He looked at the old man, who was deeply focused on Jesse's confession.

"Thank you," he said, and extended the watch out. Jesse stared back at him and tried to determine if he was about to be tricked. Jesse slowly extended his hand, then quickly grabbed at the watch and took it from the old man's hand. They stared at each other for a moment more. "I will be seeing you," the old man said. He turned toward the sidewalk and continued running on his way.

"Or not. Pinche pendejo," Jesse said under his breath and looked down at the merchandise in his hand. The howls and jeers continued in the distance behind him.

Aron II
Icy Blue Eyes

Still at his desk recounting his escapade on the Plane from only a few moments ago, Aron was sure he had been very close to Tilson's hideout, which appeared to be someone else's den: the location where someone sleeps and enters the Plane through their dreams. The putrisomn had been thicker and more detailed. The swirling glow from people's hazes could be seen flickering throughout. This was usually the case when a Reader on the Plane approached an area where many people lived in waking life.

"When a person sleeps," Aron remembered Yusef telling him long ago, "all of their mind's uncertainties, fears, hopes, desires, and other raw emotions are processed. They are manifested on the Plane in what is called a haze." Just before Aron had seen someone else's haze for the first time, Yusef described it as what a galaxy might look like if it were placed inside a blender. One had to be careful, he warned, not to get too close or listen too intently to a haze unless you were both willing and ready to be sucked into that blender of thoughts, memories, and emotions. In many ways, it was just like entering a swirling, chaotic galaxy.

Aron had made his way down the slopes and into the outskirts of town, navigating around the hives of putrisomn as best he could. He stuck as close to the edge of town as possible, gently moving vines and branches of silky, dark brown and green putrisomn out of his path, and slowly made his way through what was undoubtedly a condensed neighborhood of plebs in waking life. He recognized the structures of putrisomn, as it had grown in the same form as people's bedrooms, ceilings, and nearby rooms.

Near the top of most hives, swirling orbs and streaks of colored light spun at different speeds; the hazes of sleeping plebs in their second floor bedrooms could be seen shining through the cracks and crevices of hives across this residential area.

This was a neighborhood of expensive tract homes because in nice houses people only slept in upstairs bedrooms, and the putrisomn had no strong bottom structure when it was produced by people sleeping ten or fifteen feet up in the air. It somewhat resembled a melted, condensed growth as the putrisomn gathered from the air and fell down to the ground as it spewed from people's hazes or occasionally spattered from shadows moving about in the waking world. Oddly enough, the poorer, less privileged people in waking life often produced more structured, impressive putrisomn hives in the Plane. Since most of them live together in rooms so compactly crammed and stacked, putrisomn grew thickly and consistently.

After making his way past another large mound and being careful to stay hidden in the branches of putrisomn while avoiding the glimmer of a nearby haze, Aron saw something that made him feel both excited and fearful at the same time: a golem.

It was the size of a large dog and walked on four legs, but had two additional limbs, which appeared to be holding or even made of crude looking blades and piercing points. Its body frame and limbs were a dark metallic color, and its legs and arms looked sharp, as though a kick, swing, or poke from any of its limbs would act as an edged weapon of some sort. The presence of a golem confirmed his suspicions, after months of investigating and tracking, that Tilson was a Reader or had been infiltrated by another Reader.

The golem appeared to be quietly patrolling. As its mechanical legs clambered over a small mound of putrisomn on the street Aron saw its head jerk over in his direction. He thought it had heard or seen him. Its face turned toward him and he saw that the construct had a darkened, blank face but for four solid, glowing red eyes. One pair was located normally near the middle of the head. The other pair was stacked above and spread further apart from the one below. At the sides of its head a pair of sharp horns angled up and forward, like a bull's. Aron tensed up for a fight. Instead, the golem stared toward his direction for a brief moment before blinking its eyes in order from the bottom up. Then it looked away and kept on its patrol.

Aron saw his chance to sneak after the passing golem and took it, successfully running across a yard and into a large mound with more defined structure. There was only a faint glow from whoever's haze was in there, like the embers of a dying fire stirred up with the breeze.

He crossed the street and passed a dilapidated mailbox which had a putrisomn pole and a miniature log cabin on top. The front door was large in proportion to the cabin because it was the latch for the mail. The cabin's chimney was used as the mailbox flag. Aron thought this mailbox was peculiar for having so much detail. The putrisomn houses on this side of the neighborhood street all had more detail than normal. There was so much evidence of den activity that Aron, now hiding behind a tree layered in putrisomn, was almost sure he had found Tilson's hideout, or the den of whoever was hiding his haze in this remote location.

Anxiously, Aron crossed the lawn to the front door and tried to look through a window, but only saw thick putrisomn in its place. Then, things got noticeably quiet.

The doors exploded. Storming out of the house was a galloping, racing blur of brown fur that shook with every powerful stomp. It was a massive brown bear, whose weight and strength hung down from every part of it. Ancient-looking runes glowed purple on its limbs, chest and back. Jesse staggered and backed himself against the putrisomn wall of the house as the bear reared around on the lawn to face Aron. He looked into the beast's eyes and saw that they were human: ice blue ones. Panic struck his chest. This bear was no golem. It was another Reader who had shape-shifted, a nagual.

I've seen this bear before.

The bear charged. Aron's eyes widened and he hesitated before juking his weight left, away from the front door, then going right at the last second, as the bear crashed into the putrisomn wall of the house, powerful and giant claws first.

Retreating in a hurry, Aron began to run down the driveway until he saw the patrolling golem heading straight for him. It was methodic as it zeroed in on Aron. The golem dropped its gear-like arms, which were spiked with barbs, and also began to charge at Aron. He turned around and ran toward his only option: through the crashed doors and into the house.

Aron barely dodged the bear again as he leapt through the doorway, and it barreled against the side of the garage as it let out a body-shaking roar. The golem kept up the chase right behind the bear. Aron ran down a hallway and looked for a back door exit of some sort, but the hallway ended at a fork: left or right. He was about to attempt to go straight through the wall itself, until he realized at the last instant that all three options were pointless. There was likely something else waiting behind them. The patrolling golem, the nagual ambushing him, the fact that they were both chasing him deeper into this den they intended to protect: this was all a trap.

With the bear on his heels, Aron ran straight at the wall that ended the hallway and ran up it. He threw the top of his weight behind him and tried with all of his might to kick the air up and behind his head. His backflip was a graceful success, as he landed behind the bear, which again crashed into the wall with an agitated grunt, followed by a roar. Aron was still facing the hallway intersection.

Without looking behind him, Aron knew the golem had probably also chased after him and was right behind him. He instinctively ducked down and performed a reverse somersault, simultaneously dodging the golem's side-sweeping strike and rolled under one of its legs. Aron kicked the golem in the back and it tangled itself with the bear, which had turned around and was attempting to head back up the hall for Aron.

He sprinted for the doorway only to see the putrisomn that had been demolished from the bear's initial crash was now reforming on its hinges to close off the doorway. The putrisomn was growing the door back right in front of him, which was a normal occurrence. But it wasn't normal for it to happen so swiftly.

Such a feat had to take a lot of concentration. When a Reader chooses their Paragon path for specialty on the Plane, such as a nagual, or shapeshifter, they need to focus heavily on their expertise. A nagual uses most of their focus and willpower to maintain their beastly form. So a second Reader, a weaver, was likely manipulating the putrisomn and controlling the golem from nearby.

There was too much happening, too quickly. Aron could not process it all. He just knew that he was outmatched and outwitted. And now, possibly trapped. He charged at the door. Aron focused on his breathing and the blood flow of oxygen to his legs and his arms, and mentally tried to make them burn with energy. His speed picked up as he leaned in and pushed off with his legs, and smashed himself into the door.

A memory flashed into Aron's mind amidst the madness. *To be limitless, you must first know what limits you*, Yusef had told him many, many times. Learning about how the body works, where strength comes from, and how energy is gathered and spent are all aspects of what being a powerful guanjun, or champion, entails. The Plane was no simple dream land. Wanting to fly really badly would not make you fly here. That only worked in subconscious dreams. Readers who trained and learned how to fly on the Plane were legendary. Aron knew a lot of tricks on the Plane. But he certainly was not a Paragon, or an expert in any particular discipline. He soon wished he had spent more time focusing on and training his advanced speed and strength.

The putrisomn door splintered but did not break through. On his hands and knees, Aron was dazed as his arms groped around the floor amidst the few broken chunks of wooden putrisomn, which began to fly back toward the door to solidify it again. He had failed and was now trapped inside this den.

He felt excruciating pain in his back and right shoulder blade, screamed, and crashed flat onto the ground. The golem had overtaken him and slammed its barbed arm into Aron's back. The barbs were lodged in deep and Aron, still on his hands and knees, painfully tried to tear himself off but couldn't. He felt warm blood ooze out and creep down his ribs onto the sides of his body.

Aron glanced over his shoulder at the golem to see how he could possibly escape its grip. Past the golem, the bear nagual was charging back to him from down the hall. The golem stood ready on four legs, and while its barbed arm was stuck in Aron and held him down, a sixth limb was raised, ready to strike. Up close now, he briefly noticed peculiar etchings and markings on its body. He thought he even saw a pictograph of weapons on it, stacked in a random way. He didn't stare for long, because there were bigger things to worry about at the moment.

The bear galloped over in front of Aron and let out a deafening roar into his face. Saliva roped out from its mouth onto Aron's face, pushed by hot breath.

Tilting its barbed arm upward, the golem forced Aron's defeated body up. He screamed as his torso was lifted while his legs stretched out behind him helplessly. His face was brought high off the ground.

The bear stood up on its hind legs and began to shake. Its fur vibrated violently and it brought up its arms closer to its body as patches of fur began to fall off. Its legs began to get skinnier, and its arms got smaller. The bear began to shrink and continue to shed its fur. It took a human shape, and a tall white man formed. The icy blue eyes were still there. They stared directly into Aron's eyes.

The fit man said, "Took you long enough." Then he gave a powerful kick with the ball of his foot straight to Aron's nose. He didn't even see it until it was in his face. Then he just saw pangs of red and yellow as his eyes opened and closed. Blood gushed down over his lips, into his mouth, and down his chin. The force of the blow sunk the spikes from the golem's arm deeper into his back as he felt the tips of the barbs scrape against his shoulder blade and the back of his rib cage.

Do something, Aron thought to himself. He screamed it in his own head. *Do something, now!*

The man with icy blue eyes raised his foot high and rested it on top of Aron's head, which was a few feet from the wooden floor of the hallway. "Now I don't need to worry about you anymore," he said, as he shoved his foot and Aron's head along with it, straight down. The spiked barbs splattered blood as they were torn out of Aron's back muscles. His head smashed, face first, into the floor. There was a quick, yet distinct sound and feeling of cracking in his face.

Aron III
Rogue Readers, a Rooftop, and Ripostes

It was too much for Aron to handle. Too much pain and confusion. Things out of his control. He couldn't maintain his focus and he lost his anchoring to the Plane.

Darkness swept over him. He was being pulled through pure blackness and all around him was unseeable emptiness. He had a sensation of falling, flying, and laying flat on the ground as it swirled, all at the same time.

Then his sense of balance flipped and he was laying flat on his back. He was back in his bed in his own bedroom. By just a desk light on his desk, he gained awareness that his eyes were fluttering. He had been booted from the Plane and was awake now. The sensation of barbed hooks stuck through his skin, and their scraping against his bones in his back was faint.

Back at his desk, Aron had now fully recalled his dream and his mission on the Plane. His mind raced and he was making connections. Those icy blue eyes did not belong to Bob Tilson. Tilson's eyes were brown, and Aron had doubted from the beginning that Tilson was a Reader at all. Aron recalled more clues.

There had been so much detail at that den. The house had precise form, from its windows and doors, even down to its mailbox. This meant there was a lot of regular interaction there by at least one Reader, both in waking life and on the Plane. If the Reader with the icy blue eyes was the only one there, he must be really powerful in order to maintain himself as a nagual, and reform those putrisomn front doors. This was highly unlikely, especially considering the golem that had to be controlled by someone else.

How was it possible for a single Reader to control putrisomn so quickly and efficiently? As far as Aron had ever been taught by Yusef, he understood that putrisomn acted like organic matter in its raw form. It was not sentient; it possessed no desires or intelligence, or even the capability to do so. Of course, a Reader with advanced weaving training on the Plane would be able to manipulate a significant amount of putrisomn in such a way. But that would require most of their attention.

There had to be another Reader controlling that putrisomn; that Reader was also powerful enough to not need to be present within eyesight to see all of those pieces and rebond them back together. These Readers who ambushed Aron were terrifyingly serious since they were clearly protecting Tilson and whatever work they had been hiding there, far away from Tilson's hometown of Meridian, Idaho, and Washington, D.C.

A thought struck Aron; he had been tracking Tilson's business partners, campaign donors, Congressional staff, close friends, and associates, but none of them had proved worthwhile to follow for a trail that would point to some kind of connection to the Plane. Yet, those eyes… he had seen them before. He just couldn't remember where.

Although Tilson had been physically sleeping in Washington, D.C., Aron was not able to locate his den. Aron doubted that Tilson's privileged life put him on the path of being a Reader. He must have had help navigating the Plane and anchoring his haze to this secluded spot in what would be Colorado in the waking world. Having another Reader like Icy Blue Eyes around to keep snooping Readers away and out of his haze was a security measure of some sort, especially since he wasn't able to find him on any official security or staff lists for Tilson. But who would be trying to protect Tilson wasn't making sense yet. What was Tilson hiding, or rather, who was hiding Tilson?

He thought about the golem that had stuck him and pinned him to the ground. It was a pretty creepy construction, Aron reflected. It reminded him of something he'd seen or learned about before. Something from history, he thought. The mechanical style didn't strike him so much as the design of its arms, and its face. Those creepy eyes. Then there were those weird etchings. *Where have I seen those symbols before?* He thought as he leaned over his desk on his elbow, then rested his face into his hand.

He picked up a pencil and did his best to redraw what he had seen for one set of symbols in particular. There was a wide-bladed scimitar curved down and to the left. Then a scythe stacked diagonally across the scimitar to form a flat "x": the blade end was pointing upward left, and it was tilted so the scythe's blade angled upward to the right. At the top of those weapons was a spear laid across horizontally, its tip pointed left. And finally, there was what looked like a machine gun laid over the top of the other weapons, pointing to the right. It looked like it should have been an M60, but the top handle angled differently.

Aron looked back at the scimitar he'd drawn and wondered if the design was West Asian or East Asian. He recalled what he had seen and decided it must have been a dao, a Chinese-style sword. *But why Chinese? Are these other weapons Chinese?*

Then it hit him. These weren't symbols. It was one symbol, a Chinese character: "Security." He drew it: 安.

He put it all together as he finished his last strokes of the character: who the other readers were, why they were there with Tilson, and what they were planning. Aron recognized that security character because it was part of the name and logo of a Chinese private security firm that operated outside of China, usually helping with mining or acquiring raw materials in other countries. He was familiar with this firm because he had researched Bob Tilson's -- and other politicians' -- investments both domestic and foreign, and this company was one that more than a few politicians in Tilson's circle had commonly invested in.

Furiously, Aron began tossing papers and manila folders aside across his desk, but when he found a particular folder he held it for a second, staring at its blank front, then opened it and stared even harder at a photo that was inside. Across the top he had written with red marker "Chu Tien, Codename: Xuannu." A young Chinese woman was cradling a CS/LR17 assault rifle in a zoomed-in shot of her as she looked somewhere off camera. She wore a tactical vest with magazines and grenades attached. A tactical throat microphone dangled from her neck, and on her vest, he saw it: a patch with the 安 character made with weapons, exactly how he had seen it on the golem. Aron searched the other photos of the security agents and didn't see a similar patch. Chu Tien had to be the one who made that golem. *Was she controlling it and weaving that putrisomn?* Aron wondered.

The presence of Chu Tien's golem meant that this Chinese security firm, which Aron knew was protecting some secretive mining exploit in Africa, was collaborating with Icy Blue Eyes. The owner of the firm was also the owner of the mining company, who also owned the world's largest manufacturer and distributor of smartphones: the world's second-richest woman, Xi Wang Mu. Aron double-checked his notes. He was willing to bet that with more research and investigating, he would probably find that Tilson had additional investments of some kind in Xi Wang Mu's various companies. Chu Tien's golem -- whose six arms and four eyes most certainly had to be designed after Chiyou, the Chinese god of war -- and Icy Blue Eyes teaming up on the Plane to protect Tilson would confirm that Tilson was collaborating with Xi Wang Mu, a Chinese national who had zero interest in supporting America unless she profited from it.

He knows that she's mining for something in Africa. But he's not bringing it to the attention of the American people. He'd rather profit off whatever gain Xi Wang Mu will get. And instead of telling us, he's distracting us with this immigration nonsense, Aron processed in his head. *Distracting us. He's pitting Americans against Americans so he can profit -- so a Chinese businesswoman can profit. Was the pill even his idea?* Aron's eyes got wide. *Whose technology is it going to be that produces these pills? He's going to make even more money from this! And Xi Wang Mu will of course be creating the technology that tracks these people in our own country, thus giving her access to American databases...*

Aron shot up from his desk with the realization of what was unfolding before the American public, and he knew he had to immediately call a meeting with Yusef. He saw Xi Wang Mu and Tilson's plan right before his eyes, and it was as impressive as it was terrifying.

He clumsily gathered some of his notes, a change of clothing, and his vibrobaton, and stuffed them into a backpack. He left his apartment in a rush, barely bothering to lock it behind him. He rushed down the stairs toward the front door of the anteroom but hesitated when he glimpsed a person's darkened silhouette through the frosted glass, as a street lamp outside cast light against the figure.

The silhouette froze on the other side of the door. Aron's gut twisted and he turned back up the stairs. Then, wood and glass crashed behind him as he ran up the stairs, looking over his shoulder to see someone running through the doorway and brandishing a knife. Aron sprinted to his apartment door, unlocked it with his key, entered, slammed the door, and deadbolted it. Without missing a beat, Aron ran to his window, slid it open with a toss, and reached up for the window sill outside his apartment, two floors up from the ground.

As his bedroom door banged, he grabbed at an edge on the outside of the building and pulled himself up while reaching for another chunk of building, a balcony, and kept going until he climbed past the third floor and reached the roof with his hands. When Aron looked back down the building and into the night, he saw someone staring back up at him from his apartment window then quickly vanish back inside.

Grunting, Aron pulled himself over the ledge and onto the roof. To make his escape, he set his eyes on an apartment building rooftop next door. Aron needed a running start to clear the jump so he hurried toward the opposite sode of his roof. He began his sprint but stopped dead in his tracks at the sight of a person's silhouette standing in the way of his jump.

The silhouette flicked its arm outward and a long, slender stick popped out into the night. The familiar, rapid *chk-chk-chk-chk* and high-pitched hum of an electrical charge indicated what Aron suspected and feared: a vibrobaton. It was the sure sign of a Reader who lived a treacherous life of committing dangerous acts while trying to leave minimal evidence of themselves in their wake.

Aron reached for his backpack, and he felt his vibrobaton hilt sticking out of a pocket. He flicked his wrist. *Chk-chk-chk-chk*. Then he reached over with his free hand and thumbed the switch at the hilt. The hard, flinching split-buzz of electric energy and then what sounded like a low-volume but high-pitched ambulance siren was reassuring. The silhouette and Aron both raised their charged batons toward each other.

Aron waited for the first move. And waited. Then Aron quickly realized that his opponent was on the defensive. The silhouette was waiting for their backup to arrive. Aron thrust forward without wasting another millisecond. He now needed as many as he could get.

He lunged into the silhouette with his baton raised in his right hand

and feinted a diagonal strike to the silhouette's left shoulder, but instead twisted his own body clockwise and swung his baton around him as he crouched down, aiming for its right knee.

The silhouette quickly pivoted to Aron's left from the feint and double-kicked the air toward Aron to avoid the incoming sweep. As it landed, it brought down its baton, intending to crush Aron's head. Aron was still kneeling and threw his weight into his twisting momentum, somersaulting to his right to avoid the blow, then pushed himself back onto his feet from the somersault, his baton on guard.

He charged again. The two continued to dodge, pivot, parry, and riposte each other, each of their strikes crashing and clanging as the electricity from their metal batons crackled and whirred to recharge.

I need to end this, Aron thought to himself. His eyes desperately scanned possible jump zones around the rooftop as he kept his guard up against the mysterious foe just feet in front of him.

Then, there was a quick and heavy metallic *chk-chk-chk-chk* from behind him.

Too late. He whipped his head around to see the second person swinging at his head.

His senses closed to the unendurable, crushing pain as he was overcome with the convulsing fury of reds, whites, blacks, and yellows raging through his head and against his eyelids. Then, he felt the light gravel of the rooftop on his face. He heard the high pitch of a vibrobaton recharging.

Aron's head tilted a bit and he could see the legs of the second assaulter nearby. Then he saw the first man walk up to him. His icy blue eyes glistened as his face briefly caught some light. He golf swung his baton into Aron's gut. Aron heard the crack of extreme voltage.

All he saw was darkness.

Jesse IV
Take Me Back!

In the week that followed, Jesse earned himself two disciplinary referrals for insubordination. He was hanging out with Racha more and getting familiar with other faces he saw while ditching classes throughout the day.

Jesse realized he didn't like being stuck in class ebcause he just thought about Maria and how frustrated he had become. In order to even be noticed by her, some things about him would have to change. For the first time in his life, Jesse could not muster up the courage to approach someone. Hr was ill-prepared to converse with her. A first impression was really important and Jesse didn't want to blow it.

He found out from Racha that she had all Honors classes, of which Jesse had none. Maria was also the Freshman Class President and on the volleyball team. Jesse didn't stand out at all and was probably really unimpressive to her, on top of being new to the school and a complete nobody. As he entered his neighborhood, he saw several neighbors hanging out in front of some apartments and he instantly felt comforted. They wore large, baggy white t-shirts, black or blue jeans, white sneakers, and a cap. He looked down at his clothes, and he could have fit right in with them. "Fuck," he said to himself, "I just blend in."

He thought about how much he had found out about Maria. She was so unique, unlike anything he ever thought he would like about a girl. There was nothing he could distinguish about himself that set him apart from other guys. Sure, he was handsome, well built, and had enough luck with girls in the past. That was never really a problem for him. But Maria was different.

Jesse got to his apartment and took out his keys to open the door, but it was already unlocked. He went inside and took off his backpack, yelling out "Lita, you forgot to--"

"Hello, Jesse. It is nice to see you again," the old Arab man said from the couch, sipping a glass of water.

Jesse's eyes got big and his gut told him to fight, but the Arab's demeanor was calm.

"¡Jesús! Tu teacher está aquí," Jesse's grandmother yelled from the kitchen.

"Please, call me Mr. Abdel," he responded toward the kitchen. "I'm his tutor, Señora Ramirez. Right, Jesse?"

Jesse looked on with wide-eyed confusion and anxiety. "Uhh… what?"

Mr. Abdel put the glass of water down on the coffee table and leaned forward. "Don't you remember, Jesse? You made an arrangement with me."

Mrs. Ramirez walked up to Jesse and handed him a glass of water. "Jesús, Señor Abdel say he has many success with other students. He is here to help you," she said, her eyebrows raised with encouragement.

Still, Jesse didn't quite know what to do in this situation with this man, whom he recently robbed, sitting politely and patiently in his living room in front of his grandmother.

Alfredo walked out of the hallway as he stared into a tablet and swiped mindlessly. Then, without looking up from his device, he noticed Yusef sitting on the couch and instantly turned around and walked back into the hallway. His swiping didn't miss a beat.

A moment later, Jesse heard Marcy yell from their room, "Where's my Cheetos? You better didn't eat 'em!"

"Shut up, Marcy! Someone's here! He's weird! Go out and get 'em yourself." Then a door slammed shut.

"Jesse," Mr. Abdel said, "I do not have my watch with me. Can you tell me what time it is?" his eyes locked into Jesse's, as a stern look took over the old Arab's face. The diving watch was on Jesse's wrist at that very moment. Jesse began to understand.

"Yeah, that's right. My tutor..." Jesse said, but couldn't find any more words.

Mr. Abdel set his glass down on the coffee table and stood up. "Señora Ramirez, do you mind if I speak with Jesse right outside? I think he might be a little nervous in front of his dear abuela here."

"Ah, sí. Yes, por favor," Mrs. Ramirez said as she gestured toward the door and walked over to open it for Yusef and Jesse.

"Thank you very much, Señora Ramirez," the old man said as he put a gentle but firm hand on Jesse's shoulder as they walked outside onto the walkway, which overlooked a courtyard below with an identical two-story apartment building on the other side.

The door closed behind them and Jesse didn't wait one millisecond longer to shove off Mr. Abdel's hand. "The fuck?" Jesse exclaimed in a hushed and harsh voice.

"I am serious about tutoring," Mr. Abdel said solemnly. "And I will make sure you get into better classes, teach you how to properly condition your body, and defend yourself. Among other things," he said with a gentle smile.

Jesse stared back at him. "The fuck?" he asked again, this time with genuine confusion.

"You need these things. Maybe you realize that you need some and not others. But you need them. And I will teach you more. So much more."

"First of all," Jesse said, "How did you find where I live?"

"Well, it was not too difficult since you robbed me a few hundred feet away."

Jesse adjusted his posture a bit and looked around. There were a few people outside, but nobody of consequence, and they weren't really paying attention, anyway. "What do you want? You're not getting that watch back." Jesse hid his arm behind himself.

Mr. Abdel took a deep breath and sighed. "It is not about the watch."

Jesse looked right at him. "We had a deal. I said you'd get fucked up if you clowned me."

The old man looked away. His eyes focused on some place very far away. "I have had many students under my wing, Jesse. They all learned much and achieved great things. In doing so, they have served a greater purpose than themselves. They still do, on their own."

"Purpose? The fuck you mean?"

"You can keep the watch. You will gain things that are invaluable."

"What's the catch? You're still not telling me why." Jesse's upper lip quivered with anxiousness and annoyance.

"It is… complicated, Jesse. In time, I can explain. But you are perfect to serve this purpose. You do not know it yet, but this is your purpose. I have learned much about people. I already know a lot about you, Jesse. Just in the few days since we have met."

"¡No mames! You don't know shit, hijo de puta! You don't know nothin' about me."

Then Mr. Abdel turned his far-away gaze to Jesse and he looked right into his eyes. "I know your bed has been wet recently."

Jesse's eyes sprang wide and he felt his face get hot. "Who the fuck--" He quickly recovered from his stunned state and his embarrassment turned to anger. He fumed past the old man and reached for the front door, yelling out "¡Lita!"

Jesse's hand reached the doorknob, but then in that impressive speed Mr. Abdel grabbed Jesse's hand as it reached the knob and he came closer to Jesse. "And I know about the prison, with no windows," he continued on. "Your Lita did not tell me anything. I have seen your father, Papá drinking his beer in his undershirt," the old man came in even closer, to Jesse's ear. "I heard the voices."

Jesse recoiled. His eyes began to well up with tears. "Who… what the fuck?" Jesse stared at Mr. Abdel, slouching and feeling powerless.

Mrs. Ramirez yelled out from inside the apartment. "¿Jesús? ¿Estás bien?"

"Tell her you are fine, Jesse. You will be."

Jesse was still in a state of confusion and helplessness. "I didn't tell anyone. How the fuck do you know that shit?"

"¿Jesús? ¿Jesús?" Mrs. Ramirez's footsteps could be heard getting closer to the front door. Jesse wiped away the tears from his eyes.

"Your life will do only one of two things from this moment on. You will work the hardest you ever have and live a life you never thought possible for yourself. Or you will share a fate similar to your father and brother, and you will never have a chance with Maria. That choice is yours, and it needs to be made right now."

The door swung open and Mrs. Ramirez stood staring at Jesse and Mr. Abdel. "¿Jesús?"

Jesse remained staring right into the Arab's eyes. He stared back and did not flinch. "This fool is wack," Jesse said, as he turned away and walked back inside the apartment.

Mrs. Ramirez gave Mr. Abdel a long look of bewilderment and disappointment, then turned away back inside the apartment and shut the door. As Jesse heard Lita slide the deadbolt and the old man's footsteps fade away, he noticed a business card on the coffee table. It read:

Mr. Yusef Abdel
Social Sciences Teacher
Portola High School, Room 33

*****

The bell rang, and the hallway exploded from both sides as doors flew open and students flooded out. Skateboards clanged on the tiled floor; hands and arms flailed in the air as students greeted each other and waved to get attention. Yells, screams, and loud cursing echoed off the steel lockers lining the walls. Jesse stood next to a door on the right side of the hall, watching the mayhem of classroom transition. Someone slammed a locker shut, but it sounded too loud and alarming.

When Jesse looked around, he saw a handgun held in the air with smoke drifting out of the barrel. Now surrounded by a blue sky, a blinding sun beat down on him. A rooster cawed nearby. To his right, looking past a familiar chicken coop from the backyard of his old house, Jesse saw the quad of Portola High School below.

Suddenly, he was walking through the center, but the buildings had switched around. He was lost all over again like his first day of school. He saw buildings from junior high, and yet others that were familiar but not identifiable.

He entered a building hoping to find his way, and as he passed classrooms with unfamiliar numbers, the windows took a darker tint, became thicker and smaller. The color of the walls turned into a worn, pale white and the doors became heavy-looking and the knobs were gone. He saw metal bars replace one of the corridor walls. Someone called to him. Jesse walked over and he was suddenly face-to-face with his dead brother Erik. "Where did you go, Jesse?"

Before Jesse could even think of a response, he saw other faces and heard other voices from old.

"Homies for life."

"Let's square up."

"I love you, Baby. I love your everything."

Then, a more distinct voice that struck at the very core of Jesse.

"Ay. Escucha, pendejo. Mira," his father said from a dark corner of the jail cell. Jesse's eyes opened wide and the hairs on the back of his neck stood up. "Jesse…" but he couldn't hear his father's voice again.

Someone grabbed his shoulder from behind and whipped Jesse around. He faced his oldest brother Junior directly, looking up at him, way up. Jesse was a child again. "Jesse, you're too small. You're not tough enough," and he turned away from Jesse and walked away from the front lawn of their old house, through their gate onto the sidewalk. Erik brushed past Jesse and snickered, following Junior.

"No!" Jesse yelled out. "Fuck you! I hate you!" he screamed in his shrill little boy voice. His brothers crossed the street in the distance and were met by their friends, much older than little Jesse and very intimidating.

A hand tapped his shoulder and Jesse turned around. He was his older self again, and was standing on his apartment rooftop. The chicken coop was there, too. Yusef stood nearby, admiring the rooster inside.

"Where do you want to go?" Yusef asked, without taking his eyes off of the bird.

"What?" Jesse asked.

Yusef pulled himself away from the wire cage. He closed his eyes, and the bright blue sky turned to a dark blue, then purple as the sun dimmed and turned into the moon. With a wave of his arm, the rooftop and cage blurred and fell away like sand. As they crashed into the ground, the discolored sand bounced back up and reshaped into a green lawn, darkened by the night. They stood near a window on the side of a house. A small, white fluorescent glow dimmed through the half-drawn blinds of a bedroom, and Jesse was able to see Maria's face barely lit by her phone as she held it in bed.

"With whom is she talking? What if that could be you?" Yusef asked from behind Jesse.

Jesse looked back at Yusef. He suddenly became aware that he had been in a dream and still was. His mind bent as if adjusting to the sudden weight of the realization: he was weak and atrophied in this new world, as if he was completely unable to use his muscles and make any movement. He turned back toward Maria, expecting her to not be there anymore, but there she lay, still texting. "I'm dreaming right now," Jesse said to himself as much as he said it to Yusef. "I'm in a dream."

"Yes, you are. And I am in yours right now." Yusef waved his arm again and Jesse's surroundings swished away again. Now he was in the hot sun, draped in shiny dark blue, polyester robes. He was sweating his ass off and feeling incredibly nervous, excited, happy, uncertain, and sad all at once. Jesse was on the AstroTurf of a stadium standing with hundreds of other robed, older students, and he realized that he was older now. Bigger, stronger. He felt confident, knowledgeable… powerful.

His neck and chest were weighed down with medals and sashes. He was standing near the front of the crowd of graduates, and thousands of people stood and cheered in the stands. He caught a glimpse of a slightly older, even more beautiful Maria through the crowd. She was also draped in blue robes and heavily clad in sashes, ropes, and medals hanging from her neck. She was looking back at Jesse and smiling admiringly, adjusting the slipping graduation cap from her head. A foghorn blew from the stadium and Jesse looked to see his abuela waving from the stands, tears pouring down her cheeks as she jumped up and down in joy. The tassel from his own cap slightly blocked his vision. Yusef still stood next to him. Tears began to well up in Jesse's eyes.

Yusef waved his arm again and it all went away. They now stood in a dingy kitchen, and Jesse yelled to Yusef, "Take me back!"

He ignored Jesse and walked to the doorway of the kitchen, peering out into another room. Jesse was crying, and didn't know why. He had never felt so many wonderful and empowering emotions--he had never seen a future in that way. He had never seen himself that way, and he didn't think anyone else had either. Now he wanted the entire world to see it.

The old man looked back at Jesse and nodded for him to follow as he walked out of the kitchen.

Jesse turned the corner and froze. His father, younger than Jesse had ever seen him, stood facing a thinly draped window. A small baby was wrapped in his huge left arm, and in his other a beer bottle was held by its neck, dangling below his hip. A boy -- Jesse recognized his brother Hugo -- played with a toddler on the ground and ran around in the room near the towering mountain of a man. His father stared into the baby's eyes as it cooed, and Jesse saw a smirk come across his father's face, and a twinkle in his eye that he had never seen before.

Jesse realized that his father was holding him, as a baby. Jesse dropped to the floor on his knees, and his shoulders slumped over. There was a sudden mass of weight he felt in his chest as a cavernous part of his heart suddenly became apparent to him. The tears fell uncontrollably and Jesse's nose stung as snot flowed. His throat swelled and his head and body thrust forward, beyond his control. He reached out to his father as his words got stuck in his throat. The room fell away, and Jesse knelt on the pebbled floor of the apartment rooftop again.

Jesse took a moment as he touched the small pebbles on the rooftop floor. It was so detailed and real. He wiped mucus away and rubbed the tears from his eyes. He stood up and faced Yusef. "Take me back. Take me back to all of it."

"No."

"What?" Jesse's heart sank.

"I will teach you how to go there on your own. And so much more."

Jesse shook his head. "Fuck that. Fuck you, puto. Stay the fuck out of my head." Jesse rushed forward. He was surprised at how real this felt, and how much control he had now.

He saw a smirk on Yusef's face and it enraged him. Jesse reached Yusef and shoved him all the way to the edge of the roof, and over the ledge.

A pained look came across Yusef's face just before he vanished over the edge. Jesse leaned over to see his body but didn't see any sign of him.

Jesse V
I'm Not With Her

A week of frustrating nights went by for Jesse. He tried to go back to those dreams somehow, but each morning he woke up and couldn't remember dreaming at all. A few nights he actually went to bed a little earlier than usual, even though he spent most of that extra time tossing and turning.

Now he just wanted memes. But Jesse kept seeing social media posts about Chayne Sauze and yet another rivalry he was starting with a new up-and-coming rapper from Missouri, named ON$l0tt. Someone posted a sloppily edited video about the feud.

"This Okie?" Chayne Sauze said on a clip from the entertainment show GZN. In his signature look, shiny gold chains dangled from his toned and tattooed bare chest as he walked down the sidewalk away from his special-edition silver- and-gold-trimmed, personalized Ford Bronco. It reminded Jesse of a luxurious tank. "What a fu--BLEEP--ng Okie jokie," he said as his entourage all chortled and whooped behind him. "Nig--BLEEP can't rap! He should go back to being a farmer. Or whatever that b--BLEEP--ch did before."

Then the video cut to a dark background displaying the words:

ON$l0tt responds to Chayne Sauze shit talking

"Keep talking shit. See what happens. I ain't even gonna murder ya on the streets. Imma murder ya on the billboards, N--BLEEP," ON$l0tt yelled into a microphone on a smoky and dark stage during a performance. "You gon' be beggin' me for money, Chayne, cuz yer shit cringe. It's old, like you. I'm the new sher'f up in this bi--BLEEP!" The crowd roared.

The black screen returned and now displayed:

Who going be on top? Like if you think Chayne Sauze, Share if you think ON$l0tt

Jesse was about to press the like button, and then hovered over the share button. Then he tried thinking about what it was he'd been looking for before he saw the video, then tried to decide on who to favor again. His mind went back and forth, and he stared at his phone. "What the fuck?" he blurted out and shrugged his shoulders, almost tossing his phone out of his hands. "What the fuck was I doing?"

Within the first quarter of the first semester Jesse's grades had fallen to F's. He had ditched or managed to get kicked out of almost all of his classes at least once, except for one class that he had near-perfect attendance in: Spanish with Maria Fonseca. Now looking up from his phone, Jesse was trying to be as patient as possible for her to arrive.

When he wasn't in class, Jesse was usually walking around trying to look busy so no adults or security would give him any trouble. Really, he had his eyes out for Maria, hoping he would just happen to run into her and finally have a proper self-introduction and conversation with her. But that was hard when he would ditch with Racha.

"'Ey, kick it, Jesse."

It was Monday, and Jesse had been looking forward to Spanish class all weekend. A heatwave had come and Maria was bound to swear a skirt, something sleeveless, and would likely have her hair up. Jesse discovered that he really liked her neck. Her fair skin gave her neck a soft look, which contrasted with her toned physique. It stirred an assumption in Jesse's mind that Maria possessed an untapped passion, heated and bound by the delicate and tiny chain necklaces she would wear on any given day. When there was hair loose from her bun and it hung over her neck, carelessly and wondrously wavy like a lick of flame, it drove him a little wild. He wanted his hand to caress her soft neck and trail his fingers back up into her hair.

"Nah."

"The fuck, Jesse? Let's go."

"Mm."

Racha shook his head. "You better hope neither one of them catches you looking at her like that."

"Wha'?"

"Nothing, pendejo. You're so fucked and you don't even know it."

"Uh, excuse me, Mr. Villalobos--"

"Nyyyyeeeeeeeeeee!"

Racha kept up his screech as he got up from his desk and only stopped as he reached the door. The class snickered as usual, but only some of them turned around to watch Racha go, as they had already grown accustomed to him and were bored with his antics. Mr. Padilla rolled his eyes and picked up the phone from his desk and started dialing.

After class, Jesse watched Maria as she hurried to her next class, but first stopped at the student leadership room. By this point, Jesse had gathered that Maria was incredibly involved and interacted a lot with upperclassmen, teachers, and other adults on campus. For the first time in his life he was legitimately intimidated, and by a girl, no less.

He had kept telling himself that he needed the right place and time to introduce himself to her, because she was always in a hurry or had a friend nearby. Even though Racha had told him that she had a boyfriend, he never seemed to see her with him. Did she really like him? If only Jesse could find the right way, the right words, to explain to her how beautiful and impressive she was to him, that she was making him feel things he never felt before, maybe it would be enough for her to take notice and give him a chance. This had to be real. She would see it; she would know it.

When the final bell had rung for the day, Jesse started heading toward the practice fields. At the far end there was a gate, used for the stadium that led directly out into the neighborhood. It was his new shortcut home, which actually added time to his walk because of the maze of streets behind the school. But there was always the chance that he would see Maria conditioning for volleyball even though they mainly met in the gym.

"¡Esperaté!"

Jesse didn't need to look back. "'Sup?"

Xotchitl skipped up to Jesse as they walked on the grass. Jesse kept his eyes around the fields.

"We getting faded?"

"Nah. Well, maybe. You got some?"

Xotchitl laughed. "No! I thought you had some."

"Nah, I wish. I just… I gotta be careful, you know?"

"Yeah, yeah. I remember you telling me. Ever since you came here and shit."

"Yeh." For a few weeks now, Xotchitl and Jesse had started hanging out here and there for a few minutes during lunch or between classes. He had her in his English class, which he slept through or ditched depending on Racha being around. She had cute freckles on her nose and cheeks with olive skin, and a great body. They laughed at each other's jokes. But there was something annoying about her starting to pop up out of nowhere to chat him up. He didn't want to be seen with her and have Maria think they were a couple.

Jesse looked ahead to the open door of the fenced gate in the distance. He saw a group of slender girls running swiftly along the edge of the fields and making their way through the gate. One not-so-slender girl trailed behind.

"So what happened? You never told me."

Jesse looked back down at the dried-up grass he was trudging over. His mind was constantly thinking about Maria and all of these new, intense feelings he had for her. This was on top of the heavy guilt he constantly carried about what he had done. It suddenly felt good to talk about what was going on inside his head. "I fucked up. I, uh… I really let my family down. When they really needed me."

"Oh. That sucks. Why?"

He instantly regretted going along with her questions, and suddenly was embarrassed and afraid to tell her the truth. Although he didn't really care for her, he still didn't want her to not like him anymore. He looked away and didn't respond.

"Well, there's other things we could do," Xotchitl said with a slight grin as she leaned over to look in his eyes.

"Yeah? Like what?"

"I don't know. Something. You always look like you've got something you're thinking about."

"Yeah, you know who." Jesse said, looking down at the ground.

"Ughhhh. What? Not her again. I thought you just wanted to fuck her real bad."

"Yeh," he lied.

"Chinga tú madre. You know she's taken. And have you even talked to her yet?"

"Nope."

"Fuck that bitch. I'm right here. Talk to me!"

The pair continued across the grass, talking about their teachers, memes, and rumors, and when they passed the gate, they both stopped talking and began listening to something else from a few houses down the street.

Next to a parked car, they saw a girl facing away from them. She was curvy and coffee-skinned, wearing shorts and a t-shirt, on all fours by the curb, huffing and wheezing violently.

Xotchitl took out her phone and started filming as she and Jesse walked along the sidewalk to get a closer look. She was an Asian girl, maybe about his age, with a reddened, sweaty face. She looked like she was focusing really hard on her pain or her breathing. She didn't look up.

"Oh, shit! It's La Puta! What the fuck is she even doing out here? Ahhh!" Xotchitl bent down to bring the camera on her phone right up close to the girl, almost shoving it to her face at one point. Xotchitl laughed the entire time. "And look at those shoes! Ahhaha!"

Jesse stood on the sidewalk in confusion and looked around to see where the other runners had gone. He didn't see any sign of them. The houses on the small street stood silent and still with no signs of life. He'd started toward the girl when a small, bright green car gave a slight screech as it made a hard turn onto the street they were on. It sped to the end of the cul-de-sac, made another sharp turn to meet the curve of the street, and stopped abruptly in front of the gate, with yet another screech of the tires. Everything on the car seemed to be customized, although with what appeared to be homemade or generic kits. Some parts were uneven or off-color. The car stood still for a few seconds, the loud engine still running. Jesse tried to not look obvious as he stared, but he couldn't see through the heavily tinted windows.

Then the passenger's side opened, and over the roof of the car Jesse saw her wavy hair, her now unmistakable figure and stature: Maria.

Jesse took small steps in the direction of the car, the wheezing and huffing completely shut out of his mind. Maria stooped down out of sight as she reached for something in the car, and just then the driver's side opened and out came a hulking young man.

He had wide, muscular shoulders. His hair was faded and buzzed short, wide black sunglasses rested on his broad face, and he had a dark, thin mustache. Jesse was pretty sure he could see a tattoo on his neck from this distance, but the guy didn't stand still. Jesse knew this kind of guy. It was the same guy his father was, and his brothers, and the same guy Jesse was supposed to be. The cholo immediately walked around the car to Maria in a hurried but stocky manner.

"Oh, shit," Xotchitl said right next to Jesse's ear. "That's Raymond Bravo! I heard a rumor last week that Maria had broken up with Moises. But I saw her with him today. Sooo… yeah. True, but not true?"

Maria had slung her backpack on and hung her gym bag over her shoulder. Raymond came over and put his arm around her, pressing her body against his. His face came close to hers and he said something to her. Then he kissed her, almost smashing his face into hers as his arm quickly moved from her lower back up to a tight grasp just under the back of her head. He pulled his body back as she pressed her hand against his chest and turned toward the gate. His arm went out and his hand slapped her butt. Maria giggled and playfully skipped up the path through the gate back to the field.

Raymond slammed the passenger door shut and walked back to the driver's side. Jesse heard gears shift as the tired screeched and the car drove back up the street toward them. It suddenly halted right in front of them with a small screech. Xotchitl scrambled to put her phone away and look casual. She looked around innocently. Jesse, on the other hand, had his eyes locked on Raymond as soon as he came out of the car. Raymond briskly walked over to the curb.

"'Ey," Raymond said with a cock of his head. "What the fuck? You a tourist or some shit?"

Xotchitl brought her attention back to Raymond. "Oh, hi, Raymond! I didn't know you had a car. Sick! How fast does it go? Can you--"

"You cabróns didn't see shit. Right?"

"I didn't even -- pues, I didn't see you until right now."

"What about you, cabrón?"

Jesse didn't flinch. "Yeah, I saw you."

Raymond stepped forward onto the yellowing grass and stood right in front of Jesse. He could smell weed on him. Raymond reached up quickly and took off his sunglasses. "You wanna see me? I'll show you the ground, puto. Your bitch, too."

"I'm not with her," Jesse said, as he took the opportunity to step away from both Xotchitl and Raymond. She looked over at Jesse as her shoulders slumped down. He kept his eyes on Raymond. "But I know who that was. That was Maria."

Raymond lunged forward and swung his arm at Jesse. He barely dodged it, but he couldn't get out of the way of the second blow. Jesse was stunned; then Raymond charged and knocked him to the ground, mounting himself on top of Jesse. He was helpless.

Jesse VI
That's Some Motivation

Raymond swung his fists again and again. He stopped suddenly, as he looked over at Xotchitl taking out her phone.

"You want to be next?"

Xotchitl shoved her phone into her pocket.

Raymond looked around and got up as casually as he could. "That's just a taste, puto. Say shit and see what happens." He got back in his car and slammed the door shut. The engine revved, and then the window rolled halfway down. "Same goes for you, puta. My crew'll roll up and fuck you up, too. I don't care who says what. If any one of you says shit, we'll fuck you both up." The engine roared, the tires screeched, and the car took off and turned the corner.

Jesse got up and wiped grass off his clothes, coughing in the exhaust and smoke from the tires. He put his knuckle to his nose and wiped blood away, but it just smeared across his face. His left eyebrow was red and already starting to swell.

Xotchitl stepped toward Jesse, but he put up his clean hand in front of her. "Stop. I'm fine."

"Damn. That sucked."

"Fuck. It's starting to droop and shit." Jesse pressed the palm of his hand against his eyebrow and then felt it with his fingers. "Uh… wait. Where-- where'd that girl go?"

Xotchitl looked around. "She's gone. Just gone."

"What's her name, anyway?"

"La Puta?" Xotchitl chuckled. "Why? Now you wanna go beat down on somebody?"

"Fuck you." Jesse grabbed his white binder from the ground and walked past Xotchitl.

"Well, fuck you, too, Jesse. Fuck you!" But he ignored her and continued on alone.

On his walk home, Jesse realized he wasn't the same person anymore. At a new school without his friends or the safety of his older brothers, he felt out of place. Unfamiliar. His tough-guy-from-a- tough-family reputation was gone. This girl was all he could think about. He was weak. It angered him. Getting home wasn't a priority for him now, and he wandered the maze of neighborhood streets, deep in thought and in anguish.

He finally emerged from the maze back to a busy street he recognized and looked at his phone. A half hour had gone by. His eye felt like it was melting since his vision was now blocked by the bump and swelling. As he passed a corner house he punched a mailbox, and he felt a pang through his hand and into his wrist. "Fuck!" he screamed. "Fuck! Fuck me!" He cradled his right hand in his left and sat on the curb.

Just then, he heard loud music bumping from a truck heading down the street. As it passed with all of its windows down, he noticed a cheerleader in the front passenger seat, and through the open window of the back of the cabin, he saw Maria sitting with Moises, laughing. And then the truck raced past Jesse and was gone.

"The fuck?" Jesse said. His heart sank even lower. *Well, why wouldn't she be seeing two guys? She's so fucking beautiful and smart. Of course she has choices,* Jesse thought to himself. "What do I gotta do to get noticed?"

The group of runners had come around the corner across the street while Jesse was distracted, and were on their way back toward Portola. Jesse, embarrassed, got back up and looked away to hide his face and started walking again. The girls passed him and he came to an intersection. As he turned the corner, he heard huffing and wheezing again. Jesse looked over his shoulder and saw the Asian girl struggling to keep moving. Her feet looked like they weighed a ton.

"Huh." Jesse said to himself. "How the fuck..." Jesse paused to assess how the girl had managed to sneak away from him and Xotchitl earlier, and still catch up with the runners. "Damn. That's some motivation."

He continued on and thought more about Maria, and how nothing else seemed to matter to him in recent weeks, and it didn't seem like things were going to change anytime soon.

That night he lay in bed with eyes wide open. *I need to do more*, he thought. *But what? How do I get into her classes? How do I compete against football players and gangsters with nice cars?* Jesse thought about getting more money, and maybe jacking more people.

His eye began to throb. He touched it and felt the blob of skin drooping down from his brow. "Shit!"

It was a distraction from the pain in his heart that throbbed even more. The anxiety it caused kept building. Jesse was losing sleep every night, feeling like he was forgetting to go find something. But he also felt that whatever needed to be found was hiding somewhere within him, like there was an idea just waiting to be thought up, a conclusion that would motivate him to take those necessary steps if he wanted any chance with Maria. He thought about his life, the choices he had made and the choices that had been made for him, and hated them all because he was in a position that was meaningless to Maria. *And what if just one of those decisions had been made differently earlier in my life? How different would it have been? How different would I be?*

Then he thought about the future, and where he would be. *How could someone like Maria be with a guy like me? I can't even see it for myself. I can't give her anything!* He realized a decision needed to be made, and he wasn't going to let someone or something else make it for him. He was going to impress Maria. He would show her that he was worthy.

"But how?" Jesse whispered to himself. *How do I catch up? I can't even talk to her, and I need to stand out. How do I make up all of that work and time?*

Then he remembered Yusef. He remembered the deal he offered to him.

"Mierda. Pinche chingón."

Jesse VII
You Are Not Special or Chosen

The Southern California heat finally felt suffocating to Jesse. Wearing black hoodies in eighty- or ninety-degree weather never seemed to bother him too much before. But now he couldn't tell if it was the high temperature outside or his own nervousness and anxiety that was making him feel so noticeably warm now. He still hadn't quite figured out what to say to the old man. How to ask for something that he wanted really wasn't his thing. Nor was apologizing. And how was he supposed to convince someone that he meant it?

The usual hoodrats were kicking it and watching Jesse on the corner with mild interest. He hadn't really been coming out too often in the last few weeks to shake people down. It didn't bring him as much excitement as it once had before, and he was also recognizing that Maria probably wouldn't be too impressed with him if she found out.

When Yusef Abdel finally rounded the corner in his long-sleeved, white athletic shirt and gray running shorts, he had to wipe the sweat from his eyes to focus on Jesse, who looked right at him. He slowed down to a trot, breathing heavily as he eventually stopped in front of Jesse and rested his hands on his hips. "Hello, Jesse. It is a pleasure to see you again."

"Uh, yeah. Hey. Yusef, right?" The watch gleamed on Jesse's wrist.

"What brings you out on this fine, dreadfully hot September afternoon? I hope it is not for another watch. I am all out."

"Nah. Nah, it's not that. I, uh…"

Yusef Abdel listened intently. "And thankfully, we are not on a roof this time, either."

Jesse's eyes grew large in surprise. The hairs on the back of his neck stood straight up and he felt goosebumps all over. A chill shot down his back that cleaved right through the heat. *That dream I had… he* does *know. He was there! Inside my dream. Inside my fuckin' head!*

"Go on," the Arab encouraged.

Jesse turned to look behind him and see who was watching from the neighborhood. He nodded for Yusef to walk away with him down the street. The old man followed, and Jesse looked behind him to scope out the neighborhood really quickly. No one of importance seemed to be paying attention. "Yeah. Look. I... I thought about what you said."

Yusef stared right into Jesse's eyes and continued to listen.

"On the rooftop," Jesse said. He waited for him to look confused. But Yusef's expression didn't change. "You said you could show me more. You could teach me."

Yusef nodded calmly.

Jesse didn't know what else to say. A long, awkward silence continued as Jesse tried not to make eye contact with Yusef. But he was also trying to figure out how Yusef was feeling toward him. He needed to know how much pull he could get from the old man.

"I want to… I want to do everything you showed me. Like you said."

Yusef nodded. "Why?"

Jesse thought for a long time. "You already know why."

The old man grinned and looked right into his eyes. Jesse looked away with a bit of annoyance.

"Jesse, I am not the only person who can see right through you. Even if I was not a Reader, it would be fairly easy to know which buttons to push and which levers to pull. But other people will take advantage of that."

"A what?"

"A Reader," Yusef repeated, staring back.

"What the fuck are you talking about? Like you can read me like a book or some shit? Read this!" Jesse pushed his middle finger toward Yusef's face.

The old man didn't flinch and looked at Jesse's finger tiredly. "A

Reader is someone who has mastered themselves in our world first, then their dreams in their own world, and finally, the dreams of others in their own worlds."

"The fuck?"

Yusef stared back calmly.

"You mean like all that shit you did to me in my dream? Why the fuck do you call yourself a reader, though? Like, is there some manual or some shit you read to get all up in my mind?"

"Readers are incredibly dedicated to knowledge. If you wish to master these worlds I have mentioned, then surely, you must first learn how they work. If you are to manipulate and create in these worlds, like you witnessed me do, then you must also go beyond the typed words in our books and read what is not directly written. You must also learn to read when there are no words at all."

"Nah. Fuck all that."

Yusef began taking some steps past Jesse. "Then you have chosen to be helpless."

"Shit! Wait, wait, wait. Come back," Jesse pleaded as he grabbed at Yusef's shirt and tugged it toward himself. "But I fucking hate reading."

"You do realize that is your choice? That you can also love to read? And with some guidance and practice, you will get better. And then it will be easy. Addicting, almost. If you are lucky."

Jesse paused and thought for a few seconds, letting go of Yusef's shirt. "Ugh. Reading? Really? That's some white boy shit right there." Jesse sighed and rested his hands on his head. "You'll help me? Like you said."

"Yes. With conditions."

"Conditions?"

"Look at this as a deal," Yusef explained. "I will take time and effort out of my growingly limited time on this Earth to train you. But you must be committed, Jesse. Or else you will never become what you want to be. You will never even come close. Your potential is... astounding."

"How do you know that? I'm just… I'm just me. I ain't got shit. I never went to no nice school. Why ain't you stalking one of them white kids in south County?"

"I know this because you are not special or chosen, Jesse. Remove that rubbish from your mind immediately. I came to you because you are conflicted. You have been your entire life that much is remarkably clear. The odds have always been against you. And while you have not been making the best of choices, you are still here. For the first time in your life, Jesse, you have decided that you want something, that it will make your life better. And you come from nothing. Your intelligence is untapped and unused. Your life has been strewn with pain and bad choice after bad choice. But, Jesse, every day is new. Every choice you make is your own. Your life, your story, has not been written. Jesse is in control of Jesse's life. All you have to do is accept that, and decide to use your will toward the things you want."

"Nah, you can't tell me that. You don't know me, what I've been through. You can say that shit, but it's not that easy to just start doing."

"This world is full of distractions, now more than ever before. It is full of things that will entice you and take you off of your path. But I will be here to guide you.

"You can be remarkable in this world and grow to a unique greatness because of your struggles and your pain," Yusef continued, now looking intently into Jesse's eyes. "Do you not see, Jesse? Your pain, your struggles, your scars: those are all strengths. Those can make you smarter and stronger, if you let them. That is the advantage that you have over those other kids in the nice houses and personal cars. Everything they have has been given to them. They do not know how to struggle."

Jesse looked confused as he processed everything Yusef was saying. "Huh. I didn't see it that way."

"You, Jesse: you will work for the things you want and need. You will earn it. Because of that, you will be capable and confident. You will understand the potential of your willpower and in so doing, possess remarkably powerful strengths and abilities in the worlds of your dreams, and others. Your growth will manifest here in the waking world, further empowering you to excel beyond your physical and mental limits."

"A'ight. I get it. You couldn't just tell me that I'm going to be a badass?"

Yusef chuckled. "Yes, Jesse. You certainly will be. But it will not happen overnight. And as I said… there are conditions."

Jesse sighed. "Ughhh! Alright, what? I gotta mow your lawn or some shit? I know I'm Mexican, homie, but that shit is fucked up."

Yusef stared back at him blankly.

"What? I am. Half. And Guatemalan."

"You will not be required to mow my lawn, because I do not have one. Can we continue?"

"Alright, alright. I'm listening," Jesse assured.

"First, you will be required to meet with me six days a week. You will have one day of rest and independent reflection. At these---"

"Get the fuck out of here! Six days? Hijole!"

"Is this going to happen every time I say something?" Yusef said with a slight annoyance.

"Shit. Alright, alright. I'm listening. Damn, six days! Might as well get a fucking job."

"Moving on. At these sessions I will oversee your physical, mental, and spiritual training."

At that, Jesse was about to speak, but then he quickly put his hand over his mouth.

Yusef went on. "I will tutor you academically for your classes as well as additional literacy and critical thinking skills that you need."

Jesse's eyebrows shot up.

"These will also include desperately needed etiquette training."

"Mwahh dhaa?" Jesse asked under his hands.

"Etiquette is proper manners, habits, and customs that are expected to be used in everyday life and special occasions. Something you are sorely lacking."

Jesse paused as his eyes scowled and stared right at Yusef. A moment passed as Jesse's eyes wandered away in reflection. He nodded his head, dropped his hands, and shrugged in agreement.

"To promptly attend these training sessions and to properly take care of your body as it is about to change drastically, you will also need to follow a strict eating, studying, and sleeping schedule. This will also ensure that your dream journaling will be completed daily, and therefore, that you will sleep enough to have lucid dreams. Then you can properly explore and train in your dreams."

"Okay, that first part really sucks. But that last part sounds lit. This is going to suck, but fuck it. This is what I gotta do, right?"

"There's more."

"No mames!"

"You will need to follow each and every direction that I give you from now on. No matter how minor or major. I am not your parent. I am more than that now. I am the gatekeeper to the heavens and beyond. This training, this world I am showing you, it is *secret.* You must not tell a *single* soul, nor attempt to explore this world on your own without my knowing -- under *any* circumstances. If another Reader finds you, they can infiltrate your mind and find you, your family, and me. I will be investing and risking so much in you, Jesse. You are indebted to me."

"Oh, there it is! This is a fucking scam. I knew it. Fuck you!"

"Jesse, I do not speak about money. I speak about something I am investing in you that is more valuable than money. That has no price because it is so valuable: time, Jesse. The things you can do with your time are limitless. It is the ultimate currency in the universe." Yusef stared into Jesse's eyes intently. "Once you have spent that, you will never get any of it back. When it is gone, it is gone forever. With each passing day, each passing hour and minute... each second, Jesse, your hourglass loses more sand.

"Perhaps right now, in your youth, you probably see the sand in your hourglass as so vast that it might seem like a beautiful beach to you: limitless. At this point in my life, my hourglass runs nearly empty. Perhaps I could even count the grains of sand left until I am no more. For me, the time I am going to put into you is worth more than anything else I have spent my time on before this point, because I have so few left. Does that make sense to you, Jesse?"

"Fuck," Jesse said heavily. His eyes stared a thousand miles into the ground. "Uh, I mean… damn, or whatever."

"I will take that to mean that you do. Therefore, as my first order for you, I will ask that you enter the science contest being held at your school in January."

"Wait, what? How -- there's a science fair going on at school?"

"It is only being advertised on the sign out front."

"Who looks at that shit?"

"People who are curious and engaged with the world around them, and not just their own. I will help you with your research and the scientific method."

"Well, damn."

"Tomorrow, your new life begins," Yusef said. "Do make sure you get your rest. The first session will be one to remember."

Jesse VIII
Endless Possibilities

During announcements in Spanish class, Jesse finally heard about the science fair, now that he was actually listening. Plus, it helped that Racha was late again -- or ditched -- and wasn't distracting Jesse. Maria was also not there, since she was now helping out with morning announcements every once in a while.

"Yes, that's right, Caballeros and future scientists, you can get a free special VIP package for Winter Bash *on Valentine's Day* -- that's right, free! -- for winning the Portola High School 64th Annual Science Fair. This VIP package includes a free photo package, two song requests from the DJ and a personalized shoutout, AND reserved seating for you and your special date.

"You will also get an exclusive interview featured on the front page of our wonderful newsletter, *The Expedition,* and a featured section in the yearbook -- which you will also receive a free copy of -- and of course advancement to the district-wide science fair competition, where you could possibly go on to state! Hey, not to mention you get everything that we Caballeros crave -- that's right, Portola -- Honor, Pride, Achievement!"

The announcements went on, but Jesse tuned out as he began to think about all of that weird pressure and attention that would come with winning. *Who the fuck wants that? But that VIP is snatched.*

Someone nearby got mildly excited about it and mentioned a volcano experiment they had done back in 4th grade. But he soon forgot all about the contest as he had too much fun describing to his friend the mess of the baking soda, pebbles, and red food coloring when it foamed all over his teacher's carpet. He had said it looked like period blood and had asked his teacher if it was hers. They laughed hard about it shamelessly.

Jesse dragged himself to the rest of his classes and was only late to one of them. Seeing Maria was beginning to grow stale, since he continued to be ignored and failed to find common ground with her. He even tried ignoring her back, which only proved to be incredibly useless and might even have made his adoration of her more intense despite his attempts to suppress it.

The effort to attend his classes came from the agreement he had made with Yusef. He was a little interested to see what his first training session would be like later that day, right after school. He imagined that the old man had a few weights laying around and he'd also do some sit ups and push ups. *Probably some weird-ass meditation shit, too.*

Yusef told Jesse to meet him at Davidson Park after school, which was near Portola and only a little bit out of his way home. Jesse got there and saw Yusef waiting by picnic tables.

"By all means, you should go change so we can begin," Yusef announced. He must have come straight from school because he was wearing his white buttoned shirt and a green necktie under a gray buttoned vest, along with matching gray slacks and brown leather Oxford shoes.

"Huh?"

"I am assuming that you brought other clothes and shoes… somewhere… ?" Yusef trailed off as his eyes searched for a backpack or something that Jesse might have used to stow away his actual work out gear. Jesse was wearing jeans, a white pair of sneakers that may or may not have had shoelaces buried under his pant legs, and a baggy black tee.

"Nah," Jesse said with a quick shake of his head. "This is it. Whatchu got, man?"

Yusef's eyebrows raised and a slight smirk snuck in the corner of his mouth. "Well, we are certainly going to see. I will be impressed if those fancy sneakers actually stay on. I hope they are actually worth their ridiculous price tag."

Jesse spat on the ground. "Vámonos."

After the first hour, Jesse's pride was still holding out against his stamina. Yusef led Jesse running around a pavement walkway that circled a soccer field. It was supposed to be roughly the equivalent of a running track. After each lap, he had Jesse complete a set of either sit-ups, pushups, squats, trunk lifts, or superman lifts right along with him. Jesse trudged along his laps getting noticeably more tired, sweatier, slower, and more red in the face. After lap number eight Yusef finally raised his hand and signaled Jesse to stop. "Get yourself some water."

Jesse didn't say anything and huffed straight away to a nearby water fountain. After he finished slurping, he slowly walked back, still breathing heavily. The autumn sun was beginning to retire for the day and was getting low.

"Now we can begin." Yusef said.

"What!"

"Well, yes. Now that you are properly warmed up. It was also nice to see that your shoes actually stayed on that entire time. Impressive, actually."

Jesse was too tired to start yelling and cursing at Yusef, but he did debate walking away at that moment. Then he remembered what waited for him out there if he left. Absolutely nothing.

"A'ight, viejo. A'ight."

"I am your mirror. Do as I do." Yusef began to lead Jesse through various stretches and cool downs. Some of the stances were very awkward for Jesse. They seemed almost like ballerina movements and Yusef also had him freeze in place at weird angles. He had to look around a few times to make sure no one was around that would recognize him, but this wasn't really near his hood, anyway. Yusef also coached Jesse on his breathing and his posture while he ran. After the warm up, Yusef told Jesse to go run one more lap, but to do it in his mind first.

"What?"

"Visualize yourself running that lap inside your mind. Go through each motion, each step, and picture your posture and plan your breathing into each step. Push your stomach out and breath in, pull your stomach in and exhale. Imagine this all the way around the lap. When you have done that, you may get up and actually do it."

Jesse nodded without saying anything and had his eyes focused somewhere else past Yusef; perhaps nowhere physically at all. His eyes began to wander a bit, and Yusef told him to refocus. After rolling his shoulders and neck, Jesse closed his eyes and remained still for a moment. He opened his eyes and Yusef, with his arms crossed, lifted a hand and pointed to the track.

As Jesse took off, Yusef noticed an almost immediate difference in how Jesse carried himself, and saw his stomach push out from under his shirt as he inhaled, and his stomach sucked in when he exhaled. His arms and hands had more control and intention in their swing. When he returned from his lap, Jesse looked more assured of himself, like he had just won at something. He looked right into Yusef's eyes and nodded.

Yusef led him through light stretches and awkward poses again. "Now," Jesse was about to get up from the grass when Yusef gestured for him to stay down. "Now, you will do burpees," Yusef declared.

"The fuck?"

Yusef demonstrated for Jesse by dropping down to a push-up position nearly touching the ground, then pushed up and jumped onto his feet into a jumping jack and then dropped down into the push-up position again. From the ground he yelled out "One!" then shot up again into a standing position and gestured with his arms toward Jesse. "Now you. Five reps to start."

"That shit's easy." But Jesse was sadly misinformed by the ease with which Yusef was able to complete his burpee. On the way back up during the first one, gravity felt like it was trying to pull Jesse's guts right out of him. He actually felt the skin on his face droop down. "Oh, fuck!" Jesse squeaked out as he unevenly clapped his hands together for his poor excuse of a jumping jack.

"I suppose that counted as one," Yusef spouted.

"Uh, I… I actually have to do all five?"

"Well, now you only have four more. Right?"

"Pinche narizone." Jesse only got slower and sloppier with each attempt at going down and coming back up. On the fifth one, Jesse's face began to shift from flushed to pale.

"Unless you want to be in even more pain tomorrow, you will continue to stretch right now."

"What do I stretch?"

"What hurts?"

"Everything, pendejo."

"Well, it sounds like you just answered your own question, my young mubtadi."

"The fuck is that?"

"Apprentice. 'Mubtadi' means apprentice."

Jesse still gave him a confused look.

"I am your trainer in a craft, and you are learning a craft from me."

"A craft? Like to make something?"

"Yes, precisely."

"Well, what the fuck am I crafting right now? Sweat and a sore ass?"

"Possibilities, Jesse. Endless possibilities. In time, you could craft whatever you wanted on the Plane."

"Oh, shit! You got a jet? Where we going, homie? You didn't tell me that before!"

"No, my young mubtadi. Not an airplane. The Plane is where you go after you have mastered lucid dreaming, where you control everything in your dreams. All of those who have the desire and are properly trained, can go to the Plane to become stronger, better, and more powerful. There, they shape our reality by reshaping other worlds."

"So, we not going to Miami?"

Yusef rolled his eyes. "It is time for another lap."

"Ah, shit."

Now that Jesse was more focused and at a slower pace on the track, Yusef trailed behind him and continued to explain.

"When you dream, Jesse, your untrained mind is creating a world of its own. You are letting your mind throw yourself around in there and it is chaos, fueled by unfiltered emotion and random memory. I will train you to control that chaos, and show you how to create your own world."

Jesse continued to huff as he jogged along. "Pl… Plane!"

"Ah, yes. Only after you have mastered your own dream world will you be ready to begin training in the common dream world. Imagine if you can, Jesse, that every night when you dream, you are watching a movie on a film screen. In time, you will be the actor, director, even the writer before the dream appears on screen. In other words, soon you will be able to dream whatever you want.

"Soon after that, you will learn how to find the door and walk out of that movie theater into the bigger movieplex, where your neighbor's dreams are being screened in the theater right next to yours. You will be able to walk along the movieplex to the theaters of anyone you wanted. Once inside their theater, you could see their dreams, and assuming they are untrained, you could be an actor, director, and even a writer for their dream on the big screen."

Jesse stopped running. "That… that night," he huffed out, trying to catch his breath. He turned to face Yusef. "When you were... in my dream. That wasn't... the first time, right? You had to… you had been in my head before… you *wrote* that dream, didn't you?"

"Yes, Jesse. You can put it that way. I did."

"Did you know I was going to kick you off the roof like that?"

"I anticipated that as one of a few possibilities."

"But if you made that dream for me, then why did you let that happen?"

"Because choice and willpower are important. And incredibly powerful. You have to want this, Jesse. You have to want this so badly, as if your life depends on it. You need to want this like you were drowning and want to rush to the surface to breathe air. You have to want it that badly all of the time. Even in your sleep. Especially in your sleep."

"I'm here, aren't I?"

"Indeed, Jesse. But things will get harder. Every day, it's going to get harder."

"I guess that means I gotta want it more every day then, right, viejo?"

"That is right, Mubtadi. That is exactly right."

"So? Tell me how to do it."

"Oh, you are not quite ready for that yet. It requires a lot of mental training, and emotional preparation, as well. To control your dreams means you are in control of your mind and your own world. That means you must have an abundance of willpower. You must have confidence. And you must have imagination."

"Mierda. I'm fucked."

"Those things will come, Mubtadi, in time. With practice. But the Science Fair is a major step toward that goal. You need victories, and you need them in ways that you never really thought possible because then you will really start believing in the things you are capable of doing and even those things that you once thought were not possible for you. Does that make sense to you?"

"Yeh," Jesse said as his head hung low.

"If you do not win the contest, it is fine, my mubtadi. We must always aim for greatness. Even in failure we can be proud. When we fall from great heights we learn how to fall on our feet, and when we do not, we learn that falling on our face is not the end of the world. We pick ourselves up as tougher, wiser versions of ourselves."

Jesse shifted his weight as his hands rested on his hips. "You're gonna help me, though, right? With the project?"

"Of course, mudtabi. But I will not do the work for you. I will guide you and help you plan. But you must see it through. It has to be your idea, your hands, and your voice."

Jesse nodded sullenly. "So… when do I gotta do this by?"

"I was wondering when you were finally going to ask. Come along. We will go sit and we will make a plan. Then you will go home and do your homework before you do anything else."

"¡No mames!"

Jesse IX
No Superman to Save Us

"But I didn't do shit!"

"Maybe not recently, but you're at a new school for a reason, Jesse."

"Not this again."

"Alfredo looks up to you, Jesse. Not only are you his oldest brother now, but he looks to you as a father figure. He needs guidance." Lita stood quietly in the hallway to the kitchen. She stared into the floor as she listened to the argument unfold.

"I didn't tell him to punch that kid. He probably deserved it, anyway."

"Jesse! That's what I'm talking about. It's the things you say as well that influence him. It's the things you *don't* do that also teach him how the world works, and what a man is supposed to be and not be."

"Yeah, I bet you would know about that, wouldn't you, Dominique?"

Ms. Arcos scowled at Jesse. "You leave their dad out of this, Jesse!" She hissed as she pointed back in her room of the apartment, where her toddler, Alexia, and her baby, Antonio, were currently playing with Alfredo and Marcy, who had her earbuds in and stared down into a phone on her lap. "That is not fair to them or me. Or you!"

Mrs. Ramirez had to step in now. "Jesús! ¡Espérate! Say you're sorry. ¡Ahora mismo!

"I'm sorry I'm not perfect. And you don't know how the world works now. For me, for us. That kid probably needed to get punched, and Fredo probably needed to be the one to do it. Now who gonna fuck with him?

He needs to fight his own battles, Lita."

"He needs to stay in school and get good grades, Jesse," Dominique went on. "And now he's suspended. Do you really want him following in your footsteps? Making the same mistakes you and Hugo and your father made?"

"What's wrong with us?" Jesse threw his arms in the air. Then he looked past Dominique and turned toward Mrs. Ramirez. "We gotta make it, Lita. No one is going to take care of us anymore. We're on our own to make our own way. That's life, that's the fucking truth. The sooner Fredo knows that, the better."

Mrs. Ramirez spoke up again. "Look at where your Papá and Junior are now! And Erik, pobrecito. God rest his soul." She performed the sign of the cross over her body and head. "You want to bury Alfredo, también? Porque if something happens to him, it's your fault now."

"Oh, my God! Fuck you, Lita!" Jesse could feel his veins pumping. His muscles felt tensed up, like he was getting ready to jump into an epic fight. He stormed out of the kitchen and went to go put on his workout gear. Yusef was always telling him about turning losses into victories, turning bad into good. When you get pushed, pull in and use that momentum to your advantage. So now that he was pumped up with anger, Jesse decided to use that energy to get his daily workout done. And it was looking like this workout was going to be a really good one.

It was November now and three weeks since Jesse began his training under Yusef. By this point, Jesse had figured out a regular running route that took him through numerous neighborhoods and led him to the city hall parking structure, where he stormed up four flights of stairs to the top of the structure, then ran back down the winding parking levels and back home.

Yusef had been making sure that Jesse was being consistent with his physical training, meditation, school work, diet, and tutoring, to the point now that Jesse was beginning to keep up the consistency on his own. But it was a rough start. Jesse would now expect a call from Yusef later that night to check in on Jesse's daily progress. Yusef had a special knack for knowing when Jesse was lying or even stretching the truth a bit -- and that was just on the phone. When Jesse saw Yusef in person, he could smell the dishonesty on Jesse before even seeing him. Getting caught in such a lie meant extra physical training: extra laps around the field, burpees, push-ups, wall-sits, planks, or whatever painful creation Yusef could come up with.

Still, despite the punitive training exercises on top of his routine workouts, Jesse felt frustrated that his body wasn't reflecting the effort he felt like he was putting in. He convinced himself that he should have a six pack at this point, or at least the beginning of one. Jesse felt stronger, more energetic, and alert. But it wasn't enough. He needed to grab the attention of Maria. He felt like he was on the path to making her seek *him*. But he still wasn't anywhere close to where he wanted to be. So why put in all of this work?

As soon as Jesse got back in from his run and stretched, he went to the bathroom and took off his shirt, sucking in his stomach and flexing his core while standing up tall and straight. There still wasn't much to look at. He did notice that his body felt tighter and maybe even looked a little slimmer. Jesse wasn't overweight, but if there was a six pack, it was hiding under a subtle layer of flab. His neck appeared to be a bit thicker now, and the constant soreness in his arms, legs, chest, and back suggested that muscles were forming and getting stronger, but Jesse wanted to see it. All of that hard work and nothing to show for it! At this rate, Maria would be off to some college far away before Jesse's body was anywhere near he wanted it to be. A wave of rage overtook him and he was about to punch the mirror, but in a last-second touch of caution, opted to punch the sink counter, instead.

"Fuck!" he yelled out as he recoiled in pain and cradled his right hand. He instinctively shook it, as if to shake off the pain, but that only made it worse. "Fuuuuuuckkk!" he groaned out in anger.

"Mijo?" Lita yelled from the kitchen.

"I'm fine!" Jesse yelled back. This was now one of those opportunities that Yusef advised Jesse about: he needed to practice dealing with his pain in less destructive ways. Of all Yusef was training him to do, he struggled most with meditation. It felt like such a waste of time. But he had to admit that he sometimes did feel a bit more relaxed after practicing.

His training did come in handy at times like this: when pain was almost unbearable. Yusef had been teaching Jesse to block out pain by learning how to focus on happy memories and positive images about the future; Zen is how Yusef kept referring to it, but apparently it wasn't the right word for it, he had tried to explain. He didn't want Jesse getting too caught up in all of the weird terms. But he had remembered that Yusef explained the original word as "dhyana." At any rate, by practicing this technique with the other steps in meditation that Yusef had trained him in, Jesse would essentially be able to block out physical pain. Jesse was practicing this more and more as his physical training continued, even when not in his typical meditative poses. "Ultimate meditation and focus is when one can become Zen in any form, any place, and any time," Yusef had explained over and over.

So Jesse started taking slow, deep breaths and calmly left the bathroom and went into the vacant bedroom. He sat down and slightly leaned himself against the wall. His muscles relaxed and his exhales and inhales were full and maximized. He went deep into his mind, syncing the throbs of his hand with the pounding of his heart. As he focused on calming the beat of his pulse and imagined sunny days holding Maria's hand, festive nights with Hugo and his Papá, and somewhere in some unknown time ago smelling his mother's hair and hearing her laugh, Jesse's heart calmed and so did the pain in his hand. It would still be sore, but now Jesse could focus on other things. Like his dreaded science project.

After brainstorming with Yusef a few weeks ago, Jesse had decided to conduct his research on something that had never really occurred to him as even being a *thing*. Since Yusef had begun to turn Jesse's world upside down, he was learning quite a bit about how the world worked. Yusef was even teaching Jesse things about the Black community, and it made a lot of sense to him. When Yusef had explained to Jesse that Blacks made up about 13% of the U.S. population, but made up about 34% of the total prison population in the country, Jesse had to let that process for a few seconds before it made sense in his head. And even then, it didn't make sense.

"Why are Black people in prison so much?" he asked Yusef.

"Ah! That is a powerful question. And now I have one for you. Have you ever heard of the school-to-prison pipeline?"

"Uh… I think one of my cousins is a plumber if you've got a problem, jefe."

"I will take that as a no." Then Yusef had immediately sent Jesse off to get his phone and do a quick web search. But when Jesse didn't come back right away and Yusef had gone to find him, Jesse just had more questions to throw at him. It was instantly decided that Jesse had already started his research for his science project, and he just needed to refine his question and perhaps make it more relevant to himself.

"But shouldn't I be doing something with like, chemicals and shit?"

Yusef stared back at him for a second and thought about his response. "Let's imagine that I was your doctor, Mubtadi, and I knew you were dying."

Jesse's eyes grew big.

"Don't worry, you're not dying. Not right now, anyway. But let us continue with this hypothetical explanation. *Pretend* you are dying. I know it, you know it. As your doctor, I know how to cure you. You just need to be shown how to change some habits in your life, take some medicine, and have it explained to you why some of the things you eat or do in your life are causing you to die."

"Okay. That makes sense so far."

"Right. But, the problem is, you are not coming in to see me. I cannot show you what is wrong with you, explain to you how to fix it. You are going to keep doing the things wrong in your life that are causing you to die."

Jesse was getting bored and impatient. "So what the fuck? Am I going to die or what? Why can't I come in to see you?"

"That is the point of this project, Mubtadi. The reality is that *we* are dying. Our civilization is crumbling. Our doctors, scientists, and teachers are not able to reach and communicate with people to teach them how to fix ourselves. Because the people that can and should be making the most difference, people like you, are not learning about how to save ourselves. They are not learning in our schools. They are getting kicked out. Eventually they go to prison. Then they become part of yet another problem that we have, and that makes saving our civilization -- our people -- harder."

Jesse stood in silence, deep in thought. "I still don't get it."

"What is the point of the knowledgeable people all together in the same room showing off the typical scientific findings to each other, when the world outside is *burning*? We have to show each other why all of this knowledge matters, and why everyone *needs* to know about it. If people are not able to learn about it, then we need to find out why and *do* something about it."

"Ugh," Jesse groaned. "It *is* hot," he said with a grimace.

"That is precisely the kind of response that indicates a need to properly inform people. It is so much more than the weather feeling a little warmer or colder than usual. Those changes have devastating effects across whole parts of the world. If you cannot see it or it is not directly impacting you in ways that drastically endanger your well-being, then you are likely to ignore it. Until it actually does. But by then, it will likely be much too late. So it goes with the poor, the marginalized, and the oppressed."

"So why don't those smart people solve it? They have all of the answers, don't they?" Jesse asked.

"This is not a math equation, Mubtadi. There is no great invention that will reverse all of the damage that has been done, and will continue to be done at our current rate. We have no Superman to save us. And the causes are driven by people that profit from it."

"What do you mean people profit from it? From the world being destroyed?" Jesse asked.

"You have much to learn, my mubtadi. And much to do if we are to make a difference."

"Pues, how does changing the school-to-prison pipeline save everyone?"

"Alone, it will not. It is but one pillar of many that needed to bolster our survival. But no one person can replace all of these foundations that have cracked."

Jesse didn't have more to say or ask, but looked like Yusef's words were working their way around in his mind.

"Now, back to training. We will come back to this question. Perhaps you will begin to realize what role you will play in this life… what kind of hero you need to be."

Jesse opened his eyes from his meditative state, back in the bedroom against the wall. That conversation was from two weeks ago. Since then, Jesse had researched the school-to-prison pipeline. He was shocked at how many teens were being sent to juvie, and then prison. Sometimes, straight to prison because their judge decided to put them on trial as an adult -- just like his brother, Junior. One statistic that really stood out to Jesse was about the likelihood of going to prison, based on your ethnicity: 1 in 23 for white males, 1 in 6 for Hispanic males, and 1 in 4 for black males. Jesse wondered what it meant for his chances if members of his family had already been in trouble with the law.

My life is shitty. But it's not prison-shitty. I want to see Maria. And be with her. I guess I want to graduate and make my family proud, too.

Just then he looked down at his arm because he noticed a slight throbbing. He saw a vein which he hadn't really noticed before. He examined it and also noticed that his forearm had a little more shape than usual.

"Huh," he said. "Guess this shit working."

Jesse X
The Legacy of All Our Struggles

It started with the fight in the stands. The Knights were already leading the American West league by late November and the championship looked promising for them this year, finally. They were playing against the Corsairs, who had started out strong this season but were last in the entire league. That didn't stop their die-hard fans from showing up to the game in force, decked out in black and silver. On a nationally televised Monday Night Football game, a fight broke out between two opposing fans and their surrounding friends took sides. The melee spilled onto the field as one of the fans was tossed over a barricade, and he pulled his adversary over the barricade with him. The game had to be paused as security cleared out the fight. The tension had been brewing since last season, when a few Corsairs players took a knee during the National Anthem. A Knights player had walked the field and tried to kick one of them over.

Viral videos from the Monday night game continued from the parking lots, right after the fourth quarter ended. The Corsairs fans ganged up on a Knights fan and bloodied him and his wife. Other Knights fans came to their rescue and broke up the fight. The violence spread across the parking lot and a nearby gas station, and as the night wore on, other fights broke out across the city in various bars, restaurants, and even the streets. By the next morning twenty-two people ended up in the hospital.

Jesse was captivated with the fight videos and all of the comments, and other people recording themselves and promising to attack people on the streets if they saw them wearing Knights/Corsairs clothes or accessories. It was hard to avoid the controversy if you used the internet at all.

Jesse's eyes fluttered and he realized that his short break wasn't short anymore. He had been sucked in again.

He dropped his phone on his mattress and then rolled over the edge of his mattress to the nearby floor, right into push-up position. He did twenty and then started holding his body straight and still at the bottom position, so his body was barely touching the ground, and held it there for five deep breaths. He pushed back to the up position, and did this four more times. He kneeled up and a glisten of sweat crowned his head.

As he caught his breath, Jesse thought about a dream from last night. Almost two months had passed since he started his training with Yusef, and his lucid dreaming was becoming consistent. Yusef's sleep training methods felt corny at first, but even before they started working in his dreams the self-affirmation and visualizing felt good. Earlier in the week, Jesse had flown in his dream for a second time. He was really trying for a third last night but didn't quite get it. Instead, he ended up jumping out of control and woke up when the landing was out of his control.

His wrist hurt where he wore Yusef's watch. He loosened it and saw the underside of the watch straps dug into his skin and left an imprint of a squiggly line around his wrist. But wearing it looser didn't feel as secure. *Beggars can't be choosers*, he shrugged to himself and tightened it back up.

He reached back for his phone and saw the time, noting that his homework break was done in two minutes. He scrolled his social media some more and something about Horizon came up a few times on his different feeds. There was a meme of Mr. Moneybags from Monopoly holding a giant bag of cash behind him, and he was labeled as "Samuel Bradford, CEO of Horizon," but instead of stepping over "Go" the famous spot on the board had been replaced with "My paycheck". Jesse then clicked on a video and saw a YouTuber holding up his Horizon phone, talking about how every time there was an update, he just knew that his phone was slower, or had lower battery life, or something just wasn't right. He then swore off buying another Horizon product ever again.

Jesse searched online for "Horizon phone news" and immediately clicked on a recent video uploaded from One World News, titled "INTERVIEW: Horizon CEO Admits Faulty Products, Promotes New

Nova Nine Phone." Samuel Bradford sat on a red leather chair, leaning across the armrest and directly addressing the interviewer, who was off-camera.

"Well, of course our phones have a limited design," he said dismissively. "These products are incredibly expensive to manufacture and assemble. Not to mention the process and cost of finding and allocating the resources for this premiere technology."

"Yes, but--" the assertive female voice of the reporter started to say.

"Look," he said to the interviewer, sitting up and then leaning in closer, sticking his head out. "Can you imagine what would happen to the international market if these phones stopped being made because everyone only bought one or two during their entire lives? The industry would crash and burn with that loss in sales. There are incredibly honorable, hard-working people in other parts of the world, the developing world, that depend on the enthusiastic purchasing habits of the more fortunate, industrial countries."

"What would you say about the--"

"We're talking massive loss of jobs, opportunities, and ongoing development in other parts of the world, not to mention the sales and other related industries right here in the U.S. of A.

"More importantly," Bradford went on, "we're helping to build a middle class in other parts of the world. With that, comes a demand for democracy. So don't come in here and question our sales philosophy. Maybe we're not saving the world, but we're sure helping a lot of people survive in it. Some people might go so far as to call our marketing strategies patriotic. We're not a business anymore. We're an institution, and without us a lot of things would fall apart."

The video then cut to the interviewer, a thirty-something blonde woman with a defined jawline and broad breasts that pushed and peaked out of her low-cut blue dress. "Yes," she said with eyes that stared directly straight ahead. "But how can you justify coordinated and planned faultiness in your products, including specially designed malware -- hidden in your company's product updates -- that intentionally slows software performance and drains battery life? All the while your company continues to push sales for products that promise to *increase* performance and battery life. Further--"

"Our products *do* increase performance and battery life," Bradford cut in. "How else can we keep up with the ever-increasing demands of newer apps, games, higher quality photos, videos, and..." He went on but Jesse stopped paying attention and tried to refocus on his task at hand.

This proved a little harder than usual. As he understood it, this Bradford guy was getting away with making our phones slow and break down on purpose so we would keep buying more. Jesse pondered that for a second and came to the conclusion that people liked buying new phones, anyway.

"Mr. Bradford, I'd like to show you something. You might be familiar, of course, with the kinds of materials that are needed for all of these phones you so proudly produce," the beautiful blonde reporter said as the video switched over to footage of microchips and the inside of phones being manufactured. "But what you and our viewers might not be aware of," she continued on as the video switched over to footage of sweaty, dirty men in scraggly clothes, digging with tools inside a dark cave, "is that these phones require uncommon materials and elements, such as cobalt. Cobalt, for example, can only be affordably mined in certain places. And extracting it can be very dangerous, especially when companies such as yours, Mr. Bradford, aggressively purchase it from Chinese companies that overlook hazardous mining practices that exploit and endanger poor, desperate workers who have limited options for other employment."

The video now showed villagers in African villages with missing limbs, some laying in beds coughing up blood, and lifeless bodies being pulled out of caved-in mines. "These laborers," the journalist went on, "live in developing countries where laws can't protect them against the careless labor practices that they work under, resulting in horrendous injuries, illnesses, and too often, death."

The interview went on, but Jesse was lost in thought as he wondered what the hell cobalt was. He thought it was a color. A quick web search revealed that it was an element heavily sought after for its high use in electronics manufacturing, particularly smartphones. Then he wondered just how many phones were being made. After another search, he saw that just within the first nine months of 2018, there were already more than a billion phones produced just in China alone.

"Damn!" he exclaimed.

How many people need phones? He thought. *Wait. How many people are there?* He tapped some more into his phone and it revealed that there were currently 7.6 billion people living on Earth.

"Shit. That's a fuck ton of people!"

But how many of them actually have phones? He then realized that the 7.6 billion people also has to include a lot of babies and kids, really old people, and really poor people that probably don't all have phones.

How does this connect with the bigger picture? Jesse thought, repeating Yusef's tip about analyzing the news. *What is being gained beyond money, and who gets it?* He was learning that more money was definitely going to the elites. But Yusef warned this was an old game, and some elites want more than that. Powerful ones Yusef mentioned, like the Apostles, were focused on not just controlling money, but ideas and beliefs. They wanted votes. Souls. Total control.

DUN-DUN-DUH-NUH-DUN-DUN-DUH-NUH. A heavy and loud electric guitar riff exploded from Jesse's phone as an alarm notification titled "Breaks over fucktard" flashed across his screen. He swiped to turn off the alarm and immediately dropped his phone where he held it, and it bounced off the mattress and thudded across the carpeted floor. He ignored it and focused on his English homework, which was a set of review questions for Anne Frank's *The Diary of a Young Girl.*

Jesse had reluctantly taken his break to begin with. He was surprised by how interested he had become in the book. It was the first time he had ever sat and read anything for an hour straight. It felt really girly and weird at first reading a white chick's diary, especially since she wrote a lot about liking boys, not to mention getting her period. But he also couldn't stop. She wrote about things that Jesse always wondered about that he would otherwise not have any kind of perspective on. Like, *why did girls like certain boys? And do they feel the same way I do when I like a girl?* But then again, it wasn't like Anne had a lot of options to choose from.

As she wrote more about her deepest feelings and confessions, she also wrote about what was happening in the world around her, from the little bit of news she had access to as she hid with her family. It all sounded like a movie, and Jesse had to constantly remind himself that this actually happened, which made it more captivating to him.

Jesse also wondered what that must have felt like, to live in the same small living area for so long, with the same people. How unbearable it must have been to constantly live in fear, he acknowledged, knowing that at any minute you and your family could be swept away because awful men were constantly hunting for you. It wasn't that hard to make a connection, as he had already heard of so many stories from Lita and neighbors and the news about families getting swept up by ICE and the police, being tricked and coerced into being captured and taken away.

Then there were *Los Ojos*. From the little that Jesse had heard and paid attention to them, he knew that they did the bidding of and dirty work for ICE. Los Ojos were not officers, but just regular civilians who in their free time enjoyed hunting for undocumented people and reporting them to the authorities. Sometimes they directly teamed up with ICE and the local police, and they could be pretending to be anyone. They often went door to door pretending to sell things, or lied to people and said they were with the local energy company and needed to know who was home, and asked other weird questions. In other cases they would go into a restaurant to see if there were a lot of Latinos working in the back and would wait until the end of their shifts to take photos of employees when they would leave to go home.

Was this what it was like for Anne, almost eighty years ago? The similarities were striking to Jesse. As a freshman, he wasn't taking a history class. But Yusef had explained to him that there's too much happening in the world right now, and learning about how we got here is too important, to wait. So Yusef had begun giving Jesse World History lessons, supplemented with videos on YouTube and documentaries. Jesse hated it.

Yet, as Yusef began tying things together and making connections with the present, Jesse began to see why history mattered. In a lesson that hit Jesse particularly hard one week, Yusef had said, "We are still living in the past. We are still a part of it, and it is a part of us. The people of the past are dead but the participants of today's world are still playing their roles: the ones with the power, the knowledge, or the grit to do so, anyway. The limits of our planet have been discovered long ago. There has been a scramble to take as much from it as possible, before other competitors do. Where does that leave you, Mubtadi? Where does that leave your children? Where does that leave the legacy of all our struggles, our sacrifices, and our loves?"

"But they've been doing this forever. What the fuck can I do about it?"

"Struggle, Mubtadi! Sacrifice. Love. Fight! Fight for everything you love and hold dear! Because if you do not, someone will eventually take it from you. And if you do not know how to fight for it," Yusef had then picked up a history textbook and let it slam on the table in front of Jesse. "This is how you learn."

Now that Jesse was paying more attention to the news and observing what was happening in his country and the rest of the world, everything began to make more sense. He saw how events connected and were continuations of previous incidents: a constant flow of cause and effect that carried forward and rooted itself from decades, generations, and centuries ago. Jesse wondered how much of it was being influenced by these secret organizations that Yusef told him existed, made up of Readers around the world. *Are all those YouTube conspiracy theories a part of the conspiracy?* Jesse thought.

He was anxious now, knowing things were constantly happening around him, and just because he wasn't being directly and immediately affected by something, that didn't mean that someone else wasn't being affected at that moment. He or someone he did know might be next. If some huge change was developing that could eventually affect him, then he was helpless to do anything about it.

Jesse had been on a page from *Diary of Anne Frank* for a while now but hadn't really read any of it. He picked up his phone and dialed Yusef.

"*As-salaamu-Alaykum.*"

"Uh, hey." The other line was silent. "Ugh. Walay-come sal-um."

"You mean, '*Wailakum Salaam,*' Mubtadi."

"Yeah, right. That's what I said."

"What can I do for you on this glorious day, Mubtadi?"

"You can help me fight."

"Pardon me?"

"I'm tired of hearing about the families being taken and separated. I hate that there's Americans hunting people."

"Yes, Mubtadi. It is terrible. If only someone *did* something about it."

"I want to do something about it." Jesse said this without hesitation.

"Yes, of course. What would you like to do?"

"Whatever I have to."

"This brings me joy to hear, my young mubtadi. You are about to take your first steps in the real world. Now I will help you with your first steps in the dream world. In the Plane."

"No shit?"

"So it would appear. I am as serious as you are willing to be."

Jesse gulped on air and his stomach weighed down with excitement. 'Fu-- I mean… yes. Yes, sir."

Jesse XI
The Waste and Residue of Dreams

Jesse threw his momentum to the left, and the sliding closet door scraped open. When he looked out, Jesse saw that the walls of his room were dingy and greasy with dirt. Some parts were entangled by glossy black and brown roots. He saw Yusef standing in the middle of the dark room between two mattresses. Marcy and Lita slept on the bed in the far side of the room while Alfredo and Jesse slept on the one closer to the hallway door and closet.

Marcy and Lita were surrounded in their hazes as smoke, dust, and shards of debris swept all around them, with occasional sparks of light popping off, like the Fourth of July.

Alfredo lay in his bed, but he was a shadow of himself. When the light from the haze popped off next to them, it would not reflect on Alfredo's silhouette. Instead, it seemed like the darkness from his body just killed the light when it reached it.

"Is he dead?"

Yusef wore a very thin, dark-blue coat that went down past his knees and a white robe underneath that went down to his ankles. On his head he wore his... keffiyeh, is what Yusef had called it. It was a white cloth wrapped around his head and draped down at the back a little bit, and it was held together with a thin red rope. "No, Mubtadi. He is just not yet in the part of his REM cycle that produces dreams."

There was a second blackened silhouette of a body laying on the edge of the bed where Jesse fell asleep.

"The fuck? Is that -- is that *me*?" Jesse asked, pointing at the dimensional shadow on the bed.

"That was your chrysalis. Now it is your husk -- until you return to your body. Come. We have much to do. Stay close to me, and do not wander off. No matter what."

Jesse stepped away from the bedroom closet and out of the corner of his eye, he saw a black tentacle hanging down right above him. He instinctively ducked and hit the floor, sitting up and turning around to face it while scooting back to Yusef's feet. "What the fuck is that!"

"That is putrisomn. It's the waste and residue of dreams that form here on the Plane. It won't harm you. Mostly." Yusef let out a short sigh. "Please, Mubtadi. Try to remain calm. And let us use some more controlled language."

"Yeh. Sorry," Jesse muttered as he looked all around with wide, nervous eyes. "And why was I in the fucking closet?"

"Language."

Jesse rolled his eyes. "Why?"

Yusef shrugged. "It was the closest location I could engineer your pylon, and an image I already knew you were familiar with."

The tentacle pulsed briefly, but did not move. It was connected to more putrisomn that was entangled and wrapped around the walls of Jesse's room, like ivy. It reminded Jesse of Lita's arms and the back of her hands: of scraggly veins, bulging and glossy with the oil of her flowery lotion. "Fredo used to think monsters would come from there. Guess he was kind of right."

Yusef walked to the bedroom door and opened it slowly, taking a peek through the crevice of the doorway and waited. Jesse looked down at himself and realized he was wearing his clothes from that day, typical black hoodie and black pants, and his white sneakers.

"'Ey. What's a pylon? That how I got here?"

Yusef bobbed his head then tossed his head forward. "We will go. Quickly, and quietly."

More putrisomn stuck to the walls in greater patches, and even smothered entirely where furniture was supposed to be. Jesse and Yusef walked past the other bedroom where the Arcos family slept. The door was ajar and they saw most of them in the haze as well. There was a huge amount of lights going off where Dominique slept. The haze was moving so quickly and violently, Jesse flinched every time he heard a light pop. They were red, purple, dark blue, and even… black.

How could there be light in black? Jesse thought. He opened the door and stepped into the bedroom. Instead of giving out light, the black spheres seemed to dim the light around them. They were moving, floating shadows.

He could begin to hear other sounds as the cloudy debris swept around Dominique like a sideways tornado. Jesse thought he heard someone calling out. His chest suddenly felt like cement and his stomach felt like it dropped to his legs when the faint voice turned into a sudden scream, tearing through the haze with rage.

"Jesse!"

He turned away from Dominique's haze and rushed out into the hallway. Yusef stood at the opened front door of the apartment. With his palm up, Yusef put out his hand toward Jesse.

Jesse closed his eyes tight in focus then opened them again. He walked slowly to Yusef, as if to prove his confidence to whatever it was that had startled him, and walked past Yusef's hand and out into the pale evening. He looked up at the darkened sky, which appeared to have a strange tint to it. The sky was dark, but there appeared to be some kind of thin overcast that he couldn't exactly spot. A refraction of light through it was barely noticeable. He couldn't quite tell if it was purple, blue, green, or a mix of a lighter color like yellow or orange set against the darkened night sky. The moon's position flickered across the night sky in different phases of its cycle and in differing hues of white and yellow.

"What's up with the moon?"

Yusef now walked past Jesse, who was lost staring up into the sky, and started walking down the concrete stairs that jutted out from the second-floor walkway. "It is there. Find the one not moving."

"Wha'?"

"What you see up there is putrisomn. Since everybody sees stars and the moon in the sky when they are dreaming, but no one really seems to know exactly where they are in the sky, the putrisomn up there reflects a scattered projection of what everybody perceives in their dreams."

Jesse was halfway down the stairs and came to a stop. "The eff did you just say?"

"Come here, Mubtadi. Sit." Yusef motioned for Jesse to join him on the grass outside the apartments.

Still looking around with wonder, Jesse did as he was told as he focused his eyes here and there along the way. "Is this real?" he asked, grazing his hands across the grass after he sat down.

"In a way, it is. That grass is a natural substance in the waking world that is connected to the Earth. So here on the Plane, it exists just as it does in the waking world, and cannot be altered. Go ahead, try pulling that grass out."

No matter how much he yanked and twisted, the grass bent but did not break. Not even the dead parts. There was a greasy, black and green residue on his fingers. "You messing with me?"

There was silence as Yusef allowed Jesse time to look around and process what he was seeing. He squinted here and there, moving forward and backward, side to side, as he focused on certain places around the apartments and beyond around the neighborhood.

"Why… What…? Are those holograms?" Jesse pointed at the cars that lined the curb at the far end of the apartments.

Without looking, Yusef replied. "In a way, yes. Go investigate, Mubtadi. You are doing what all intelligent people do: asking questions. Go on, be curious. Do not mind any walking shadows. They are not ghosts, they do not see you, they cannot harm you."

Jesse stood up and made his way to the curb. He did notice a few shadows, like the ones of his family and the Arcoses, floating through the street in the distance as if they were riding in a car. A few walked on the sidewalk.

As he approached the parked cars, they shifted. The cars stayed in place but some looked like they switched places or disappeared then reappeared only a few feet further down the curb in either direction. Some were fractions of a car. All of them changed type and color as he walked and his visual perspective changed. He stopped and looked back at Yusef.

"Go on. It is fine."

As Jesse approached, the car continued to shift around. It reminded him of when he was a kid and he looked into a cheap kaleidoscope at the Mexican mercado. The twisting of the tube caused pieces of color and shapes to dance and morph, rotating and repeating in a complex manner. This same function was happening right in front of him, before his very eyes.

He got close and reached his hand toward a car. Or two? The image of the cars continued to shift and switch around.

"That's close enough. For now." Yusef said, grabbing Jesse's hand.

"Where the fuck did you come from? This isn't *my* dream anymore, right?"

"Correct. We are definitely on the Plane."

"So you can't do crazy shit like that here. That's what you told me before. How did you move that fast?"

"Focus. And *practice*, Mubtadi. Lots of focus, and lots of *practice*."

"Wack."

A blur, then he was gone. "You expect greatness from nothing? You wish to be born a mage or a mutant with innate abilities, undiscovered and unearned?" Yusef yelled from the middle of the grass lawn.

"Fuck yeah."

"Such fantasies of hidden gifts and natural power are for the weak-minded, the weak-willed: the plebs."

"Okay, sabio. What the fuck is going on here?"

"Before, I was able to construct and control your entire dream because we were inside your head, inside your haze. Those same 'rules' and abilities do not all apply here on the Plane." Yusef appeared next to Jesse again in a blur. "These are not cars."

Sighing, Jesse slumped his shoulders and stared toward the street.

Yusef lifted his arm and twisted his wrist. A car was lifted and as it left its place, its sides began to change, like it was made of a multitude of screens that were all changing pictures and video at the same time.

Jesse's eyes grew large as the car lifted higher from the ground. The images of cars blinked away from the car and in its place were blackened screens… no, a greasy black body of a car, with no clear design or angles. It hovered there as Yusef held up his arms. "Name an object."

He stood there with his mouth slightly hanging open at first, then his jaw snapped shut. "AK."

Now Yusef returned an odd stare. "Pardon me?"

"AK-47."

"I was afraid that is what you meant." Yusef closed his eyes for a second or so and then reopened them with intense focus. His arms were outstretched and his wrists and fingers danced.

The levitating car crumbled. Huge chunks fell to the ground and they immediately lost their illusion of a car as it turned into a black mass.

One chunk remained in the air, and smaller pieces broke off. It appeared to slowly lose its shape. Then it seemed to melt. It formed an oblong figure and then edges began to mold. Black sludge drooped off here and there. Textures appeared, and there it was: an AK-47.

As it drifted toward Jesse, the rifle took on colors. By the time it reached his excited hands, it was unmistakably an AK-47.

"Holy shit."

Yusef stood relaxed, with his hands clasped behind his back.

"I can… I can shoot it?"

"You can try. But it--"

The rifle clicked. Jesse was poised with anticipation, frozen in place waiting for a powerful recoil that never came.

"What the fuck?"

"... But it will not fire any rounds."

Jesse stared at the AK-47. "It *feels* real. Not like a toy. Uh...." his fingers fumbled around the sides of the rifle and along the magazine. The clip angled and slid out of the rifle. Jesse looked inside through the top. It was hollow. There wasn't even a spring. He shot a look at Yusef that bled with betrayal.

"A combustion of a primer on a metal-shelled cartridge followed by the sudden release of energy from another chemical combustion using the gunpowder inside it, requires numerous elements. Those need a bit more time and focus to manifest, Mubtadi."

"So you didn't bother making this with all its parts because I wouldn't have bullets anyway."

"That is correct. You do not seem impressed."

"I was just excited to finally shoot one of these effers." Jesse stared back at the black chunks on the ground. They, too, had started to lose the hardness of their form, as if they were beginning to melt.

"What's up with--"

A loud shriek erupted from an apartment building behind them, followed by rumbling and crashing of heavy things.

"Her again. Jesse, come. We must go now." Yusef extended his hand and turned toward Jesse's apartment building.

"What was that?"

"Nevermind th--" A large window and its surrounding wall exploded open. Jesse instinctively threw an arm up for protection, dropping the useless rifle on the ground. Blackened debris and huge chunks of putrisomn flew all over the apartment complex's grass courtyard, headed straight for Jesse.

Jesse XII
Atop a Drifting Staircase

Yusef was holding his arms up while shrapnel hung suspended in air, mere feet in front of Jesse. Chunks of putrisomn fell harmlessly to the ground in front of Jesse when Yusef dropped his arms.

Smoky tentacles shot out from the giant hole in the wall and groped its edges. Long, bony fingers transformed from the tentacles and as they found their grip, they pulled forward and shifted into talons. A sooty, purpled beast thrust out of the wall.

It belted out a monstrous scream with its huge head. Long, jagged, and brown teeth jutted out of its wide mouth. It had no eyes.

"The fuck?"

"A wraith. Mubtadi -- *now*!" Yusef was already halfway back up the stairs.

Jesse turned and began to run back toward the apartments.

The dark monster launched itself out of the building and landed on the courtyard grass with four strong, clawed legs. Red and purple ooze dripped from its teeth and jaw. Its snout jutted up and sniffed in the air. Dark smoke and mist continued to swirl and shift around its muscled body.

"Hurry, Jesse!"

The wraith turned its head toward Jesse, who was dashing across the other side of the courtyard. It yelped out a horrendous howl and galloped toward Yusef, who was already at the top of the staircase.

Jesse was nearly there. Then the beast scuttled to a sudden halt at the foot of the stairs and hesitated to climb up, instead turning to Jesse. His momentum was too strong to make a sudden stop.

The fiend roared and shrieked simultaneously. Its toothy maw shot open farther than it should have. Then the creature's skin exploded into smoke that shot out toward Jesse like a blanket, reaching out to swallow him. He screamed as his chest suddenly weighed heavy with the fear and anxiety of his deepest nightmares being yanked out of his subconscious.

He felt a sensation of his weight being suddenly thrust forward and the sound of crashing thunder in his ears. He felt anger directed toward him from all directions. His dad's wife beater smudged with black dust from the asphalt. Yelling and shouting. Lightning and booms and crying and anger.

From the top of the stairs Yusef thrust his arms, launching a still-screaming Jesse backward.

The wraith's attempt to pull Jesse in was foiled as the groping smoke crashed like waves against itself. Multi-colored sparks and bolts sizzled inside the wraith's twisting form.

Without skipping a beat, Yusef adjusted his footing and prepared for the inevitable counterattack.

The wraith sprouted a multitude of spiny legs which began creeping up the stairs. Fangs jutted out from a tiny head at the front of its thorax. Smoke slipped out of its tail end.

Yusef twisted his wrists and fingers upward. The staircase broke off the second story landing and was lifted up and away, the wraith now stunned with apprehension as it floated along. It shot out a tentacle toward Yusef but he had already carried the staircase far away enough to barely be out of its reach.

With his other arm, Yusef reached for Jesse, who was still on the ground. Jesse's eyes grew wide as he felt himself being lifted up. He flailed a little bit, but felt sturdy enough and relaxed. As he was elevated and brought toward the second story landing, Jesse kept his eyes on the wraith.

It began swirling atop the drifting staircase. The wraith reverted back to its first form with muscular, clawed legs. Taking powerful strides across the tilted steps, the wraith leapt off of the staircase, claws outstretched toward Jesse, who was still floating toward the landing.

As the wraith bounded across the stairs, Yusef began to twist his wrist and arm again. The steps and railing crumbled away into black chunks of putrisomn. His right hand and arm danced quickly while his left continued to guide Jesse closer to him on the second floor. Putrisomn rocks fell beneath its feet but the wraith had already leapt forward.

Yusef was already scrambling to adjust his footing. He leapt off the broken ledge and flung himself forward, intercepting the path of the wraith.

The beast exploded as it sunk its claws into Yusef. Black smoke swallowed Yusef up.

Jesse, helplessly witnessing everything, suddenly fell to the ground twelve feet below.

Jesse woke up screaming and with pain faintly pulsing in his back where he landed. He was out of breath and panicked.

"Aye, Dios mio. Jesús, again?" Lita asked from the dark room.

"I gotta call Yusef."

"Que?"

Jesse searched for the glow of his phone plugged into the wall. He dialed and there was no answer. "Fuck."

"Jesús! Que pasa?"

"Lita! What's wrong?" a tiny girl's voice asked in the dark.

"How the fuck do I go back? I need to help him," Jesse said to himself under his breath. He punched his pillow, then dialed again. Still no answer.

"Jesús! Hablame!"

"Fuck!"

Jesse XIII
Carolina

Yusef's eyes were red and dark. Puffy bags were under them. There was a fatigue about him that seemed to weigh down Yusef with more than just a lack of sleep.

"What the fuck happened?" Jesse hadn't slept the rest of the night. He rushed to school in the morning and barely made it through his classes (he could have sworn that Maria gave him a glance today, so that helped with his motivation). He met Yusef at Davidson Park after school as usual.

Yusef sighed. "I am sorry, Mubtadi. That did not… go as planned. I failed you."

"You fucking saved me, 'Sef. Right? That's what happened? What'd it do to you?"

Yusef's face became sullen and his eyes drifted downward. They looked like they were staring at something deep below the ground.

Jesse stepped forward. "'Ey. Are you… you okay?"

Staring for a second more, Yusef shook himself back to attention. Jesse couldn't tell if the shiver was from the cold winter breeze or something else. "Yes, Mubtadi. I will be fine. It had just been a while since a wraith got the better of me. I forgot… how good they were at making you remember things."

Jesse nodded his head. "Yeh. When that thing got close to me I had memories come back to me. But it's weird."

"Which part?"

"I can't remember some of them. Like, they were my memories by they weren't."

"That is because not all of those terrifying memories were yours."

"Huh?"

"That wraith was a ten-year-old girl who lives in the apartments across from you."

"The fuck?"

"Her name is Carolina. She does not know she is a wraith. She knows nothing about the Plane. But she does know that every time her uncle Alejandro drinks tequila that she has to get as far away from him as possible. She has known this for as long as she can remember. She also knows when it is football season and when the Corsairs get close to playoffs. If her father runs out of beer and her mother is not around, then she will have to hide the bruises for weeks."

"Were you in her dreams, too?"

"Yes. When I first started to visit you, I came across her. That is her den -- where she sleeps and enters the Plane."

"But why is she like that? How?"

"She does not choose to be. Do you remember when we first got on the Plane? You saw the shadows of your grandmother and siblings?"

"Yeh."

"While encased in their haze, a person's shadow is called a chrysalis. That is how people normally appear on the Plane -- when they do not know about it or are not on it."

"You've called them plebs."

"That is correct, Mubtadi."

Jesse stared back at him.

"A plebian. In ancient Roman times, thousands of years ago, a plebian was a commoner. Uneducated and limited in power, they were meant to stay that way and were used as the main economic and military source for the republic and later, the empire.

"It is a phrase that stained non-Readers through the millennia to describe modern commoners who are aimless dreamers. Plebs are ignorant of the Plane and Readers. Their dreams are usually easy to infiltrate and manipulate."

"Okay, I didn't need a lecture."

Yusef let out a sigh. "When a pleb is under constant fear, pain, or distress, their existence on the Plane changes. How you saw your grandmother and siblings was fairly normal."

"What was with all them lights?"

"We call it the haze. Memories, emotions: the stuff of dreams. And nightmares," he added with a grim face. "They spew and swirl around a shadow as the dreamer subconsciously recounts their innermost fears, desires, memories, and so forth. When there are too many raw, powerful emotions and troublesome memories, they destabilize a pleb's shadow in their chrysalis form. A storm of those emotions and memories manifests into what we encountered: a wraith."

Jesse became focused and he looked lost in thought. "I -- *she* was raped. I saw it for a split second when she got close and smokey."

"Not just once, Mubtadi."

"And beaten. Those motherfuckers."

Yusef let the realization sit in the air between them.

"What you -- we -- encountered was a mixing of our worst nightmares, fears, and memories with Carolina. As a wraith, she is on the hunt for our dreams, and memories; our hope, and happiness that drives our willpower -- and thus, our very ability to access and anchor ourselves to the Plane."

"So… can we go back?"

"Yes. You were not very affected by Carolina's wraith. I, on the other hand, will need some time to recover and clear my mind -- and heart -- from that dreadful experience before I can return."

Then Jesse frowned. "Hold up. Why aren't you helping her, then? Or going into her dad's and uncle's dreams to fuck them up?"

Yusef looked like he smelled something bad and looked away. "To help her directly would require an immense amount of time and focus. The subconscious is powerful, Mubtadi. And *dangerous*. Infiltrating the dreams of her abusers would be easy, but to correct their behavior would take a lot of time."

"What about getting even! You always tell me how important justice is. There it is! Justice is waiting and you could give it!"

"Even then, the damage has still been done to Carolina. Are we ever truly even, Mubtadi?"

"Nah!" Jesse kicked the grass and a muddy patch of it flew. "You could do something. I would."

"That is exactly why I am spending this time with you, Mubtadi. Because I know you would seek out that justice. But you must understand," Yusef stepped forward and closer to Jesse. "My time is limited. The hourglass drops its last grains of sand for me. We must leave something behind that's greater than ourselves. We have to be sure to leave this earth in a better condition than how we first encounter it. There has to be hope, and people that are willing and strong enough to carry it forward."

"But why me? I can't be the only one you've taught this crazy shit to."

"This is true, Mudtadi. There are others. Some continue to spread hope as I have wished -- *Alhamdulillah*. Still, others took… a different path."

"How do you even know all of this? Who taught you? Like, how do you know how to build an AK-47? That didn't just appear. You like, made it."

Yusef sighed and looked far off into the distance. "Sergeant Haseem Nusaybah. Well, he was actually a corporal when he taught me."

"You were in the army?" Jesse's jaw hung open.

"I should have been at university. Instead, I joined the PLA: Palestine Liberation Army. The Ayn Jalut Brigade in Gaza."

Jesse's jaw still hung open, but now one eyebrow was confusedly raised.

"Add it to your homework for tonight. I was not in the army long. There were many horrors that I witnessed, was a part of, and unfortunately, was directly responsible for. Sergeant Nusaybah kept me alive through it all."

"What about the AK? Did you fire any RPGs?" Jesse asked excitedly.

"I was given an AK-47 to use when I joined the PLA. It was my responsibility to take care of it, because in actuality, it belonged to the Palestinian people. It was my responsibility to defend the people. And to seek *justice*." Yusef looked directly into Jesse's eyes.

"Against who?"

"Our sworn enemy, the Israelis. Ever since *Al-Nakba*, The

Catastrophe. We were enemies before then, too. I fought the Israelis with pride, courage, and hatred in my heart. They probably did the same against me and the rest of the PLA."

"So.... RPG? Or nah?"

"No, Jesse. I never fired an RPG. I was more… up close and personal."

"Were you in people's dreams?"

"No, not back then. I was a lucid dreamer. But I had not been taught the way to become a Reader back then. That came after."

Jesse waited.

A distant look returned to Yusef's face. "Another story for another time, Mubtadi. Now, we must meditate to recover our willpower and prepare ourselves for the Plane. We must be stronger and wiser, and more prepared for the next time we encounter Carolina, or any of the other countless wraiths and horrors on the Plane."

Jesse nodded. "Bet."

Jesse XIV
Nice Dream

The alarm on his phone blared at 6:00 am. Lita hadn't come to wake him up in weeks, maybe even months, as he thought about it.

And now Jesse was even more motivated by Yusef's words and more of his life story. In the weeks that followed the chaotic incident on the Plane, Jesse focused on his schoolwork and bringing up his grades. Even Math class was now pretty easy since Jesse had begun paying attention, did his work, and asked the occasional question in class. Yusef had started making him ask at least one question in every class, no matter how stupid, every day.

Aside from school work, Jesse was also busy with science fair research, physical conditioning, and lucid dream training.

In his dreams, he was getting better at not just remembering and recording his dreams in the night and in the morning (Yusef bought him a light-up pen and a journal he kept at his bedside), but also being self-aware in his dreams. He was getting closer and closer to full lucidity. A few entries from his dream journal read:

> *Started after school. played NBA Live like I use to. Was I playing the game or actually playing b-ball? I was good. Then Racha was on my team. Then the other team. Couldn't tell which.*

> *Was trying to train at home, school. Kept ending up in a*

bathroom to pee. Woke up fr, ran to piss. Think I drank too much water before bed.

Maria. Again. She's in my kitchen. We standing next to each other at the sink. There's something out the window we're looking at. But I don't see it. All I can think is reaching over to her. I want to hold her. Fuck. I want to hold her.

He had also done a lot of research. There was so much info on the school-to-prison pipeline. Too much. It became overwhelming for Jesse after a few days and he found himself starting to avoid it and procrastinate. Getting up early in the morning allowed him time to record his dreams, do a quick workout, eat a decent breakfast, and *try* to get some studying or research done before heading into his classes. But he was still working on that last part.

The hot weather had finally subsided and the sunny Southern California days were now interspersed with some clouds and occasional polar winds. Back at Portola, Maria's skin-revealing wardrobe changed but she took to wearing form-fitting workout pants. And her hair. She let it down in waves of mahogany. The shine of her thick locks caught the light every time she turned and carelessly tossed her hair over her shoulders.

"Señor Ramirez!"

"Huh?"

Mr. Padilla stood next to Jesse with a clipboard. "I was just complementing you -- en español -- on how you've brought your grade up in this class. I peeked at your other grades and noticed that you were doing better in all of your other classes, too. Muy bien, Jesse."

The desk next to him was empty and that made Jesse grateful. "Uh, yeah. Thanks." If Racha had been here today, he never would have let Jesse live this down.

"Is everything alright?" Mr. Padilla went on. "You seemed to be a million miles away a few seconds ago."

Again, so grateful Racha wasn't here. "Yeh. I'm good." Jesse straightened up and shook off a blank look from his eyes. "Let's conjugate some shit."

Padilla raised an eyebrow. "Muy bien, Señor Ramirez," he said sternly. Then he walked to the front of the class and announced he was done with grade checks.

Jesse tuned out again because Maria was tuned out. He saw a book opened in her lap. Yesterday it had been a poetry book by some white dude from back in the day. Keats, or something.

He had looked it up later and read some of his poems. He barely made it through "On First Looking into Chapman's Homer." He read "On Seeing the Elgin Marbles" twice and gave up on the third try. Didn't even make it past the first line of "Ode on a Grecian Urn."

But "Ode to a Nightingale" caught his eye. He didn't understand a lot of its references and the centuries-old language was too archaic for him to fully grasp. But he recognized that desire and yearning for something beautiful -- something that would bring completeness and some other kind of reality. Maria would be that doorway for him. His guide and light through the dark forces that dictated his life.

Now he was trying to see what she was currently reading. It was an old book with a plain, worn scarlet cover. There was small gold lettering on the front cover and the spine. He waited for her to close the book when she'd occasionally look up from her lap to pretend to pay attention. There was no title. *Or was that the title?*

"Oscar Wilde? The fuck?" Jesse cursed under his breath.

When lunchtime finally came later, Jesse quickly made his way to the library. He needed to know who this clown was. A search on one of the computers brought up some photos of another white dude. More poetry. One stood out, probably because it was short and easy to read: "In the Forest."

Out of the mid-wood's twilight
Into the meadow's dawn,
Ivory limbed and brown-eyed,
Flashes my Faun!

He skips through the copses singing,
And his shadow dances along,

And I know not which I should follow,
Shadow or song!

O Hunter, snare me his shadow!
O Nightingale, catch me his strain!
Else moonstruck with music and madness
I track him in vain!

The nightingale again, also in a dark forest. *Was it a guide?* he thought. *Something that fights against dark forces? That's definitely her. But why would she want to be my nightingale? I need to show her that I'm worthy: something more. More than everyone else. I need to be a nightingale for her. And we'll lift each other.*

Jesse closed the web browser and clicked on the library's inventory app. He searched for "poems" and the search brought up more than a hundred hits. He sighed. "Chingame."

Ms. Irons, the peppy school librarian, had shown Jesse how to narrow down his search and look up books on the shelves, among other tricks. He'd been to the library quite a few times -- careful not to be seen by Racha -- for his science fair research.

"Back for more?" Ms. Irons' gentle but firm voice asked from behind the check-out counter. Her thin-rimmed glasses hung at the tip of her nose.

"Uh. Kinda," Jesse replied as he looked around the library to make sure she was talking to him. And to make sure that no one else of note was listening.

She walked over and locked her eyes on Jesse's computer screen. "New project? Did you finish your report on the school-to-prison pipeline?"

"Uh. Kinda."

Ms. Irons looked away from the screen and then at Jesse with a fair amount of surprise in her eyes. "Is this for English class now?"

"Uhhh... kindaaa." He went on to make up and explain a fake assignment to her. "So I need to write a poem. I just don't know a lot about them."

She politely nudged Jesse away from the keyboard and began to scroll up and down the screen. After some more clicking and clacking of the keyboard, she turned to Jesse. "Yes, there are quite a few poetry books currently checked out at the moment. Nevertheless, I can still help. Follow me!"

He followed her down and around a few aisles before she slowed down and grazed the spines of books with the tip of her finger. She grabbed a book here and there; then lifted her hand for him to follow her back to the check-out.

There were old-looking books, like the kind he saw Maria with, colorful new ones that were small and compact, and one wide, flatter paperback.

"Alrighty. Hopefully this does the trick for you," she said over beeps and clicks as she checked them out.

"Yeh. Hopefully."

"And don't forget to update your works cited page if you add these to your research. For whatever project this is." She deliberately looked at Jesse now, searching his face for a reaction.

He nodded. "Huh. Yeh."

Ms. Irons grinned. "Maybe this is one of those personal projects, huh?"

Jesse quickly stuffed the books in his bag before anyone could see he had them. He didn't respond and shuffled away, then tried to remain calm and casual as he walked out of the library.

Later that night, Jesse sacrificed his dream training and recovery time to skim through the books. An idea struck him and he took to paper, writing a poem around the idea, and what would later become the title, "Nice Dream." It began:

I wake up
To the sound
Of heavenly bells
I look around
To see a different me
With a different you.

It went on for lines and lines, one continuous giant stanza reflecting his unrequited love, and how bright and wholesome his life would be with "her love" in it; by the end the narrator wakes up back in his stale, boring life.

"Nice Dream" was placed in the back of his binder, where hopefully no one would see. It was yet another distraction and reason he was continuing to procrastinate on his research for the school-to-prison pipeline report he really needed to finish for the impending Science Fair.

The other big distraction was his progress on the Plane. He couldn't wait to get to sleep so he could train more. Tonight Yusef had a challenge waiting for him. Jesse was eager to crush it.

Jesse XV
My Nightingale

The western sky was orange, pink, and blue. Violet vastness began to settle over the San Vallejo Mountains to the east. A rooster clucked passively despite Jesse's growing frustration, and the anxious prodding of his feet caused the rooftop gravel to make muffled crunches. He hurried toward the chicken coop, opened the door, and walked in.

Still, the rooster remained and belted out a caw.

"Fuck!" The bird panicked and fluttered its wings. "I thought I had it this time."

Yusef stood well behind Jesse near the ledge of the rooftop, observing him. "I know, Mubtadi. You became too eager. You need to complete your focus, not jump to it as soon as you feel it, or think you feel it."

Jesse sighed, then walked out of the giant cage and slammed the door behind him. The sky shuddered. Then the skyline of surrounding rooftops and buildings began to lose focus, as if a mirage.

"Calm, Mubtadi. Come sit and focus."

Shutting his eyes, Jesse put his arm out toward the floor in front of the coop. A cushioned mat appeared and he set himself down, sitting on his legs.

"And let us work on making that language… more *intelligent*, Mubtadi."

His eyes closed, a half-smirk came across Jesse's face. "You trying to turn me into a goodie, old man?"

"Oh, I would never dream of such a thing, Mubtadi." He cleared his throat with a forced cough. "Now remember where you are. Take control of your dream."

The horizon calmed and the surrounding skyline returned to focus. The rooster settled back down and clucked again.

This was the third night that Yusef was overseeing Jesse's practice on creating and opening his very own pylon. Before, every time Yusef brought Jesse to the Plane he had constructed a pylon specifically for him, and he created a way for Jesse to open it within his own dream without him really knowing. Jesse learned that it required a lot of preparation and focus because a pylon was a permanent way that a Reader could manifest a portal from the subconscious of their own dreams to access the Plane. The more the design of the portal resembled something within the den of the dreamer, the easier and safer it was to access and exit the Plane. Jesse insisted that the chicken coop from his old house reminded him of being home more than anything, so he was attempting to imagine it here at the apartments.

He also learned that losing a connection to the Plane abruptly or by force could be problematic, as was the case with Yusef when he was attacked by the wraith. Even without a wraith, if a Reader felt enough pain or distress they would be forced to awaken and booted from the Plane, experiencing aftereffects similar to Yusef's. Not being able to access the Plane for a length of time then left a Reader susceptible to infiltration, because their haze would be accessible and unprotected on the Plane. To make matters worse, there was a visible essence that evaporated from a Reader's avatar, the bodily form they inhabited while on the Plane. This colorful essence would begin to make its own way back to the defeated Reader's haze, leading anyone willing to follow and track down the essence straight to their den.

Now Jesse had to envision a portal that he constructed from within his subconscious. It was something that represented or reminded him of his core self: the person he always was before he grew up, or as most people do it, force themselves to grow up. The time was coming for Jesse to take charge of his own destiny and manifest his will deep beyond his subconscious to a breaching point into the Plane.

Jesse steadied his breathing. His psyche formed various images on the back of his eyelids but he avoided the temptation to explore them. Instead, he used his mind's eye to push past the visages and illusions. The rooster crowed and the shrillness brought him back to his childhood. Before everything changed. Before he did. He was trying to retreat within himself, a trust fall backward into his own id.

Maria's face, then her body appeared briefly in his mind. Then Portola's campus, Racha, Xotchitl, Moises, Raymond, and Carolina's wraith. The thunderous violence of that encounter reminded him of pale, fluorescent-filled nights in the old house when the family was still together, except for Mamá, of course. The sudden silence before Papá would act out and throw a beer bottle. The scraping of the chair against the ugly linoleum and the rumble of the flimsy kitchen table getting shoved aside by an angry mountain, suddenly reddened and awakened. It would explode with steaming magma and giant dark clouds that filled Jesse's eyes and heart with doom.

And yet Junior stood by, a statue without a hint of fear or anger. No matter what age Junior was in Jesse's memory -- even when he was younger than Jesse now -- his brother always seemed bigger and older than him. Then there was Erick, who would witness the eruption with brooding, his face getting hotter and holding back a rush of lava just beneath the surface.

"Jesse!"

His eyes fluttered open. He and Yusef were no longer on the rooftop. Jesse was sitting in the old kitchen. The cheap, shadowy lights and the broken beer bottle both drenched the walls. Yusef stood in the doorway behind Jesse. "Shit," Jesse said.

Yusef cleared his throat and said nothing.

"Fuck. I meant, 'shoot' or some shit."

"Well, I suppose that is progress. We will call it a night here, Mubtadi."

"Yeh. A'ight."

"Ah. There is one more thing, Mubtadi. My apologies, I almost forgot."

Jesse looked up and didn't get an immediate response. "What? What is it?"

"You have progressed. Not just spiritually on the Plane, not just physically here in the waking world, but mentally as well. I am very proud of you, Mubtadi. You are ready to advance further."

Jesse didn't realize it at first, but his eyebrows suddenly felt like they were going to float off of his forehead. He furrowed them downward and put on an intimidating look. "Yeh, what?"

"I am going to arrange with your counselor to change your schedule. It is time to put you in some more challenging classes."

"Aw, fuck."

"Beg your pardon?

"Ah, fun. Fun. That sounds… that sounds great, 'Sef." Jesse said, deflated. Then a thought came to him. "Honors classes? Like, English?"

Yusef gave Jesse an inquisitive look. "Yes, that is one class I was thinking about transferring you to. Or perhaps Honors Biology."

"Yeh… English," Jesse repeated, a far-off look in his eyes now. He thought of Maria's shiny legs and her careless fingers twirling her hair in his new Honors English class. He knew she had his same English teacher, Mr. Klinkhammer, but for Honors. Replaying her in his mind from Spanish class, Jesse loved watching her flats hang off the tips of her toes as she let a shoe dangle from her crossed leg under her desk. Having another class with her would improve his chances so much, not to mention just being around her was an intoxicating thought. What if she was in *all* of his new classes?

"Jesse!"

"What!"

"You were ignoring me. I was trying to ask if you thought that would be too much for you to take on next semester."

"Oh. Yeh, I heard you. I was just trying to think about it. Yeh. Do it."

In the morning, Jesse ignored the notifications on his phone and crawled out of bed to power through a ten-minute round of dumbbell curls, push-ups, crunches, and weighted squats. He knew he had failed again last night. But he also had come to realize that failure was a part of success. He realized he was uncovering and facing things his mind had buried over the years, both knowingly and unknowingly. This, too, was progress.

He felt good about his advancements. Checking over his homework and putting it in his folder, he was also pleased and impressed with himself in his academic improvements.

Jesse was about to zip up his backpack when he spotted his green spiral notebook, in which he was compiling the various poems and free-writes about Maria.

The unfamiliar positivity he was feeling this morning spurred a moment of inspiration and he needed to put pencil to paper. He needed to get down the clear image he saw in his heart of how this love he felt for her was most genuine and powerful. If it could change him this much, what would it do for her? Where could this love take him once he finally was with her?

Looking at his phone, he cursed as he realized he wouldn't have enough time to finish this poem before he had to leave for school. Jesse grabbed the notebook, tore out a sheet of paper and titled it, "My Nightingale." Then he hurriedly creased the loose paper into his hoodie pocket.

"Imma finish this shit before I even get there," he vowed to himself with a clenched fist in the air. He chuckled at himself. It was crazy to think how far he had come in such a short time -- and how far he was going to go in just that day. "Maria Fonseca is finally going to know who I am."

Jesse XVI
Today's the Fucking Day

"Today's the fucking day."

Jesse stuffed his completed poem into his hoodie pocket as he punched the crosswalk button with his free hand. He did this both hurriedly and nonchalantly as Xotchitl approached him down the sidewalk. Jesse did his best to avoid staring at her dimples. Her eyes shone just as brightly as her smile.

"'Eyyy, what it do?" she greeted with an open hand that waited for Jesse's to meet hers.

Jesse quickly brought his hand out of his hoodie and greeted Xotchitl. "What's up, Loca?"

"'Ey, fuck you!" Xotchitl socked him in the arm and quickly followed up by lightly shoving the side of her body into his. "I'm no loca." She made sure that her hip bounced off him. "Ohmygod, did you see that post from Chayne Sauze? That fool is gonna straight up bop ON$l0tt if he see him on the street." The crosswalk light switched on and they began crossing.

"Did you see the video of that terrorist? The one that blew himself up in Iraq? That shit was nasty."

"What? When?"

"It happened yesterday. In Baghdad, I think."

She giggled. "Where?"

"In Iraq. You know, that country we've been fighting for decades?

There's like, another civil war there or some shit."

Xotchitl stared at Jesse with a suspicious look. "So you didn't see the post?"

Jesse sighed. "Nah." They reached the other side of the street and started walking onto campus in an awkward silence. Then someone yelled out from across the street behind them. "Who that?" He turned to see a girl with bronze-tan skin and long curly hair on crutches awkwardly waving an arm, and someone else waiting at the light behind her.

"Heeyyy!" Xotchitl yelled while jumping and waving an arm in the air. She turned around but kept walking forward, turning her body toward Jesse in the process and shoving her breasts into his bicep. Jesse forced an uncomfortable grin with just his chin, not even bothering to smile with his lips. "Huh," Xotchitl said as she turned back forward. "Cervantes was excited to see me this morning."

"Who is she again?"

Xotchitl whipped out her phone. "Oh! Did you see this meme?"

The conversation -- if that was what Jesse could call it -- dragged on through campus until they reached the entrance of the cafeteria in the quad area. He barely paid attention to Xotchitl's rambling about various memes, the Knights in the playoffs, and whatever else she talked about excitedly in order to spill her hands and body onto Jesse. He worried Maria would see them and get the wrong idea. "'Ey. I gotta go turn in some shit."

"Oh, yeah? I'll go with you. Breakfast here is gross, anyway."

"Uh. I think my teacher wants to like, talk to me," Jesse lied. The first bell rang obnoxiously. But also conveniently.

"That sucks."

"Yeah. I'll see you later."

Xotchitl said something back to him, but Jesse had already turned away and walked quickly to Spanish class. He began planning what he would say to Maria and how he would say it.

"Nyeeeeee!"

"Fuck me," Jesse said to himself.

The raucous roll of Racha's board rumbled from behind. "Newwwwwbieeee!"

"Fuck off, Racha. Not today."

They were at the front of the electives building now. "Aw, you're such a fucking schoolie now. What a bitch."

Jesse pulled the door open and then stopped to stare down Racha. "Say it again to my face."

"Jesse!" Xotchitl yelled from far behind.

"Goddamnit." He pretended not to hear her and continued into the Humanities building.

""Eyyy. You slapping that shit or what?" Racha asked sleazily.

"Not today, Racha!" Jesse warned again with a stern finger.

The door closed slowly behind Jesse as he hurriedly entered the building. "If you don't hit that shit I will!" Racha blurted as the heavy door shut between them.

"I'd be impressed," Jesse said to himself. There was another distant yell from Xotchitl in the distance, this time more desperate sounding, just before the heavy door shut closed.

He went back to fantasizing about the moment he would read Maria his poem, right after class. He would call her to the side of the hallway. She would probably be too surprised to say anything at first. He would play it off coolly and say something like, *I didn't have words when I first saw you. Now I have too many.* He would smile wide while looking down like he couldn't help it, but was also too tough for it.

As he neared the door to Padilla's room, Maria Fonseca veered around the corner of the hallway. To Jesse it was life in slow motion. The warning bell pierced his ears and he tried desperately to think clearly. He continued moving normally but felt frozen inside. He knew he was seeing her right in front of him but he couldn't react, even though he knew the time to do so -- to take action and finally drop the charade of ignoring her -- was about to happen at this very moment. It was now or never. He might not have another chance like this alone with her without distractions, her friends, or Moises around. Or Raymond. It was actually kind of perfect.

"Maria," Jesse said. Even he was surprised he actually called her attention. He went past the classroom door to meet her.

Her eyes were focused on her phone. "Huh?"

This was it. The moment that would change his life -- everything -- forever. He reached for fate into his hoodie pocket. Then he felt nothing.

"Are you okay?" Maria asked. Her phone was still held right below her face.

"Uhhhhh..." Jesse patted down, then went into each and every pocket on him in search of the poem he had so carefully constructed that morning. It was a product of his entire first semester filled with change, growth, struggle, progress.

Maria was now giving Jesse her full attention, and her face frowned in awkward disgust. "I don't want any." Then she trudged past him to the classroom.

"What the *fuck*!" he uttered to himself. More classmates began to arrive. Continuing to grope and search every possible place, Jesse failed to find his life-changing poem. Panic overtook him before he could realize where it was.

Where the fuck did I drop it? he asked himself. Jesse replayed every move from the morning, trudging to the classroom as if in a trance. His classmates continued to arrive and push past him impatiently. He contemplated ditching first period so he could retrace his steps and find the poem. The tardy bell toned annoyingly. "Fuck me," he said and walked back down the hall toward the exit.

As he reached the doors and began to pull them open, he heard then saw Racha racing toward him on his skateboard from the quad. "Nyyeeeee!"

"Fuck me!" Jesse waved his arm in the air.

"'Eyyy, Schoolie. Where's your Nightingale? Did you hear her song already?" Racha picked up his board and started embracing it, as if it was a woman he was dancing with and getting ready to kiss.

Jesse's heart plummeted and his knees nearly buckled. "The fuck did you just say?"

"Nyeeeee!" Racha screamed. "I don't fucking know. It's just what I saw posted."

"What!"

"I guess you don't follow Cervantes."

"Who?"

"Roger!" A large school security employee yelled from a distant golf cart.

"Fuck. Po-po. Gotta dip." His skateboard slammed the cement.

"Racha! Get the fuck back here!" Jesse yelled out louder and more frantically than he had intended. The beaten-up golf cart sailed between the Humanities buildings and gave chase to Racha. The security employee and one of the assistant principals held onto the golf cart grips with intensity.

Jesse sighed and turned back around toward his first period class. He accepted that it was gone and in someone else's hands, spreading around as he walked. But he still searched his pockets desperately, as if finding it would wake him from a terrible dream.

When the principal's serious voice came through the speakers and instructed teachers to read their prepared statements to their students, Jesse was sitting in his seat in the back corner of room 811 with his head down. Mr. Padilla greeted the class with "Escuchen, estudiantes. ¡Escuchen! This will be the only time I won't speak in Spanish because of the significance of this news. The House of Representatives has voted in favor of the Tilson Plan. As of now, it is not law. The Senate will reconvene after the holiday recess to vote on it, where it is also likely to pass. Just so you know, since I am paid partially with federal funds, according to the Tilson Plan I am considered a federal employee. Therefore, if and when this law passes I will be mandated by the federal government to report anyone who is living here in the United States without proof of citizenship or legal residency. If I fail to report potential illegal residents then I am under the jurisdiction of the federal government to be prosecuted for treason and will face high fines and prison time."

The classroom became quiet in one of those moments where the silence was so obvious it was distracting. People wanted to break it, but no one dared to do so, to challenge this new order that was forming -- and power that was being established by the highest officials in the country.

One of these days, Lita could be gone forever before Jesse got home, and he wouldn't be able to say "sorry" or "thank you" or "I love you."

He would have to find a way to pay the rent and feed his siblings. His entire life could change in an instant.

Finally, Maria looked back at Jesse for a moment. She held her phone just below her face, as if she was just reading something closely. She looked bewildered and as soon as she saw Jesse staring at her, her face flushed red and then she looked away quickly. There was a flash of annoyance in her face before it went out of view.

Nothing would ever be the same from now on.

Jesse XVII
We Have an Important Mission

Finals week for the first semester had felt like it would never end. Jesse's focus and drive to complete his projects and prepare for his exams had not been this bad since before he started his training under Yusef. He trudged through it, distracted by the onslaught of taunting and meme-making that had become his life in the wake of his poem being posted online.

I finally got my wish to be noticed by Maria, Jesse thought.

On top of that, the Science Fair was finally right around the corner, after the second semester started, in mid-January. The typical energy drain of mentally checking out just before winter break was typically washed away when everyone came back after the recess. But that wasn't the case this year. Students were still on edge from the Congressional vote on Tilson's SENTRII Act. Even the teachers weren't completely back to normal, especially considering the new power, responsibility, and tension that all came with their possible new roles as enforcers of federal immigration policy.

Attendance during finals week, which was the week right after the Tilson Plan had been passed in the Lower House and announced, hadn't dropped dramatically. But there were definitely noticeable empty seats in his classes. One of his group members in Math had just disappeared after December tenth, or "The Tenth" as people were starting to refer to it.

Lita started putting more of the shopping and parenting responsibilities on Jesse now that she was at risk of being detained under the new policy. She also mixed up her work schedule with a few other house cleaners, coordinating with them to go to different houses on random days every week. This was a precaution to prevent capture in case anyone was watching or tracking her.

Christmas was quiet this year. Dulled and stale, there were few parties and gatherings especially since ICE agents made a lot of arrest raids on entire families as they met together for the holidays. Jesse was jolted by the various videos shared over social media of families having dinner or otherwise enjoying themselves and then being suddenly invaded inside their own homes. Terror-stricken women and children screamed amid loud yelling and commands from men, then camera views swung violently and were cut off abruptly.

The added responsibilities and anxiety that the Tilson Plan put on Jesse were both draining and motivating. The Senate's return from winter recess was fast approaching along with the inevitable passing of the SENTRII Act into law once the President signed it. Some days were fatiguing while others spurred his anger to dedicate himself to learning so he could be readily equipped as a force for change, to undo all of the damage that was about to be, and had been, dealt to his people and the country he thought he knew.

Yusef had anticipated this lull, of course, and was ready to counteract it right on The Tenth. Really, the only reason Jesse made it through that last month was Yusef's discipline. In retrospect, Jesse felt ashamed of his inability to meet the demands of the circumstances laid in front of him. After actually studying history, he had grown to admire the game-changers who willed themselves beyond their boundaries, took advantage of the uncertainty of their times, and made legitimate reforms and changes: Siddhartha, Alexander the Great, Julius Caesar, Ashoka, Napoleon, Mahatma Gandhi, Martin Luther King, Jr. He especially admired Siddhartha and the last two, since their influence was so great they didn't require taking power for themselves to bring about the changes they sought.

Jesse didn't see himself as one of them, but their impact certainly brought him some hope that he could at least achieve some kind of change that would impact people around him, if not his country or the world. One of the few voices that spoke out against the SENTRII Act had been Junius Levin, a maverick senator from the east coast who planned to run against the President in next year's election. Jesse thought since he couldn't vote for him yet, maybe he could help some other way.

Winter break was a welcome escape from the taunting Jesse was receiving at school and online. Lita was stressed from her constantly changing work schedule due to the holidays and the precautions she was beginning to take to avoid being tracked by ICE or Los Ojos. Jesse found himself stuck at home babysitting so Lita could pick up odd jobs as other households needed cleaning for holiday parties. He used the time as best as he could to workout, read, work on his research project, and occasionally beat up Fredo and Marcy to remind them who was boss.

Christmas was good, for once. The Arcos family left on Christmas Eve to open gifts and party with their extended family and Lita was home, which gave Jesse some alone time to be productive. That night Jesse and his siblings opened their gifts.

Jesse had managed to sell another one of his video games and a pair of sneakers to finance his holiday shopping. He bought Fredo a pair of youth boxing gloves and when he opened them Jesse promised to teach him how to fight *properly*. For Marcy he found a mini-tripod for her phone, which was an old, cracked hand-me-down and wasn't activated but she still used it for social media on a Wi-Fi connection. When Lita opened her gift, she stared at the opened small box and she wiped away a tear as she said "Gracias, Jesús. Gracias." She lifted the modest and delicate-looking metallic chain necklace out of the box and put it on right away. Lita looked down to center the pendant while centering the clip of the necklace on the back of her neck.

"Which one is that?" Marcy asked.

"San Miguel, nieta," Lita replied somberly. "El nos protege."

"Protects us from what?"

"Fucking ICE," Jesse blurted. "And other pendejos."

"Jesús!" Lita scolded. She hesitated. "Pero, es la verdad," she conceded with a shrug.

The rest of the break wasn't so smooth. Jesse still couldn't completely get away from the social fallout before break. He received a message from @raym._.nd who forwarded a screenshot of Jesse's poem and threatened to kill him if he even tried talking to Maria again. As if that wasn't enough, Jesse saw another post of his screenshot poem (with a GIF of a sad clown crying on it) and Moises was tagged on it. A comment was added: "Who tha real clown, tho?"

These were going to lead to an inevitable problem, Jesse realized, because Jesse was now in Honors English this semester -- with Maria. He was excited when Yusef told him he'd made the switch. A fluttering sensation took over his belly. But then he quickly became anxious when he thought about what the reality of the situation would actually be. It would look self-serving and disingenuous to others if he, of all people, were to suddenly join an Honors class that Maria was in. Everyone he had ever met always doubted his intellectual abilities; now, they would accuse him of creeping on Maria.

Jesse missed Maria over the break and was worried that without a proper opportunity to explain how genuine his feelings were, she would continue to assume the worst about him, which would cement her misunderstanding over the break. He feared coming back to a hopeless situation with her. He had constantly gone back and forth in his mind about whether he should try to contact her over the break. The unknowing and assuming was excruciating.

So during the first week back at school in early January, Jesse dug into his science fair research both as a distraction and as insurance to impress Maria rather than annoy her. He was still delving deep into it through the first weekend of the second semester, while also doing his best to keep a low profile and play it cool around Maria. Yusef had sent a few news articles his way to help him with his research, and they were proving useful.

One article in particular struck Jesse's attention. It was from the *New York Times* but the news report was right out of his native Citrus County, California. A local judge had earlier in the year ordered a man and his family -- a four-year-old daughter, six-year-old son, and his wife -- arrested and sent to one of the many immigrant detention camps that had sprung up in recent years. Judge Thompson had issued the decree very early in the hearing, as soon as he had a chance to clarify the defendant's home address. The judge pressed him on how long he lived there, where he was before, and finally, where he was born. As soon as the man said Guatemala, the judge asked for citizenship and residency status. When the defendant responded honestly by saying he had none, the judge slammed his gavel and ordered him and his entire family to be immediately detained and sent to the camps -- without even inquiring about the status of the children and wife.

When civil rights lawyers appealed the court case weeks later, it was already out of the hands of Thompson and the federal courts. ICE responded weeks after that by saying that the family was in one of their camps, but their newly issued identification numbers had been "lost in transit" while en route to one of the detention camps in ICE's vast network across the country.

Of course, Jesse wanted to find them. But he thought about what Yusef had told him before, about trying to see beyond just immediate justice, especially on the smaller scale. He became more curious about who this judge was, how many other severe rulings he had given out, and what had made this man so cruel to begin with.

9:19 PM Sunday, January 12

hey. you ready to go back yet?

sef: Good evening, Mudtadi. Yes, I am ready for the Plane.

I wana find judge thomspn

sef: Why?

Need to know y they hate us

sef: You might end up with more questions than answers.

what else is new?

sef: Try your pylon. Meet me in the alley. Avoid Carolina

* * * * *

"Really, Mubtadi. It is fine. You are still learning. It will take time and struggle to establish your pylon. It is no trouble to help you in the meantime."

"Whatever. I was so close this time." Jesse walked with Yusef down the alley behind Jesse's apartment building, the side opposite where Carolina sleeps. The purple sky of the Plane subtly glowed above them.

"Your Judge Thompson lives in south County, Mubtadi."

"Yeh, but where are we going?"

"To his home. His den, where he sleeps."

"But… how the fu-- how the hell are we getting there? All these cars ain't real. Right?"

"Correct, Mubtadi. A very astute observation. While the highways of the waking world are the most common form of transport in the waking world, here on the Plane there are other forms of quick travel. The more astute and dedicated Readers are able to become Paragons in teleportation along leylines."

"A'ight. Now you gotta tell me. You been mentioning this shit but not tellin' me."

Yusef smirked. "Have you ever wondered why pyramids are a common phenomenon across the ancient world before human civilizations even interacted with each other?"

"Aliens."

"Vortices."

"Huh?"

"A vortex is a natural and sometimes man-made structure designed over a naturally occurring point of energy that boosts one's abilities on the Plane."

"And that other thing?"

"Ah. When you have a specific focus of your abilities, you achieve a Paragon status of mastery in your particular field of focus." Yusef looked at Jesse to make sure he wasn't wasting his own breath.

"Uh-huh. Still aliens, but sure."

"Excellent. Back to transportation and teleporting. Some vortices boost your travel speed from one point to another along a leyline. Depending on your training you might be able to directly teleport a Reader from one point to the next without a problem."

"'Without a problem'?"

"Hm. Yes, on occasion if a summoner is distracted they might end up sending their target to a different destination entirely. This is why it's crucial for Readers to have someone solely tasked with summoning. This is why you are here."

"Imma be a summoner?"

Yusef nodded his head. "We have an important mission, Mubtadi. This role will be both highly integral for this mission and the least dangerous. *Mushiiyat Allah.*"

"So I can go anywhere I want on the Plane?"

"Theoretically, yes. Even in and out of people's subconscious, if you dedicate yourself enough."

"That's fuckin-- I mean, that's sick."

"I am glad that you are pleased."

"So what's this mission?"

"We are going to stop a civil war before it happens. You and I will save the United States of America from killing itself."

Jesse nodded "Órale."

Jesse XVIII
The White Bishop's Pawn

"I fucking knew the Illuminati was real!" Jesse blurted out.

"Shh! Not so loud," Yusef said with a finger to his lips as he looked around.

"Oh, shit -- Shoot. I forgot." Jesse looked around, too. He and Yusef were sailing just above the low rooftops of San Vallejo at a speed comparable to a car. Yusef had woven together an ornate boat out of putrisomn. It was just big enough for the two of them sitting on simple seats with no backrests. The small boat had curved edgings and wavy siding with no sails or oars. The boat was simply sailing through the air by the mental focus and command of Yusef. Jesse observed the surrounding skyline while shifting uncomfortably in his seat.

"The Illuminati you speak of is not what we are up against. There are many secret groups, not just the one, all vying for power, influence, and control. But more on that later. Return your focus to meditating, Mubtadi. You need to focus on your presence here. Listen to the sky. Close your eyes and try to hear the swirling hazes as we pass them. See the putrisomn in your mind's eye as it can see you."

Jesse slouched over, closed his eyes, and sighed. "A'ight, whatever you say." He fidgeted again. "Ay, what's up with these seats? Can you fix them?"

"Yes, I can. But I will not."

"Ooookaaayy."

"But you can."

Jesse opened one eye and used it to stare at Yusef.

"Focus, Mubtadi. There is plenty of putrisomn on this boat to use."

The ride was mostly silent from that point on. Yusef watched Jesse struggle as he grimaced and winced every few moments. Then he heard the boat creaking near Jesse. As his eyes scanned the vessel, Yusef spotted the edge of the boat near Jesse occasionally shaking. The creaking began sounding like brittle cracking. Then, silence and stillness. He looked back at Jesse, whose face was now demonstrating extreme focus with his eyebrows furrowed and his back arched erect.

"I can't. I fucking can't, because I keep thinking about Maria-fucking-Fonseca."

"Ah, yes. Her."

"Yeh. Her," Jesse said with a sigh.

"You will never reach your potential or even really grow from this point until you seek resolution."

"What?"

"A definite decision to take action and work toward an ending. Before this you must also realize and embrace your *purpose*, Mubtadi."

"My purpose? It's not to be such a fucking loser."

"No! No. It must be much more than that. Why have you put in all of this work, time, and effort? This is about more than you. So much more, for so many more people depend on what you and I will be able to accomplish."

"I love her, 'Sef. I'm in lo-- I like her a lot, and I hate it."

Yusef shook his head vehemently. "You must rid yourself of these thoughts if not permanently, then with temporary but immediate conclusion. We do not have much time left. You must be ready, Mubtadi."

"You think I like this? I want to feel this way all of the fucking time? I already try not to think about her. It's been driving me fucking crazy! I don't even know how I've been able to get as much sleep as I've gotten since you started training me. Probably because I kick my own ass from training so fucking hard that my body doesn't have a choice."

"Well, I hope you recognize that this infatuation has served you in that manner, at least -- that you have been motivated to push yourself to your limits and beyond."

"Infatuation?"

"Yes. How much --"

"Fuck you."

Yusef cleared his throat and let the moment pass, looking away into the horizon. "How much do you really know about her, Mubtadi? How many conversations have you two had? How many of those were deep and meaningful? What are the secrets you have shared between yourselves?"

Jesse shook his head quickly. "I've never felt this way about a girl. She's special. This is special."

Yusef raised an eyebrow and lifted his nose, as if he smelled something unpleasant. "Trust me when I say this comes from a place of care for your well-being, and from experience -- so much terrible, terrible experience. You have plenty of time and opportunity ahead of you. Who you are now, who you have been, and who you will be -- is special.

"When two paths do not align atop one another," the old man continued, "you have to accept and respect it: no matter how strongly you believe it should not be the case. When two paths converge, you will know without any doubt that you are exactly where you should be. Knowing when and where that path ends or splits is a topic for another conversation entirely."

Jesse had his mouth open like he wanted to say something, but then he slowly closed it and continued to listen.

"If you refuse to accept your separate path from another and attempt to force it, you risk losing your own way. You will alter who you are, who you will be, and re-interpret who you were before. You risk losing yourself and your purpose entirely. No one is worth that, Mubtadi. No one. *You* are the special one. And you must not ever forget that."

Jesse was looking away at this point, staring far off into the violent, eerie ether of the Plane. A silence seemed to extend Yusef's words. "Thanks, 'Sef," he finally blurted out. Jesse tried to lean back while putting his hands behind his head, but quickly remembered he had no backrest to lean on.

Yusef waved his arm and a few slivers from the boat that Jesse had previously loosened flew off. They melted in air and reformed together into a flat surface as they floated behind Jesse and then were set onto the back end of his seat.

Jesse leaned back with a smile. "Thanks."

"It must be so frustrating to feel so strongly about her and not have that feeling returned or even acknowledged. But if you are to take these next steps in your training, you will need full focus."

"Should I just shoot my shot, then?"

"You mean, tell her how you really feel about her?"

"Yeah."

"I do not know why you failed to do that to begin with."

His mouth agape, Jesse stared at Yusef and scowled. "What? I thought you were like, helping to build me up and shit."

"You are built up. You will continue to do so. But without the burden of your infatu -- infectious feelings."

"So -- what, I can either love someone or go down this path with you? I can't do both?"

"This path, Mubtadi, this purpose that you have, it is bigger and more important than you or me. Some quests call upon us to sacrifice."

"All I've been doing is sacrificing!"

"It must feel that way, I can see that. Your effort, attention, trust, and so forth. All important aspects, but minor in terms of the other things you have yet to sacrifice. Look at how strong you have become. How much better you are. Imagine the change in you and the power you would have on the Plane -- the power to stop this unnecessary war and change our country for the better -- if you sacrificed more? If you gave all of yourself, the ultimate version of you would be beyond your own imagination and comprehension."

Nodding slowly, Jesse replied with an uninterested, "Yeah, I guess."

"I suppose we will have to conclude this discussion at a later time, when I can properly explain the implications of what -- and who -- I believe we are up against. But we have arrived at your Judge Thompson's den."

"Oh, fuck yeah," Jesse said, wringing his hands together. "Let's infiltrate the shit out of this motherfucker."

Jesse hadn't noticed the steady rise in elevation he was traveling in the boat until it began to rise a bit more suddenly. By that point it was clear they were nearing their destination.

Judge Thompson lived atop a quiet-looking hill that overlooked a canyon with a lonely highway crawling through its floor. His house looked like it was on steroids. As Jesse and Yusef exited the boat and approached the den, Jesse realized that the typical two-story house was in this case three stories. It was accompanied by an expanded garage, and at least one additional guest house behind it.

"Must be fucking nice," Jesse said under his breath. He and Yusef walked up the winding brick walkway to the front door. Yusef stood in front of the door and held out his arm in invitation to Jesse.

"I… do you want me to knock?"

Yusef blurted out a laugh and then covered his mouth and calmed down. "No, Mubtadi. Do you want to try to remove this putrisomn?"

"Oh. Right. Yeh, sure."

Jesse positioned himself in front of the double doors and extended his arm out, his fingers stretched with intensity.

"Relax, Mubtadi. Stop trying to force it with your mind, and your fingers. You have to remember that the putrisomn is made of the residue -- the leftovers -- of our dreams and emotions. It will listen to you if you listen to it."

Jesse put his arm down. He closed his eyes and relaxed. He focused deeply and listened. He heard nothing. But as he focused more, there was almost a buzz in the air. He couldn't quite tell if it was coming from a far or from somewhere nearby. Or both. He listened more intently, trying to separate the stillness from the subtle humming: he hadn't noticed it before. Jesse looked up at Yusef, who was staring back intently. "Has it always been there? The buzzing, or whatever?"

"Yes. As long as there have been humans on this planet that have dreamt. It is always here, all around us. Keep going, Mubtadi. This is wonderful. Just wonderful."

"A'ight." Jesse closed his eyes again and was able to quickly return to separating the reverberations. He focused on trying to slow down the humming, then speed it up. *What if they're voices?* Jesse thought to himself. *Maybe they're in a different language.*

"Now speak to it. From deep, behind your mind. But do not tell it what you want. Refrain from using your inner voice. Instead, will it, Mubtadi. Want it, need it to follow your will and command."

The doors vibrated and began to crack. There was little progress beyond that. "I fucking can't." The doors stood still again.

"Jesse. You can and you will. You have to try again. But when you return to this point you need to find a better way to communicate with the putrisomn. Remember that it is the byproduct of our desires and fears. So you, too, must use your emotions to command it. Focus on something that has meaning to you. A memory or a desire that moves you and drives you."

Jesse nodded slowly. "Yeah, I can do that." A minute passed and loud cracks began to come from the doors. Shards of wood peeled off in long splinters. Squeaks and shaking emanated from the doors. Finally, they shattered and broke apart from their centers, leaving chunks of debris scattered about the entryway. Jesse touched the door, which had a rubbery skin and muskiness about it that the putrisomn could not completely hide.

"Fuck yeah!"

"I normally would not approve of the ugly language, but in this instance I will let it slide. Congratulations, Mubtadi."

As they stepped over the debris and entered the home of Judge Thompson, Yusef held out his hand, swirling his fingers. Pieces of the putrisomn debris flew up to his hand and melded together into a long cane or walking stick. He finished weaving it together and began using it immediately. The staff stood tall to his shoulders.

Jesse walked into the family room and looked around, putting his hands on his hips as he took it all in. A few veins of dark putrisomn lined the walls. Framed photos had been strategically placed in ideal lighting and viewing space. They included Judge Thompson with his family and attractive or successful looking people, deliberately arranged on key shelves and furniture. These artifacts attempted to tell a story to visitors entering his home: Judge Thompson was very successful, he knew lots of successful people, and he was powerful. "Fuck this guy," Jesse said out loud, his hands still resting on his hips as he looked at the walls and raised ceilings all the way up the staircase and elevator. A few blackened vines of putrisomn hung down from each landing, and more putrisomn nestled together like cobwebs underneath each landing.

As Jesse began trudging up the stairs he stopped to notice they were soft, almost soggy.

"Putrisomn. Sometimes in dens with fewer inhabitants the structures are not as solid. Sometimes not every part of a den is as complete or as detailed as it is in the waking life. Not enough people to properly reflect the entire home in all of its intricate details. We should venture carefully, as the top floor might not hold our weight."

"Yeah. So I'll just, like, hope for the best and not fall through the floor. Got it." Jesse gave an overly enthusiastic "okay" sign with his fingers to Yusef.

"I will take lead, Mubtadi," Yusef said with a sigh.

They made their way up the stairs, slowly, avoiding use of the railing since Yusef said it was probably quite unreliable on the Plane. Carefully, they continued while Yusef used his walking stick to poke the floor, testing its sturdiness.

The master bedroom had double doors, and the left one was already open. Jesse saw moving reds, blues, and purples reflecting off the open bedroom door and on one wall.

"Stay close, Mubtadi. Wait for my direction."

"Yeah," Jesse said while catching his breath.

Both blinding and mesmerizing, the two hazes of Judge Thompson and his wife together in bed caught Jesse's eye and he lost focus. The blackened bodies of the Thompsons lay peacefully while a separate haze swirled around each of them. Judge Thompson's haze swirled at a faster speed close to the center, and then it had a slower, calmer speed at the outer rim of the haze. It was rhythmic without a beat, almost hypnotic.

The sight reminded him of a memory from long ago. He had been huddled as close to the bonfire as he could get without burning while his backside felt frozen. His pants were soggy from his wet chonies and he couldn't help but still feel his body swaying and being rocked by the waves he had fought all that day. Sand crunched in his ears and irritated his inner thighs from when Papá had buried him in the sand earlier. Junior had thrown him into the ocean more times than he could count and Erik had chased him into the sea all day, trying to throw slimy dark green, smelly seaweed on him. He would have caught Jesse if he hadn't been laughing so hard the entire time. Mamá was roasting marshmallows on straightened metal clothes hangers and trying to free her hand of one by giving one to Jesse while Fredo and Marcie fought each other to try to claim it. Jesse couldn't look away from the glowing embers and the crackling of the wood inside the barbecue pit. Every time he had thought he was ready to return to the world, a pop or a flame would flicker, curling like a whip and cracking Jesse back into submission.

"Take my arm. Do not let go. I also suggest you close your eyes, but we both know you will not."

Jesse XIX
The White Bishop

Jesse grasped Yusef's arm tightly and brought himself close to him. They walked to Judge Thompson's side of the bed, and a few of the orbs of light encircling him began to pop off. Jesse saw flashes like photos and felt unfamiliar emotions sway him like passing waves. Lights floated around him and strange images flooded before him. Scenes from outdoors, indoors, daytimes, nighttimes, summers, and winters, all new to Jesse. He saw himself moving and talking in Judge Thompson's memories. Time felt old, foreign, frozen, moving, and malleable all at once.

An image stuck. It was an old-looking school hallway with a waxed wooden floor and steel lockers painted dark red. The walls were cream colored with a gold and crimson band painted across them.

Jesse saw Yusef move next to him. Then he moved his free arm and looked down, realizing he was no longer merely seeing one of Judge Thompson's memories but was now *in* one of them.

A white teenager walked in view from around a corner down the hall. Yusef gently pushed Jesse to the side and they pressed themselves against a classroom door with frosted glass. The doorway created a nook between the line of lockers and they were able to hide while they watched the teen make his way to a locker.

"Is that him?"

"Yes, Mubtadi," Yusef whispered.

"What--"

"Shh. Please, save your questions until after. We must not distract ourselves or be detected."

"But how--"

"Shh."

"Ugh."

High-pitched feedback from loudspeakers near the wood ceiling blared, and Jesse hunched his shoulders up and covered his ears with his hands, eyebrows raised and eyes alert. Yusef remained steady and calm, only slightly wincing.

An angry, deep, and crisp male voice with a slight Southern drawl thundered from the walls. "Don't turn your back on them. These illegals, they'll take everything from you when you're not watching. Just look at everything they've taken from us *while* we've watched."

The teenager, wearing pressed navy blue slacks and a tidy white dress shirt rushed to flick open his locker. A bright light shined from inside and he was gone. The locker door slowly swung on its hinges, remaining open, and darkened once again.

"Come. We must not lose him."

Jesse followed Yusef closely down the hall. The loudspeakers squawked again and the same overconfident and cocky voice yelled through the speaker. "Even if you wanted to quote-unquote 'keep the peace,'" his voice turned into a mockingly wavering and wimpy tone at this phrase, "you would be the weakest link in this whole ordeal -- our struggle. Because there isn't any more peace. The war has already started, people! They've already invaded us; they've already started stealing our precious resources, our hard-earned property, our space, and goddamn air!"

"Who--"

"Shh. Later, Mubtadi."

The locker was about to close when Yusef reached for it with his walking stick and kept it open. He pulled it back and the blinding light returned only for what seemed like a camera flash to Jesse.

They were now in a courtroom, wooden and carpeted, with fluorescent lights and no windows. A man sat at the prosecutor's table, his back to Jesse and Yusef who were standing at the rear of the courtroom.

"No, this is not it."

"Huh?"

"Stay with me." Yusef grabbed Jesse's arm and they turned to the double doors at the back of the room. The old man opened the door and hesitated before leaving, as if he was waiting for something. An armed security guard calmly patrolled the hallway. "Hm," Yusef said quietly as he closed the door. "That is not the way. Perhaps we took a direct route."

Looking around, Jesse saw the only other door to be behind the Judge's bench. The man still sat at the prosecutor's table, facing forward. "'Sef. What about over there?"

"Ah. I suppose we are where we need to be." Yusef quickly walked up the center of the courtroom toward the bench. "Keep up." When they walked past the man, Jesse saw that it was an older version of the teenager he had seen in the school hallway. He didn't seem to notice them. Until they crossed him and approached the bench.

"These men are absolutely one hundred percent guilty, your Honor," Prosecutor Thompson proclaimed, now standing up. Jesse looked behind him toward the bench and saw an even older version of the same man, Judge Thompson, who looked more like the man in the photos Jesse had seen earlier in the family room.

"Present your evidence and argue your case, Prosecutor," Judge Thompson declared.

"We do not have time for this," Yusef said, his hand grasping his forehead.

"Well, Your Honor, this Mexican boy and this terrorist have no business being here. I mean, just look at them. The evidence speaks for itself," Prosecutor Thompson bellowed out.

"Just keep up, Mubtadi. Ignore them." Yusef started toward the judge's chamber door behind the bench.

"Yes, well we know the defendants were caught taking from you. We know they would take everything from us if they had the chance," Judge Thompson confirmed.

"The fuck?" Jesse said, staring at Judge Thompson.

"Yes, Your Honor, the audacity of these people. Even when they know we're watching they'll take everything from us. They're fighting a war against us. And it must be stopped. It must end here!"

"Order!" Judge Thompson barked. "Your argument has been heard and saved for the public record. And it's nothing new. We have been under siege for decades. This war they have brought upon us is being waged on the streets, in our schools, in our places of work. There's no escaping their invasion!" Judge Thompson's face and ears were turning red now. He went on after taking a breath and straightening his posture. "My judgment will be severe. Any effort to keep the peace with these aliens would be seen as a weakness and their resolve to take everything from us would only strengthen."

Pressing his hand to Jesse's back, Yusef said, "I think we have heard quite enough, Mubtadi. That way," his staff pointed at the judge's chamber redwood door behind the bench. The two of them walked toward it while both Prosecutor and Judge Thompson glared angrily at them.

"You are in contempt of court!" Judge Thompson and Prosecutor Thompson both yelled in perfect unison. But a third voice spoke as well, Jesse thought.

As they reached the chamber door, a set of jail bars shot up from the floor and blocked it. Jesse turned around to look at the judge and another set of bars shot up to block his path, then another on the opposite side. They were locked in a jail cage. He turned to Yusef and wondered if he should panic.

The old man lifted his staff and waved it from left to right. "We do not have time for this." The cage shattered into pieces, flying off into different directions of the courtroom. Both Prosecutor and Judge Thompson stared with blank looks. The main courtroom doors burst open and two armed guards entered, carrying automatic rifles.

Yusef opened the chamber door and motioned for Jesse to go in first. He rushed into the opulent office and Yusef followed closely as loud gunshots rang out. The chamber door closed behind Yusef, thudding and splintering with a few hits of high-velocity rounds before closing shut.

At the judge's walnut desk sat a large, overweight white man with thin-framed glasses resting at the tip of his nose and with a set of headphones on his head. Glare from multiple monitors reflected off his glasses and the sweat or oil gleaming from his forehead. He bawled into a professional microphone which was attached to a suspended mic stand that arched down from above his head. A video camera was set up on his desk, placed to record him. His voice boomed out from his thick, heavy body. Jesse put his hand on his chest.

"¡No chingues! Do you feel that?"

A framed photo on the wall next to Yusef shook and vibrated with the man's voice. He stared at the man behind the desk with eyes that Jesse never wanted directed toward himself. "Erik Peters. I would have guessed as much."

"Who--"

"Later." Yusef stepped past Jesse. He stood in front of the desk and raised his staff and free hand in the air. Erik Peters blew away like dust.

They turned their attention to a computer monitor featuring a news video clip of a handsome man in a suit waving from a podium. The chyron below him read "Representative Tilson (R-ID) Speaks at America First Rally."

Then Yusef turned to the mahogany bookcases that lined the walls of the judge's chamber and raised his staff, concentrating for an extended time at each one. The video clip from the monitor continued to play: "Yes, we will prosper! Our best years are still ahead of us…"

By this point, Jesse kept quiet and observed. He saw the books and photographs on the shelves and walls change. There were frames that contained beautiful, articulate Arabic lettering in black, green, and gold. Framed Bible quotes. Titles of books that Jesse didn't recognize laid in gold type on leather-bound, thick book spines. A few thinner ones grabbed his attention: Marcus Aurelius's *Meditations*, Hesse's *Siddhartha*, and *An Essay on Crimes and Punishments* by Cesare Beccaria.

"Standard fare for scrubbing someone's subconscious, and a few select choices for Judge Thompson to reflect on in particular," Yusef commented to Jesse as he finished the last wall. "Hopefully he will recall some of these titles, remembering the lessons and messages they offer. Perhaps he will even seek some of them out in the waking life to remind himself."

"....We will have a new day. And a new future!" Tilson's voice went on. Applause followed.

Yusef turned to the computer on the desktop and swept his staff across it, melting the entire setup. Tilson's voice was no more.

"'Ey. You gonna explain all this shit now?" Jesse threw his arms around himself.

"Not yet."

A deafening bang combined with the sound of splintering wood burst from the chamber's door. Jesse instinctively fell to the ground and covered his face with his arms. Yusef had turned and faced the doors, pushing his chest forward with his arms outstretched. The flying splinters and debris were pushed backwards with an invisible wall that shot out from Yusef.

A cadre of commandos armed with assault rifles and grenades on their tactical vests began to storm the office, yelling grunted commands and affirmations at each other.

An aggressive forward thrust from Yusef's staff launched the charging assault team off their feet and back out into the courtroom.

"Time to go!" Yusef sang aloud. He grabbed Jesse's nearest limb, then tapped his staff on the floor twice. Jesse felt like he just dipped on a roller coaster. Then he was laying on the floor back in the school hallway with Yusef.

"Arise, Mubtadi. I believe you have witnessed quite enough for one night."

"You mean there's more?"

Yusef grinned, leading Jesse by the arm to a locker against the wall. "Yet another lesson I would have hoped to have stuck with you by now: there is always more."

Jesse didn't have time to respond. Blinding light shot out from the locker Yusef opened and he was gone, thrust out of Thompson's subconscious and back out to the Plane. Jesse stepped in front of the locker and waited his turn to get sucked back out. The flashing light returned and Jesse braced himself for another wild ride.

Instead, something flew toward him through the flash and he tripped backward to the ground. Dalisay Morcilla now stood in front of the locker, feet apart, and her fists clenched at her sides. She scowled straight into his eyes.

Jesse XX
The Black Knight

He was on his back when the heel of Dalisay's foot came shooting down to his face.

"Bahhh!" he belted out and snapped his head out of the way just in time. Dali's foot slammed into the polished wood floor. A flat kick to his ribs quickly followed.

"Fu--!"

A second kick flew to his face. He got his guard up and broke some of the hit at her ankle, but he still absorbed a fair amount on his face. *At least I hurt this puta's shin. I think*. In between his shielding arms he scanned the hallway of Thompson's subconscious and saw no sign of Yusef.

Jesse scrambled up on his feet while shuffling backward, keeping his arms up to parry and block a flurry of blows coming at him. He heard sharp exhales and grunts coming from her as she kept her chin down close to her chest.

How is this the same person I saw struggling to breath on the street just a few motnsh ago? Where the fuck is Yusef? Jesse's back slammed into a wall of metal lockers. Dalisay's jabs started slipping through Jesse's guard and he took some shots to the face and one to his liver, which actually hurt the most.

"Time to die, bitch!" Jesse used his leg to push himself from the lockers and threw a jab at her face. She dodged it, which he anticipated, and a stronger right hook followed. *Goodnight, Puta.*

Jesse's arm swung hard and fast. Bracing his fist for impact, he instead felt pain in his whole body and he fell to his knees. His hands were on his liver. "Fu--fu--ugh," Jesse gasped for breath and grimaced as he kneeled helplessly in front of Dalisay.

"Stay away from me, Jesse. And from Moises." Dali threatened as she stood above him.

"Wha--"

Dalisay reached back with a clenched fist then sent it crashing straight into Jesse's nose.

"Arrgghhh!" he screamed from red and yellow lights of pain that flashed all over his vision. Jesse grabbed his nose, which he was sure had been broken and bursting with blood. It was fine.

"Jesus! Pobrecito! Again?" Lita cooed as she rushed over from her mattress.

"Shut the fuck up, Jesse!" Alfredo griped over his shoulder as he tried to scoot further away from Jesse so that he was practically flat against the bedroom wall. He shoved his only pillow on top of his head.

"The fuck?" Jesse sat up and looked around. Marcy was sitting up on her mattress, studying Jesse with concerned eyes. He caught her stare, which was deep and seemed to come from afar, even though she was only seven feet away or so. "Shit. I'm sorry, guys."

Lita and Marcy stared silently at him.

"It won't happen… I'll try..." Jesse kicked off his blanket and pushed himself off the mattress. "Imma get some water." He unplugged his charger from the wall and took it with him, along with his phone. He snuck down the hall, trying not to disturb the Arcos family, at least not more than he already had. He could hear murmured voices and shushes through their door as he passed.

In the kitchen, Jesse drank a glass of water with his eyes half open then went to the living room and plugged in his phone. He collapsed on the couch, ready to start figuring out what had just happened.

The blaring, penetrating tones from his phone yanked Jesse from deep slumber. "Ohgoddamnit." He reached over from the couch and snoozed the alarm.

It hit him again, and it was even harder to get up this time. He felt exhausted, like the morning after the first time Yusef had made Jesse run five miles of hills near the beginning of his training. He slowly sat up after turning off his alarm and rested his head on his hand. "Pinche La Puta."

Jesse's energy level hadn't been this low since the beginning of the school year, before he started his training. He slowly got ready for school and slumped his way there. Taking his stiff pancakes and a cold, old sponge of scrambled eggs from the cafeteria, Jesse wondered how he was going to survive the day. Klinkhammer's diatribes on Shakespeare's *Julius Caesar* had been engaging for Jesse in the last week, but now he considered how long-winded they typically were, and he worried about falling asleep and slamming his face into his desk or even falling out of his seat.

Barely lifting his feet, Jesse slowly shuffled to his first period class, holding his breakfast in front of him. "Fuck me," he said, grabbing his liver which didn't actually hurt, but still echoed pain.

"Nyeeeeeeeh!" he heard from behind.

"Really?"

"Jessseeeee! What up, foo'? Long time no toke. Nyeeh!"

"I'm fucking tired, Racha."

"Were you beating it too much last night?"

"Yeah, to your mom."

"Nyeeh! Still got it, pendejo. You gonna need that comedy act when Raymond comes around. Your best chance is to make that foo' laugh so he doesn't fuck you up so hard."

"What the fuck are you talking about?" Jesse asked irritatedly, shoving his cardboard basket of breakfast outward as he threw his arms out in a big shrug. His scrambled egg sponge flung to the edge of the basket.

"Your poetry is popular, Homie. It's good. So good that Raymond read it. And he wants to let you know how much he likes it. Because, you know. You got a big tiny boner for his girl. Nyeeeh!"

Jesse froze and stared at Racha, his arms still stretched out to his sides. The egg sponge teetered off the basket and bounced off the ground, landing against Jesse's white sneakers.

"Fuck."

"I hope you're ready for a fight, homie. I'd have your back, pues… It's Raymond." Racha shrugged as he drifted on his skateboard around Jesse. "I like my face how it is, you know? In one piece. Nyeeeeeh!"

Jesse XXI
Wherefore Art Thou, Romeo?

"What the fuck, 'Sef?"

"Mr. Abdel."

Jesse glared at him from across the desk as the bell rang. This already wasn't the best way to start a Monday.

Yusef patiently returned the stare. "I am sorry you have so many unanswered questions. All in due time."

"Let's start with 'where the fuck were you?'"

Yusef paused and studied Jesse's demeanor which was threatening at the least. "Hmm. You might remember me mentioning Erik Peters once or twice before. I thought I had warned and prepared you well enough for that kind of interaction."

"Oh, yeah? To get my ass kicked by fucking Dalisay Morcilla? You prepared me for that?"

Yusef closed his eyes and took in a deep breath. He looked down at his tie and straightened it under his thin sweater vest. "You mean to say that you did not return safely to the Plane or your own den? That you were somehow intercepted?"

"What the fuck, 'Sef? Where were you?"

Yusef leaned back in his desk chair. "I suspected another Reader was operating nearby. Judge Thompson had to have been enthralled at some point."

"Enth-what?"

"Enthrallment is when a Reader consistently infiltrates the haze of someone to alter their memories, their fears, and their desires. They do this to influence and control the victim's decisions and actions here in the waking world," Yusef explained.

"The fu-- uh, how?"

"It requires work. After learning how the victim thinks and feels, a Reader must weave dreams for the victim that deconstruct and recreate their desires and objectives. In some cases these are dog whistle phrases or subliminal imagery that trigger responses from the victim in the waking world. A person is essentially brainwashed and can be controlled to think and act in a certain way."

Jesse stared back in shock, trying to connect the things he'sd seen with what Yusef was explaining to him: the announcements, the security measures, the multimedia broadcasts of Erik Peters, and all of the photos and books and propaganda in that deep subconscious of the judge.

"I saw no sign of recent infiltration, but clearly Judge Thompson had previously been influenced by an outside force -- the Apostles, undoubtedly -- and they were able to create a sustaining influence in his subconscious."

Jesse was still too angry to listen. "Who? Dalisay? Why didn't you say something before if you thought there might have been someone else around?"

"You already had too much to focus on. And again, Mubtadi, I did not know for sure. But now I do. What did she say to you?"

"I was too busy getting my ass kicked to take notes, 'Sef."

"When we are around others, you must refer to me as Mr. Abdel. Where were you?"

"Back in Thompson's dream. In the fancy school hallway. She effed me up."

"Yes, you do look rather… spent. Remember our run-in with Carolina? You are suffering a similar aftereffect as I had. You were ejected from the Plane because you took in too much pain for you to endure. A decisive defeat -- whether in someone's subconscious or on the Plane itself -- can be debilitating on your willpower. But it is temporary, as long as you are willing to put the work back in. Plus, you will be tougher and wiser now.

Defeats are necessary for growth, Mubtadi."

"Whatever. Can you write me a note so I can go home and sleep?"

"No. Go to class."

"'Sef!"

"'Mr. Abdel.'" Knocks erupted from the door along with muffled yells and rubber screeches from shuffling shoes from outside the classroom. Yusef stood up from his desk and made his way to the door as he scooped his keys from his pocket. "We shall continue later. Chin up, Mubtadi. Endure. Grow!" He opened the door and unlocked it as his students began pouring in with frowns on their faces. "And rest! I know you have not forgotten about tomorrow, Mr. Ramirez. The big day is finally here."

Jesse's eyes shot open wide and then he quickly forced them back to a normal size. "Oh, you mean the Science Fair?" he nonchalantly confirmed. "Psh. Yeah, it's whatever. I got this."

"You are all prepared, yes?" Students began lightly pushing past Jesse to get to their seats as he slowly walked away from Yusef while still looking over at him.

"Of course!" Beads of sweat began to appear above his lip and on his forehead. "'Kay. Bell rang. Gotta go, bye!"

"Send me your final draft when you get home, Mr. Ramirez!" Yusef yelled as Jesse ran outside the classroom, impolitely shoving past students.

He cleared them and found a wall to lean against as he hunched over and rested his hands on his knees, breathing heavily. "Fuck!"

Heavy footsteps neared Jesse. A large Asian guy whom Jesse recognized as Phi walked by holding only a folded up school agenda and spotted Jesse. "Aw, did you get your heart broken again, Romeo?"

Jesse looked up and then stood straight. "Fuck off."

Phi chuckled and flipped him off, then made sure his baseball cap was straight and went back to looking all around him for potential administrators or campus security as he trudged down the hallway. He turned back and yelled, "I hear Raymond *and* Moises are looking for you. Can't wait to see that shit go down! Romeo!"

Closing his eyes, Jesse took a deep breath and sighed. He rushed over to Mr. Klinkhammer's classroom and borrowed a laptop, promising to return it by the end of the day. "Yes, yes," the English teacher grumbled as he waved his hand. "What's it matter to me? They're not mine."

In the rest of his classes that day Jesse was scribbling in his notebook and scrambling on his laptop. "Fuck, fuck, fuck," he kept mumbling under his breath as he worked and went from class to class, multi-tasking with whatever assignment he had to do that day or ignoring it altogether.

The laptop was about ready to die when he returned it after sixth period. "I hope that was helpful," Klinkhammer said from his desk as softly as his deep, loud voice could get. He leaned back in his chair, resting his hands on his belly, which was swollen like a beachball. There were photos and holiday cards from students, staff, and family pinned on the wall behind him. A few book posters were taped to the high parts of the ceilings around his classroom, but it was mostly student work that was on display around the room. One whiteboard was completely full of notes from *Julius Caesar*.

"Yeah," Jesse responded as he crouched down and finished plugging the laptop back into the computer cart.

"You're ready for tomorrow?"

This time Jesse turned to Klinkhammer and gave him a quizzical look.

"Just because I teach English class doesn't mean I don't follow what happens outside of it. I understand you're working on a lot of research and it's justice-related. That's quite admirable, Jesús."

"Yeh." Jesse rubbed his saggy, dried eyes. "The research has been more, uh, intense than I thought. I don't know if Imma be ready."

"That's unfortunate, especially if you've already put in so much work. A student in one of my Honors classes has also been working hard on a research project for the Fair. I proofed it earlier this week. It's phenomenal, truly impressive."

"Uh-huh," Jesse uttered, shifting his weight and rubbing his neck. He wondered just how much more work he had to do still.

"You might know her. Dalisay Morcilla? A very promising young lady. You kind of remind me of her, actually. I don't know why."

Jesse scowled and clenched his fists.

"No? You don't know her? Huh. I thought you might have. You smarties all run in the same circles. Anyhow, good luck, Jesús. I hope you have your own victory at Philippi."

"Oh, I'll have it done. Imma be ready tomorrow. Dead a— uh. Bet."

Jesse rushed home, trying to stay angry and motivated to beat Dalisay in order to fight off the exhaustion from the previous night. Lita saw how focused he was when she got home later and avoided nagging him about chores or watching his siblings. She brought him dinner while he worked at the kitchen table, hardly looking away from his notebook and his phone as he shoveled food into his mouth.

Alfredo and Marcy called for Lita from the living room, their homework splayed out on the coffee table. "Ya voy."

After some time she heard Jesse call from the kitchen. "Lita."

"¡Ya voy!" She walked to the kitchen entryway. "¿Qué?"

Without looking up at first, Jesse said. "Thanks." Then he twisted around from his chair and forked the last of his fajitas into his mouth. And just as quickly he turned back and went to work again.

"De nada, nieto." Lita stood there and stared at him for a moment. Then she walked over behind Jesse and gently grazed his scalp with her fingernails. "Estoy orgulloso de ti, niño."

Jesse stopped for a second and asked, "What's that? 'Orgullo'?"

Lita took a moment. "Es 'proud.' I am proud of you, Jesús."

Pausing again, Jesse nodded. "Dinner was good."

"Si, si." Lita returned to the living room and checked back on Alfredo and Marcy, who were wrestling and slapping each other for the TV remote.

The alarm on his phone blared and Jesse's gut twisted when he noticed the early morning blue gray outside the living room window. He shot up from the couch and saw his notes scattered across the coffee table. "Fuck, fuck, fuck. I knew I shouldn't have left the kitchen last night."

Mrs. Arcos rushed through the living room from the kitchen, dangling her keys and clutching her purse and her lunch in a knapsack. She cleared her throat loudly and walked out of the apartment without saying a word. Mrs. Arcos locked the doors behind her.

Jesse wiped the slobber from his chin and rubbed the sleep out of his eyes. He lifted his arm and sniffed his armpit. His nose wrinkled and he shrugged. "Fuck it." Then he went right back to his notes and typing into his phone.

"¡Jesús! ¡Jesús!" Lita called from the hallway. She walked into the living room still tying the cord of her sleeping robe around her midsection. "Ah. ¡Pobrecito! ¿Quieres breakfast?"

Taking a long moment to finish typing something in his phone, Jesse finally replied, "Nah. You got work, no?"

Lita flung her arms at Jesse as she began hustling to the kitchen. "You have school. Today es muy importante."

The soft banging of cabinets closing and the clanging of dishware on countertops drifted from the kitchen as Jesse continued his work, hardly stopping to blink or even look away from either his notes or his phone.

Before he knew it, Jesse had to go so there would be enough time to find somewhere on campus to print out his project, then make it presentable. He grabbed his project supplies from his room, which he had bought with money he got from selling his NBA Live video game to a neighbor the week before. The rest of the money he would save so he could buy some heavier dumbbells.

"¡Tu desayuno!" Lita called out from the kitchen as Jesse was already opening the front door, holding his bag of supplies in the other hand, while trying to put on his hoodie over one shoulder and balancing his backpack on the other.

"I gotta go!"

"You're not hungry, nieto?"

"No, I'll eat later. Imma be late!"

Lita rushed over as Jesse waddled out of the doorway with all of his things. She put a hot burrito wrapped in a paper towel inside his hoodie pocket for him.

"Get the door," he barked, kicking the outer screen door shut, almost in her face. Then he rushed off.

"¡Que Dios esté contigo!" he heard Lita yell from behind him.

An hour later toward the end of first period, Mr. Padilla had largely ignored Jesse as Jesse in turn ignored him, frantically trying to make his project presentable. He was able to use two empty desks in the back of the room to work. A few more students had not returned from winter break, in addition to the ones that left after The Tenth. He ended up using only half of the supplies he bought due to lack of time. When the bell rang Mr. Padilla walked over to Jesse and he prepared himself for a scolding or a lecture from the teacher. "Buena suerte, Señor Ramirez."

"Huh? Oh. I mean, uh… thanks."

Mr. Padilla nodded and walked back to his desk as the rest of the students drained out of the classroom around him.

Jesse was now excused from the next few periods, as check-in time for the Science Fair participants was expected to begin soon. He rushed to the gym with his printed research pasted onto a large poster board. "What the fuck am I forgetting?" he snarled to himself. He couldn't shake the feeling that he forgot something. Jesse racked his brain and then thought about anything he might have forgotten at home. *Too late for that*, he thought. Jesse didn't slow his frantic pace at all. He didn't have a free hand to check the time on his phone but he knew check-in time had to be starting about then.

A folding table with a taped sign that read "Check-In" was set up just in front of the opened gym doors. It was being manned by Ms. Irons, the school librarian. "There he is! You did it! You made it!" she exclaimed with her hands high above her head in celebratory triumph.

Jesse forced his eyebrows up in a tired expression of fake joy. He wiped his brow of sweat he worked up from jogging across campus while juggling all of his materials.

Then Ms. Irons quickly scanned a roster laying in front of her and satisfyingly marked a check. "Table twenty-four, dear. I think the rest of these are no-shows. That cold/flu is going around. Anyway, now I can leave!" and her arms shot up again, but with slightly more enthusiasm this time. "Go on in, Honey. And I hope you formatted your works cited page in the same format style of your research paper. That always loses points for a lot of students. Good luck!" Ms. Irons cheered with a dismissive wave as she stood up and began shuffling papers together.

Jesse's stomach dropped. He forgot his works cited page. Fresh beads of sweat began gathering on his brow and he felt a line of sweat fall down his lower back. *I'll be disqualified,* he thought to himself. *They won't even look at my research. I'm fucked.*

Jesse XXII
The 64th Annual Portola High School Science Fair

All of that work… all of that time and stress and bullshit. For fucking nothing?

"Jesse. You can go in," Ms. Irons repeated, standing awkwardly while hugging her belongings. "Are you okay?"

"I'm fucked," Jesse whimpered.

"Excuse me?"

Jesse continued standing in front of the gym doors, staring inside aimlessly.

Ms. Irons' tone became more conciliatory. "Oh, don't be intimidated by all of them. I've seen your research and know your thesis -- you're going to be great. Get in there and give them a going!" She gave him a gentle and light shove toward the doors as he slowly stumbled through them. Then she closed the doors behind him.

I don't have it completed. Don't even got it formatted. There's no time, I can't do this. Why am I still walking? Barely picking up his feet and with the color drained from his face, Jesse might have been mistaken for a zombie as he slowly lumbered toward the display tables. Jesse went on debating in his head. *What if they don't look closely? If I can find a printer or buy some time… maybe I can pull this off. They can't stop and read EVERY paper here, right?*

A giant poster on the back wall of the gym read "Welcome to the 64th

Annual Portola High School Science Fair". Jesse wandered past tables topped with various displays of colorfully decorated poster boards, dioramas, scaled models of various structures and futuristic-looking vehicles, circuit boards with blinking lights, a miniature hot-air balloon, and at least two papier-mâché volcanoes. But he hardly noticed any of it, or the students nervously waiting behind them -- until he reached table twenty-four.

Behind the table across from him stood Dalisay Morcilla with two poster boards propped up. On the left was a larger poster board with a clear title header that read "Why You Need to Leave: The Next Ten Years of the Climate Crisis," and on the right was a smaller poster board that read "Works Cited". It displayed various print-outs of a long, detailed bibliography. Dali caught him staring and looked right back into his eyes. A small smirk rose on the side of her mouth.

"Pinche puta," Jesse hissed out under his breath.

Ms. Clifton, who Jesse knew was the AP Biology teacher only because Maria had her, used a handheld megaphone to loudly squawk over the murmuring students in the gym, who were anxiously socializing with one another or nervously practicing their presentations. "We are about to open doors and let the judges and audience in. Best of luck to everyone!"

Dalisay looked cool and calm. Prepared. Not worried in the slightest, especially about Jesse right across from her.

"Fuck this." Jesse briskly walked to the interior doors on the other side of the gym where the boys restroom was, and the boys locker room just beyond. He let the gym doors close behind him before walking past the restroom to go inside the boys locker room. There were still a few students milling about in their gym clothes and as he passed the wide windows of the coaches' office, he could still see the P.E. teachers at their desks, getting rosters, clipboards, and mini three-ring binders in order before they headed outside to meet their classes. Jesse looked around the walls of the locker room and spotted it. He went over to the red fire alarm on the wall, glanced around to make sure no one was watching . . . and pulled it.

A loud, obnoxious siren blared from different directions somewhere up in the high exposed ceiling of the locker room. It echoed in places beyond, too. Jesse casually walked back to the gym, avoiding the windows of the coaches' office. When he reached the gym doors, he peeked inside and saw everyone looking around shrugging at each other.

"Please evacuate the gym in a calm and orderly fashion," Ms. Clifton said sternly through the megaphone.

Jesse knew he didn't have much time before someone would take a count or roll call and realize that he was missing. He waited for everyone to leave before he went out to the gym floor and bee-lined straight to Dalisay's works cited board. As he grabbed it, he smiled. "Didn't put her name on this one." But as he picked it up, his smile faded. He envisioned what would happen with Dalisay standing right in front of him while the judges came by to read his project or hers. He would have to beat her down before the judges got here. He touched his liver, remembering his encounter with her last night on the Plane. "Pinche puta. She's too strong." Jesse heard doors or lockers slamming shut down the locker room corridor. "Fuck it. Fuck all this." He put her poster board back on Dalisay's table and ran back to the restrooms, leaving his project behind, too.

On the way, he passed by the miniature hot-air balloon table and grabbed a kitchen lighter that had been left there. Then he rushed over to the girls' side of the gym and right into the girls' restroom.

There, he scooped some quarters from his pocket and put them into a steel dispenser on the wall that was labeled "Sanitary Napkins". A pad packaged in thin cardboard fell into a metal tray and Jesse quickly grabbed it and tore apart the cardboard, throwing the pad into the sink and then the cardboard pieces into a small pile on top. Then he went into a stall and tore some toilet paper and added it to the pile in the sink. Jesse clicked the lighter and set the pile on fire. He quickly ran back out on the gym floor to the table to return the lighter. As he reached the table the fire sprinklers burst open, and water rained down in the gym. Jesse sprinted to the heavy exit doors and ran through them, his hair and clothes drenched.

The entire Science Fair, judges, teachers, and school administrators included, all stood a short distance away and stared with mouths agape. Their eyes were gawking with surprise at Jesse. Panting, he belted out, "Bathroom. I was in the bathroom."

No one said anything, and he felt the stares get deeper.

"Explosive diarrhea," he said with a shrug, as water dripped from his t-shirt and ears.

As the crowd glared suspiciously at Jesse, only he noticed the side entrance door to the boys locker room closing behind them all, out of their view. Racha had just walked out and casually joined the distracted onlookers. He carried a backpack and a sports bag slung over a shoulder and eyed Jesse with a giant smile on his face. Then he pointed at Jesse and nodded, his smile getting even bigger. Racha slinked away and disappeared behind the crowd.

"He fucking saw me," Jesse muttered under his breath.

Jesse XXIII
Gonna Get Worse

Dr. Sanchez uttered a series of uh-hms and nos into the phone handset that was pressed to his ear with his shoulder. Jesse and Dalisay sat across from his desk. Dalisay sat straight up and did her best not to be nervous. Jesse slouched in his chair with his head tilted up at an angle, and he stared mindlessly into a corner of the ceiling.

"Yes, thank you so much, Chief. And again, we are so sorry to waste your time," Dr. Sanchez apologized. "I'm sure you have actual fires and emergencies to tend to. Of course, we will do that. Thank you." He lightly slammed the handset back on the phone console and immediately blurted out, "Hijole!" and froze in place for a few seconds, his eyes enlarged. Still not moving, his eyes adjusted to a scowl and they shifted to Jesse and then Dalisay. "Both of you are suspended for the maximum amount possible: five days."

"A'ight, peace." Jesse grabbed his backpack from the floor and got up from his seat.

"That is unfair! Uh, sir!" Dalisay protested. "I had nothing to do with the fire alarm. There is no proof I pulled the alarm or had any connection with it -- because I didn't."

Jesse was almost at the door and stopped. "Yeah," he chimed in and then slowly turned back around to the principal. "Yeah, me too. Where's your witness?"

Dr. Sanchez's face began to flush red. "Both of you were the only ones from the fair that were unaccounted for."

"Sir, there were students in the locker rooms from P.E. Anyone who had access to the locker rooms could have done it. I was out on the exhibit floor when the alarm went off. Did you even interview people? Uh, sir?"

"Yeah, and I was on the shitter. Since when do you get suspended for having *chorro*?"

"Of course we interviewed. That's why you two are here. I am willing to reduce your suspension if you admit to it right now."

"Fuck that. You got nothing." Jesse turned back around for the door.

"If you don't have any evidence that either of us actually pulled that alarm, sir, then we shouldn't even be here right now beyond answering your questions to help figure out who actually did it. Sir."

Jesse's hand was on the doorknob when he heard this last part and froze. Dr. Sanchez opened his mouth but hesitated to say something. The doorknob turned and Jesse jumped back as the principal's secretary shoved the door open while quickly knocking on it.

"Dr. Sanchez? Dr. Sanchez, sorry to interrupt. You need to watch the news. Right now."

"Which?" he clarified.

"Any. Come out here, we have it on." Then she hustled back out to the main office lobby, where a large flat screen TV was on the wall.

Dr. Sanchez gave Dalisay one last stern look, then pressed his tie against his chest as he scooted his chair out from his desk and stood up. He walked to the door and Jesse had already started his way out. Various secretaries, office staff, counselors, and even a few students stood scattered around the office, all frozen in place and gazing at the television.

The headlines across the bottom of the screen read, "Tilson Plan Signed by POTUS." The president himself sat behind his desk in the oval office. He had already signed it and was shaking hands with his Cabinet and Republican members of the House and Senate. He then folded his hands in front of him and stared directly into the camera, waiting for an imaginary audience to end their imaginary applause.

"Today marks a momentous day in our history as a nation and as Americans. Today, I have signed into law the Secured Entry of National

Territories and Reintegration of Illegal Immigrants Act, or SENTRII for short. And, standing next to me is this genius bill's author, Senator Tilson. Great job, Bob." The president paused to reach out and shake his hand. Bob Tilson gladly and enthusiastically shook it with a smile that went ear to ear. The president continued. "Today, a new era begins in the United States of America. No longer will illegals feel the need to run and hide from this government. Today, we embrace our illegal population in an unprecedented legal package that will guarantee them the right to live and work in this wonderful country the rest of us call home. Today, I will order ICE to begin accepting pre-registered applicants into the SENTRII program while simultaneously seeking out non-registered applicants to bring registration to them. Today, we move forward as a united country and Americans can take pride in their country's progress. Today, we look to tomorrow -- and it looks brighter already." The President smiled and showed his teeth, then swept back to a smug grin as he took more handshakes from the small audience crowding his desk. He leaned over and his grandkids jumped on him for hugs. He stood up and began awkwardly embracing his wife and children.

"We'll continue this later," Dr. Sanchez said, his eyes still glued to the TV screen. Or to something beyond it.

"Yeah," Jesse said absently.

"Yes, sir," Dalisay said. She picked up her bag and brushed past Jesse on her way out of the office.

"Nancy, hold my calls except for district personnel. Take messages from local or federal agencies. I need to call in the APs, counselors, and campus security."

"Which ones?"

"All of them."

"Yes, Dr. Sanchez," the secretary responded, as she wiped a tear from her face.

"Jesse. Time for you to go back to class."

"Yeh," he responded while still staring at the screen.

"This isn't over."

"Yeh," Jesse uttered again. Dr. Sanchez closed his door and that seemed to snap Jesse back to awareness.

From the main office, Jesse headed to Yusef's classroom since it was now his conference period. A campus security staff member sped past Jesse in a golf cart with one of the assistant principals riding as a passenger. She clutched her radio in one hand, the other gripping the roof of the cart. She squinted hard into the distance, but there was no sunlight on her face to squint through.

In the social sciences building, Jesse walked past the bathrooms and heard two girls sobbing as he passed by. A classroom had its door open and everyone inside was quietly watching the news broadcast projected on their pull-down screen. The President was now taking questions from reporters.

When he got to Yusef's classroom Jesse's excitement from the morning's events fired him up and he swept himself through the door, ready to start blabbing away about his calamities.

"...Next steps are now immin-- " Yusef cut himself off, holding his phone's handset to his ear and now staring at Jesse. "We will have to continue this later. Ma' al-salāmah." He put the handset back on the phone's switch hook. "You should be back in class, Jesús. Especially after all of the... excitement, from today."

"Ah, shit. You heard already?"

"How could I not?" Yusef asked, standing up at his desk. "All of that work and preparation, Jesús!"

"Aw, shit," Jesse said under his breath with an eye roll. He knew he was in for it now.

Yusef took a quick breath and was about to begin his next bombardment when the high-pitched tone of the P.A. system chimed. Jesse closed his eyes and sighed with relief.

"Good morning, Caballeros," Dr. Sanchez's deep, Latino accent crooned out of the speaker. "Just a few moments ago, the President signed into law the SENTRII Act, also known as The Tilson Plan." Dr. Sanchez's tone now switched from authoritarian principal to caring-adult-talking-to-kids. "This means that ICE, the U.S. Immigrations and Customs Enforcement agency, will now begin actively seeking undocumented residents, wherever they may be, in an effort to collect them for processing in the government's new tracking program. Any local or federal officer can now ask residents for identification and proof of citizenship if they suspect that someone is not living here with proper paperwork. But rest assured, your teachers, counselors, Portola's staff, administrators, our district personnel, and I -- we are all here to support *you*. You shouldn--" Dr. Sanchez's voice broke and he cleared his throat. "You should not feel unsafe here at Portola," he continued. "We will do anything and everything we can to ensure the safety and privacy of our students and families. Caballeros: be smart, be safe, look out for each other." There was another pause and something slightly muffled over the microphone. His voice returned, shaky but determined. "We love you all. We will get through this. Together. God -- good day." There was a click and the P.A. system turned off. It was now completely silent in Yusef's room, and Jesse found himself now sitting down at a desk.

"Damn," Jesse said, gazing into a spot on the floor far off somewhere.

"Everything will be fine, Mubtadi. Eventually."

"What does that mean?"

"It is like I have stated before. Things will need to get worse before they get better."

"This isn't worse?"

"We are getting closer."

"What do we do now?"

"Your training will be intensified, especially now that the Science Fair is over." Yusef paused and inspected Jesse carefully. "You were responsible for the debacle today, were you not?"

Jesse looked Yusef right in the eyes and kept a straight face. "You're gonna read my mind later anyway."

"I can read you from here. You were not prepared, were you?"

Jesse shook his head. "I was! I finished it! I stayed up all fucking night. I just… the *pinche* works cited."

Now it was Yusef's turn to shake his head. "Your solution was to set the school on fire?"

"La Puta Dalisay. She was right across from me, 'Sef. I couldn't let her win again. Or any of those stuck-up *maricons*."

"Calm yourself. You only belittle yourself when you resort to name calling."

Jesse was about to go on but shut his mouth instead.

"You were upset because you put in all of that hard work. Then at the very end, it would have meant nothing. You felt like your work was worth more than anyone else's there, because it was hard for you. And you know it was easier for everyone else there. You feel like they all had an advantage. A head start. Your work would not even have been looked at. Dismissed, like yourself, and every other positive thing you have attempted to do in your life." Yusef let that last sentence hang in the air between them. "Is that accurate?"

"Yeh."

"Excuse me?"

'Yes! I said 'yes.''"

"So, if you could not have your hard work finally validated, no one else could. That was your solution. Or your revenge, as it were."

"Yes."

Yusef, still standing, hung his head down in thought, and rubbed his brow with one hand. "What will you do now?"

Jesse shrugged. "I dunno."

"I will not lie for you, Jesse. If I am asked a direct, specific question I will answer it honestly."

Jesse nodded solemnly.

"After all, I only have my own assumptions and no evidence." Yusef shrugged. "No one knows that you are here, correct?"

Shifting his eyes in thought, Jesse shook his head. "Nah."

"Then perhaps it is best you leave before someone does, and asks questions."

Jesse nodded and did his best to hide his grin, then briskly walked to the door. He peered through the glass left and then right, and left again. Then he slightly opened the door and peeked out. Not seeing anyone in the hall, Jesse slinked out and casually walked back to class.

The rest of the school day was somber and his teachers were not that focused in class, so Jesse was extra eager to get home and try to take a short power nap before his physical training.

On the walk home, Jesse wondered what Maria was up to. He wondered if she noticed that he wasn't in class this morning. He wondered if she was ever going to notice him now that he blew it at the Science Fair. Well, if he got suspended she might start to notice him then. Assuming he didn't get caught for the fire alarm and wouldn't get fast tracked out of Portola, considering his long record of referrals, parent meetings, suspensions, arrest, and expulsion. "Fuck," he said out loud to himself. "This was all for nothing. I'm still a piece of shit on her goddamn shoe."

A notification on his phone chimed. Someone from an account he didn't recognize tagged him in a meme post. It featured a close up of William Shakespeare's very serious face and his pupils were replaced with emoji skulls and eye liner had been added. Black hearts floated around him. *This fucking poem bullshit*, Jesse thought to himself. *I gotta find out who this was and bop them. In front of everyone.* A new post popped up on his feed, from Chayne Sauze. It started to autoplay:

"'Ey, yo. This Tilson shit is fucked. Why we still keeping these fucking freeloaders here? We gon' go through the trouble of findin' 'em, just go the extra step of kickin' these foo's out. An' that's a fucking blessing. I find a foo' in my fucking house an' he ain't welcome, that nigga gettin' shot." Chayne Sauze then threw up his free arm. "This country our fuckin' house. Why we not shootin' these foo's?" The video ended. Jesse saw that it had been posted a few hours earlier, probably right after the President's announcement, and the video already had over four million views and tens of thousands of comments. This wasn't even Chayne Sauze's actual social media account, either -- it was a meme account, one of many that had probably reposted his monologue.

Jesse scrolled through them and saw that people were debating all kinds of things, from the law itself to whether or not someone like Chayne Sauze should be commenting on it at all. People were threatening each other. Whatever he saw, it was laced with anger. No matter what reasonable thing or compromise someone suggested, there were at least two other people who demonized it and swore to fight it.

"Yusef was right," Jesse said out loud to himself. "This shit is gonna get worse." He continued to scroll and hop across different social media platforms, and even checked the news for a little bit. He wondered: *just how worse does it have to get? And then what? Even if someone came along as a new president or whatever and took away the Tilson Plan, there would be a shit ton of people angry about that and want it back.*

Then a thought entered his mind and with it his knees got weak for a second and his body felt like gravity doubled on him. *What the fuck does Yusef want me to do about it? How am I -- how is anyone going to stop this or make this better?*

Tires screeched from a flashy green car that had sped past Jesse as he continued on the sidewalk. Out of the rear passenger side window he saw an arm and a pointed, painted fingernail sticking out toward him. For a split second he hoped it was Maria, but then he didn't recognize that arm or hand. The smell of burnt rubber reached his nostrils before the smoke did. Then the car abruptly pulled into reverse. Jesse couldn't ignore this, as he remembered this was Raymond Bravo's car. He stopped walking and got ready for anything.

The lime green Accord stopped next to Jesse. The windows were tinted, but through the passenger door he saw the familiar shape of Maria's face and hair. Behind her, with the window still down and the pointing hand still sticking out, was Xotchitl. She looked at Jesse and then looked away as soon as he made eye contact with her, instead dropping her focus to her phone in her lap. Jesse heard the rapid clicking of a handbrake being pulled back and then the driver side door swung open. The gleam from the shaved head of Raymond Bravo was disturbed only by the black shades that he now pulled off and tossed back into the car before slamming his door shut and coming around the hood toward Jesse without saying a word.

Jesse knew what was about to happen. He had just enough time to drop his backpack off his shoulders. Raymond's Air Jordans stepped over the curb. His eyes deadlocked on Jesse's, and then he hurried his pace toward him. Raymond seemed shorter compared to the last time he saw him.

Just as Jesse's backpack hit the ground behind him, Raymond reached striking distance and swung a giant right hook. It was pretty easy to read and as Jesse was ducking under it, he realized that it was *too* easy.

Jesse saw his right shoulder coming back and his left foot pivoting. Raymond had adjusted his weight to throw a left cross, his sneakers screeching against the sidewalk cement while he did so. As he was already in motion raising his head back up, Jesse swerved his upper body and stepped to the left toward Raymond. A sharp and powerful exhale hissed from Raymond's nose. The tatted left cross shot straight out and barely missed Jesse's head. Now, Raymond's right arm was too close to Jesse to have any good momentum to strike him.

The advantage was now Jesse's. He threw a right jab at Raymond's face.

Raymond brought up his right forearm and parried the punch, but was now off balance and he had his entire right side exposed.

Jesse followed up with a left uppercut to Raymond's liver. His body jolted and Raymond let out a breathy grunt. His arms instinctively dropped to protect himself and Jesse hissed an exhale and pivoted, throwing a right cross. Raymond tried bringing his guard back up but Jesse connected with Raymond's nose and right eye. Raymond flinched and threw his upper body backward, taking a few steps back. Jesse didn't relent and moved in.

Raymond threw out a jab, connecting with Jesse's face. He threw another but Jesse guarded against it with his forearm, then bobbed left, threw a fake body shot, and bobbed right with an uppercut to Raymond's jaw. It was a risky move, but Raymond wasn't ready for the speed and already had his confidence shaken. He slumped into himself and fell back, his body falling on the sidewalk and his head slammed onto the grass of whoever's lawn had turned into their own boxing ring. Raymond's chest expanded and sank down in big motions, and his eyes were open. But nobody was home inside.

"What the fuuuck, bruuuhhh!" Xotchitl yelled from the car. Jesse looked over and saw her hanging out the car window, recording with her phone. She brought her arm back in to open the door and stepped out to get a closer shot of Raymond on the ground, then she pointed her phone's lens toward Jesse. He was now staring at the tinted front passenger window. He saw a hand tightly pressed against the window and Maria's silhouette behind it. The hand disappeared and there wasn't any movement or sound. Jesse stood and stared to where he felt her eyes must be. Then he moved to retrieve his backpack, put it back on, stepped over Raymond's body, and continued down the sidewalk toward home.

He felt warmness on his cheek and wiped it with the back of his hand.

Blood was smeared all over it. He touched his cheekbone and felt a cut. Jesse smudged it with his hand and continued on. He wanted to look back at Maria, but knew if he did he would just see her cradling Raymond in her arms. And his face was now a mess. But not nearly as much as Raymond's was. Jesse smirked and straightened his posture. He picked up his pace and calculated the time he would lose from training now that he had to ice his face when he got home.

Jesse XXIV
Vortices, Leylines, Secret Societies, and Blackmail

The sparring pads were barely staying in front of Yusef as Jesse bobbed and weaved in between each jab he threw. Yusef alternated bringing forward sparring pads on his hands after each connecting hit from Jesse would knock them back toward Yusef's chest. "In three, two, one, rest," Yusef belted out.

Jesse corresponded like clockwork. He hunched over and leaned on his knees, panting heavily. In his mind, he tried to focus on the other things he had to do today, a Sunday. The cut on his face was healing quite nicely, but he knew he would have to add a little bit of time into his schedule to clean it, ice it, and dress it once he got back home. Jesse had to rush home after training, too, so he could watch Fredo and Marcy when Lita left to work for a few hours.

"We must continue on the trail for Peters and undoubtedly, to the Apostles," Yusef declared.

"Yeh," Jesse huffed out with a single nod.

"He is not local, however. His studio is based in Texas."

Jesse took a few more breaths. "We -- we going on a field trip?" he asked, not looking up.

Yusef thought and then shook his head. "Yes and no."

Glancing up now, Jesse asked, "You got a faster boat?"

Yusef's eyebrows raised. "Yes and no." A subtle smirk came across his face.

Jesse jabbed at him, but Yusef brought up a sparring pad to block it, then brought the other around as a hook to Jesse's head. He barely weaved out of the way in time, then backed away.

"Aye! Whoa! We throwing hands or what?"

Yusef gave out a hearty laugh, deeper and fuller than Jesse had expected the old man's lanky body to produce.

"No, Mubtadi. I would not dare. Now you are too fast for this old man. But maybe on the Plane, you can ask me again."

Jesse, seemingly satisfied with this response and self-consciously touching his cut, returned to his line of questioning. "So how we getting there?"

"With your new ability you will be learning, starting tonight."

"The fuck is it?"

"You are a natural fighter, Mubtadi. This is clear," Yusef said as he gestured toward Jesse's face. "Not in the sparring sense. If you had no arms, you would still fight. Do you understand me?"

Jesse shoved his shoulders up. "Yeh."

"That kind of determination can be focused in other ways on the Plane. Your stubbornness has value. The more sustained and difficult -- but powerful -- abilities on the Plane can be found in an area of study known to some as Alteration. More specifically, you will learn how to teleport and summon individuals on the Plane."

Jesse stood perfectly still and didn't blink. "Huh?"

"All across our precious Earth, Allah -- God -- has seen fit to both place and guide humans in the construction of vortices. A vortex is a holy place. It is a wonder of natural beauty: a mysterious site created by ancient Readers whose secrets have been lost to time. Vortices are tears in the Plane which bleed out an energy that flows to other vortices, creating an interconnected web, or highway system, across the Plane. We call these leylines."

On the surface, Jesse's eyes were wide and his face showed surprised interest. But the smallest look into and past his eyes showed that everything on the inside was currently melting.

"You know the Great Pyramids, of course. And you have heard of

Stonehenge? The Grand Canyon? The Forbidden Palace in China, Machu Picchu in Peru… I could go on with other natural and man-made wonders, both widely known and barely known. These are all locations that enable a Reader to harness more power and thus have attracted Readers on the Plane. And of course, in the waking world as well."

Jesse was rubbing his knuckles while staring off somewhere, his mind trying to process this new information. "'Kay."

"With the right kind of focus -- and practice -- one can teleport and even summon other willing Readers between these vortices, and beyond."

"So we're going after Peters?"

"Yes. But not tonight, Mubtadi. Soon. Tonight, I will begin teaching you your new skills."

"Andele."

On the way home, Jesse checked his phone and his social media was still blowing up. The night before, Saturday night, someone had tagged Jesse in a posted picture of Maria at a mall with Erika Gomez. A picture of a wolf-like dog barking ferociously toward the edge of the frame -- labeled as "Jesse" -- was edited next to Maria and a caption was added for the picture: "Why is @moysoy hiding?"

Another post featured Jesse, blurred from what looked like a screenshot of a video -- of him in mid-punch against Raymond. But in place of where Raymond's head should be was an edited graphic of the cartoon character Arthur's face. Above it was typed in colored font "tha simp is next" and alongside that, "@moysoy" had been tagged. Jesse knew that the username belonged to Moises.

He read the comments, which were a mix of disbelief that Jesse had beat down the legendary Raymond, and a massive outpour of shittalking about Moises. He hadn't responded to any of the comments, but they collectively and conclusively warned him that he would be beaten well beyond embarrassment if he ran into Jesse. Everyone assumed Jesse was on the hunt for him, naturally, since everyone also knew that Jesse had the hots for Maria and assumed he was obsessive at this point, now that he had defeated her "secret" side boyfriend. Numerous people commented that they hadn't seen Moises with Maria at all since last week.

Now that Jesse thought about it, why couldn't he just knock out

Moises? Doing so would probably put social pressure on Maria to dump him. Moises would be seen as a weakling not able to defend the honor and safety of Maria. Then Jesse could finally make his move. It was finally happening. To hell with academic glory. Jesse was going to get Maria the only way he truly knew how to with anyone and anything: with brute force.

Even though he had slept a full eight hours, Jesse still felt exhausted the next morning. The extended time and focus he spent on the Plane with Yusef that night really took a lot out of Jesse. He felt like he either slept way too little or too much. It was the kind of fatigue that left him restless but also longing for more sleep. The remedy would be physical activity or some other catalyst for adrenaline.

He packed a few extra books in his backpack to add some weight, deciding to make his walk to school a workout in itself. As he built up a sweat, Jesse recalled other pertinent background information that Yusef explained to him while they were traversing the Plane and exploring local vortices and ley lines.

As soon as Jesse had awakened in the morning, he made some notes before he could forget. Now he took out a yellow pocket-sized, bound notebook. He flipped the lined pages filled with notes: workout routines, poem ideas and drafts, notes from class, to-do lists, and other random things. He found his recent entry from Yusef's lesson to him on secret Reader organizations and read it as he trudged along the sidewalk.

> *The Apostles (1945-Present) AKA "The Family"*
> *Mostly American (some European) elites--CEOs, politicians, pastors, etc., mostly conservative and pro-business. Very "Christian," use it to gain support and spread influence. Goal = politically and culturally strong collection of Western countries united by conservative policies sold as Judeo-Christian values, backed with strong military and limits individual freedoms for its citizens. Economic system that favors wealthy class ← they are God's "chosen." Immigrants & "non-natives" serve as working/ lower class caste, promised chance into heaven with hard work, obedience, and loyalty. Ideals and influence can be traced back to the Templars.*

The International Workingmen's Association/Progressive Alliance (1864-Present)
Creator, gatherer, & organizer of labor unions. Socialist, anti-capitalist. Particularly strong in Europe. Mission: resist & counter the growth & influence of The Apostles; promote education for developing countries & oppressed people.

- *Also founded International Workers of the World (Wobblies) and became active with socialist and communist uprisings throughout the first half of the twentieth century.*

His mind wandered a bit as he stared at a series of doodles in the margins of his notebook. They were almost like cursive, if he had ever learned it. There were random words he'd written and connected together without lifting his pencil. "Homie," "Portola," "Ramirez," and "Maria." They were repeated with multiple attempts at making a smooth link between each letter. He was about to make another attempt when he caught a familiar and alarming color pattern in his peripheral vision.

A white and green Border Patrol truck raced down the street, followed by a police car. Even though their sirens weren't on, they still sped with impunity. Jesse was able to see that the men inside the truck wore ski masks, a new trend that had begun with the passing of Tilson's SENTRII program. Intended to instill fear, the federal agents instead acted as motivation for Jesse. He now felt more empowered than he'd thought possible. The course of history itself was now at his whim.

He continued with his notes about how to summon a Reader from one point on the Plane to another. There were various stages of progress as a Reader honed their abilities in Alteration. To start, Jesse would need to be at a vortex and both he and whomever he was summoning would need an identical sigil marked on their bodies. Yusef didn't go into much detail beyond this stage, but Jesse looked forward to the day when Yusef would show him how to summon people anywhere on the Plane -- even to and from another person's subconscious.

At the crosswalk traffic light across the street from campus, Jesse saw a few kids looking at him. He checked his face and felt the Band-Aid on his cheek. It didn't feel wet. He stared back at them but they didn't look away.

"That was you last week, wasn't it?" A pudgy, short Mexican kid asked. He pointed a plump finger at his own cheek to mirror Jesse's face. With his other hand he gestured a punch.

Jesse remembered that Xotchitl had her phone out and was recording. She must have posted it on social media. "Yeh, I guess so. Can I see it?"

The kid quickly took out his phone and swiped his fingers a bunch of times. "Let's see… yeah, here it is." He held it up for Jesse to view.

He saw footage from the back of Raymond's car. Xotchitl had the phone on herself with one arm hanging out the window. She said, "There he is. That gay-ass bitch."

The camera switched view and it was now recording forward. The camera angled forward as tires screeched. Raymond's muscular and tattooed arm reached to the center console and adjusted the gears. The car whirred in reverse, then stopped again with a slight screech. Raymond gave one quick look over the passenger seat out the dark window as he adjusted the gears again and put the car in park. Maria's head turned to Raymond but he didn't return the look and grunted, "Finna end this boy right here," as he swung his door open and then got out.

"Yeah, fuck that boy up," Xotchitl said from behind the camera. "*No one's* gonna want yer punk ass now." Maria's head swung back over to the window toward Jesse as the camera followed Raymond walking past the hood to the sidewalk. The brightness of the video adjusted as it pointed outside to Jesse, whose backpack had just dropped to the ground and he brought his guard up and ducked the first blow from Raymond.

At the end of the fight when Jesse made the knockout and Xotchitl screamed out, a text came over the video that read: "oh shit watch out @moysoy". Then as the video left a closeup of an unconscious Raymond on the ground it went to Jesse staring at the car window and another text came up: "the simp coming 4 u next". The video ended with Jesse walking over Raymond and the text still superimposed over the video shot.

"When are you fighting Moysoy?" a scrawny Mexican kid with shaved eyebrow slits asked. The shorter pudgy kid put away his phone and listened.

"Huh? You mean Moises?" Jesse clarified.

The two kids stared back and nodded.

"That's not… I never sai--"

"Jesse got lucky with that sucker punch! That bitch won't fight Moises," a loud female voice yelled over. The walk signal was on and Cervantes was already limping ahead of everyone into the street, her long curly hair bobbing with her uneven motions. She had an ankle brace now but carried her crutches in one arm. An image came to him, like déjà vu, of Cervantes standing at this crosswalk and yelling over to him. He and Xotchitl, on the school-side of the street.

The two kids shrugged and walked with the rest of the small crowd of students that had gathered to wait at the traffic light as other kids jumped out of idling cars stopped at the signal and hustled to the school gates.

In first period, Jesse did his best to stay focused on the lesson and not stare at Maria. He was eager to see if she was upset at him, or impressed, or still ignoring him. Plus it was harder to stare at her without it being obvious since Mr. Padilla had moved everyone around in a new seating chart when the second semester started.

Jesse had, before last week, looked forward to his new third period Honors English, which was still with Mr. Klinkhammer. The class was divided in half, each side facing each other. Maria was in the front row of one half, while Jesse had a front row seat on the other half. They did not sit directly across from each other so she couldn't tell when Jesse was ogling at her unless she looked over at him. A few times she had and Jesse's eyes had almost fallen out of his face when they briefly made eye contact. But since the fight, he anticipated an even higher degree of awkwardness with Maria coupled with a fair amount of coldness from her.

After Spanish class, Math was a bore, but Jesse powered through it. During the passing after second period, Jesse's phone jingled. Racha, known as @kushcums2luv online, had forwarded him a post. Jesse opened it and saw a story update from Portola's Associated Student Body profile. It was just text that read: "Winter Bash will be canceled due to safety concerns if guilty parties from the Science Fair are not found," followed by a sad face emoji.

Racha included a message: "Imma tag u and repost if u dont come find me. Gotta talk".

"Fuck," Jesse spat out. He shoved his phone back in his pocket. He adjusted his heavy backpack and picked up his pace, all the while trying to anticipate what Racha wanted from him.

Jesse found Racha with Phi in the boys' restroom inside the 800 building. Vape smoke filled the air, giving the bathroom a thick, musty smell of piss, shit, and body odor that stuck to his nostrils.

Phi eyed Jesse as he entered and then chuckled. He put out his hand in front of Racha next to him, and Racha placed the vape pen into Phi's open hand. Jesse stepped aside as Phi brushed past him and out of the restroom.

"I hope you didn't want any," Racha said to Jesse. "I mean, I'd be surprised since you're a schoolie now."

Jesse sighed but didn't say anything. He just stared at Racha and waited for him to get to his point. Jesse did his best to look tough as he breathed through his mouth and not through his nose.

"You see, I would've offered if it was mine, but it wasn't. Because mine got taken away this morning. By that gordo borracho, Klinkhammer. And you're getting it back for me before he turns it in at the office today. If you don't I'll let everyone know who it was that fucked up the gym and the Science Fair." The one-minute warning bell rang with a horrendous dull pitch. Racha's eyebrows shot up twice as he continued to stare at Jesse, who was doing his best to not appear nervous about it.

"Fuck that. I'll tell them that I saw you."

"Go ahead. But I hear some things were also stolen from the lockers that morning. It would be a shame if one of those items suddenly appeared in your bag or something, and Dr. Sanchez knew about it."

Jesse's faced turned red. "You bitch!" Jesse lunged forward to grab Racha, but as he sprung a booming voice echoed from the doorway. "Campus security. Everybody out and get to class. Let's go, move it!"

Racha smiled. "Never thought I'd be happy to hear that. Nyyyyeeeeeeee!" Then he brushed past a speechless Jesse and walked out of the boys restroom. "End of the day, guey!"

Jesse XXV
Say Hi to the Love of Your Life

"You're late, Mr. Ramirez."

"Yeh. Uh, sorry. I wa--"

Even from the distant corner of the room where he sat at his desk, Mr. Klinkhammer's large hand was effective when it came up to stop Jesse. "Don't need to hear it. I was just making sure we were both on the same page."

Jesse went to his seat near the center of class, sliding his bulky backpack under his desk on the dusty tiled floor. He shot a quick look at Maria who had her notebook out in front of her but was staring into her phone, subtly nestled in the crook of her arm on her desk. *I might as well be a fucking ghost.* And she might as well have been while sitting there, minding her own business in her own world. Her back was to Klinkhammer's desk so it seemed to him like she was deeply engaged with her notes.

The P.A. system pinged and Dr. Sanchez's deeply accented voice apologized for the interruption. "A decision has been made by the administration team to cancel this year's Winter Bash. We are concerned for the safety of our students and staff attending the event, in light of recent events involving the unresolved matters with the science fair."

A collective but mixed murmur of "What the fuck?"s and "Seriously?"s and "fucked up"s pinballed around the classroom.

"Quiet! Settle down!" Mr. Klinkhammer shouted.

Dr. Sanchez's announcement continued. "Of course, if we were to catch all parties involved and responsible for the locker room theft, and the fire and water damage in the gym, we would no longer have the need to cancel Winter Bash. We would be safe to continue as planned. In addition, since we did not have a winner for this year's science fair, the unused first place prize of free tickets will now be offered as rewards for any information leading to the disciplinary action of the person or persons responsible. Any students with information about the guilty party or stolen items are encouraged to come talk to any adult or administrator. You may email if preferred. Thank you, Portola. I believe in you to do the right thing. ¡Todos Los Caballeros! Honor, pride, achievement!" The P.A. system clicked off.

The classroom was visibly upset from the announcement. Arms were crossed, heads shook, a few students flipped off the P.A. system. Jesse remembered that this was an Honors class and wondered what the regular classes looked like right now. "Settle down, damn it!" Mr. Klinkhammer thundered. "You're upset, I get it. Try getting drafted to Vietnam. Take out your notes."

Klinkhammer resumed his lecture from yesterday on how ambition and loneliness are directly linked, weaving Mary Shelley's character Victor Frankenstein into his argument. He continued on about how ambition can drive us to creating monstrous things with little care or concern for their repercussions, just as long as we can accomplish them in the first place. Further, he pointed out how the absence of essentials to our humanity, like love, can drive our ambition or twist our morality when we fail to get them. Klinkhammer wrapped up by leaving an open question: Who is more morally corrupt by the end of the story, Victor Frankenstein or his creation? Then he instructed the class to open their *Frankenstein* books to chapter twenty along with their literary analysis guides.

Jesse's eyes quickly shot around the room as he took his guide out, which was mostly blank compared to his classmates'. It's not that he wasn't reading the book. Just the opposite. He was so into it that stopping to complete his guide was distracting and annoying. Jesse rushed to fill it out while Klinkhammer turned on an audiobook reading of *Frankenstein* and sat at his desk in the corner of the class with his book open.

In the back of his mind, he was still trying to figure out how to get into Klinkhammer's desk and get Racha's vape pen. Assuming it was even in his desk at all. Jesse took out his phone to message Racha. He texted:

Foo. Where did Klink put the pen?

Jesse hit send. He looked up and saw Mr. Klinkhammer staring at him. "Mr. Ramirez," he boomed out. The class all looked up from their desks in unison.

Mouthing a profanity, Jesse slinked into his desk and shoved his phone into his pocket. "Uh, yeh?"

"I suppose being late today wasn't exciting enough for you, was it?" Klinkhammer stood up with his belly protruding over his desk.

"Wha -- I don--"

"Hand me your phone right now, please."

Jesse closed his eyes. "I didn't bring it today."

Then his phone jingled in his pocket.

The class couldn't help themselves and some students giggled.

Klinkhammer walked over with purpose. His brow was furrowed and the corners of his mouth were arched down. He towered in front of Jesse and laid out his open hand, palm up, to him. "Now, Mr. Ramirez. You need to submit your phone right now."

Jesse was silent for a moment, magnified by the collective silence of the entire class as they all watched with anticipation. "I can't."

Letting a little tension pass, Klinkhammer replied. "Are you sure? This is your last chance before I let campus security take over."

Jesse's eyes bored into the wall across the room, creating a very vacant and apathetic expression. But on the inside, his blood was boiling. "Do you what you gotta do."

Mr. Klinkhammer sighed and went to his desk to dial for campus security. After his curt phone call, he reminded the class to continue completing their analysis guides as he turned on the audio reading of *Frankenstein*.

Well. You're sure getting her attention now, tonto. Jesse looked over at Maria. She was looking at him and as soon as she saw Jesse look her way, she lazily rolled her eyes away and shook her head. *Fuck.*

As he sat there, sunk in his desk waiting for campus security to come to the classroom to get him, Jesse felt his face and ears getting hot. It seemed like after all of his hard work, he kept moving backward, not forward. Had anything really changed between him and Maria? If anything, it was worse now.

The classroom door pounded with a quick *knock-knock* before swinging open with jolting force.

"Jesús Ramirez." A giant of a man took the entire space of the doorway, wearing a navy blue jacket with yellow lettering that read "SECURITY."

Jesse sighed, stuffed his analysis guide into his backpack and then swung his pack over a shoulder as he got out of his desk and calmly walked to the doorway. It was left wide open by the large ogre of a campus security staff member. Jesse was escorted out of the Humanities building to an awaiting golf cart.

The campus security ogre gestured a brown open hand toward the passenger seat of the cart, then plopped himself into the driver's side. The golf cart tilted down toward him. Jesse climbed in, swinging his backpack around onto his lap.

"Watcha got on the phone?"

Jesse lifted his pelvis up off the seat and dug into his pocket to fetch his phone. He unlocked it and immediately deleted Racha's message before the ogre could see it. Jesse didn't get a chance to read it. "Nothin'. I just hate Klinkhammer," he lied casually.

"Hm," the ogre acknowledged as he scratched his bushy facial hair. A short moment passed and he continued. "I had him when I came here, to Portola. He wasn't so bad. As long as you don't get on his bad side."

"Yeh."

"I guess you got on his bad side."

"Guess so."

"What happened to your face?"

"Shaving accident."

"Hm."

The rest of the ride was silent. Jesse closed his eyes and tried to focus on keeping his cool. He anticipated the questions he would be asked and began playing out different routes his responses might take him and the consequences that would follow. He needed to get back to Klinkhammer's room and find that vape pen. *What if Klinkhammer didn't wait until the end of the day, and turned it in at lunchtime instead? Another fire alarm would be legit.*

The ogre walked him to the administrator's office and knocked before entering, but this time opened the door a lot more carefully. Assistant Principal Ngo was a plain but intelligent looking Asian woman. Jesse would typically call her a chinita, but he knew better now than to use that blanket term for all Asians he saw. She sat at a crowded, cherrywood desk. A few framed photos stood on a shelf behind her. The ogre leaned in to whisper in her ear. She nodded and then he left her office.

"Hi, Jesús. Tell me what happened--" the woman's eyes spotted the bandage on Jesse's face and she hesitated for a second, "--in Mr. Klinkhammer's class today."

"I fu--" Jesse stopped himself. "I messed up today. Uh, Ms…"

"Doctor. Dr. Ngo."

"Dr. Ngo, I messed up. It was my fault. I'm just having a shitty day and I was -- oh, sorry, sorry. I didn't mean to say that. I was waiting for my moms to text me back. She was scared that Immigration was going to come ask for her papers before I left for school this morning. I didn't hear from her all morning. So I was just trying to text her and check in to see if Immigration came. Because she…"

Dr. Ngo was nodding her head the entire time, her eyes bent with concern and empathy. "Because you were worried. Oh, Jesús. I understand. It's terrible that you have to go through that anxiety this morning. But it's still not a good excuse for being disrespectful and insubordinate to your teacher."

"Yeh. I know. Like I said, I messed up. I can say sorry to him. Or write it or whatever."

"Well, our school policy, which is aligned with the entire district, states that we'll need to take your phone and have mom or dad pick it up from us."

"Uh, nah."

"Excuse me?"

"I mean… my moms. It's just her. And what if she had to leave work to come get my phone and Immigration gets her? Won't I like, never see her again? What would I do by myself?"

"I, uh…"

"Here. You can take it," Jesse said and craned it over her busy desk, dropping it on a pile of papers and manila folders in front of her. "You can call her. Tell her. I'll deal with her punishment at home. If she's still there."

"Jesús," Dr. Ngo said gently. "If you can write out an apology to Mr. Klinkhammer right now, then yes. I think we can work this out according to your… concerns. The last thing we would want to do is put you or your family at risk."

"Thank you, Ms-- Dr. Ngo. It's just like the principal said the other day, on the announcements. I guess you guys really are trying to protect us."

"Of course. But I also need your assurance that you'll abide by class and school rules at all times unless you get permission otherwise. What if you explained your situation to Mr. Klinkhammer beforehand? Do you think that might have prevented all of this?"

"Oh. Huh. You know, Ms.-- Dr. Ngo, I didn't think about that. But you right. I should've. And next time, I will."

"That's good to hear, Jesús. I'm very glad to hear that you understand things from Mr. Klinkhammer's -- and the school's -- perspectives."

"Uh, should I go write that letter now and go back to class? Or do it tomorrow?"

"I think now would be good, Jesús, since it's fresh in your mind. Mr. Klinkhammer could probably use some time to refocus himself as well. He's probably not expecting you back so early, especially with an apology."

"Yeh. Right." Jesse paused and thought. "A'ight. Should I sit in the hall and write that letter, then?"

"Yes. You can go to your next class when the bell rings. And be sure to come by right after school to get your phone. I'll need to leave pretty quickly. District meeting."

"Yeh. A'ight."

"Thank you, Jesús."

"Uh, yeh. Thank you, Dr. Ngo." Jesse grabbed his backpack and headed out to the hallway. He opened his backpack, pulled out materials, and started writing his letter.

As he wrote he tried figuring out how he was going to distract Klinkhammer. His options all involved high risk and would likely put him into an even bigger, darker cloud of suspicion than he already was.

And all for Racha.

"Fuck this shit," Jesse muttered. "Finna fuck that boy up." He finished up his letter and put his stuff away. He waited until the bell rang and then made a beeline for the vape room. When he got to the boys' restroom he went into one of the toilet stalls and waited.

He heard other boys come in and out, bantering, giggling, bragging. One of them yelled out, "Oh, fuck. This dude taking a shit up in here!" followed by laughter with someone else. The minute-bell rang.

"I heard there's gonna be a fight at lunch," a voice declared.

Another boy responded, "They say that every day."

"Nah, it's Moises."

"That boy ain't fightin' nobody. Especially Jesse. I hear Moises don't even go near Maria now, ha!" Shoes started scuffling and boys started leaving.

He should have showed up already.

It became quiet and Jesse peered through the cracks of the stall door and didn't see anyone. He opened the door and walked out of the bathroom. Jesse looked down the hall left then right, and left again. Students were scurrying to their classes and he saw no trace of Racha. He then made his way to the main doors, trying to remember or figure out what class Racha had this period.

The tardy bell chimed as Jesse exited the Humanities building. He was now technically late for P.E., but who really needed to be there on time, anyway? He racked his brain, trying to sift through all the bullshit Racha had spewed out in the school year, trying to sift through it for a clue to what class he had right now. Either way, what would it matter if he did figure it out? How was Jesse going to get Racha out of a classroom to intimidate him? He decided to keep walking and hopefully he would either see Racha or something would come back to his memory.

Now Jesse found himself on the other side of campus, by the Math and Sciences building. He knew it was a matter of time before a security staff member -- perhaps the Ogre -- would come along and find him out of class. He had to make a decision about which building he thought Racha was in and stick to it.

As he turned around to go back to the Humanities building, he heard the rhythmic and metallic clank of crutches coming toward him. He saw ankle-braced Cervantes powering her way up the unsteady, dilapidated concrete, daring to not look down at the cracks and uneven pavement. Instead, she stared straight at Jesse the entire time as they got closer to each other. They both knew what was about to happen, and there wasn't any avoiding it. The only mystery was who thought they'd enjoy this moment more.

"You. I saw you that morning. The day I lost my poem. You posted that shit, didn't you?"

"Leave Maria alone, you fucking creep," Cervantes spat out with a feisty tilt of her head, which was accuentuated more by her squared shoulders that held up her weight on the crutches.

Jesse shook his head. "You fucking bitch. Why'd you do that?"

"Because you're fucking stupid. Maria is way out of your fucking league, and Xotchitl literally threw herself all over you and your dumb ass won't give her the time of day. That's some fucked up shit. I got my girls' back. What you gonna do?"

He took an aggressive step forward and lifted his back foot, ready to kick her crutches. As he did, one of the doors to the Math and Sciences building swung open well behind Cervantes. Maria, carrying her school-printed agenda as a hall pass, glided out.

Cervantes saw Jesse frozen in place, his mouth and eyes opened wide, so she turned her head to look. "Oh, hi, Maria!" She shifted her weight and let a crutch lean into her ribs as she lifted an arm and waved.

"Hey, Cervantes," Maria replied. She saw Jesse and his eyes quickly fluttered away.

Cervantes turned back to Jesse and raised an eyebrow. "Well. Aren't you going to say hi to the love of your life?"

"Fuck you," Jesse hissed, as his face got red and hot. He quickly turned and walked away.

"That's right, pinche pendejo. Walk the fuck away!"

Jesse heard the girls talking to each other but couldn't make out details as he hurried to the nearest building, which was Electives. "That bitch. Imma fuck her up tonight. Make her piss herself in her bed or some shit," Jesse grumbled to himself. She was probably talking about him to Maria that very instant. He swiftly pulled the door open and lunged into the building, trying not to make any eye contact with Cervantes or Maria off in the distance.

Not wanting to be discovered by security, Jesse gently closed the door behind him and carefully made his way down the hall, subtly peeking through classroom door windows. When he approached the middle of the building where the hall split a corridor to side exits, he heard a muted commotion and the awkward silence that screams tension. It came from the corridor around the corner.

Carefully and as inconspicuously as he could, Jesse crept to the corner and recognized Racha's voice as he neared. He sounded tensed and aggravated. But restrained.

"Nah. Fuck that, Puta. What are you gonna do?"

There was more tense silence. Jesse peeked around the corner and saw Dalisay Morcilla leaning in close and speaking softly, but sternly, to Racha. Racha's eyes shot wide and his stature appeared to crumble a bit. Jesse retreated and hid around the corner again.

"Nah, fuck that! How do you know about that? Who -- I never even told anyone. The fuck? That ain't right. That ain't right, you feel me?"

Eager to see, Jesse carefully leaned out from the corner to see.

"And no one has to know, Racha. You just have to do what I asked and your secret stays safe with me."

Racha shook his head. His black and silver Corsairs cap even loosened a bit and he reached back to adjust it. "I ain't no snitch. Jesse kind of a bitch now but I still no snitch."

"You know why everyone calls me La Puta?"

Racha hesitated, trying desperately to read her face. He nodded. "Because you a slut. You kept telling all the dudes at a party you'd get with 'em. Moises got first dibs and when it came time to do the dirty with everyone else you ran out like a bitch."

Jesse heard Racha's body slam against the lockers. Dali's hands were wrapped around the collar of his bold colored, mixed-pattern t-shirt. She leaned in close to whisper in his face, out of earshot.

"... And now because of it I'm 'La Puta.' That's how a rumor ruins your life. That's how I'm going to ruin your life with your secret if you don't tell the principal what you saw Jesse do. He has to get caught."

Jesse's ears actually perked back enough that he felt the skin on his forehead stretch back. "¡Puta la madre!" he hissed out.

Both Dali and Racha looked over to Jesse with wide eyes. Dali let go of Racha instinctively. He stood there for a few seconds, a cockroach frozen by the sudden surprise of lights getting turned on, then he scurried away down the corridor and out the side door, not looking back once.

Dali didn't take her eyes off of Jesse. She didn't blink once.

"I came to fuck up that boy. But now I can just fuck you up." Jesse stepped into the corridor and faced Dalisay head on.

She turned her complete attention to him, standing her ground. A smirk came across her face. "You really are stupid. You couldn't beat me on the Plane. And you won't beat me here. Or anywhere, for that matter."

"Bitch. That wasn't a fair fight. You sucker punched me. I'll fuck you up anywhere."

"Alright," Dalisay said calmly. "Tonight then. On the Plane. You'll get your fair fight. Then when you're out of the way, I'm going to visit Racha's dreams and make him tell the principal tomorrow."

There was one more moment of tense silence in the corridor, then Dalisay turned her back to Jesse and walked out the side door. He was still standing there when the door clinked shut.

"Fuck."

Jesse XXVI
Our Sunset is Upon Us

They met in the quad at Portola that night. The purpled overcast sky above glowed down on them as they faced each other on the Plane. Across the wide space, lunch benches were scattered around the quad, with an occasional tree peppered about the sections of lawn. A gentle breeze blew across the Plane, mimicking the same one that blew across the waking world at that very moment.

Jesse stared into her eyes, trying to catch her flinching. If he could get her to look away from him, he would know she was scared and done for with just a little bit of aggressive force. But he couldn't catch her gaze.

Instead, Dali's eyes were racing to every part of Jesse's body. She even had make-up on, here on the Plane. Perhaps this was her warpaint. Her mascara was thick and her eye shadow was a bright purple -- or was it luminescent? He noticed her stare at an arm, a foot, or his body for a second or so at a time before moving on to the next body part. She kept still the entire time.

"Why you keep checking me out? You gonna fight me or fuck me, Puta? Like you did all of those dudes. Even for you, I'm enough man." If he could get her emotional, he could be in control. This fight would be over before it started.

Dali lifted her eyes to meet Jesse's stare.

Got her.

But Dali's face was emotionless.

Shit.

Her eyes didn't blink even after she started to rush forward with a speed Jesse wasn't prepared for, despite staring at her and waiting for this very moment.

Jesse didn't have time to move up to meet her or take the offensive, as was his original plan. He realized he needed to adjust his footing as quickly as he could and be prepared to dodge or block and then hopefully counterattack as quickly as possible.

Dali moved in fast, straight toward him. He couldn't tell where her strike would come from. Before he knew it she was in perfect striking distance. Jesse instinctively threw a jab to her nose in hopes of stunning her, but right when he thought he had connected and was gearing his stance for a follow-up punch, Dali's face wasn't there anymore.

By the time he realized to which of his sides she had pivoted -- or just appeared -- Jesse had expected to be hit already. The delay caused him to recoil for a split second, expecting a sudden strike to anywhere on his body, especially now that he remembered how surprisingly strong she had been during their last fight in Judge Thompson's subconscious.

Still, there was nothing. He turned around to find Dali in a striking stance with an arm cocked back and ready to launch, but her head was sunk a little lower than it should have been, as if she was deep in thought. Now was as good a chance as any to flatten her.

Facing Dalisay, Jesse placed his feet and stepped forward, determined to ram his fist right through her face. As he began to throw his punch forward, he noticed that Dalisay was looking right at him, but seemed almost frozen in place, her guard barely up.

Then as he really put muscle into his punch he felt his eyes twitch. When he stopped blinking he was somewhere else. Masked police in riot gear rushed out of trucks and vans. There were crowds of loud and anxious people who cheered the police on down a large street. In the distance above people's heads waved handmade signs, banners, umbrellas, and bobbing poles. "I thought we had an agreement," a smooth voice said from nowhere.

The silhouetted crowds and the black-uniformed police swept together into a giant shadow. There were faces, clothes, limbs, claws, eyes, hair, fur, weapons, scales, and more reflected off shifting prisms within and outside the shadow as it swirled, recoiled, clouded, shaped, seeped, and creeped around Jesse.

A gunshot rang out and empty bottles clanged on the ground somewhere and echoed off distant walls. The sound resonated after the vision Jesse saw disappeared as abruptly as it came. He thought he heard the clanging still somewhere behind him, on the Plane. But they echoed in his mind just as much as he thought he heard them echo behind him.

When he came to he was back in Portola's quad. His arm was lowered and Dali's body was more relaxed, non-threatening. But her eyes were open with wonder -- and fear.

"The fuck was that?" Jesse gasped.

"What did you see?" Dalisay asked.

Jesse snapped out of his confusion. "Whadda ya mean? How do you know I saw something?"

Dali paused, and her eyes seemed to lose focus. "I saw something, too. I had seen it before."

"Yeh," Jesse agreed. "This feels like that déjà vu shit."

Dalisay nodded. "It did. It still kind of does." They stared at each other. "Well?"

"Pff. You go first."

She paused. "I dreamt it a while ago. I think… I think I've been dreaming it. I don't remember when I had the dreams after the first one, but it feels like I've dreamt it and seen it over and over. Maybe in pieces."

"What, puta?"

She scowled and for a split second Jesse thought her purple eyeshadow got brighter. "People. In the streets. They're angry and yelling. Protesting something."

Jesse's stomach felt like it had been sucked out of him: he was the helpless kid strapped into a roller coaster seat and plummeting down a sudden drop. He gulped for air and couldn't feel it in his lungs. Finally, he mustered out a word. "Police."

"Yeah," Dali confirmed with a slow nod. "Riot police."

"But who are they going for? They never attack the crowds."

"It doesn't make sense. The crowd is armed. They have guns. They're so angry."

"But it's like the police are there to help them."

"Right. You didn't see any clues about who the police are there for?"

Jesse shook his head. "Nah. Every time, they all vanish. Because the--"

"The shadows." They both said in unison. Looking at each other, Jesse tried to decide if this turn of events with Dalisay Morcilla was comforting or worrisome. It was both, he decided.

"I need to go," Dali said as she walked away and sat on the grass.

"What? Where? You're going back?"

She had just closed her eyes to concentrate and opened them back up again. "You know what this means, right?"

Jesse raised his hands and shrugged, shaking his head. "I don't know. We're fucking 'chosen ones'?" Jesse said sarcastically with air quotes and an annoyed face.

"Yes. That's exactly what it means. But not by fate. By our masters."

Dali stared at Jesse, who just had a blank look on his face.

"Why didn't you punch me, Jesse? You really wanted to, didn't you?"

"Uh. Huh. Yeah, I did. But… it was like… I don't know. It suddenly felt wrong. Like I was about to hit a dog or some shit. And then I was just…"

"Distracted?"

"Yeh."

"We've been set up, Jesse. Yusef Abdel and Sharonda Williams are working together."

"Who?"

Dalisay shook her head slowly and frowned. "How did an idiot like you end up being trained to be a Reader?"

"Psh. You think I can't read good?" Jesse said, straightening his posture and sticking out his chest.

Dali shook her head again. "I don't know what Yusef -- and Sharonda -- must see in you."

"There it is again. Who is that?"

"She trained me. Like I'm sure Yusef Abdel has been, er, *trying* to train you."

"Huh. When did you start training?"

"You're not asking the right questions. I have to go."

"Why?"

"Because, Jesse. If we were both set up to react this way -- if we had these dreams planted into us -- then our mentors anticipated us fighting each other. They didn't want us to. And these images, this vision that we both have... " Dalisay propped her head up with her hand. "They have to mean something. And no offense, but, I don't think I'm going to figure out what that means with you."

"Wait, Pu-- I mean, wait, Dalisay," Jesse's eyes were half-opened, trying to process and concentrate on so much. "Why did you train to be a Reader?"

"Now you're asking the right questions."

"Y que?"

"Huh?"

"So what? Why?"

"Because. I have my own reasons."

Jesse thought for a moment. "Everybody does. But why us?"

"Everybody wants something, and will give a little to get a lot. But it never looks like they're getting a lot. It always looks like they're not getting anything. I think I really see that and understand now. What Sharonda has been getting me ready for... I thought I was at war with everyone at school. But none of that matters. She's been getting me ready for an actual war. Here."

"At Portola? Or on the Plane?"

Dalisay shook her head again. "The war on the Plane has never stopped. You already started fighting in that war. No, I'm talking about the civil war that's ready to erupt. In our country. I see it now. It's already begun, Jesse."

"What the fuck are you talking about?"

"I have no idea why anyone would want your help for anything," Dalisay said with a sigh. "This thing with Maria, and Moises. We're going to settle it. But not right now."

"She's mine. I've worked too hard for you to get in the way. Moises needs to get stomped. By me."

"Ew! 'She's mine'? Are you kidding me? She's not property. She doesn't belong to you, or anyone for that matter. Look, we have bigger things to worry about now. I know you can't see that, but if you talk to Yusef tomorrow and tell him what happened tonight with us, he's going to need to explain some things to you. It sounds like things that he should have explained to you. Or maybe you're too stupid and weren't paying attention when he did."

"Fuck you!"

Dalisay closed her eyes again. "Leave Moises alone. He won't be a problem with Maria anymore. I think he's finally seen her for what she is."

"Oh, yeah? And what's that?"

A smirk curved Dali's face while her eyes were still closed, her back up straight while sitting cross-legged on the grass. "You're so stupid. You'll see it, too. I hope. You think she's this really bright thing, and it blinds you." Dalisay quieted and was still. "And I was really looking forward to framing you for that locker room theft." She legitimately sounded disappointed. A silent moment passed as she kept her eyes closed and her body turned into a flash of white light. Only a black mist was left behind, trailing off through campus and into the distance. The misty essence began to dissipate into the breeze of the Plane.

Jesse looked around and confirmed he was alone. "Damn. Guess she really had to go. Hijole, that was close. She would have kicked my ass." He stared at the empty Portola campus, shards of putrisomn occasionally glinting in the purple light as they depicted alternating renditions of the campus in different hues of colored paint, student-made banners, plants, and trees that probably existed on the campus at different times. "Guess I'll go fuck around in Racha's head now."

* * * * * *

Cradling his breakfast in his arms -- which consisted of a plastic tub of sealed dry cereal, a small milk carton, a juice box, a plastic tube of yogurt, a tiny green banana, and a cellophane-wrapped package of plastic spork, straw, and a stiff napkin -- Jesse juggled to get Mr. Abdel's classroom door open and rushed inside just as his breakfast poured out of his arms and onto a nearby desk. "They ran out of fuc-- of damn trays again."

"Good morning to you, too, Mubtadi."

Jesse looked around and noticed he was the first and only student there. He scowled at Yusef. "Who's Sharonda?"

Yusef leaned back in his black leather office chair but remained focused on inspecting Jesse. "I see you and Dalisay finally met each other."

"You *do* know shit! Chinga tu madre!"

The doorknob turned noisily behind Jesse and was lazily pulled open. An Asian student walked in.

"Yes, that does sound like an excellent plan, Mr. Ramirez. I shall see you after school, yes. Have a good day. Good luck with breakfast. Ah, good morning, Mr. Li. What can I do for you on this glorious day?"

The student's eyes glanced at Jesse as he passed him and then quickly darted away. He put space between himself and Jesse and walked to the front of the class to Yusef's desk. "Uh, I just had a question. It's about last night's homework."

Jesse began scooping up his breakfast into his arms again and left the class to first period Spanish. The weather had turned cold again, so he was getting himself ready to be disappointed in Maria's attire. *I hope it's leggings at least.*

He was the first one there, again. Señor Padilla had welcomed him in and sat at his desk working on his computer. As Jesse ate his meager breakfast he took out his phone. *Let's see what kind of* mierda *awaits me today.*

A few news accounts were now a regular part of Jesse's social media feed, and they were citing a recent report that was published about a growing number of deaths within the federal immigration camps that had been set up across the country to hold and process undocumented people, according to the new Tilson Plan that had been adopted, the SENTRII Act.

A video had been leaked, which Jesse watched, of secret footage from inside one of the camps. Detainees overfilled containment cells, huddled and sleeping on each other with a few silvery emergency blankets scattered about the crowds. Jesse wondered why they looked cold and so tired when they were inside and the lights were on. He read a little bit and learned that the footage was taken at night with air conditioning left blasting. *But this is from January,* Jesse thought. *Why is the A/C on? Why would they…? Oh. The government* wants *them to freeze*. Jesse imagined Lita in one of these camps, stuck grasping onto strangers and never knowing when it was daytime or nighttime. Always being tired, cold, confused.

People are probably getting sick, too, he thought. When he read more his suspicions were confirmed as the report stated that a growing number of detainees were not receiving proper food, sanitary supplies, showers, or medical treatment. Then Jesse realized that there weren't any children in the video, in the cells with the adults.

A second video featured armed guards patrolling a chain-link fence. A tiny dirt yard on the other side of the fence was filled with children sitting down, dusty knee to dusty knee. A few kids, no older than Marcy for sure, were crying, calling for their mothers. One of the guards taunted them. "If you guys start over at the same time maybe we can make music out of this." He waved the barrel of his gun toward them like a composer conducting music with his baton. The children howled.

"Jesse!"

He looked up from his phone at Señor Padilla who was alertly and annoyedly looking at Jesse from around his computer monitor.

"Lo siento. I'm sorry, Señor Ramirez. I tried calling you but you weren't listening."

Feeling tension in his face, Jesse released the pressure from his jaws, which were clenched tight. He realized his legs were tapping up and down ferociously, and they were exhausted. One of them was tapping against the desk in front him. "Oh, shi-- shoot. I'm sorry. Lo siento, lo siento, Señor Padilla."

"Esta bien, Señor Ramirez," Mr. Padilla said, more relaxed as he slowly took his eyes off Jesse and went back to work.

Jesse took a deep breath and finished reading the report, which stated that multiple events were planned across the country in coming days and weeks to protest the SENTRII Act, ICE, Tilson, and the President. A few detainee camps were being targeted for these protests, aside from most major U.S. cities. The report ended by stating that counter-protests were also being planned by supporters of the Tilson Plan.

The anxiety was coming back to Jesse, even as he was trying to control it. *I have power now. I can fix this. I can fuck up that guard. I can… I can free those people. Right?*

Then he checked his notifications. There was an add-request from Maria. *The fuck?* Jesse stared at his phone in disbelief. He checked her profile to make sure it was actually her and not someone pranking him. He opened up and zoomed a selfie of her from the summer, laying out in a white bikini at the beach, cleavage pouring out onto the sand.

"Did you get my request?" Maria asked, standing right behind him.

For what had to be a whole, eternal second, Jesse couldn't find his stomach. It certainly didn't feel like it was where it should be. He pondered looking on the ground for it.

"Wha-- uh. I-- you're here early, no?" Jesse sputtered, dropping his phone on the table. Maria's photo was still zoomed in. He quickly scraped it back up and tried to shove it in his pocket while turning off the screen, but being seated made it difficult and awkward. He couldn't do either while sitting at his desk and ended up thrusting his hand into his pants quickly and repeatedly with no results.

"The bell rang."

"Oh, yeh. Ha. Right." Jesse emptily agreed while trying to focus on fitting his phone inside his pants pocket and also trying to figure out where his stomach had gone. And maybe his lungs were missing.

Other students trudged in and took their seats. "I'll catch you later, I guess," Maria said and went to her desk.

"Yeh. Good later. See ya, talk." Jesse took a few breaths. He grabbed his breakfast trash and raised it up high in the air for Señor Padilla to see, who saw and nodded. Jesse took it out of the classroom to a trashcan in the hall and dumped it. He hunched over and tried to decide if he was going to throw up.

Okay. Pull yourself together, Jesse, he thought to himself. The warning bell chimed and Jesse took a few more deep breaths and focused with his eyes closed. He took out his phone and checked the notification again. He accepted the add from Maria Fonseca. *I don't know what's happening right now. But this is good. Right? Right. Don't fuck it up*. He walked back to the classroom, returned to his seat, and did his best to focus on the lesson, or at least appear that way. Really, all he wanted to do was check his phone. But he had to play it cool and unimpressed even though everything in his body -- the parts he could still feel -- churned to move him toward Maria and to hear her voice, to smell her, to see her eyes up close and connect with his own. She would finally see into his heart and soul and feel for herself how deep and pure and different this feeling for her was than anything else he or she had ever felt before.

"Señor Ramirez?"

"Yeh?"

"Te puedes ir."

"Huh?" Jesse looked around to an empty classroom, except for Señor Padilla standing at the podium in front. The classroom door was still slowly closing after the last student had left. "Ah, shi-- shoot. Class is over already?"

Mr. Padilla replied with a grinning nod and went back to his desk.

I guess I played it cool, then, Jesse assured himself. He made it through third period Honors English a bit more focused: he at least was paying attention when the bells rang this time. He was also trying to anticipate his conversation with Yusef later. It was really difficult though, as he could have sworn he saw from his peripheral vision that Maria looked toward him a few times, maybe for just a split second. Or was she looking at someone behind him? He dared not look at her to confirm.

Checking his phone again during lunch, Jesse caught up on the news. Raging forest fires in Australia and Brazil had finally subsided. A Chinese city was in a forced quarantine from a weird new flu while the government still struggled with the unrest in Hong Kong. Arrests had been made on leaders of a group of armed Americans who were gathering for a gun rights rally at the Virginia state capitol while also protesting the Democratic-led state government. The arrested individuals were attempting to incite violence and had gone so far as to plan the use of explosives at the event.

How normal is this? Jesse thought to himself. *Pues... I've been gaining superpowers in a secret dream world. So… I guess I shouldn't feel surprised. But still. What's everyone else's excuse?* Jesse looked up and around him, watching boys trying to do kickflips on their skateboards, a group of girls running around the corner of a building, another group of students huddled around and laughing at something on one of their phones.

When Jesse got to Yusef's classroom after school had ended, there were students talking with him. "Ah. My 2:45 appointment has arrived. Ma' al-salamah. Go with peace, young ones. I will see you tomorrow."

"Bye, Mr. Abdel," a few of them said as they picked up their backpacks and headed past Jesse and out the door.

"Make sure that door is locked, Mubtadi."

"Yeh." Jesse did and walked back to a desk near Yusef's and sat down. "A'ight. Spill it."

"Your entanglement with Dalisay was no accident. It was an inevitability."

"Are you telling me that you knew about her the entire time, and what? You were planning on us fighting each other?"

"Ms. Williams and I found it in the best interest of everyone that you and Dalisay did not know about each other for as long as possible."

"Who?"

"Sharonda Williams. Dalisay's mentor."

There was a pause. "So… that night in Judge Thompson's head. You... you set that up? You knew she would kick my ass?"

Yusef nodded slowly. "Dalisay began her training before you did. It was likely that she would have the advantage, on top of the element of surprise. It was an exercise for you both."

"Like I need my ass kicked more in my life?"

"On the Plane? Absolutely. Your abilities on the Plane are unfathomable for most people. You need to learn how to fight and how to lose. Learning to do that under controlled circumstances would be ideal. Instead of another situation like Carolina. Or worse."

"What could be fucking worse than that monster?"

Yusef gave Jesse a slightly stern look.

"Sorry. You just got me heated, 'Sef."

"I understand how you must feel, Mubtadi. Betrayed, untrusted. But please try to understand that it was done with the best of intentions and you were always safe. Things are moving fast now. Supporters of the government's plan to hunt down immigrants are more emboldened than ever. Plus, there are other developments unfolding that are beyond the control of anyone. An unseen clock is ticking, Mubtadi." Yusef's eyes grew wide as his eyebrows raised. His tone was the most serious Jesse had ever heard it.

"Whaddaya mean? Is it happening? Are we all gonna get strapped up and go all Call of Duty on each other?"

"No, hopefully not. If we can act swiftly and find the root of what is influencing this wave of aggressive paranoia and control from the government, and shut it down as quietly as possible, then we just might be able to turn the tide. Otherwise, Mubtadi, I fear the worst for our country. A portion of our people will feel backed into a corner, voiceless, powerless, and desperate. Meanwhile, the portion with the power will continue to take as much power and control as possible, especially if they feel supported by the President. It is a perfect storm for civil strife. And it will rip this country apart. We will never recover as--"

"A'ight. So, what's next?"

Yusef straightened up. "We must follow the source we found in Judge Thompson's subconscious. We have to infiltrate Erik Peters."

"No mames!" Jesse exclaimed excitedly. "He's in Texas, no? So you gotta finish training me to be a summoner."

Nodding and taking a quick swig from his water canteen, Yusef gently cleared his throat. "And we will be working alongside Ms. Morcilla and Ms. Williams on this quest."

"No mames!" Jesse grunted angrily.

"Not for the training. That will still be you and I, over the next week. The infiltration operation will need to happen by then. Whatever we find out from Erik Peters will be helpful for Sharonda's operation."

Jesse shrugged. "Yeh, whatever, 'Sef. If you say so."

He nodded again. "Until then, we cannot risk anyone catching on to you and Dalisay. You must avoid her in public when possible. You will need to check in directly with me on the Plane every single night. If we ever separate you will need to safely exit the Plane and do not return to sleep after doing so. It is imperative that you are either always under my protection or not asleep. Do you understand?"

"Yeh. I got it. Don't be friends with Dali, which won't be hard. And you're my babysitter."

"I encourage you to coordinate privately with Dali for training or school-related matters."

Jesse looked at the time on his watch and got up. "Oh, Imma *fuck* her up, 'Sef."

Yusef shot Jesse a glaring look as though he could pierce him with lasers from his eyes.

Jesse stuck out his tongue between his teeth and laughed at Yusef on his way out the door.

Before heading home Jesse checked for more notifications from Maria, but there was nothing. He figured he really blew it earlier today. His mind wandered and he instead caught up on more news.

The New York International Auto Show made a headline with a photo of sightseers storming out of a convention hall in disgust. Their faces, clothes, and arms were splattered with black-brown goo that looked like crude oil. The headline read, "NY Auto Show Shut Down Over Eco-Terrorist Scare." He went on to read about how an environmental protection group calling themselves "The Sunset Brigade" had infiltrated the event as paying participants and snuck in gallons of chocolate syrup. In a timed operation, they simultaneously doused headlining speakers, cars, show screens, models, and crowds, all the while decrying the continued use or "worship" of fossil fuels, warning of complete global environmental collapse. They made sure to use the viscous chocolate syrup to graffiti in large letters on the front wall of the main convention hall: "Our sunset is upon us."

"Híjole chingao," Jesse said to himself. "Who the fuck does something that crazy?"

He rounded the corner to the apartments, the same corner where he once tried to rob Yusef in what felt like a lifetime ago. He stopped in his tracks when a white and green ICE truck slowed at the stop sign, on its way out of the neighborhood. Jesse's eyes locked a gaze through the ICE officer's sunglasses as the agent scowled at Jesse through his driver side window. He waited for the officer to roll down his window and threaten him, like clockwork, but he drove through and left the neighborhood instead.

A second ICE truck came, and this time Jesse saw a set of familiar eyes through a window in the rear of the truck. It was Lita, whose face was wet with tears, and she looked terrified like death was imminent. When she saw

Jesse her face stretched and scrunched and although he couldn't hear her screams he felt them at the bottom of his gut. The truck drove away.

Fredo and Marcy were wailing as they ran to Jesse, on the corner. They ran into him, almost knocking him over. He then realized he was kneeling on the ground, and his knees were throbbing but he couldn't feel the pain. His brother and his sister held onto him tighter than anything he had ever felt in his life, and they screamed into his body.

Jesse XXVII
You're a Hero

Jesse mindlessly scrolled through his feed as he trudged down the sidewalk and came within Portola's WiFi range, seeing images and words but not really piecing any of them together into anything cogent. He didn't know if he should be laughing at or learning whatever it was his fingers glided across. He just realized how cold it was and that he had forgotten his black hoodie.

"Joining militia groups…"

"Chayne Sauze Responds."

"... Asylum Seekers."

"No Police Charged in Fatal…"

"... Prompts Local and… into Crisis Mode."

"... Stuns in Dress on Red Carpet."

"Antifa… 'Rebels' and 'Terrorists'."

All he thought about was what Lita was doing at that very moment. What was happening to her? Jesse imagined her frightened, huddled against strangers in a cramped, cold room. Was she hungry? What does she have with her, to bargain with or keep her safe? Is she in a hell within a hell, wondering about how she's failing to keep her grandchildren safe, after so many other failures her children and grandchildren had? Is she worrying herself to white hairs and scarred wrinkles about the safety of her kin, her legacy, her last chance at leaving something good and meaningful in this awful world?

For now, things would go on as normally as they could. Jesse started skipping his early morning workout to make sure Fredo and Marcy were up and got ready for school. They looked like shit when he dragged them out of bed on the first morning. Marcy had come to Jesse and Fredo's mattress at some point in the middle of the night, sobbing. Jesse wanted to switch and take the empty mattress so he could finally try to sleep and meet Yusef on the Plane. But he knew he had to stay there and hold Marcy, and Fredo. And once he did he didn't want to let go. With all three of them there on the mattress along one wall, the rest of the room felt so empty.

As he picked up his pace on campus, Jesse went to his camera app and switched it to selfie mode. He looked like shit. Jesse couldn't stop thinking about Lita and worrying about how to keep taking care of his brother and sister. Yusef had very sternly instructed Jesse to either meet him on the Plane or not sleep. So he hadn't slept much, except for a few coordinated -- and awkward -- training sessions with Dalisay. They practiced infiltration and subconscious manipulation on Racha.

Jesse had gotten out of bed earlier that morning to get ready first, then he woke up Fredo and Marcy. He helped them get ready for school and scrambled some eggs, while also helping keep an eye on Ms. Arcos's daughter, little Alexia. Jesse tossed the eggs into tortillas for the kids, then quickly rinsed the pan and dishes he used. In the fridge there was the last of some roasted and blended salsa that Lita had made. Not enough for him to have, even as he poured it into the burritos he wouldn't have, he knew he might never taste that salsa again. He took one last whiff of it before wrapping up the burritos. He did his best to make them like Lita, but they quickly became unfolded.

"Here," he told them. "School breakfast sucks. And this week sucks."

They had nodded, looking down at the ground and said, "Thanks," without looking up.

Now at Portola, Jesse was still racking his brain trying to think if he forgot anything before he left. He kept thinking all night about his new responsibilities, big and small. Ms. Arcos talked with him before bed last night, about the few things she could help out with, but the biggest, hardest part of the conversation was that she would need to find someone else to live in his room, who could pay rent. She asked Jesse to start calling family, friends, anyone that could look after him and his siblings.

"I'll… I'll drop out. I'll get a job." Even as he had said it, he didn't believe it himself.

"Don't be ridiculous," Dominique had responded. She had her baby, Antonio, bouncing on her lap. "I know you could do it, Jesse. But you've worked so hard and turned everything around. I've seen you put in all that work! You changed. And in the best way. You can't turn away from that now. Make some calls. You'll find help."

Jesse had felt like he should argue, but he didn't want to. He was shaken hearing Ms. Arcos compliment him and encourage him to stay in school. And he wanted to now, which was a realization that also shook him. "Yeh. I'll, uh, I'll make some calls."

"Good. You have some time, but I'm going to start interviewing people to take the room in March. Luckily, your abuela paid for the last month in advance. I remember arguing with her about it when you first moved in. I guess I was right on that one." Ms. Arcos shook her head and stared into Antonio's eyes as he giggled and bounced, "But that doesn't happen often enough."

"Yeh. I know what that's like," Jesse agreed. "And uh, thanks. You could have not told me about the last month's rent being paid already. But you told me the truth."

Dominique nodded. "I know what it's like to have your life turned upside down," she consoled as she stood up and held Antonio above her head and looked at his face and smiled. "But we did alright, didn't we?" She said in a high-pitched and playful voice to her son.

Jesse was now at the Portola cafeteria. It hit him that he actually had almost forgotten an important detail. He texted Dalisay.

7:36 AM

You here yet?

He headed straight to the library to try and get some homework finished, which he didn't touch at all last night. But then, a building down the way, he saw Maria walking toward the quad.

She was wearing workout pants with meshed sections that accentuated her muscular legs even more than usual, and even from here he could see the curves of her ass sway from side to side, as if her butt cheeks were trying to burst out of her black leggings. Her brown hair was tied up in a high ponytail which tossed about as she walked.

"Ffffuuhhh," Jesse exhaled. "Locker. Gotta go to the locker," he justified to himself as he changed course to follow her to the quad. She walked out of view. *I'll just casually, uh, apologize for not messaging her yet because my abuelita got abducted by federal agents and now I'm in charge of two small human beings. It'll be a great ice breaker.* He turned the corner around the cafeteria, trying his best to avoid a crowd of eboys and egirls hanging out and now saw the quad.

His eyes scanned the crowds. Then he looked to the cafeteria line to his right and saw Maria waiting there with Erika Gomez and Cervantes.

"Damn it." He decided this was a stupid idea and needed to go back to do some homework.

"Nyyeeehhhhh!"

"Really? This early in the morning?" Jesse asked no one in particular as he pressed his hand to his brow in frustration.

The deafening roar of his skateboard caught everyone's attention as Racha came to a scraping halt right in front of Jesse. "You fucked up. I've got an on-campus suspension today. And you still didn't get my pen. Bitch." It seemed like almost the entire cafeteria line turned to look at this brewing confrontation.

Jesse's phone chimed and he checked it really fast.

7:41am

dali: Yes, should I get into position?

He smirked and didn't bother to look at Racha as he quickly replied and put away his phone. Calmly, he responded. "Chill." Then he turned to him. "I got you."

"Yeah? Pues, dame."

"I don't got it on me. I'm not stupid."

"Then what the fuck? You gonna tell me it's at your house? Fuck that. I'm gonna rat you out right now. Get me that reward."

"I said chill. It's in my locker." Jesse reassured Racha.

"When did you get a locker?"

"Don't worry about it. I'm borrowing it," Jesse said with a nod to follow him.

"If you fuckin' with me, you gonna regret it." Racha warned as he started gliding on his skateboard and followed Jesse away from the quad and to the Math building.

"Uh-huh. Hey, show me one of those cool tricks."

"This one's called, 'Fuck off'," Racha lifted his arm toward Jesse's face and extended his middle finger.

"I seen that one already."

"Tha fuck you know? What tricks can you do?"

"I know one or two. Just not on a board."

Racha snickered. "Yeah, you *are* really good at embarrassing yourself, Romeo. And being a fucking loser. But I don't need to learn those tricks."

"Yeah, I guess you already know those, too," Jesse responded coolly as he opened the Math building doors and walked in with Racha.

"Fuck you, bitch," Racha snapped back as he scooped up his board and carried it against his hip.

Jesse sniggered. He checked his phone one more time and then zeroed in on a set of lockers against the wall.

"Ay, whose locker you using? It's right by mine."

"Oh, excuse me!" A female voice blurted out over the loud tumbling and crashing of Racha's skateboard.

"What the fu--" Racha yelled out after taking a few stumbling steps and looking up from his skateboard that had skittered across the hall from his arm. "Oh, shit! Es La Puta! Lookit here, Jesse!" Racha pointed as Dalisay stood in front of him so that his back was turned to Jesse. Dalisay looked back and forth at Racha and the building entrance down the hall. Her head bobbed a little bit to get a clear view between the various students in the hall who were walking, hanging out, and accessing their lockers. "Jesse?" Racha asked again.

Racha turned around and saw Jesse turning the combination on Racha's lock. "Ay? Is that… is that my locker? What the fuck?"

Dalisay, staring toward the building entrance, said aloud, "Jesse. They're here."

Racha turned back around to Dalisay. "Who?" Then he looked over and in between the heads and bodies of students at the Math building doors and saw them open. A golf cart could be seen outside. The campus security ogre and Dr. Ngo walked in.

"I got it," Jesse said with a metallic click and swung the locker door open after swiftly removing the lock.

Racha looked back, and maybe for the first time in his life, was speechless. Finally, all that he could muster out was, "You bitch." He glanced back at Dalisay who had her phone out and was video recording. "You. You fucking bitch, too. Pinche Puta." A small crowd of students were starting to gather and watch.

The ogre picked up Racha's skateboard and the assistant principal went straight to his locker and looked inside. A sports bag was stuffed inside. Dr. Ngo grabbed it and had to wrestle it out because it was full of various items inside. "That shit ain't mine. I don't know how it got there," Racha protested with his hands up.

Dr. Ngo zipped it open. "Jordans, wireless headphones, a tablet, a letterman's jacket." She kept digging. "Yup. These are the stolen items. You're coming with us, Rogelio." The ogre stepped over and he beckoned Racha with his big hand to come with him. Racha looked around for an escape. He saw a crowd of students surrounding them, all staring at the locker, the sports bag, him, and talking amongst themselves. Some of them had their phones out and were recording. He sighed. "You can't call me that." Then he trudged over toward the ogre and they walked through the crowd toward the golf cart waiting outside.

Dr. Ngo stuck her palm up in front of Jesse. "I'll take it from here."

Jesse put Racha's lock into her hand. The first bell rang out. He locked eyes with Dalisay across from him and they nodded at each other. She put her phone away and disappeared into the crowd. Jesse began wading through the crowd of students and headed to his Spanish class when he heard, "Bravo." His stomach sank to his feet. He looked around and saw Maria giving a gentle but sarcastic applause.

"Oh, shit. You saw that?"

"When I saw the AP and security rush toward your direction I knew there was something I didn't want to miss out on, haha!"

"That was -- that's not something I would normally do. I ain't no snitch," Jesse said apologetically, but with a touch of inflated defiance toward the end.

"But you did it to save the dance. You realize you just saved the dance for the school, right?"

Phi emerged from the crowded hallway and came around Jesse to put his heavy hand on Jesse's shoulder. "Fuck Racha. That bitch always takes too many hits off my blunts. That dance finna be litty." Phi reached out his hand and offered a dap to Jesse, which he accepted. After he walked away, Phi threw up his arms and yelled out, "We finna tear up that shit!"

"See? You're a hero!" Maria teased with a laugh. They were walking out of the Math building now and seemed to be headed toward first period Spanish class.

Jesse felt unreal being this close to her, casually, in a welcomed manner. He looked down and saw she was wearing her thin, gold watch bracelet. He pointed at it and asked, "Are we going to be late?"

"Huh? Oh, that. I don't know, this stopped working a while ago. It's dead. You'll be fine with me. Padilla never marks me tardy because he thinks I'm always doing student government stuff," Maria explained with a snicker. "He won't mark you tardy if you're with me because it's not 'equitable,'" she added while motioning quotation marks in the air along with an eye roll. "Anyway. You going to get those free tickets, too?"

"Huh? Oh," Jesse said sheepishly. "I don't know. It just sort of happened. I don't even have someone to ask as a date."

"You? Really?"

"Uh, yeah," Jesse almost snorted as he nervously scratched the back of his head.

"What about Xotchitl?"

"What about her?"

"I thought you two were a thing."

"I didn't think you knew I existed."

"Hard not to notice when you're always staring at me. Or trying to beat up my boyfriends."

Jesse's eyelids shot up. His eyes grew wide and he bit his bottom lip. "Fuck. Did I just get called out?"

"Haha! Yeah, you did! But try to come at me and I'll hit you back, boy!" She raised her fist playfully and the thin, gold watch rattled lightly on her wrist.

"Hehehe," Jesse chuckled. "I bet you hit hard, too."

"And fast!" Maria turned toward Jesse and threw a jab at his arm.

"¡A poco, guey! ¡No me chingues!" Jesse yelled out sarcastically and dramatically rubbed his arm.

Maria laughed hard, baring her white teeth and a wide smile that stretched her red lipsticked mouth across her beautifully smooth, milky face. Her eyes smiled and even seemed to have dimples at the ends. She pulled her hair tie and let her ponytail fall. Jesse forgot where and when he was. "You might as well be asking me to go with you since you're already walking me to class," she said as she peaked a look at him through her hair tousling in front of her face.

A prickly, sudden sweat beaded across Jesse's lower and mid-back, then he felt the perspiration starting to break through on his hairline and his upper lip. His armpits were swamps. "Ah… ha-ha…"

Be cool, *pendejo!*

Jesse continued, "Don't get your hopes up. You're just lucky we got the same class right now. And that you're cute enough to walk around with."

"Pshhh! This guy! Haha!" Maria shook her head and smiled even bigger than before. They were now almost to their class. "Well, you'd better find that date." She looked over at Jesse again. "Don't forget it's a super special dance because it's also on February fourteenth."

Gritting his teeth, Jesse slowly nodded. "Oh, yeah. That. Valentine's Day. Every guy's favorite holiday."

Maria laughed as she got to the classroom door first and opened it. "You're funny." Her dead watch dangled as she held open the door. She walked in and Jesse couldn't help but smile, and then he tried to stop and hide that as fast as he could.

The rest of the day went by just as fantastically for Jesse. He kept thinking he was going to wake up back in his bed. At the end of second period he got called up to the front office, received an apology from Dr. Sanchez, and was told that his dance tickets were being added to his student account as a reward for recovering the lost items, as well as for finding the person responsible for the gym damage and theft. Dr. Sanchez even went so far as to call Jesse a hero. He was really liking the sound of that.

Later, more students greeted him warmly and he was tagged in a few social media posts, praising him for saving the dance. There were a few students and posts that called him a snitch, but he didn't really care about any of it. Maria had talked to him.

When he checked in with Yusef at the end of the day, Yusef immediately noticed something different about him. "Ah! *'Alaykum as-salām*! You seem much... *brighter*, today, Mudtadi. All went according to plan, I take it?"

"Yessirrr!" Jesse said. "A little earlier than expected, but Dali came through. I don't ever want to be on her bad side again."

"Well, let us hope that you actually are not on her bad side anymore."

Jesse froze for a second as he really thought about it and then raised his eyebrows. "Shit. You right." He shook himself out of his sudden but playful shock and plopped down into the desk in front of Yusef's desk and doodled on it with a pencil. "What's next?"

"We need to get you ready for the infiltration of Erik Peters by the end of next month. You need to get your teleportation abilities under control, your quick escape skills need to be smooth, you have some geography to learn, and we need to make sure you understand the operation plan. This will not be like Judge Thompson. There will definitely be resistance."

Jesse nodded. "I'm ready, 'Sef. Whatever it takes to save mi abuela. I'll be ready. Andalé."

Jesse XXVIII
The Black Pawn Moves Forward

In the weeks that followed, Jesse was able to clear some hurdles and make significant progress as a fledgling Reader on the Plane. He knew a large part of that was having the Science Fair and all its drama out of the way. Not dealing with Raymond was also a relief, although he was still making threats online, mentioning he wouldn't need his crew to back him up in another confrontation, but Jesse wouldn't take the bait. He let it be.

Besides, Jesse was busy taking care of his brother and sister, which required a rather considerable transition that he still wasn't sure he had completed, even after three weeks. There was cooking, washing dishes, laundry, making sure they got to school and did homework every night, making sure they brushed their teeth, getting them into bed, managing their fights, cleaning the bathroom, grocery shopping, and selling their own things to afford groceries. He was running out of valuable things to let go of, but one item remained that he had realized he didn't want to sell: Yusef's watch.

Then he had all of his own responsibilities on top of that. He managed to get Fredo and Marcy to help out with what they could around the house, but that usually took more time and effort than it saved. The first week was survival mode with an adrenaline rush. The second week was difficult as the fatigue and frustration definitely caught up with Jesse. By the third week he was over it.

Jesse was also still trying to track down his Tia Claudia. He had recalled Papá mentioning his hermana a few times when he was younger.

All he knew was that Papá never really got along with her and he would say that she always acted like she was too good for the family. She would prioritize other things over la familia and would never be around when she got older, and he said she was selfish for trying to be a slutty college girl over staying home and working. Jesse apparently met her once, but he was too young to remember.

Since Lita never mentioned his estranged grandfather, who was somewhere back in Mexico, Jesse didn't really have any other contacts on his dad's side of the family. He did his best to work contacts through his deceased mother's side in Guatemala. Everyone he spoke to expressed their worry and concern -- even though they had never met him or his siblings -- and offered their own homes to them. He kindly refused them all in his Americanized, broken Spanish, and they assured him they would do their best to contact Claudia.

Yet, the frustration and fatigue seemed to sit well in him because of all he *was* accomplishing amid the new responsibilities he was handling, and almost entirely on his own. He tended to forget about it, mostly, when he was back at school. Jesse was still getting his assignments done, paying attention and actually participating in class, and was really enjoying doing well, especially as more of his peers and teachers noticed and validated him.

As an extra bonus, he didn't need to worry about Dalisay creeping around at school or on the Plane this week. She was out on an all-expenses-paid, week-long trip to Washington, D.C. The National Bar Association sponsored an annual youth leadership academy, and Dali was one of twenty finalists from across the nation who had been accepted.

Still, he credited his clearer conscience and new luck to Maria Fonseca. Jesse was walking her to her classes, chatting with her for small spurts during lunch, and interacting with her more on social media. Jesse smoothly got around to asking her out to the Winter Bash by teasing her about not having a date. She happily agreed and Jesse was in shock for the rest of that day. Then the shock wore off when he got home and realized he was going to need a babysitter for that night. He asked Dominique to see if she could request that night off from the restaurant and babysit the kids instead, but she wasn't confident since it would be on Valentine's Day, one of the busiest serving nights of the year.

However, there was one slightly tense moment when Jesse walked Maria to first period one morning and she brought up the poems he had written, and she asked if they were really about her.

"Uh… maybe," Jesse responded sheepishly. "Look, I only started getting into poems and shit because I saw that you liked them."

Maria looked up from her phone in her hand and stared back with a puzzled face.

How can she look so beautiful even with that look on her face? Jesse thought.

"Huh?"

"Your poetry books. I saw that you were reading them. So, I -- uh -- I got some inspiration."

After a moment she exclaimed, "Ohhhh! Hahaha!"

"What? What?"

"I was carrying those stupid things around for weeks and barely read any of those dumb poems. It was for English. We had a project last semester, before you were there."

Jesse's brow furrowed. "Huh?"

"Pendejo. Your poems were cute, though. I didn't really, like, *get* them, but who else gets poems written about them these days?" Maria tossed her hair and grinned. Then she brought herself closer to Jesse as they walked. "Hey, are you coming with me to the basketball game tonight? It's a home game."

"Ah. Nah, I can't."

"What? Why? Don't you want to hang out with me?"

"It's not that. You know I have to watch mis monstruitos."

"Ugh. That's right." She went back to swiping and tapping on her phone and didn't say anything. When Jesse texted her later that night to check in on her at the game, she never responded.

The next day she pretended like nothing happened and just said, "The game was fun!" Then she quickly talked about how much she liked the new ON$l0tt track that dropped and how Chayne Sauze was garbage now, and a Tik Tok dance she was practicing for the new song and all of the followers she was getting. He had felt dread the entire day before, sensing she was mad at him, and he was ready for a fight but instead they just moved on.

It was unreal how much his life had changed since the beginning of the school year, and just within the last few weeks. On top of becoming an impressive student, and essentially becoming the man of the house -- for now -- Jesse was also on the verge of becoming an essential part of bringing the country back from the brink of self-destruction, as Yusef had put it.

As his busy weeks went by, Jesse did his best to keep up with headlines. A shootout in a St. Louis nightclub apparently started over the Chayne Sauze and ON$10tt beef. An increased presence of Russian forces spread along its western borders and in the Norwegian Sea. Senator Levin was gaining more support in his election bid against the President while receiving numerous death threats from the president's supporters. Rising concerns from the World Health Organization about the virus originating from China had already begun to spread to other continents. Yet most countries, including the U.S., did little to nothing in response to the warnings.

The Supreme Court ruled on a case where an unarmed black man was murdered by a concealed-carry permitted white man in New York. The Court's decision allowed citizens to use lethal force if they felt their lives were in danger, similar to Florida's Stand Your Ground Law, but now in every part of the country. The black community immediately voiced their dissent, as black athletes and other celebrities rallied to decry this new federal law.

Jesse's favorite headline was from Nevada, where a team of protestors splintered from a main group and found (or likely made) a hole in the fence of a Customs and Border Protection containment facility, while a separate and larger group of protestors created a disturbance at the front entrance to distract the facility's security forces. The infiltrating group caused a breakout, but many of the freed prisoners were recovered, according to CBP. Still, they wouldn't release an exact number of unaccounted-for detainees, but just described it as "very sizable."

Jesse was quickly disheartened to learn that it likely wasn't the facility where Lita was being held, as she was probably somewhere in California. The agency was very vague and inconsistent in responding to phone calls and emails, and now they had permission to keep the detainee's whereabouts unknown since they were awaiting "installation" of the new tracking nano-chip that was currently under massive production and awaiting distribution across the States.

With the recent escape of detainees, various militias and armed groups across the country were coordinating with federal agencies to help hunt for "escaped criminals" and "violating aliens." Many of the groups were already well-seasoned from years of hunting and detaining immigrants who attempted to cross the southern border. Bands of civilian militants armed with assault-style weapons and tactical gear now began roving across the interior of the United States.

Combined with the recent Stand Your Ground ruling, the increased presence of armed civilians who felt empowered by the federal government's new laws and recent court rulings, prompted a resurgence of the Black Panthers. They began appearing in a few cities, brandishing firearms on the streets in black neighborhoods. One member was quoted as saying, "We're done dying while our back is turned or while our faces are pinned to the ground. We're done with the America you took from us. We'll build America, again: our own black one -- better, safer, and that actually cares for its people."

The increase in public uproar, protests, fear, and anger was palpable.

On the Plane, this was also evident. Jesse and Yusef were coming across so many more wraiths. On some nights they had to call off their training mission for the night and navigate safer routes which allowed for Jesse to just further his practice of teleporting along ley lines, and learning where they lay, too. Other nights, Jesse was able to put some of his improved defensive skills to the test, lightly skirmishing with a wraith alongside Yusef. While terrifying, the close encounters tempered Jesse's will and confidence, and his quick thinking. Jesse was grateful for once that he didn't have good drawing skills, aside from his doodling, because he didn't want any way of recreating the horrible things he saw from the wraiths.

Still, he felt much more experienced and confident now than he had upon his first encounter with Carolina. Which was important, since the big night to infiltrate Erik Peters was coming up in a couple of weeks. It would be his first attack on the Apostles. Second, if he counted Judge Thompson.

Jesse, of course, didn't feel completely ready. *But when do you ever?* he thought to himself. He was grateful that at least it was going to be well past Valentine's Day. With his mission still far away, he could be free to dance his ass off and have the time of his life with Maria, where he would be hailed as a hero.

"We are very fortunate, Mubtadi," Yusef said when they met on the Plane Thursday night. "Mr. Peters left Texas and has come to *us*!"

"Wait up. He's here?"

"It is a two-night visit. Mr. Peters is here to support a fundraiser for the Los Angeles County Sheriff, and to air a special edition of his show tomorrow and on Saturday morning during a Second Amendment rights rally. With the time change, Mr. Peters will need to get up early for his show tomorrow and now he should be tucking himself into his hotel bed. Assuming he has been infiltrated and influenced by other Readers, this is the most opportune time to strike since Mr. Peter's den is now reset in a new place."

"Huh. So… so I did all that training for nothing? Like, that's… that's what you're really telling me right now, right? Right, my man?"

"Nonsense," Yusef dismissed as they made their way across the apartment courtyard, Carolina growling and barking loudly from her room upstairs across the way. "Your skills and abilities have grown exponentially in the last few weeks. There is more to come, Mubtadi, after this." Yusef reached the street and effortlessly pulled putrisomn from the cars and concrete around him, and Jesse automatically moved his arms and assisted him as they built a sleek boat in midair, but with very comfortable backrests. "We are only at the beginning of this great battle for the republic! Once we discover who else Peters is connected with, and perhaps what plans he is aware of, then we can strike and bring relief to this country. We can find a way to help save your grandmother. This is wonderful, Mubtadi!"

Jesse nodded his head as he climbed into the boat. "Yeh, alright. Let's do this ish."

Yusef verbally guided Jesse north on the Plane, toward Los Angeles, as Jesse used his powers to move their vessel first to the nearest leyline that ran north-south. North was new territory for Jesse since they had been getting ready for a long excursion east, all the way to Erik Peter's home studio in Southeast Texas.

A northward leyline wasn't far from them. A major one ran right along the entire coast, Yusef explained on the way there. The Spanish monks of the 1700s were led by Junipero Serra, a Reader himself, and he established the California mission system along this leyline. This aided his impressive control and management of the missions immensely as he was able to secretly micromanage his subordinates along the California coast. The route, of course, had long been used by native shamans for thousands of years before Serra, all along the coast from the bottom tip of Argentina to the northern wilds of Canada, where the leylines splintered off into a green-blue-violet web of minor lines. As was the custom of the European invaders, they took and used everything of value that the natives had and claimed it for themselves.

Jesse definitely felt the ancient power of this leyline when he connected to it, and even sensed it before they approached its glowing purple streaks. Yusef took control over the boat to let Jesse shift his focus to anchoring themselves to the leyline. Since this was new territory for him and he had not been to a vortex in the area, traveling along the leyline was their quickest option. An incantation was needed to move speedily along the leyline, and Jesse recited what he knew best: rap and hip-hop songs.

He found that his more current favorite songs were not as effective as some of the older hip-hop songs he knew. Yusef explained that emotion is tied with spirituality, and when Jesse invoked the intense feelings of oppression, hatred, love, and more that were imbedded deeply into hip-hop songs, as opposed to the vanity and banality of more recent rap songs, Jesse was able to pull them much faster along the leyline. It required his focus, but more importantly, his emotional presence to feel the words and sounds coming out of him in order to access this ancient power. He had to emotionally place himself into the experiences and hearts of others so he could invoke that emotion and the raw power which emanated from it.

When Yusef first performed an incantation, Jesse witnessed him sing songs in Arabic. He clearly had no idea what words Yusef was using but he *felt* what he was saying. He had tried to ignore it, but he had to wipe away his tears after a few minutes of listening to Yusef's deep and sorrowful embodiment of pain, reverberating his long life of struggle and echoing the sacrifices of generations before him.

Nearing their destination, Yusef began to bear the boat away from the pull of the leyline toward a southwest direction as he instructed Jesse to end his incantation. "Sit and regain yourself, Mubtadi. We are not far from our prey." He steered them through the cavernous streets of downtown Los Angeles. Jesse did his best to practice etching some of his sigil scribbles onto the boat but he was too distracted with what he saw around him.

Large swaths of San Vallejo and Citrus County back home had occasional unclear or collapsed putrisomn structures along the wider spaces of the city and suburbs. But unlike there, the Plane's version of Los Angeles was crowded and seemed solid. Yet fluid. As they traversed the streets, Jesse felt at times as if he was inside a silvered and rainbow kaleidoscope. The buildings and streets were dark and gray, the edges of which were often grotesque and uneven. Windows appeared constantly and disappeared on the faces of buildings, sometimes shadowy or bright with yellow-orange light. Fluorescent signs flashed one split second and entirely vanished the next, only to reappear in a different place.

Visions of people walking on the sidewalks and cars snailing on the streets pulsed on and off. The shadows of people actively moving in the waking world trekked the sidewalks and moved across glowing windows. They lined the streets as if sitting in their carseats, hands on steering wheels, but their cars were not present here. As they flew across the city blocks, Jesse heard all kinds of grotesque groans, moans, growls, and howls from countless wraiths near and far in all directions.

"Jesús!" Yusef hissed through a forceful whisper.

He shook himself back to attention.

"I was trying to explain that you need to be ready for a fast exit back here to the leyline, in case we are separated. You must not be captured or defeated. Do not attempt to fight. It is likely that Mr. Peters has brought security with him, especially here on the Plane, if my instincts are correct. If they can trace you back home or to me then our entire operation is at great risk, and we have lost our element of surprise -- and likely an opportunity to infiltrate him again tomorrow night. Do you understand,

Mubtadi?"

"Yeh. Quick escape. I got it. I'm memorizing how to get back here."

"Take a look at that building there," Yusef commanded with his arm jutting out.

"The one with the big tree in front and the weird gate at the bottom?" Jesse asked as they flew by. He looked back behind as they passed. "Wow, shit. I just felt that. The one with the little like, clock tower at the top?" he confirmed.

"Yes, Mubtadi. If worse comes to worst," Yusef hesitated for a brief moment, "and you cannot reach the leyline, you can go to either the bottom floor or the penthouse at the top of that building. It is a minor vortex, and you can use it to teleport yourself back to the leyline in the least."

"Huh. I thought vortices were like, organic and shit."

"You mean, not man-made? No, Mubtadi. That is not always the case. But that is why it is only a minor vortex. There are more, and what you felt before as you passed is something you should remember for future encounters."

"Oh, snap! That the Staples Center up there?"

Yusef cracked a small smile, "Yes, Mubtadi." He slowed the boat and brought it to a stop. "But perhaps you can visit it another time, in the waking world when there are actually interesting people inside of it. The hotel is around the corner." He climbed out and with his hand he sucked putrisomn off a nearby car and constructed his staff. With his other hand he took more putrisomn and constructed a platform that he stepped on. "I shall return. Do not move."

He elevated the platform closely along the wall of a nearby business building. Jesse looked up and estimated that Yusef had to be about ten stories off the ground. He remained at that height for a few moments as he moved around the corners and sides of the building, and ventured out a little but in different directions. Then he returned to his first position and descended.

"The outside is clear," he said in a softened voice. "Now I do not want any arguments from you. I am going alone."

"Pinche--"

"Jesús!"

Jesse was silent, but stood with his arms crossed and biting his lip.

Yusef continued. "I need you to protect my rear and flanks. You are overwatch on this operation. If this turns out to be a trap or a quick escape is needed, I need you a step ahead of everything and able to help me if needed. You are essential in this position, do you understand?"

"Do I got a choice to understand?"

"It would appear not." Yusef climbed off the platform and with his free arm motioned for Jesse to step on it. You are my eyes in the sky, Mubtadi. Protect me."

Jesse sighed and nodded. "A'ight." Then he stepped on the platform. "What do I do if we get made?"

Yusef extended his hand and the platform turned a dark and cloudy translucent color, like glass. "Toss this as far as you can in a different direction, and then evacuate back home as quickly as possible. With any luck you might draw security away and give me a safe escape route."

"That's it? A distraction?"

Nodding, Yusef already began walking away. A wraith roared from somewhere behind a wall in the alley behind them. "Mierda," Jesse said to himself, looking around. He stepped on the platform and slowly ascended to a vantage point that hugged the side of the office building, but he stopped short of the very top so that he wasn't visible from the skyline.

He watched Yusef, tiny in the distance, reach the hotel and then rise along the outside to the top floor. Yusef swung an arm a few times and chunks of the hotel wall peeled off, exposing a large hole. He guided the broken-off chunks and silently grafted them back onto the surrounding exterior of the hotel, and then entered through the hole.

Jesse's eyes and ears scanned the streets and the exterior of the hotel from his observation point a hundred feet in the air. His eyes searched for movement along the windows and rooftop of the hotel down the block, but he didn't notice anything. Minutes passed and he felt the patter of a raindrop on his hair.

"The fuck?" Jesse gasped as he patted his head and felt a small pebble slip through his fingers. He looked up at the top of the business building and saw, silhouetted against the purpled mist of the Plane's night sky, a rounded but mechanical shape leaning down from the roof's edge. A subtle blue glowed from its head but suddenly shined like a spotlight. The figure leapt and raced straight down at him. "Shiiit!" he screamed, lurching away from his platform and into freefall.

Panic struck and paralyzed his entire body as he plummeted toward imminent death. Reflections flashed into his eyes from the tumbling glassed platform falling next to him. He reached out and controlled the putrisomn, putting every amount of focus into stabilizing the platform underneath him. The ground rushed right beneath him and the best he could do to break his fall was angle out the landing of the platform in as much of a horizontal direction as he could, along the street below. With a loud crash of shattering glass across the rough pavement, Jesse's body skidded and skipped across the ground about fifteen feet, spreading out the impact of his fall.

Immediately following Jesse's erratic landing, a loud thump and cracking of cement emanated from his original drop zone. Prone and writhing in pain, Jesse looked up and saw a giant robotic-looking figure standing on two legs, crunched concrete surrounding its boot-like feet. It was bulky and armored with decorative streaks of blue and magenta, immediately reminding Jesse of the cartoonish, anime-inspired mechas he might have seen on Fredo's t-shirts or school folders when he was younger.

He got up as fast as he could, still slightly stunned from his fall, and tried to assess his situation and figure out which direction to run. Shadows continued about their business unaware and unaffected by this intimidating, hulking figure. The mecha's single eye, a large convex blue light, stared right at Jesse. The mecha reached an arm behind its wide waist and revealed a coiled, dark blue knotted rope. "Okay, nah." Jesse turned away in the opposite direction and took a few running steps before stopping completely.

A white woman dressed in a skin-tight pale jumpsuit had glided down to the street. She did so with an arm extended from inside of a blue, symmetrically webbed cage. But it wasn't as closed off as a cage, Jesse thought, perhaps more like a protective shell, or a chassis. She wore blue lipstick with a vertical streak of vibrant, magenta-pink down the middle, horizontal blue streaks of paint under both of her eyes, and a vertical streak of the same hot pink painted down the middle of her forehead. Her blond hair was cut evenly at the length just past her shoulders, and as it waved in the air Jesse noticed a streak of pink on one side and a streak of blue on the other. "Lazavik," she called out past Jesse. The tone in her voice was guttural and harsh, familiar to Jesse from video games and violent movies about Russian gangsters. "Ponyat' tsel'," she commanded.

The thumping and cracking resumed behind Jesse. He looked over his shoulder and saw the mecha named Lazavik march toward him. The rope it held in its hand dropped at its side while it still held on to one end, which he now realized was a handle, and revealed the knots to actually be barbs along a thick and heavy-looking whip. "Oh, no mames," Jesse said under his breath.

Still looking over his shoulder at Lazavik, he reached his arm out in the direction of the shattered glass along the street and thrust his arm toward the woman. Then Jesse ran as fast as he could to the sidewalk, leaping over some mounds of putrisomn cars on the side of the street, and back toward the alley where the boat was docked. As he ran to the sidewalk he glimpsed her recoil and heard her scream. The open spaces within the chassis's frame suddenly encased together, creating a shell around her, and glass putrisomn broke and deflected off it. But he was certain at least a few pieces had made it inside.

Ungodly screams and roars echoed around street corners and from behind walls all around them as the countless wraiths in the city responded to the sudden sound of the woman's scream and the commotion that had erupted.

Jesse reached the alley and jumped up to climb into the boat. He looked down the alley back toward the street and saw the mecha meet the woman's shell, which was now returning to its opened chassis form. Towering over the woman, Lazavik kneeled and its chestplate opened forward and down, creating a ramp. Jesse could see tears in the woman's suit, revealing milky skin and streaks of blood across her body and limbs. Now her makeup was joined by a streak of blood across her cheek. As she climbed into Lazavik, the chassis crumbled to the ground and began shrinking into something else. Its chest closed back up to encase her inside.

Grated slots and small holes along its torso turned out to be vantage points for the pilot inside. Lazavik reached its free hand to the ground where the chassis had fallen and picked up what had now become a shield, which looked like a small buckler compared to its size.

“Fuck, fuck, fuck, fuck,” Jesse quickly stammered as he tried to focus on lifting the boat up and away, attempting a takeoff further down the length of the alley. The stomping became very fast paced and closed in on his position as the boat began gliding and cleared a couple stories in the air. Jesse heard silence and shot back a look. He only saw Lazavik’s feet as the rest of the mecha jumped underneath the boat and out of his view. The buckler shield crashed through the bottom of the boat, shattering the entire bottom of it, seat and all.

"Podtverzhdenny khit!” he heard the pilot yell out excitedly from inside Lazavik.

Jesse grabbed onto the top rim of the boat, the only thing still flying in its intended direction, and dangled. He heard the loud thud of Lazavik landing in the alley below. Its momentum gone, the boat wreckage hurled back down toward the ground, in yet another crash landing for Jesse. He cleared a cinder block wall and ended up in a separate alley surrounded by different buildings that belonged to the next block over. This landing was smoother as he was able to roll into it this time and actually end on his feet. The remnants of the boat, however, crashed loudly into one of the buildings flanking him. A low, deep growl reverberated from behind a side door, inside the building.

The pounding thuds zeroed in on Jesse from the other side of the alley, and the cinder block wall crumbled into chunks as Lazavik smashed through it, wrestling with and bending the exposed iron rods out of its way.

He heard screeching from behind the nearby door now, and scratching. Lazavik cleared the tangle of rods and wall chunks and began toward Jesse with its whip arm extended. Once it reached the side door Jesse stepped forward, which caught Lazavik off guard. It raised its shield but kept moving forward. Lazavik’s big blue eye shined right at Jesse.

With both hands extended out, Jesse grunted and used all the control he could muster to splinter the door. It fractured outward and a hellish shriek followed it. Lazavik stopped to get into a full defensive position, but

the wraith already had it in its sights. Its eyes were amber and reptilian. A pointed snout, heavy with snarling and curved teeth, jutted out and led its long slender body out of the doorway. It slinked on four legs, and a bladed tail waved and curled around its body. When it emerged completely from the building it extended its scaled and horned wings, taking agitated flight. It hovered over Lazavik, scratching at it with its long sharp claws.
"Pizdets!" Jesse heard the woman yell from inside Lazavik.

The wraith and Lazavik began fighting: a melee of claws, teeth, whip cracks, glaived tail swinging, and shield bashes. Jesse backed away but could already see that the wraith wasn't going to last long. Which meant he wasn't, either.

He focused again, this time on a nearby large chunk of cinder block that had been flung nearby. He waited for the wraith to move out of his way and to the opposite side of Lazavik, then waited for the right moment that Lazavik would be bracing with its shield. With its back to Jesse now, and the wraith about to lose this fight, he forced the cinder block to strike right behind Lazavik's knee as it held up its buckler to defend against the swooping wraith. Its back leg buckled and Lazavik tumbled to the ground, allowing the wraith the best possible advantage.

Behind the fight and beyond the broken wall, he saw a dark cloudish figure skulk into view. Another wraith. He turned to run out of the alley toward the street and heard more screaming and yelling from the woman he now left behind him.

He was now on a different block than where he and Yusef had first deployed, but he found his sense of direction and began running northeast, toward the leyline. Jesse ran past and through more shadows of people, and had to avoid the sidewalk entirely due to numerous homeless people sleeping and projecting their hazes. It was difficult to discern what were harmless shadows of people all around him or stalking shadows of wraiths. He felt exhausted and didn't know if he could muster the focus required to pull more putrisomn and pull himself on it any faster than he could run.

Silhouettes crept along darkened doorways and alleys. They were the projections of conscious people in the waking world. But this city was also full of wraiths. He spied an arm here, a set of eyes there as he ran through the streets for blocks. Glancing behind him, he felt something following him but saw nothing. He continued running and looked back again. This time he noticed that along the side of a building a giant spider with shiny black legs and a head full of blinking, reflective tiny eyes pattered quickly, giving chase to Jesse. The kaleidoscope of reflecting putrisomn altered rapidly as he ran.

The air in his chest felt like it got sucked out and Jesse's eyes bulged. Now he just wanted to cry. At the intersection ahead, a small roving black swirl of cloud yelled and screamed; muffled flashes of red and white light flickered violently from inside. The swirl intensified and this wraith took form as a large, middle-aged white man. He was disheveled and disoriented, pointing threateningly at Jesse and yelling angry nonsense. Behind him down the street ahead, more dark clouds floated about. *Okay, okay. Not going that way anymore*, Jesse thought to himself. He turned the corner at the intersection as the man also gave chase to Jesse.

The screeching, yelling, and howls that were erupting from the chase echoed through the canyons of downtown, and panic began to overtake Jesse. He felt light-headed, and confusion set in. Over his shoulder he saw through his blurring vision that the man was catching up with him. As he looked away and back in front of him he no longer saw a middle-aged white man but his own father thundering toward him.

You can't run. He grabbed the side of his abdomen in pain, but kept pushing forward.

You're going to lose it, Pendejo, Jesse thought to himself through his clouded mind. *Come on!*

You need to be the man now. Jesse.

The spider was now skittering the building right alongside Jesse, and was pulling ahead of him.

Mamá! Another dark swirl swooped down from a nearby rooftop and joined the chase.

You're fucked. He turned another corner away from the spider and it jumped down but crossed the street and climbed a new set of buildings flanking Jesse.

It's just business. A tentacle stretched out from the swirling storm.

The man behind Jesse was at his heels, and he could smell the alcohol on his breath and felt his spittle as he yelled. The spider jumped down from the building and closed in on Jesse.

... day. And a new future!

The man let out an exasperated profanity. The spider hissed, and the swirl slowed to a halt.

Jesse felt it again. He looked around and saw the oddly designed gate and looked up past a tall tree and saw the little clocktower on the roof. The wraiths had stopped, but still prowled around Jesse, who was right in front of the gate. It was as if he were protected by a cage of unbreakable glass.

Breathing heavily and walking backward to keep his eyes on the wraiths, Jesse groped the gate handle and navigated his way behind it, never blinking away from the wraiths. "Holy fuck," he burst out amid deep breaths. "What is this place?"

He stood in front of an opened room that faced the street. The floor was marbled in pale yellows and a black symmetrical web design connected the tiles together across the polygonal room. The amber-colored ceiling was a three-dimensional design that had triangular shapes jutting in and out like a frozen, pixelated wave. On the walls a few signs read "Cicada" amidst golden curtains behind glass and gold-black zigzag designs. The energy that Jesse felt was on par with other vortices that Yusef had shown him in the previous weeks. But there was something... *more*, to this energy he felt.

The wraiths on the street screamed. The man and the spider looked upward and then all three rushed in the same direction: back toward the direction whence they came. Jesse didn't want to find out if the reason was Lazavik, or something else entirely.

Jesse went to the center of the powerful room and sat with eyes closed, beginning his incantation to teleport to the leyline. He heard a commotion somewhere outside, perhaps on the rooftops but it was hard to tell with the echoes from the buildings. He felt some kind of jolt in the energy around him, but it didn't feel threatening. He refocused and after a few moments, he felt weightlessness and a sensation of getting pulled out of his own body. He fluttered his eyes open as the teleportation began. In a split second he saw the mecha pilot running up to the building. She was in worse condition than when he left her, with entire portions of her jump suit torn off and she was covered in grimy smudges, scrapes, and cuts of dirt and blood. She held a broken portion of her shield in one harm, and the end of her mecha's heavily barbed whip that appeared to have snapped off. She looked pissed. The spider returned and dropped down behind her. It got ready to pounce as she lifted her shield and turned around to face it.

In a flash of purple streaks all around him, Jesse found himself sitting on the ground back at the leyline, but he felt like he was lurching forward still and had to splay his hands out on the street to steady himself.

"You made it! I knew you would, Mubtadi!"

Still on the street, Jesse turned onto his back and breathed heavily. The purple streaks of the leyline glistened in reflection off the sweat of his face, neck, and arms.

"Come. There is no time to lay down and get lazy, Mubtadi. We must go."

He clambered up as Yusef gathered more putrisomn and constructed another boat. "Yusef! That was too fucking close! Like, a few times! You said it was all clear!"

The boat came to completion with a ramp and open portion that allowed for easy boarding. Yusef bowed and invited Jesse in with his arm. "My apologies, Mubtadi. These poor eyes of mine must be slipping in my old age."

Jesse sighed. "You've got some explaining to do, bruh," Jesse warned with a pointed finger as he climbed aboard and sat in the front seat.

"Oh, I sure do, Mubtadi. I sure do." Yusef climbed up and used the ramp to seal the side of the boat. "It appears we will have to pay the infamous Mr. Tilson a visit, as soon as possible. And our friend, Mr. Peters," Yusef said with a distant look in his eyes. "He is in deep," he continued, "and he will have to be dealt with."

Jesse turned around in his seat and looked at Yusef. "Yeah?"

Yusef stared back and nodded slowly with an intense look in his eyes. "For your grandmother, Mubtadi. For all those who suffer."

Jesse returned the nod. "I want to do it."

Jesse XXIX
The Winter Bash

"Anna Baronova," Yusef confirmed, standing behind his desk. "Without a doubt. I do not know how you managed to escape, and almost unscathed. Truly impressive, Mubtadi."

"Who?" Jesse asked.

"I have had at least one former apprentice come across her before. Ms. Baronova was trained by a camp of Readers that stemmed from a series of Russian secret organizations, most of which were actually public learned societies but with private inner circles, reaching back to the mid-1800s --"

Jesse loudly cleared his throat with annoyance.

Yusef gave Jesse a frozen stare. "Right. I shall give you a crash course in Russian history later. Ms. Baronova was trained by The Divine Servants of Ilya Muromets. But she found this camp had lost its traditional roots, and had become yet another weapon in the arsenal of the Russian oligarchy that morphed out of the Cold War."

Jesse stuck out his finger accusingly at Yusef, pursed lips on his hardened face.

Yusef raised his hands in defense. "That is all I was going to add."

"And now? Who she with? Why was she there last night?"

He thought for a moment before responding. "I doubt that her loyalty to her mother Russia has faltered since our last run-in. If I recall correctly from a visit to her subconscious, she had a certain --'affinity' for President Putin. That would be putting it very lightly, too," Yusef said, as his face turned flush. He pulled out his desk chair but didn't sit down yet.

"Ew! She has wet dreams about Putin?"

Yusef looked away and regained his composure. "So… I doubt that her overall loyalties have changed much. Now we must ask ourselves if the Apostles are allied with foreign groups. What do they gain? What are they willing to give a foreign force that is helping to orchestrate the misinformation and brewing tensions in their own country?"

"Damn. 'Ey! Is this how Hitler did it? The Nazis, the Holocaust, trying to take over the world? He was a Reader, right?"

Solemnly and painfully, Yusef responded, leaning on the backrest of his chair. "No, Mubtadi. No. Unfortunately, humans do not need a lot of coercion to give in to their fears and insecurities. Most of our great atrocities and failures in our history were not the fault of secret societies or powerful abilities. Humans can be terrifyingly manipulative and selfish on their own. Hitler had no help from the gods, demons, or Readers. It was a dark time in the world, and many people chose self-preservation and obedience over standing up for what was right. That is all that it takes for darkness to consume us all."

Jesse's brow was furrowed and his posture was slumped over as he sat in a desk at the front of the classroom. "That's effed up, 'Sef."

He nodded.

"So what chance we got then? If everything's been shi-- I mean, crappy for a while, and there's a-holes trying to eff up peoples' heads on top all that?"

Even more muted and pensive than before, Yusef slowly pulled out his chair to finally sit. He also gave this moment a longer pause as he nodded, perhaps trying to convince himself of what he was about to say before it came out of his mouth. "What do you think the purpose is in putting immigrants in cages?"

Jesse resisted the urge to open his mouth with the obvious answer first. *Because they're fucked up and hate brown people.* He sat and thought. *They're not killing them, like the Nazi concentration camps. That we know of.*

After Lita was taken, Jesse's research found that most immigrants were detained in Customs and Border Protection jails for about a month or more before being deported. Assuming they weren't also accused of terrorism or other illegal involvements. But with the SENTRII Act in place, the new process of "catch, tag, and release" was taking longer because of manufacturing of the new tracking nanochip pill. Approval of the pill was currently being rammed through the Food & Drug Administration. Also, the large-scale production required a large demand for rare earth elements to produce the smart dust. *I just read an article the other day about the Chinese companies making the pills and mining the metals. This shit worldwide.*

"To get us used to it," Jesse finally responded.

Yusef didn't say anything, but he leaned back on his chair in approval.

"We finally doing shit, attacking the camps and freeing people. But this has been going on for years, right? Since Obama."

"Yes. Things were bad then and grew worse," Yusef nodded.

"If that can happen here, it can happen anywhere."

Yusef nodded again. "It already is, Mubtadi. China, Russia, Israel, North Korea, Chechnya, Syria, France, Uganda, Greece, and the list goes on. Immigrants, Muslims, gays, lesbians, ethnic minorities, trans people, political enemies, and more. The marginalized are being targeted, tracked, and captured. In some of these countries, they are being killed."

Jesse was quiet again, taking it all in. "People keep getting sick. This flu that's hitting right now. What's going to happen? What's going to happen to all of those people being detained? What's gonna happen to save us?"

Yusef got out of his seat, put his hands on his desk to lean on, and got closer to Jesse. "Nothing."

His face contorted in annoyance and then he shook his head. "Nah."

"Pandemics are not quick matters. Humans are impatient and foolhardy. Prideful. Selfish. The proper measures will be suggested and even mandated in some cases. But Americans live to break the rules and boast. Here, the government has no interest in protecting the well-being of its people. Only inasmuch as will keep them docile. Just content enough and hungry enough to keep us focused on one thing: chasing our dreams in a system that allows only a few into the winner's circle and leaves everyone else out in the cold to fend for themselves -- and against each other, more importantly."

"So what? We're just going to be screwed?"

Yusef nodded again, "Yes. Most of us will one way or another. Those select few, however, will prosper even during a plague."

"Why's it always like this, 'Sef? Why are my people always getting screwed? Why does my generation have to clean up the mess of yours? You've shown me how the ones with the dreams most denied are the ones that just want enough to live comfortably -- to work hard, earn what they deserve, and have the respect and rights everyone else has. But no, they can't even have that. This shit, *everything* is rigged. We're just living in the shadows of these giant ass monsters who feed on us."

Looking down, Yusef seemed to remove his mind to somewhere else, nodding to himself and gave out a short chuckle. "You remind me of myself, long ago. I argued the same thing with Haseem Nusaybah, my old sergeant. By this point he was a lieutenant, and it was the night before he turned in his bars. He was quitting the PLA and wanted citizenship in Israel -- our sworn enemy. 'How can you do this?' I asked him. 'You are literally joining the enemy. You would become one of them? We are outmanned and outgunned -- they take everything from us! We need you to *fight*!' And you know what he said to me, Mubtadi?"

Jesse stared back with anticipation, not bothering with a response.

"He said, 'Fight? Where has that gotten us, Abdel? What have we gained in our war against Israel? We have lost more land, more people, and more resources. No, Abdel. We do not need to fight. We need to live, to dream! Look at us. We are ravenous, skirting around this relentless giant as we fight for scraps in its shadow. They take our land, our children, our dignity. But they cannot take our dreams. For what shadows may dream shall make giants fall."

Staring right into Yusef, Jesse quickly retorted, "Yeah, well this feels like a fucking nightmare. How long is this plague gonna last? Once it's here?"

Yusef leaned back again and rubbed his gray, bearded chin. "At least one year, under the best circumstances."

"What do you mean?"

"Whether by design or destiny, this might be the final stroke to bring this country crashing down." Yusef got back out of his seat to walk as he spoke, as if giving one of his lectures. "This 21st century of ours has brought us many miracles in science and technology. But with those have also come distractions. With all of the means we have to save us time and energy, we still find ourselves too busy to learn, to reflect, to pay attention to the things that really matter to our future and our wellbeing. It is too much energy for us to even fake caring about them. We have television shows to catch up on, and personas to portray in our online lives."

Now it was Jesse's turn to lean back into his desk. His brow was furrowed with agitated thought, as guilt began to settle in. He was culpable of these things all of his life.

Clearing his throat, Yusef continued. "While there will be an attempt to keep people calm and focused on staying safe once the pandemic strikes, the forces you and I are fighting against will continue fomenting misinformation and discontent. There will be attempts to defy science and the experts in the name of liberty, for the sake of the economy and justifiably so, to keep money moving. People will still need to eat, even when everything eventually shuts down." Yusef paused as he was now facing away from Jesse, caught up in his foretelling. "I am doubtful that our current administration in the White House will take quick or effective action. When people are out of work and are forced away from their distractions, they have time to observe, to discuss, to learn, to get angry, and to take action. In due course, there will be a boiling point. Another cultural controversy, another extreme political act, or another tragic killing, and then…"

Hanging onto every word, Jesse was impatient. "Then what!"

Yusef turned and looked back at Jesse. "Chaos."

He didn't argue or ask more. Yusef had already taught him about the French Revolution, and the American Revolution, and the Civil War, and the Russian Revolution, and more. None of them were just started on a battlefield or in a monarch's throne room. The elements of economic disparity, cultural and class divisions, and political conflicts were boiling under the surface for decades before these big events. Food shortages and high inflation, acts of violence from the state, a new law that goes just a bit too far: these were the catalysts to changing history.

Always, it was someone whose name we don't even know that threw the first stone, or fired the first shot, or started the first fire. Someone else of entitlement always stepped in to fill in the void of power once it was displaced by the people. They relabeled everything the people had fought so hard to tear down, and after so much fighting and instability, people were always eager to go back to their work and their distractions and accept the new normal.

"So we're going back to take down Erik Peters, right? We gotta shut him up. That crap he keeps spewing out every day: it's what's making people do all this crazy ish. Judge Thompson, the shooters, the SENTRII Act. It's him and the Apostles, right?"

"Yes, Mubtadi. Exactly," Yusef agreed as he eagerly walked back to his desk. "But our time is short. Erik Peters is but one head of many on this giant monster that is breaking us apart. The presence of Ms. Baronova, as well as the defenses and traps I encountered inside Mr. Peters' haze, definitely indicates a wider plot. This goes beyond him. In his dream last night, very similar to what we saw in Judge Thompson's subconscious, was an outside influence. He was being enthralled by Representative Tilson."

"¡Venga!"

Yusef flinched at Jesse's coarseness. "Even then, Mubtadi, I do not believe it ends at him. With a foreigner like Ms. Baronova, we will need to keep moving up the ladder of this conspiracy. And as quickly as possible," he emphasized as he gripped his chair. "We must move again tonight!"

"We going to D.C., dawg?"

"No. Representative Tilson's den is not there."

Jesse thought for a moment. "It's back in Idaho, where he's from?"

Shaking his head, Yusef said, "Colorado."

"Huh?"

"Some time ago, I received a coded message from a former apprentice of mine. He was updating me on an investigation he was doing. He was nervous about the potential danger and stated that he was on the verge of locating Representative Tilson's den, as a part of a corruption scandal he was attempting to uncover. I did not pay much attention to it because it seemed like such a minor matter at the time, compared to what we have been dealing with."

"Wait. Who is this guy? You mentioned him before."

"It was a long time ago, and we saw our roles in this world differently. We went our own ways, and occasionally sent each other valuable information. After that last letter, I did not hear from him again. He either found what he was looking for, or it found him."

"Sounds like you gonna have to give me a few more tips about quick esca-- oh, fuck. Fuck, 'Sef! Tonight's the dance!"

He slowly turned his head at an angle, not wanting to look at Jesse when he said it. "It would appear that you will have to leave early."

"Ah, shit, 'Sef! Really? How early we talking here? I'm going with Maria Fucking Fonseca!"

"Language!"

""Sef! Come on!"

"Colorado is one hour ahead of us. And who knows what we will encounter when we arrive. You will need to be extra vigilant and perceptive tonight. I cannot stress enough just how fortunate you were with Ms. Baronova."

"What. Time?"

"Meet me by ten o'clock."

"Aw, what? You can't be serious! That means I'll need to leave the dance… by like, what, nine?"

Yusef shrugged. "You would know better than I would, Mubtadi."

"No mames! It just starts bumpin' at that time."

"Need I remind you, Jesús, that the fate of this country, and the wellbeing of your grandmother, relies on the actions we take tonight?"

With a loud, aggravated, and forced sigh, Jesse conceded. "Goddamn it, 'Sef. Fine. I'll be there. At ten."

"Excellent. You will be able to catch up on your sleep in the morning since tomorrow is Saturday. You see? It all will work out in the end."

Under his breath, Jesse muttered, "The fuck it will." He got up from his desk and grabbed his things.

"What was that?"

"With luck it will, 'Sef," Jesse said as he made his way out of Yusef's classroom.

"Ma' al-salāmah," Yusef Abdel replied with a wave as he stood and prepared to welcome his students.

The red, pink, and silver Mylar balloons suffocated the hallways all day, and blinded everyone outside when they reflected the California sun.

Passing periods were clogged with people hugging, making giant displays of affection toward each other, and grabbing each other close in pairs and groups for selfies. Everywhere he looked, he spied a couple kissing and wished that was him and Maria already. Candy wrapping littered the ground and the floor of every classroom in every period. In each of his classes, Jesse noticed at least one girl lugging around giant, oversized stuffed animals with embroidered phrases like, "I luv you" or "Valentine Cutie" or something of the sort.

He couldn't afford any of these things for Maria today, but he managed to write her a poem and sent it to her in a Val-O-Gram that got delivered by the Associated Student Body to her fourth-period class. But she approached him during third period to thank him.

"Ohmygod, Jesse. Thank youuuuu," she said coolly when she walked in before the bell rang. Her arms were up and she closed in for a hug as she dragged out the last syllable.

"I, uh," Jesse stammered.

"Your poem was the best! It was so cute."

"But how--"

"Erika sent me a photo. She saw it in ASB when she was organizing the Val-O-Grams."

"She reads them?"

"Oh, not *all* of them. Just the ones she thinks might be interesting. Us gals gotta look out for each other, right?" Maria reasoned as she plopped her stuff down by her desk and sat. She had balloons, a stuffed animal, a rose, and a small cake in a disposable tin and plastic covering that was decorated with frosting and read, "Happy Valentine's Day" along with a fire and a pair of pointing fingers emojis that were directed at each other.

Jesse stood in front of her desk and stared at everything then looked at her. He felt his face getting hot and focused on trying to keep his embarrassment and hurt pride under control.

"What? They're from friends." She tossed her hair back over her shoulder. "And maybe a few losers who are totally not in our league," she reassured as she reached and grabbed his hand. "My hero."

The bell rang and Jesse pulled his hand away. "Right," he said. "Well, I can't wait for tonight. It finna be snatched! And I got a big gift waiting for you later, too," he lied with forced confidence. "All this shit 'ere is grade school. Huh, no offense to your 'friends.'"

"Alright, alright! To your seats, already!" Klinkhammer boomed. He walked to his podium, big belly resting atop. He shook his head. "Damn it, I hate this day."

Jesse hurried to his desk but barely paid attention to Klinkhammer's lesson. Within a minute he saw that Maria posted on her social media about how excited she was for tonight's dance and her special mystery gift from him, and she even tagged him in her post. *This shit is getting real*, he realized. *And now I gotta figure out what the fuck I'm going to get her that's so big. And how 'm I gonna get it?*

It didn't leave his mind much until the end of the school day, just after he had snuck a short walk with Maria out in the field during her Track practice. He hesitated to give her a kiss goodbye, but figured he'd have plenty of time to make his move later that night.

Heading home, Jesse began brainstorming ideas about this amazing gift he was somehow going to just conjure out of thin air, because he had absolutely no money set aside for such a thing. To help with ideas he thought he would browse online so he took out his phone and hopped onto the school's Wi-Fi.

As his fingers hovered over the screen, frozen in his complete cluelessness about where to even start looking on the internet, he received an instant message notification through one of his chat apps: Dominique Arcos.

Aw, shit. This can't be good. She never messages me. Did Fredo get in another fight? If he did and his school finds out that Lita is gone, then now I gotta worry about CPS!

Friday, Feb 14, 3:12 PM

Dominique Arcos: Jesse im sorry but the restaurant called me in. Half the staff is sick and they need everyone tonight im so sorry ! I need to leave in 15 mins pls hurry and sorry

"Fuuuuuck!" Jesse yelled out with a raised and clenched fist. He tried to think of some reply that would save the day for them both, or at least stall Dominique, but nothing came to him. Nothing worth lying about, anyway. He understood now how important a job was and keeping that stability. He didn't want to jeopardize that for Dominique, or lose her as one of his very few remaining adult allies. He hustled his pace to get home so she could leave for work, and now he was brainstorming how to break the news to Maria that he would be stuck home babysitting and not take her to the dance, on top of this miraculous gift he apparently had waiting for her.

When he fumbled into the apartment, Dominique was already waiting on the couch in her uniform and adjusted her purse strap on her shoulder as she stood up and jangled her keys. "Antonio is napping and I already helped Marcy with her homework. Alfredo is all yours." She nudged past a sweaty and panting Jesse to the door. She opened it and stopped in the doorway. "I'm sorry, Jesse. I know tonight was big for you. I'll make it up to you." Then she walked out and shut the door behind her, locking it from the outside. He heard her do the same for the metal screen.

He was so overcome with anger, disappointment, frustration, exhaustion, anxiety, nervousness, and bewilderment about his next moves. He wanted to yell or punch a wall. But he remembered he was the adult now, and punching holes was bad for the security deposit. He took a few deep breaths and focused as Fredo chased Marcy across the living room, and Alexia was yelling about how her TV show wasn't working.

Alright, pendejo. One thing at a time. What do you gotta do first? What do you know for sure and can't be helped? You're stuck here. You got no favors, no money, and probably no time to find someone to watch these kids. On Valentine's Friday Night. Nope, that's definitely not happening. You gotta tell Maria.

His face grimaced at this thought. This was the type of night he had fantasized about the entire year. This was the magic moment he was waiting for. It was here! And about to fall between his fingers.

He messaged her to explain the situation and apologized profusely, stressing how everything was out of his hands at this point, she should go without him and have a great time, and how he promised he would bring her the gift tomorrow. That last part was a bit of a relief since he had more time to figure it out. While waiting for a response, he wrangled the kids, sat Alfredo down to do his homework, and constantly checked his phone.

Expecting Maria to be angry or really disappointed, when she finally messaged back about a half hour later she brushed it off and asked about the tickets. Jesse's stomach dropped. He realized yet another problem he didn't anticipate: the tickets were under his name in his student account. This meant that he would need to physically be there to let Maria into the dance, otherwise she would have to buy her own. Assuming the dance wasn't sold out. He checked the Portola High School ASB's social media feed to check. Sure enough, the dance had just sold out. *I could have been there taking care of this problem. But now I'm fucked.*

"Jesse!"

"What!"

"Tell me! What do I do?" Alfredo stared at him from across the small kitchen table with his pencil in his hands. He looked miserable. "Come on, I can do this on Sunday! Let me go play."

"Do it now, maricón. We both know you're not doing it Sunday." Jesse reinforced as he held his phone in front of his face and stared at it, stuck in thought.

"Ugh!" Alfredo then clicked his tongue. "Qué soso eres."

"Shut up. This message is more important than you'll ever be."

"How do I do this!"

Jesse reached for his paper and skimmed the directions. "¡Ponte chingón! This is basic math."

"You're basic."

Jesse shook his head. "I'll help you in a minute."

"Come on! I don't want to sit here while you drool on your phone."

"Fuck. Alright, go play. But just for a few minutes while I figure this out."

Alfredo was already flying out of his seat and running to their room before Jesse even started his last sentence. "Maaaarrccyyy! It's my turn on the tablet! Jesse saaaaaid!"

Jesse scanned the living room and saw Alexia watching TV on the couch and playing with her toys while little Antonio, now a year and a half, sat in a playpen with his toys, also watching the TV and blabbing away. *Gotta check that diaper soon.*

His phone pinged. It was Maria. He opened the message:

Friday, Feb 14, 4:33 PM

Maria Fonseca: a friend is gonna take me and sneak me in. Sucks about babysitting. Ill give youa shout out on the dancefloor, tho. See ya manana!

Jesse looked up from his screen. "Well... Shit."

The rest of the night Jesse was a dizzying mix of referee, tutor, parent, and big brother as he uselessly attempted his own homework amidst constantly checking his social media feeds, watching everyone at the dance have an amazing time. It was hard to avoid since people kept tagging him in their posts and eventually people were asking where he was.

He obsessively tried to track Maria through the feeds, tags, and stories. She did tag him in one post, on the dancefloor like she promised. It was a three-second selfie video taken from above her head and looking downward on her face and cleavage as obnoxiously loud and incomprehensible music blasted through his own phone speakers. The dance floor around her was filled with shouting students bouncing and throwing their arms amidst lasers shooting across fogged air and blue-red lights. Toward the end of the video a guy appeared from behind and started grinding on Maria as her head turned toward him and the video cut.

From Phi's feed he eventually saw Maria in the background of one of his videos, dancing with the same guy from her post. Jesse couldn't recognize him, but his blood began to boil.

In Erika's story, Jesse saw her and Maria screaming excitedly in the girls' bathroom mirror. They hugged, smashing their faces and bodies together with huge smiles. Then they pretended to kiss each other on the lips, giggling the entire time as other girls screamed and scurried about behind them.

Jesse checked the time yet again. "Alright, niños. Time for bed!" He announced from the couch in the living room.

"No, it's not!" Alfredo yelled back as he ran from the kitchen to their bedroom.

"Damn it, 'Fredo! Get your ass in the bathroom and brush your teeth. Now!"

Marcy leaned her head out into the hall from the bathroom doorway. With toothpaste all over her mouth, she blurted, "Yeah, 'Fredo! Stop looking at inappropriate things on my tablet and go to bed!" Then she quickly ducked her head back into the bathroom.

"Ughhhh…" Jesse groaned out through his hands, now covering his face and trying to massage his forehead and temples. He put down his phone and began the real challenge of the night: getting all the little ones to bed so that he could get himself to sleep in time for his meet-up with Yusef.

Considering the triple anxiety of Maria unguarded at the dance, putting four kids to bed early, and anticipating the huge risks involved in tonight's mission on the Plane, Jesse boiled some water for valerian tea to help him get to sleep. He eyed a bottle of Nyquil on the counter, but tried to remove the thought.

Yusef warned him a long time ago about the dangers of addiction and the reliance on drugs to sleep. While it might work well for a few times at first, the convenience stretches a Reader's willpower, allowing them to stay on the Plane longer but with an inflated sense of control. Since this makes them more susceptible to staying on the Plane longer than normal, their need to sleep longer for recovery after leaving the Plane increases. This further throws off their sleep cycle and numbs them in the waking world. Then they crave the feelings and experiences from other people's subconscious, blending with the buzz of deep sleep. These addicts, who usually become power hungry on the Plane and use their extra time to infiltrate the hazes of plebs to consume memories and secrets, were known as Dream Eaters.

By the time he got everyone to bed with Alfredo being the last one to go down, Jesse's phone had to be recharged, he had finished his entire cup of valerian tea, he hadn't finished a single piece of homework, and his anxiety wasn't anywhere close to being gone. He quickly got himself ready for bed and then checked his phone as he carefully crawled onto his mattress and under the covers. Alfredo and Marcy had become accustomed to sleeping in Lita's old bed together with their heads at different ends. They insisted the mattress still smelled like her.

When Jesse finally swiped through all the feeds he could find from the Winter Bash, then went through them again to find no more clues or signs of affection from Maria, it was already close to 10:00 PM. He typed out a message to her, hoping she had a great time, he apologized again for not being able to make it, he expressed that he missed her and had been really looking forward to this dance, and then wished her goodnight. Staring at his own message and seeing that it hadn't been read made him unnerved, and he thought about the mystery guy taking her somewhere to put his hands and face on Maria. Jesse shook his head with frustration. *Imma be so late to see 'Sef. Goddamnit.*

He got up from the mattress and went to the kitchen, grabbed a spoon, and took a dose of Nyquil. Trying to relax and distract himself from the social media feeds, he instead switched to news feeds.

Earlier that day, a regional militia calling themselves the Augusta Legion used their guns to attempt a citizen's arrest of a small group of the escapees from the Nevada CBP facility. With the help of local Ojos, the militia found them hiding out on in an RV parked on the driveway of an American citizen's home in Elko, Nevada, who was providing refuge. The homeowner, 68 year-old Alyssa Torlakson, her family, and her allies attempted to protect the refugees, and a standoff developed where the Augusta Legion found itself supported by the local police and ICE when they arrived on the scene with a tank. Although unarmed, two American citizens were shot and killed, including Alyssa Torlakson, three others were shot and hospitalized, and the refugees were detained. The police and ICE did not acknowledge whose guns fired on the American citizens, whom they were quick to label as Antifa members. No investigations had been opened into the case.

A white woman was thrown off a flight before it left the tarmac in Florida. She was caught on video as she erupted in a racist tirade after seeing an Asian and Black couple in the seats in front of her kiss. The headline was "Love Is Not in the Air."

Erik Peters' special Los Angeles radio broadcast and pro-gun rally drew in Second Amendment rights advocates and White House supporters from all over California, as well as Arizona, Nevada, and even Oregon and Washington State. Counter-protestors gathered as well in a futile attempt to thwart the demonstration. Peters' crowds surrounded the counter-protestors, attacking them. One counter-protestor was sent to the hospital in critical condition after being run over while marching in the street. The suspect, whose truck was heavily decorated with "Don't Tread on Me," "We the People," and "III," decals, and a giant American flag, was still at large.

Multiple states began issuing mandatory use of masks for their hospital workers and first responders as cases of the new flu were being confirmed in major cities and numerous deaths had been announced linked to the virus.

Big protests were being planned in cities across the country tomorrow to speak out against the new federal Stand Your Ground law, as well as the SENTRII Act. Counter-protesters were also being encouraged to come out in support of the new laws and to enforce open-carry gun laws where applicable. Jesse barely found a report about the FBI arresting a member of a Georgia militia for obtaining explosive materials in an attempt to bomb one of the protests. There was no information about what happened to the rest of the militia members, if anything.

A 6.1 magnitude earthquake hit Mexico, where a towering concrete prison building, gray and windowless, collapsed. A sole survivor emerged from the rubble, wearing black baggy pants and a wife beater. He was quoted as saying, "You need to be the man now, Jesse."

A gunshot rang out and echoed. Sirens were all around. Metal doors opened and clanged shut behind Jesse. He turned around and saw masked police in riot gear leaping out of trucks and vans. They charged past Jesse as if he wasn't there.

"You got my back, hermano?" he heard from over his shoulder.

His eyes followed the police force while crowds of loud and anxious people, watching from the sidewalks, cheered them on down a large street. In the distance, the lines of police marched toward a crowd wearing face coverings and dark clothes. Above their heads were handmade signs, banners, umbrellas, and waving poles of various colors and designs.

Hundreds of heavy boots rumbled on the asphalt as they marched in unison. The tide of black tactical uniforms began to vibrate with the roar of the marching, the crowds, the tear gas guns, the pounding of sticks against make-shift shields.

Jesse shook himself to attention as he recognized these familiar sensations and images. He reached an arm across his body and extended his arm out, as if he were pulling a curtain open. The entire scene around him vanished like dust being blown away.

After it cleared, he was in his room. Anchoring a pylon in his closet just seemed more familiar to Jesse than the rooftop; there were less distractions and less things to recreate. The beds and dressers were there, but no one else was. He walked to the closet and like before, extended his arm in the same motion, this time pulling open the sliding closet door. He entered his pylon and focused, closing the door with the same motion of reaching out and extending his arm across his body.

He was weightless in a vacuum of darkness. Numbness, then a feeling of wind not on his body, but through it. When he felt his limbs again and the rest of his body, he impatiently reached his arm out again and pulled across. The flashing, spinning, swirling of colored lights surrounded him as he flew.

Gravity returned and his forward momentum sent him into a sloppy, somersaulting tumble onto his bedroom carpet. The swirling lights from his haze were gone now and his husk lay on the bed as a shadow, still moving as it breathed in the waking world. Both hazes of Alfredo and Marcy were active, however, casting lights across the room as well as occasional putrisomn mist that floated out of their haze's spin.

"That landing was less than graceful, Mubtadi," Yusef quipped from a padded chair in the corner of the room. One of his hands gripped his staff, which he held upright with one end on the floor.

Jesse clambered up. "Ah, sorry, 'Sef. Crazy night. Dominique had--"

Yusef raised the palm of his other hand and shook his head. "No. We do not have time for your excuses. We must go. Now." He got up and brushed past Jesse as he left the room.

"'Sef! I'm sorry!" Jesse apologized again as he trailed him.

They made their way down the stairs to the apartment courtyard. No sign of Carolina tonight. "The boat awaits us in the alley. We have a lot of ground to cover and you have a major teleportation to cast at the end of it all. We cannot leave a single trace of ourselves behind, Mubtadi. We are very close to the top of this conspiracy." Yusef stopped on the concrete pathway just before they reached the parking alley and turned around to look Jesse right in the eyes. "Everything may very well depend on tonight.

Do you understand, Jesús?"

He scoffed, but then saw the serious look in Yusef's face. "Psh. Yeah. Yes. I get it, 'Sef. I'm ready. I'll do what I have to. For Lita. For my family. For the country… for us."

Jesse XXX
The Black Pawn's Gambit

The evening scenery was impressive and exciting when Jesse was first making his practice treks with Yusef, but that got really old, really quick. The first ley line they traveled on sent them east over the modest San Vallejo Mountains, and then up and through the San Jacinto Mountains to a vortex on the ridgeline not too far off San Jacinto Peak, almost eight thousand feet in elevation. Here, above the sprawling signs of civilization below, was an ancient sacred site that the medicine-men of the Cahuilla tribe used for secretive rituals and accessing the Plane themselves. Only a dilapidated putrisomn foundation of a ring-like structure remained near the vortex, the remnants of what was probably a tower at some point.

The area crackled with a subtle buzzing sound and there were phantom rumblings like thunder in the distance. From here the wispy, flowing leyline splintered: one leyline went north along the ridgeline and eventually fell off the mountain into Morongo, while a thicker leyline continued eastward over the ridge and down the mountain. It continued to drop in elevation and made its way across the Coachella Valley, skirting the Little San Bernardino Mountains, and went further eastward.

In this small clearing on the ridge Jesse scooped up as much dirt as he could and sandwiched it in his hands. He began the ritual incantation by singing and moving his body, waving the dirt sandwich in the air as he focused on breaking down the putrisomn dirt in his hands into a pure form of putrisomn. His hands glowed purple and he began pouring the putrisomn out in a line on the ground, continuing his incantation. He continued this process until the line completely surrounded their boat.

When this ritual "circle" -- which was actually more oval to surround the boat -- was connected Jesse climbed back into the boat, where Yusef waited. With eyes shut, Jesse focused as he started the last part of his incantation. There was a pull to the eastern ley line like a magnet he felt tugging at a center inside a body within his body, or perhaps behind it. He held his body, Yusef, and the boat in place within the ritual circle until the pull was strong enough to take them all. When he released, the glowing purple putrisomn that surrounded them blew apart in a flash, almost like flame being thrown by the wind. It dissipated back to normal dusty dirt as it settled back to the ground.

Craggy rocks that jutted out of the earth in odd, crashed shapes suddenly surrounded Jesse and Yusef. They were now at a major vortex inside Joshua Tree National Park. The horizon was a mixed silhouette of bumpy mountain tops and spiky groves of trees. Dust flew about and swirled around the boat as Jesse clumsily buried his face in his hoodie, and Yusef already had his cloak over his eyes. The buzzing was here, too, and even though he couldn't identify it or explain it, the static sounded different here. Yusef cleared his throat while Jesse jumped out of the boat and started the teleportation ritual all over again. He began to shiver as he worked.

Yusef crafted a dark gray and forest green poncho with white blotches on it for Jesse since this night was unusually cold and it became too unbearable for Jesse's pride to hide. By now, Jesse was able to weave less complicated objects with a moderate hardness. But fine materials like cloth were well beyond his skill. Jesse was wearing what he had envisioned for himself in his subconscious when he entered his pylon: loose, dark jeans, a large black t-shirt under a black hoodie, a thin gold necklace, and white sneakers, which were all becoming dusty at this point. He thought ahead about keeping a low profile, but failed to anticipate just how cold it was going to get.

From this major vortex, Jesse could pull enough energy to take them to Phoenix. Weeks ago, Jesse had begun sailing on a network of ley lines across the Sonoran Desert, stopping at each vortex to practice his incantations. Doing so strengthened his sense of direction, or bond, to those vortices. This not only made teleportation possible, but as he connected more together he was able to teleport at further lengths, skipping through vortices where he had practiced his incantations and had grown familiar with their magnetic-like pull.

The doodles that Jesse had been mindlessly leaving on his notes, desks, and anywhere else he could let his mind wander, were practice for personalized sigils. Conjurers of the Plane used these personalized signatures, enchanted by putrisomn, to leave markings on the Plane for teleporting from a vortex or even for teleporting another Reader to their own location at a vortex. Another Reader with the same exact sigil marked on their body while on the Plane could be summoned by a conjurer, or teleported elsewhere. A sigil needed to be unique and the design interlinked in one contiguous pattern. Some Readers had sigils tattooed on their bodies to make the tracing of it while on the Plane that much easier and quicker to do, particularly for more complex sigil designs where accuracy was important. Other ancient tricks of the trade had Readers etch their sigils into stones or trees while in the waking world so that their marks were permanently available on the Plane.

Temporary sigils, or markers, could be left on the Plane. But they eroded after their first use or after three days, whichever came first. The marker was also useless if the sigil was disturbed in any way or if the conjurer changed the location of their den in that time.

Dust flew all around again in a purple-white flash, but it seemed to blow right back into the boat. Unable to avoid it this time despite covering his face with the loose sleeve of his white jubbah robe, Yusef sputtered out, "I guess-- *qaf* -- you made it inside the cavern -- *qaf* -- this time."

Hunched over and nearly gagging, Jesse took a few moments to reply as he blindly waved dust away from his face and eyes. "God -- *kaagh* -- damnit! *Kaagh!* You were right. Cave wasn't -- *kagh* -- worth it. Should have stuck to the mountaintop clearing. *Kagh!*"

"Still, your accuracy is getting precise, Mubtadi. I am impressed." Yusef stood up in the darkness to lean over the edge of the boat and tapped the tip of his staff on the cave wall. When he found the wall he pressed his staff against it and hummed or mumbled a tune. The tip of his staff lit up a soft, yellowed white. "There is more about you than meets the eye,

Mubtadi," he added as he turned back to the bow of the boat, the light of his staff casting stretching shadows across the small cavern walls, floor, and ceiling. Ancient petroglyphs of animals, people, and other symbols lined the cavern walls. "This, I always knew. When I first set eyes upon you."

Jesse took the seat at the stern of the boat. "On the street corner. By my place."

A moment passed as Yusef's back was to Jesse before he turned around. "Yes. On the street corner. That seems like such a long time ago now, does it not?"

"I was just thinking the same thing."

Yusef grinned and turned forward again. "You rest now, Mubtadi. I will manage us northward as much as I can. You may have to navigate again at some point. It has been a long time since I last traversed these old canyons and plateaus."

As Yusef prepared for the next teleport, Jesse ignored the crackling and subtle rumbling of the vortex and stared out the cavern entrance, down the mountain and into the Valley of the Sun. It was littered with the artificial lights of metropolitan Phoenix. Jesse thought about what it looked like a few thousand years ago, when it was just the Salt River Valley and its only inhabitants were the Hohokam nation. On the top of the mountain they were inside of, there was a rectangular clearing with subtle ruins: traces of crumbled rock walls, mortars and cisterns carved into the mountaintop, and indistinct stone carvings of oversized heads and crude faces. Jesse had tried to teleport into this cavern because those face carvings creeped him out. The way their eyes were sunken, and deep. They stared back at him, and *into* him. It was as if they could see everything about him, and everything in his past that made him who he was -- it made him feel naked.

From Phoenix, Yusef teleported them north to a vortex in Sedona. After an incantation there amongst the dark rocks, they landed on one of the cliffs overseeing the Grand Canyon. Amidst its dark depths, the river's waters on the cnayon floors subtly sparkled with the Plane's myriad reflections and rarely bright moonlight. Jesse nearly threw up, then nearly passed out after Yusef completed the next incantation, which took them to the mesmerizing layers of Vermillion Cliffs in Marble Canyon. "One more teleport and then you will have to navigate a leyline to the next stop,"

Yusef informed over his shoulder.

"You got it, 'Sef. No more caves or cliff edges, please."

"No problem."

When the dust cleared, Jesse felt like an ant. He was surrounded by a wide, empty vastness, save for a few dark stone towers and spires that jutted straight out of the flat desert. A few purple leylines snaked their way through the buttes, stretching out in various directions and disappearing in the distance. The weight of how small he felt in comparison to the emptiness and the giant monoliths pressed down on him.

"Monument Valley, Mubtadi. When I first arrived in this country, this was one of the first places I traveled to, both in the waking world and on the Plane. Breath-taking, is it not?"

Jesse now noticed a nearby rock with petroglyphs similar to the ones drawn by the Hohokam on the cave walls in Phoenix. "Damn. These *are* everywhere, huh?"

Yusef chuckled. "Yes, Mubtadi. In many ways, even aside from drawings on stones. Since before we have recorded history humans made their marks and told their stories everywhere. In a way, these are the first recordings of our history, as a people. As humans." He stood up from the bow and offered the seat with his arm stretched out. "When you are done with your incantation, we must go East."

Jesse nodded and jumped out of the boat onto the dusty, graveled ground which was littered with sage, rabbitbrush, and brittlebush. He completed his incantation and returned to the boat, taking one last long look at the mesmerizing space around him, illuminated by the purple dim light of the Plane's night sky.

With an arm extended out, he steered the boat on a ley line eastward. The ley line eventually took a northeast route as they passed by a few towns and gained elevation into foothills and then mountains, some of them snow-capped. There were more putrisomn ruins here, many of them towers, still partially or fully intact. They sprouted from ridgetops and some statues jutted out from cliff faces. Jesse finally looked back at Yusef with a shocked face.

"We have reached the Canyons of the Ancients, Mubtadi. Wondrous." There were more petroglyphs etched into the putrisomn towers and statues. As they moved through the canyons, they saw the putrisomn on the rock faces reflect images of hikers and beasts, and even the occasional native in a hunting stance or in mid-dance. The Plane's buzzing was loud here, and Jesse thought he could hear thunder in the distance. He was hesitant to get out this time.

"Are those… Indians, are they ghosts?" Jesse asked uneasily.

"These? No. Just reflections of the past. These are not lost spirits. I do not know of any here. This vortex is too strong and sacred."

"Wait. Hold up. I was kind of kidding. Whadda ya mean?"

"There are vortices that are… disturbed… by immured wraiths, some of them ancient. The terrified and haunted subconscious of a very unfortunate soul sometimes may get captured or caught here on the Plane. Unlike normal wraiths who manifest when a pleb is asleep in the waking world, an immured wraith is stuck here indefinitely after the death of their host."

Jesse's jaw dropped. He was frozen trying to process this new information. Finally he made a realization. "That weird building. In LA. The one you told me to escape from. That shit was weird. Was that place… haunted?"

Nodding slowly, Yusef confirmed. "Some people would call it that, yes."

"What the fuck would you call it?"

Yusef stared back at Jesse with wide eyes. "Interdimensionally occupied."

Jesse shook his head. "*¡Ay, dios mio!* You're gonna kill me one of these days, 'Sef."

"Come along," Yusef redirected. "Time is of the essence."

When Jesse was done with his ritual, Yusef took the bow again. "This should be our last stop: Wilson Peak." They continued northeastward into more snowy mountains and valleys, now capped with dense pines and Douglas firs, and eventually aspens.

"When we arrive you will not need an incantation there. Aside from attracting attention to ourselves, I do not think you will need to return here anytime soon."

Jesse nodded.

"When I have completed my extraction from Tilson, I will cast a brightened chunk of putrisomn into the sky as a signal. From the point of leaving this vortex, just up this last ridge, it should take me twenty minutes to locate his den, infiltrate him, and return to the Plane. At that point, begin your incantation and be ready to teleport me back here." Yusef pulled his sleeve back and revealed a few sigils on his forearm. He pointed at one that Jesse had been practicing doodling for months.

They cleared the snowy ridge and arrived at the vortex atop Wilson's Peak. They were surrounded by valleys and other mountaintops in the distance. A freezing wind howled from the east, rustling his poncho. Jesse shivered and looked at his watch, which was not ticking. "How am I going to know when it's twenty minutes?"

Yusef gently landed on the ridge and walked to a rock that poked out from the snow. The moonlight cast a shadow of it against the snow. With his staff, he carefully drew a line. "When this rock's shadow reaches this line, it should be about twenty minutes." Jesse climbed out of the boat to get a look. Yusef drew a second line close to the first one. "This should be about thirty minutes. If there is no signal, extract me. And hope that I am still here. If I am not, then you must make your way back home alone, as quickly as possible. You must not leave any trace of yourself!"

Flipping his hoodie on and tightening it around his face, Jesse squinted, sunk into his shoulders, and nodded. "Got it. We got this, 'Sef." Jesse reached his knuckles out for a bump, but his hand was inside his sleeve.

"Yes, we do," Yusef agreed as he reached out and pressed his knuckles against Jesse's and left them there. "Let us hope that this night leads us to the everlasting change we have desired and worked so hard for; that our sacrifices would be worth it all. *Bil-tawfeeq*."

Nodding, Jesse returned the expression. "Bill-towfeek." He finally dropped his arm and hugged himself in the cold.

"And no fires, Mubtadi," Yusef warned as he turned away and made his way down the ridge, collecting putrisomn with him as he went and eventually making a platform that he glided on the rest of the way down, and out of sight.

"I don't even know how to make a fucking fire," Jesse grumbled. He climbed back into the boat and huddled inside, trying to hide from the wind. He stared up at the sky and saw the stars through thin clouds and the purple fog in the sky. They were exceptionally bright. His mind wandered as he thought about how the stars were still there back home, even though he never saw them. He thought about a poem he could write about it, for Maria. And the big gift he needed to get her! Would it be an epic poem? He could write about this night -- as a metaphor, of course -- and how great his struggle and will is to get back home to her by following the stars through obvious dangers and terrifying mysteries. In his head he started listing a lot of the things he had seen and trying to form lines and rhymes. The buzzing and odd rumblings that were always in the background of the Plane became soothing. His eyes got heavy and his mind went to his warm bed. He felt weighed down, or weightless in a current that ebbed and flowed like a tide, tugging him about. Was it time for school already? What day was it? There's a test tomorrow. Every day. Every day is a test.

A presence, like someone watching him. Flinching heavily and opening his eyes wide, Jesse jarred himself to attention. "Fuck!" He scrambled out of the boat's bottom to look at the marks left next to the stone in the snow. Immediately his eyes caught something darkly cast against the snow to the side of the ridge and he ducked back down into the boat, holding his breath. Then he realized he was inside a putrisomn boat at a vortex on the Plane, and hiding inside the boat at this point was useless. He shot himself up, ready to spring into action. It was the living shadow of a wolf, wandering the ridge in the waking world. "Fuuuck," Jesse sighed out with terrified relief. Another wolf's shadow tramped through the snow, catching up to the first one. Their paws left tracks in the snow as they edged along a nearby thick patch of trees. They kept moving down the ridge, completely unaware of Jesse's presence there on the Plane.

Jesse rubbed his eyes and saw the stone's shadow was just barely about to reach the first mark. He set himself up in front of the boat and gathered some rocks, trying his best to avoid the snow, and prepared his materials for the summoning incantation. After breaking them down into glowing purple and green putrisomn, Jesse was set up and ready. "Alright, 'Sef. Let's go." He waited, facing the north and keeping his eyes above the distant ridgeline for Yusef's signal. Then he waited some more.

The stone's shadow was well past the first mark and was almost touching the second mark. "Come on, 'Sef!" He waited to see the signal soar through the air, to hear a distant pop or explosion like a firework. He just heard the howling of the wind in his ears, and the constant buzz of the Plane. Rumbling like distant thunder. Again, louder than usual. He looked at the mark, which was now touching the shadow. Jesse shook his head. "Damn it, 'Sef."

Another rumble, but it sounded close. *An earthquake?* He looked at the shadow to see if it shook. Instead another shadow shot from across the snow, a large spot. It was large against the moonlight but shrank, as if flying down from the sky. He recognized its shape in the split seconds as it zeroed in on the vortex and its big shadow took over the stone. He turned around as it landed on the boat and crushed it into splinters, a rounded blue light shining amidst the wreckage. Jesse dove for cover. Shards of the boat flew everywhere like daggers.

He scrambled up and seeing the destruction of the boat and what stood in front of him, he also acknowledged the destruction of his mission. His eyes carefully scanned the slats in Lazavik's armor and confirmed Baronova was inside. She used the mecha to unravel her whip with one giant arm and reached over Lazavik's shoulder with the other, pulling out her shield. "There are no wraiths here to save you this time, *hooy morzhovyy*!" Anna Baronova bellowed from inside Lazavik.

Jesse reached for the purified putrisomn he had been waiting to use for the incantation. He would have no safety in performing a teleportation ritual while Baronova was here, and even with the boat, he stood little chance of outrunning her on a leyline. He was sure she used her mecha for traversing leylines as well. And at this point, Yusef had probably been made or bailed out. Jesse was on his own, with nowhere else to go.

He moved his hands quickly and angrily. The putrisomn separated in front of him. One chunk flattened out and formed into a crude shield as the wind whistled through its arm fittings. The other chunk stretched out, becoming pointed and thin with a gripped hand guard at the opposite end. He put his left arm through the floating shield and grabbed the shortsword with his right. With his shielded left arm he pulled his hoodie back, then he twirled his sword and settled into a guard stance. "Let's do this, puta."

His dark poncho whipped in the wind as he kept his eyes on Lazavik's feet. Its blue eye flashed bright and Jesse brought his shield up to cover his vision while peaking out from under it to look at Lazavik's feet. They remained in place but he saw Lazavik's left shin and knee straighten up and then bend again. He lunged forward and to the right, keeping his shield up while he shoulder-rolled into the snow and closed the distance.

A deafening whip-snap from behind clapped at his ears and he felt the shockwave reverberate in his shield. The blinding light stayed on him. Under the shield he spied Lazavik's feet pivoting. Then its rear foot backed up a little bit and he saw its weight go on it. He kept taking steps to the left flank of Lazavik and prepared to jump up as high as he could. As if clearing a high jump hurdle, Jesse threw his weight up and flattened out. He heard the violently fast whoosh of the whip just underneath him. Kicking his feet up and over his head while in midair, Jesse flipped backward and landed crouched in the snow. He instantly somersaulted to the side, again closing the distance as another whip strike landed next to him and splashed snow and dirt everywhere.

Yelling angrily, he pushed off the ground and shield-bashed against Lazavik's shield, immediately pivoting and striking at Lazavik's left arm with his sword. Lazavik countered and adjusted its balance, barely blocking his strike with the edge of its shield.

Baronova grunted from inside the mecha and while still gripping her whip, punched at Jesse. He dodged it and sidestepped to her right, striking at her exposed right leg. It connected and a coin-sized chunk of armor chipped off. She laughed. Then she swung her shield across at Jesse and he jumped back to clear its giant swing.

Now Jesse was back at square one. Lazavik twirled the whip in the air, and Jesse panted. "Pinche puta."

I'm outmatched. What the fuck do I do now? Another whip strike came in and Jesse dodged it, but the following thunderclap left a ringing in his head. *Fuck! I can't get through this armor. I have to get this sword in between that grating and stab the bitch.*

The whip snapped again above Jesse, and it jarred him. Lazavik quickly followed with a low, side-swiping whip toss. Jesse stepped forward and lifted his feet high under his body like he was playing jump rope, barely clearing it. Lazavik immediately came back around again a little bit higher and Jesse ducked down and charged forward. His shield dropped for a second and Lazavik's eye blinded him.

He heard the mecha shift in the snow to the side. There was a split second of silence and Jesse braced his shield. The whip snapped and crashed against his shield, popping his left eardrum and numbing his left arm. He felt ice on the side of his face and remembered he was still holding a sword, but he couldn't lift it.

There was cackling laughter. "Ahahaha! That was cute. Not as exciting as last night, but still pleasuring." Lazavik walked to Jesse where he lay. "Any time I can crush a pathetic American dog is pleasuring. I really like it when they are dirty dogs, like you. The ones that *think* they are Americans, ahahaha!"

Jesse started moving and realized he was lying on his sword underneath him. He began to scramble. Jesse had a split second's flash in his mind of sitting in his old living room in his underwear on a hot summer day. Papá sat behind him on the coach, a beer dangled from his hand as he watched in silence. Little Jesse was planted in front of the television and his eyes were glued to the roadrunner eating seeds in the middle of a road. A dot of a shadow appeared next to it and grew in size. High above him the coyote looked down from a cliff and was watching a giant grand piano, tied to a giant anvil, tied to a giant boulder plummeting down toward the roadrunner.

The pain was sudden and then numbed out into heavy throbs. He heard multiple snaps and cracks and yelled out. He looked down at his legs and saw Lazavik's shield, bordered in blue and fluorescent pink, had buried them in the snow. His head swiveled and he felt like he was being tossed and pulled down a drain.

"No you don't!" Baronova griped as Lazavik threw the shield aside. It reached down to flick snow onto Jesse's face. "You're not going anywhere. I need to see inside that disgusting little head of yours."

Jesse's eyes fluttered. More snow got tossed on him and he felt it on his neck and slipping down his back, riling him. Lazavik holstered its whip and scooped Jesse's body up and held him with both of its hands. His mangled legs dangled and grazed the snow as droplets of blood began to paint it red. Blood also streamed from his left ear, and only one arm band remained on his lifeless, left forearm with only a small chunk of the splintered shield remaining on it. His right hand was caught in his sword's handguard. Even if he had the will to lift his sword, Lazavik's grip was tight around his upper arms.

Lazavik's chest opened down and Anna Baronova stepped out. She inspected Jesse and spat on his face. "Now I have to come up with name for you, my new pet." She ripped the velcro off her white driver's gloves. Jesse took this moment's distraction and lifted his sword with his wrist and drove it toward Baronova's body. She had nowhere to go. Swaying her hips, she dodged the desperate strike and then snapped a quick jab at Jesse's nose, whipping his head backward. The sword fell from his hand and landed flat in the snow. More blood flowed from Jesse, now from his nose. Baronova reached out her hands to grip his head on both sides. Her right hand became bloodied. "Ugh. Disgusting." She brought her face in close to his. "You disgust me!"

Jesse tried to move beyond the pain and think. He couldn't give up and leave the Plane; that would expose a trail back to his den. His mind and willpower was already critically weak, but that was the only place left he had to fight. Before he could brace himself, he already felt her penetrating his psyche and swimming in his mind.

He knew what she was looking for. Why he was there. Who he was with. He had to protect-- no, he had to change his thinking. She was there, in his thoughts. *I have to protect my secret. She can't get to it.* He tried splitting his thinking somehow, putting an inner voice at his forefront and thinking ahead somewhere in the back of his mind, without words. *Protect my secret. Guard it.* He thought of something that would catch her attention, something he legitimately wanted to keep secret. Anything to keep her away from the information she was really after. He dug it deep, encasing it and dropping it into an ocean of his subconscious.

Everything turned upside down. Water fell into the sky. Baronova's colossal hands appeared from the abyss of his mind like a leviathan. She cupped the water as Jesse's secret plopped into her grasp. She smashed its encasing with a slap from her other hand. Jesse's voice screamed from the sky below, "Noooo!"

The clank of empty glass bottles echoed, and angry yelling followed it.

A younger Jesse searched, but he was surrounded by darkness and strange voices. A giant concrete building loomed behind him and he turned to face it. His lungs felt solid and his chest felt like exploding. He needed to get away from the gray and windowless edifice. Other familiar voices called out to him.

"You can't run."

"You need to be the man now, Jesse."

"You're fucked."

"Mamá!"

"... day. And a new future!"

He stumbled into the garage, kicking over a box of empty beer bottles. The clanking on the cement floor was dulled in his ears and he didn't realize he had knocked them over until he was already past them, still stumbling along to Papá's Impala. Middle school-Jesse took another hit from his pen before trading it in his pocket with the keys. His phone chirped. Unlocking the car and climbing inside, he took out his phone and tapped. "Yeah, yeah. I'm coming to get you, heina. Fuck." He carefully closed the car door and tapped the garage door remote attached to the visor. An old photo of his mother was clipped next to it, forever youthful and beautiful in his mind.

Tapping the breaks and adjusting his seat as the car crept in reverse out of the garage, Jesse struggled to get to a comfortable height. He had only done this once before, also when Papá was drunk and his older brothers weren't home. He was in the driveway and squinted to find the remote again above his head. After groping for a bit the garage door closed. Jesse made his way down to the dark street and successfully backed out. Groping for the shift to first gear, Jesse pressed the gas but the car didn't move. It rolled backward, toward the cars parked on the side of the street. "Shiiiiiit," he slowly mumbled and covered his eyes from blinding headlights down the street. The gear shift fumbled while the car revved loudly. Jesse never lifted his foot off the petal.

He blinked. The yelling was annoying and he just wanted it to stop. And the asphalt hurt. His pants were torn at the knee and there was blood. Papá was drunk and arguing with the neighbors. A police car arrived. He heard the officer call for backup as he stood from his opened door, surveying the scene. The silhouette of the officer was set against his blue and red lights. Jesse blinked and Papá was telling the officer that he was taking full responsibility. The officer said something about a DUI and wanted to see papers. The neighbors yelled and pointed at Jesse. Papá barked back at them angrily and slurred his words. "... No witnesses!"

A car pulled up and stopped in the street behind the Impala. Junior and Erik ran to Jesse and leaned down to ask if he was okay. They didn't bother asking what had happened. They looked at each other and already knew. More blue and red lights arrived. They looked over and saw Papá getting cuffed. Junior looked at Erik. "Got my back, Hermano?" Erik gave a confident nod.

The two brothers started yelling aggressively as they approached the arresting officer. The cop was asking about Papá's citizenship status and papers. Erik yelled at Papá trying to talk sense into him, he was being an idiot. Junior yelled at the policeman to stop, he was being an idiot. Junior was almost in the officer's face, as the cop used his hands to apprehend a handcuffed Papá.

More yelling behind the new blue and red lights. Junior screamed as he was tased and hit the floor. Bystanders booed. Erik let out a roar and charged at the second officer. The tasing stopped and there was a struggle between Erik and the officer, silhouetted by blue and red. Bystanders screamed.

A gunshot rang out, echoing off into time. More screaming and people ran. "Nooooo!" Junior bellowed. He tried getting up, but the first officer was tackling him back down. Papá had collapsed on the street, sitting upright as he stared at Erik's body slumped face down on the street, a pool of blood surrounding him.

Enraged, Junior punched the officer's face, screaming the entire time. Papá whimpered, "Nooo." The red and blue lights reflected off his glossy eyes and tears streamed down his face.

Jesse blinked and he was beside the cracked open rear window of a squad car. Papá stared out somewhere past Jesse. "You need to be the man now, Jesse."

Another blink and Jesse stood outside a Mexican prison, next to Lita and beside her little Alfredo and Marcy holding each other's hands in the hot sun. He was frozen in place, staring at the gray, windowless building. Deported, a stranger in his birth country, and convicted, Jesse knew how likely it was that he would never see Papá again alive or as a free man.

He wasn't able to bring himself to see Junior back home, either, who was locked up with maximum sentences for multiple misdemeanors and felonies from that night, ranging from interfering with a police investigation to assaulting a police officer. He was just about to turn eighteen during the month of the incident, so he was tried as an adult. Jesse didn't want to acknowledge that Junior probably didn't want to see him, either.

"Ah-Hahahaha!" Baronova's cackle echoed inside Jesse's mind. "The real men in your family protected you and looked out for each other, to their own doom. And you, you disgusting dog, just sat there and caused it all. Ah-hahahah! So pathetic."

The limpness and throbbing pain returned to the forefront of Jesse's mind, along with the biting wind. He heard a mechanical trill from the side of the ridge. Baronova's hands were off Jesse's head and she was looking off to the side with a look of surprise.

Next to the treeline, a bronze golem had trekked up the ridge. It was almost like an insect, with six barbed limbs and a head that had two pairs of red eyes in a V-shape. It produced a trill again, flashing its red eyes in an upward pattern. It reminded Jesse of emergency exit lights.

"*Chto*?" Baronova blurted out, her brow furrowed. "*Seychas*?"

The golem made another trill and continued to flash its lights in a hurried pattern, and waited.

"No time to waste, dog," Baronova muttered to Jesse.

"Fuuhhh…" Jesse forced out painfully. "You."

She reached out her hands again to Jesse's head with an annoyed but determined look.

A green and blue flash erupted from the trees behind the golem. Jesse turned to see along with Baronova. The golem's eyes all turned red and wide then it turned around to the dense treeline right behind it. Earth groaned and churned as if something were being rejected by its bowels. Trees splintered in an explosion and pine needles flew everywhere, like an enormous dandelion puff being blown. Two giant, slimy tentacles shot out and grabbed the golem, lifting it off the ground. It used its sharpened limbs to cut and slice at the tentacles. A deep, cavernous howl erupted and trees shifted. An enormous amber and brown eye set in tree bark, half covered in drooping vine and surrounded with blotches of moss, emerged amidst the trees. The warm scent of decayed fish and manure invaded Jesse's nostrils and throat. He tried not to throw up or pass out.

A tree trunk stepped out of the tree line. A massive, heavy arm bent and shaped like wood with patches of wet scales swung at the golem, still held aloft by one tentacle. Uselessly, it tried to block the blow. The arm smashed it again and again. The golem's red eyes eventually shattered or popped out of its head. The tentacle then flung it against the other trees repeatedly and a few of the barbed limbs snapped off. Finally, it slammed the golem into the snow and then the beast lifted its tree trunk of a leg and crushed the golem, a chunk of its body flying off and down the ridge. Its dented and smashed head popped off and skipped across the snow in the other direction, clinking against the foot of Lazavik.

Baronova's eyes were wide. She stepped backward without taking her eyes off the beast and sat back into Lazavik, closing its chest. Jesse fell into the snow as Lazavik picked up its shield and whip.

The beast let out a terrifying bellow, rooted from rage and somewhere deep and ancient. It trudged forward through the snow, fully emerging from the treeline. It was a hulky mass of barked wood and stray branches, intermixed with slimy and fleshy scaled hunks of body parts. One limb looked like it couldn't decide whether to be a leg or a massive, fish-like tail. Slimy, dark vines or tentacles protruded from under and behind it.

Returning the battle cry, Baronova yelled and charged Lazavik forward. Jesse couldn't see from where he lay, but out of his good ear he heard roars, the thunderclaps of Lazavik's whip, the slaps of the beast's tentacles, the stomping of its trunks. Then something caught his eye. Pieces of the smashed boat moved. They began to come back together and mend. "The fuck?" Jesse whispered.

His sword floated up and drifted away, opposite the battle. Jesse watched as a young-looking black man, somewhere in his late twenties or so, snuck up the ridge and willed the sword toward him. He reached out and weaved it, extending the sword out into a fine, flat tip: a spear. The man grabbed the spear from the air and hustled over to Jesse, placing his index finger over his own lips with his eyebrows stretched up high. Whispering through the wind and over the hellish sounds of the fight, he asked Jesse, "If I can push you toward Canyons of the Ancients, can you make it the rest of the way?"

Jesse nodded. The man willed a last large chunk of broken boat over to them and laid it next to Jesse. Then he pushed Jesse onto it, using the wreckage as a stretcher. The man guided the stretcher over to the half-destroyed boat and held Jesse on it. Jesse grunted and moaned. He was rolled into the boat as the man mended this last piece of wreckage into place.

Behind them, the beast gave a deafening shriek. The man looked back with concern. He was about to turn and leave when Jesse grabbed his arm. "Who are you?"

"My name is Aron." He looked back behind him to check on the battle as another thunderclap echoed and a shriek followed. "Ebisu! Shit, I gotta take this bitch out. Good luck." Aron shoved the boat into the leyline and extended his arm out to send it on its voyage. His eyes grew big as he remembered something. "And don't tr--"

Baronova's barbed whip snapped around Aron and yanked him back. His spear in one hand, he still extended his free hand at the boat and forced it forward with his willpower, even as Baronova pulled him away. The dilapidated boat shot in the opposite direction along the leyline and down the backside of the ridge, back to Canyons of the Ancients. Jesse caught a glimpse of a bloodied and uniform-torn Baronova next to her crumpled and broken mecha reeling Aron into her as he sailed quickly off the ridge and out of view.

Jesse XXXI
The Black King in Check

Panic struck: he couldn't move his legs. Jesse tried to kick wildly and he felt them. Looking down, he saw that they were wrapped tightly in his blanket. He moved his right arm to untangle himself, then shook his left arm and reached his ear to check for blood. Everything was fine.

Glancing over in the gray morning light, he saw that Alfredo and Marcy were still sleeping. He sat up and unplugged his phone. Multiple notifications were waiting for him.

10:52 PM Friday, February 14

maria fonseca: omg, so high rnnn

maria fonseca: where are u? we needd apic dengit. hungry

11:19 PM

maria fonseca: got a fuckin burgr we gettin kikked out tho, lol

Still laying in bed, Jesse scrolled the rest of his notifications and then opened his social media apps to search for any other messages from Maria, clearing most of his notifications in the process. There was nothing. He swiped through her feed and saw short clips of her getting ready, then footage burned white by her camera's flash while dancing on the crowded dancefloor; posing in the bathroom mirror, more dancing, tons of pics and tags with other people on the dancefloor and other spots in the classy-looking venue; that *fucking* guy again, who Jesse didn't even recognize. Next was her yelling and singing out the window of a speeding car, laughing with a guy driving and another guy in the passenger, and Erika laughing next to her in the back seat. Then a bright, white fluorescent clip in a fast-food restaurant filled with giggling and slowly stuffing food in each other's faces, apparently unable to avoid it. Finally, her arms pushing open the doors to the restaurant, laughing terribly along with the two guys and Erika with a text graphic that read, "guess we dun for the night lol".

He laid his arms down flat on the bed with his phone still in his hand, and he stared at the ceiling. *What the* fuck*? Why do I feel farther away from her now than I did six months ago? I just fought a fucking mech piloted by the toughest, meanest bitch I never knew possible. AND outsmarted her in my head. I think. Why can't I out-maneuver Maria? This -- whatever this is with her -- doesn't feel real. Is she trying me on for size? Or just using me? She's already replacing me. And I'm just letting her. Am I the next fucking Moises? How does Maria have so much power and control over me?* He hung on that thought. *Does she, though? I fucking fought Anna Baronova -- twice! And I'd do it again. Could I do all that shit on the Plane if I didn't have this sense of control with Maria? Have I just been so cocky -- or delusional?*

Another notification was from a new contact on Dolen, an app for encrypted and secure messaging that he had already been using with Yusef. The awaiting message was from "RunToRuin." His breath held hoping it was Maria.

8:12 AM Saturday, February 15

RunToRuin: Jesse, this is Dali. Things really went south over here. Don't contact me anywhere else. Got rid of my phone. It looks like I'll be taking an extended trip. Meet me back on the Plane where we last saw each other there, in exactly two months. That should give me enough time. Things are going to get crazy. I messed up, bad. I'm such an idiot. Don't tell anyone you've heard from me. Don't respond to this message. Just send me a thumbs-up two weeks before we meet. BE CAREFUL.

It was awkward not to reply, especially when she sounded like she was in trouble and he really wanted to know more. Jesse shook his head. "Can't be crazier than my night," he muttered to himself. Still on Dolen, Jesse opened up Yusef's message.

7:54 AM Saturday, February 15

sef: It was a trap. I barely managed to escape. We do not have much time. We will need to get away for a little while. I fear we now have become the hunted. Pack your belongings, enough for a few days. Fortunately, President's Day on Monday can afford us an additional day. Meet at Davidson Park at 10:00 AM. We shall briefly discuss our plan at my apartment before we head out.

Christ, I thought I had a bad night. This Aron guy really saved my neck. I've got to figure all this out. Jesse looked at the time: 9:35 AM. He shook his head. *On my way to the park.*

He was about to get up in a rush but he decided to check another notification that was nagging at him: a personal email from a new contact. Jesse left for the kitchen while looking through his inbox for this message. There were so many news bulletins and spam emails, not to mention the clutter of his mind at the moment. He was also trying to figure out how to ask Dominique to watch the kids for the next few days. There wasn't a single good excuse, and he clearly couldn't tell her the truth.

He heard a kid's show on the television, as well as Dominique moving around in the kitchen. There was too much to figure out right now and all he wanted was some clarity and peace of mind with Maria. Jesse flipped back to Maria's message trying to figure out how to respond as he sat on the opposite end of the couch from Alexia, who was engrossed in watching a cartoon.

"Good morning, Jesse. Thanks again for covering last night. I'm really sorry. I'll make it up to you, I promise. I'll start with some eggs for breakfast. It's gotta be fast, though. I have to go back to work."

"Uh, thanks. Yeah, it's all good. It was fine. I uh, needed to get some sleep, anyway." Jesse's gut twisted with anticipation on how to explain that he was running away for a few days, but he couldn't figure out if Maria's messages and her feed were making him more anxious.

The bustling and smell of eggs and chorizo woke up Alfredo and Marcy in no time. They ran out and jumped on the couch with Jesse and Alexia, almost immediately fighting for the remote and what to watch while little Alexia cheered them on and started jumping on the couch cushion. Antonio, in his playpen, also started yelling in excitement. Jesse aimlessly tried to calm them as he stared at the messages on his phone. He shook his head and decided he wasn't going to figure out this reply to Maria at that very moment. The nagging in his gut raged on as his mind wandered back to his situation with Yusef. "Shit."

"Ooooo, Jesse said a bad word!" Marcy teased, pausing the battle for the remote. Alexia, still on the couch and trying to stare ahead wide-eyed, continued to pretend like nothing was happening right next to her.

Alfredo joined in. "That means we can say it!"

"Yay!" Marcy agreed.

Shutting his eyes in frustration and shaking his head, Jesse said aloud, "Why do we keep making more of you?" He left for the bedroom.

"Bye, Shitface!"

"Smell you later, Shitbreath!"

"That's enough!" Dominique yelled from the kitchen. "If Alexia starts that, I'll make sure the both of you aren't even able to speak anymore."

Alfredo swiped the remote from Marcy's hand and they both leaned back into the couch, eyes forward, and pretended like nothing just happened.

Jesse grabbed his backpack and was trying to decide what to prioritize: his clothes for a certain amount of days or his folders and textbooks. He decided that the circumstances were unique, and maybe it was okay to miss homework this weekend. After all, he had come from all failing grades last semester to straight As by December. He felt indomitable. So he packed his bag with clothes and toiletries. He brushed his teeth and rinsed his face. *What about the little ones?*

He picked up his phone and replied to Yusef.

9:52 AM Saturday, February 15

Imma be a little late. Trying to figure out what to do with Fredo and Marcy.

sef: Hurry.

As he finished packing and zipped up his bags, he stared at the watch on his wrist. He still saw it as Yusef's. For the last few weeks when he was selling and trading things for food and bills, he had hoped it wouldn't come to this. But he always knew it would. Jesse also knew what he had to do now, what he would tell Dominique and how messed up it was of him. But he didn't really have any other choice, and after all, it really was the most believable excuse.

He walked back out to the living room in a rush and headed for the front door. "I'll be right back. 'Fredo and Marcy, be good. Listen to Dominique. And stop cussin'!"

"You first!" Marcy shot back.

"Don't be long! Your breakfast is almost ready and I have to leave soon."

Ten minutes later, he returned. Jesse was shaking the cold off with some deep exhales as he went straight to his room. He yanked out the two wadded twenty-dollar bills from his pocket and tossed them on his bed, next to his bags. Opening his wallet, he stared at forty dollars and hesitated to take any of it out. Finally, he took a ten dollar bill from his wallet and added it to the two other bills on his bed. He rubbed the soft spot on his wrist where the watch had been. It still left imprints of where the straps were. They had an odd design that left a squiggly pattern on his skin.

His backpack was already on and he gripped his gym bag in one hand and the money in his other when he came back out to the living room.

"Jesse, your breakf--" she stopped when she looked up and saw him. "What... where are you going?"

Jesse's face scrunched to one side as he prepared himself. He kept his eyes away from Alfredo and Marcy as he walked to the kitchen counter and swapped the cash for the egg and chorizo burrito that awaited him. Looking at Dominique directly in the eyes, he said, "I fucked up again. There's uh.... There's some guys that want to fuck me up." An image of him punching Raymond flashed before his eyes. "I took something from one of them." Maria walking with him to their classes. "I can't stay here." Racha skating somewhere, plotting his revenge against Jesse. "I gotta leave for a few days."

Dominique stared at him, stunned. "You can't. You're not serious. And right now? Jesse, I have to go to work. Who's going to watch these kids?"

"Should you? That flu already knocked out your work. You gonna bring it here, too." Jesse walked back to the living room and bit his burrito in his mouth while he used both hands to bring his gym bag's strap over his head and onto the neck of his shoulder.

"Jesse!"

"I got to, Dominique. I don't want any of them coming here and fuckin wit' y'all." He finally looked over to Alfredo and Marcy who were trying their best to pretend like they weren't listening. "This is the best I can do right now to protect you. This is my problem, not yours. I'm gonna come back. I promise. I wouldn't leave y'all like that." Alfredo and Marcy were staring back at Jesse now. "Look. None of y'all can say you saw me today. You were sleeping and I was already gone. You understand? That's important. You even have to go ask around and pretend to not know."

"But, Jesse," Dominique interrupted. "Where *are* you going?"

"I don't know yet. And if I did I wouldn't tell y'all. For your own good." Jesse crouched down to Alfredo and Marcy. "I'm serious. You can't slip up if anyone asks. I'm gonna come back. it's just a few days. But you aren't supposed to know that either. You got it?"

They both nodded.

Jesse looked at Alfredo in the eyes. "You're the man now, 'Fredo." His brother stared back with wide eyes. "Don't fuck it up." He rustled Marcy's scalp and tossed her hair around. "Keep him out of trouble, okay?" Then he stood and went for the door.

"Jesse," Dominique said. "Thank you for the money. Be careful."

He nodded and closed the door behind him.

On his hurried march to Davidson Park, Jesse was able to listen to a daily news podcast that automatically started downloading every morning. The lead story was about the flu and early scientific estimates about how much it had been spread the night before for Valentine's Day. There was an interesting bit of facts on just how much bacteria gets swapped from kissing.

Protests against the SENTRII Act and the Stand Your Ground law that were organized in various cities across the country today were already expected to be contentious, but were now anticipating even larger crowds. A police report had been released yesterday, summarizing an incident weeks ago about an unarmed black woman who was killed by a SWAT team in her own home in the middle of the night while sleeping. Apparently, the police had entered the wrong home.

Polar winds were sweeping into the Midwest and were creating yet another record-breaking winter for low temperatures and snowfall.

And lastly, there was a breaking and ongoing story concerning the emergency hospitalization of an unnamed politician in Washington, D.C. Paramedics were called to the scene, but information was still unclear.

He shook his head. Yusef and him weren't doing enough. Jesse was eager to hear what Yusef had managed to discover, and how Baronova being at Tilson's den was connected to other things he had yet to learn about. And this trap: Yusef said Tilson probably wasn't a Reader, so who set this trap? Whose weird golem was that? Just what in the hell was that monster? And who was Aron and why did he help him? Yusef had a lot of explaining to do.

Jesse passed by an elementary school and hopped onto its Wi-Fi. His phone pinged: a new message from Maria.

10:16 AM Saturday, February 15

Maria Fonseca: heyy, when r u bringing me that vday gift u promised? 🤨

Immediately, Jesse tried to figure out how he could buy more time from Yusef. And more time to write a poem, or run to the store. Or both. He opened his wallet and thought about how much money he might be needing for the next few days, to who knows where.

Then he saw the marks on his wrists from Yusef's watch, just barely there now. He thought about the money he left behind for Dominique and the kids. *What if they ever knew that I could have left more and instead I spent it on Maria?* He dropped his arms as he kept walking. *Was she worth that watch? And for what? What could I possibly get her with thirty bucks that would make her happy enough to ignore all the other dudes out there? Even then, how long would it last?*

He brought his phone back up and started strategizing a curt response about how he was leaving for a few days. Then he thought about how it probably wouldn't matter, and she would be in some guy's car tonight, and maybe a different one tomorrow night, no matter what he wrote. He would never be enough for her right now. She would never be satisfied.

A wave of sadness swept over him, flushed with anger. He felt like such a fool. He was angry toward Maria. Angry at everyone who had gotten in his way. Angry at everything that made his life the way it was. He should have been at her level; he should have been beyond. After all of that work, he still felt like such an ant to her. *You're a fucking joke. And everyone knows it. Everyone always saw you for what you are. You're just barely in on the joke--it's you!*

Laughter thrust out of him, like vomit. He calmed to a chuckle. *All of that struggle and growth? A total waste. You didn't get her, you didn't defeat any bad guys. You didn't' save the fucking day. You're a loser. Just how everyone knew you always would be. And here you thought you were a hero. Everyone called you a hero!*

Cackling came out of his throat. He stopped walking and hunched over, leaning on his knees, laughing uncontrollably. *Oh, I'm such a loser! I should have listened to Racha on that first day of school. And everyone else who warned me and made fun of me. They all knew! And I was the idiot. They're all laughing at me now.*

A realization that he wasn't angry at Maria, or Racha, or anyone else settled in. His laughing suddenly changed to a whimper. He hated himself. He hated himself for being so foolish and naive. Tears fell from his blurred eyes and he quickly wiped them away. He hated himself for always being an idiot, and always making things in his life -- and things in the lives around him -- so much worse.

He took one last look at her message, then blocked her as a contact. He opened his social media apps and did the same across them all.

Davidson Park was on the other side of the elementary school. When he rounded the campus to the park side, he saw Yusef standing and waiting far off at the other end. His phone pinged. It was a breaking news notification: Representative Tilson was dead. Murdered. In his own Washington, D.C. apartment. Jesse's jaw actually dropped. Details were extremely limited. He thought about the protests today, and how angry the counter-protestors were going to be and how many more of them were going to come out all over the country. Did he and Yusef fail completely now? Were they too late to prevent a great conflict? It looked like the country was ready to tear itself apart.

How can I worry about Maria at a time like this? Jesse was attempting to bolster his recent decision. He already wanted to go back and check her feeds. He sighed and instead searched for more information regarding Tilson, but he lost his Wi-Fi connection.

"Did you hear?" Jesse asked as he hustled up to Yusef, who was already turning to the parking lot. "About Tilson. He's dead!" Jesse exclaimed, not wanting Yusef to ruin the shock of the moment.

"Yes, yes. I saw. Terrible, Mubtadi. Just terrible."

"What do you mean? This is good in the long-run, right? He was one of the bad guys."

"I would not wish for our political leaders to be murdered. No matter how much I disagree with them. It is barbaric and detrimental to a functioning democratic republic, held up not only by laws, but by a society that agrees to follow them. Such mindless barbarism will only lead to more chaos."

They reached Yusef's modest car and got in. Jesse plopped his bags in the backseat and sat up front with Yusef. "Today is going to get crazy, right?" Jesse asked.

"Mushiiyat Allah," Yusef said under his breath.

"Huh?"

"God protect us," Yusef said after he backed up and drove out of the parking lot. They headed to his apartment, which was downtown. "I must apologize to you, Mubtadi. They were waiting for me. Were you discovered as well?"

"'Discovered'? 'Sef, I got my ass handed to me by that bitch, Baronova."

"Tell me everything. Spare no details."

Jesse was scolded after Yusef inquired about him nearly falling asleep in the boat, and he made Jesse confess to taking Nyquil the night before. Yusef let the lecture slide so he could hear the rest of the story. When Jesse got to the part about being rescued by Aron and a tree monster, Jesse stopped himself to ask questions.

"Aron Franklin," Yusef sighed. "One of the most promising apprentices I ever had. He was the one I mentioned before, who had reached out to me last year." There was a moment's pause as Yusef appeared to refocus on the road. "I am... relieved to hear that he is okay."

They passed another park, one of the bigger parks in the city, where there were lots of people with signs and, backpacks, huddling in small groups within the stretched crowd.

"Well, he didn't look like he was going to be okay last I saw him." Jesse finished explaining how he had crawled out of the boat and performed his teleportation ritual from the ground at the vortex in Canyons of the Ancients. Then a flurry of questions followed, about the golem, about Aron, Baronova, about where Yusef was the entire time.

Yusef pulled into a parking garage and raised his hand. "Alright, Mubtadi. Yes, I will explain. Let us continue once we are in my apartment. I do not want any stray ears listening in."

"Ugh. Fine." Jesse grabbed his bags from the backseat.

"You can leave them there. We will come back and leave shortly."

"Psh. You clearly never lived in the hood, 'Sef. They coming with me."

"Very well. Come along." Jesse followed Yusef out of the garage and through a tight canyon of tall stylish apartments, three stories tall. Small balconies jutted out among the white-framed windows. They walked up a staircase to the second floor. "Here we are. Welcome." Yusef unlocked his door and opened his arm, allowing Jesse in first.

The apartment was minimal and clean. Wide open with no walls separating the bedroom. There was simple, cheap-looking furniture, a workspace in the corner with a laptop. A basic television. No wall decorations, but the kitchen looked busy with what looked like a science experiment: a massive collection of unlabeled, half-filled bottles and tiny jars in a rack that he spotted over the bar counter that separated the living room. A solitary barstool stood at the bar counter. There were a few cardboard boxes Jesse saw sitting in the bedroom by Yusef's closet, which was partially hidden by a dividing wall that Jesse assumed led to the bathroom since there weren't any hallways. There was just a sliding glass door, covered with blinds, that went out to one of the small patio-balconies he saw from outside. This was not at all what Jesse expected. "Uh, nice place."

"Thank you," Yusef replied as he walked in and locked the door behind him.

"Hey, where's your remote? I want to check the news really fast. See if there's more info on Tilson." Jesse dropped his bags by the door and spotted the TV remote on a small table next to the small couch and sat down.

Yusef didn't bother with a response. He walked over to his worktable in the corner and grabbed a rolled up poster, then walked back across to his closet. "I will get us ready. But we cannot waste much time. You did make sure not to tell anyone about our retreat, or leave any clues or hints behind. Right? No messages to your friends?"

"How do I…?" Jesse fiddled with the remote and the TV finally beeped on. "Got it. Yeah! I mean, no! I just made up something vague and told Dominique I had to get away on my own for a few days. That really sucked." Jesse yelled from the couch as he flipped loud channels for news.

"Excellent," Yusef said, almost to himself. He reached deep into the closet to grab something else and walked over to the kitchen-side of the bar counter, awkwardly reaching over the stove to unroll the poster. It was actually a map. He set things down and aside to make room and placed a few items on the corners to keep it flat. "Mubtadi, please. Come along now." He raised his voice over the TV.

"He's dead," Jesse said from the middle of the living room; his eyes were unblinking as he stared at the television. "Erik Peters. He was killed early this morning. In his hotel room." He waited for a reaction from Yusef, but there was silence. He turned around and saw him staring back without any surprise in his face. "Where *were* you last night, 'Sef?"

His brow furrowed. His silence was magnified by the ongoing reporting blaring from the TV. "Jesse, we do not have much time. Come here, please. You need to see the plan."

"No. Not until you tell me what happened last night. I already told you everything I saw. What about you? Why is Peters dead?"

"Do not be ridiculous, Mubtadi. You should not insinuate such things. We need each other now, more than ever. I was with you last night."

"For part of it."

"Come here. I will show you on the map where I was and what happened. Then you will see where we need to be tonight."

He and Yusef stared at each other for a long moment. Jesse looked back at his bags on the floor next to the door. Then he looked back at Yusef standing in the kitchen behind the bar counter, with one arm out inviting him to the map. "Please, Jesse. We have come so far. We cannot let it all fall apart now. Please."

Rolling his eyes, Jesse walked over to the bar counter. "Fine. But don't dumb this shit down. I want to know everything."

"Sit." Yusef had one finger pointed on the map. "You see that small town, there? Telluride?"

"You making that shit up? No."

"Look closer. It is there."

Jesse squinted and brought his head closer to the map. He heard a muted, metallic crunching sound from behind him. He whipped around and saw the doorknob turning. In panic, he looked back at Yusef. Behind the counter, he saw that Yusef held something like a short stick in his other hand, dark and heavy-looking.

The front door swung open and a blonde woman rushed in. Her clothes, jacket, and gloves were dark and her eye shadow was a magenta pink. Following her a gloved, tall white man with blonde hair and icy blue eyes locked the door behind them. He placed thin utensils that looked like dental tools into a jacket pocket and pulled out a black dagger. Baronova reached into her jacket and pulled out a thick, black handle. She flicked her wrist -- *chk-chk-chk* -- and the handle extended into a baton.

Jesse XXXII
Pyrrhic Victory

Yusef charged forward from the kitchen. "Jesse, run!" he yelled. When he passed the counter there was a *chk-chk-chk* and he swung a cumbersome-looking black baton at Baronova. She blocked it with her baton and Yusef immediately turned his body and brought his baton toward the man with the icy blue eyes, who dodged it and stepped back in toward Yusef with his dagger, which barely sliced only air. Yusef brought his baton up to block a blow from Baronova.

Jesse grabbed the barstool and launched it at her. "Bitch! Let's go!"

Baronova tried to move out of the way and had to block the chair with her forearm as it thudded on the carpeted floor. The TV set crashed over sideways onto the floor but still blared out the news. Her attention was now on Jesse.

He reached over the counter and grabbed one of the bottles in the kitchen. He flung it at Baronova. Odorous liquid that reminded him of lawnmowers and go-karts spilled out from the thick, capless bottle as soon as he brought it over the counter. It trailed out as Baronova used her baton like a baseball bat to bunt it down. Jesse quickly turned to grab another one.

Out of the corner of his eye, he saw Yusef continuing to struggle with the man, coming very close to being stabbed. He spotted a red slice across one of Yusef's wrists. "Go!" Yusef yelled at Jesse.

Jesse heard a whirring and high-pitched tone coming from the baton Yusef held. Jesse grabbed a bottle by the neck and smashed the other end against the marble counter. More oily liquid exploded everywhere along with bits of glass. Baronova's baton began to whir and made a high-pitched, fading tone.

They scowled into each other's eyes as Jesse closed the distance, holding out the broken bottle in a fighting stance. Baronova stepped in and swung down at Jesse's head. He barely dodged and dived in with his bottle shank. She swerved her hips, just like she did on the Plane the night before. Jesse hadn't learned his lesson. Her baton came crashing down. Jesse flinched and caught the blow partially on his head though most of it went into the top of his left shoulder. He fell to one knee and swung his bottle again. It grazed her shin and tore her jeans, revealing freshly torn flesh, and blood dripped onto the white carpet.

Baronova blurted something in Russian while she brought her baton back for another swing. Jesse lifted his arm in defense. The baton crashed into his forearm and then into his head. There was an immediate crackling noise and he felt his toes stretch and curl. There was nothing in his hands but he felt like he was gripping gravity itself. His body convulsed as it helplessly fell sideways to the ground. The electrocution from the baton continued as his head hit the carpeted floor and his perspective was now even with the sideways television that had been knocked over.

The news was displaying two smiling portraits, side-by-side, of Representative Tilson and Erik Peters. Jesse lost consciousness as he watched digitized American flags wave next to them both with a black ribboned chyron below, captioned with "Remembering Our Proud American Voices."

The rumble and muted clanking of glass, like a refrigerator being shut, echoed in his mind. His father stood in the kitchen, with one hand keeping the refrigerator door open and the other holding a brown bottle of cervéza. Jesse watched Papá stare into the open fridge and Jesse said hello, but Papá kept staring, like he didn't hear him.

He ran over to jump into his arms. The fridge was a building now, dark and gray with covered slits for windows. The clank of glass bottles echoed. Angry yelling reverberated in his ears.

The giant concrete building loomed behind him and he turned to face it. His lungs felt solid and his chest felt like exploding. Other voices called out, familiar and foreign. He wanted to run.

"... day. And a new future!" Jesse opened his eyes. The newscast featured Representative Tilson finishing up one of his fiery speeches.

"Alright," the Asian anchor said. "We're now taking you, live to Washington, where the Secret Service and federal police have now arrived on scene to control the growing and sudden unrest happening there." Jesse heard scuffling and yelling from behind him.

The broadcast switched to live footage of masked police in riot gear rushing out of trucks and vans. They formed lines in the wide street, shields brought up into a wall. People stood on the sidewalks, holding signs that read, "RIP Tilson," "For Peters!" "We Won't Let Them Win," "Tilson Forever," and more. They cheered on the police as they advanced on the street toward a mob down the block, who were wearing face coverings. Some sat in the street. Some yelled at the police and others began backing away. The camera crew was too far to see in detail the handmade signs and banners they had. The crowd also held umbrellas and in the distance held up flags of various designs.

The female anchor's stern voiceover went on, "And of course, we can only wonder what kind of extra added danger these protestors are bringing to themselves and those around them with the risk of this flu that is sending so many people to the hospital."

Another rumble and shake from the kitchen with the sound of clanking and things falling over from inside the refrigerator. Jesse was still prone on the floor, chest down. He slowly and painfully turned his head to see Yusef's baton next to small puddles of blood in the carpet which smeared and trailed to the kitchen. His cheek rested near the smelly oil from Yusef's bottles. Baronova stood between Jesse and the kitchen, feet away with her back to him as she watched.

Behind the bar counter, the blonde man with the icy blue eyes stood in the kitchen, looking down aggressively. Yusef's legs peeked out from behind the counter, one foot solidly set against the bottom of the refrigerator. He was also on the ground. "You pathetic, dirty, old fool!" the man yelled down and spat.

Baronova said something in Russian.

"Niet. He will talk. Break one of the boy's arms." Jesse couldn't place his accent. At best, he knew it was European.

Baronova replied back in Russian.

The man glanced around the kitchen and tossed her a dishtowel.

She caught it and turned to Jesse. He quickly closed his eyes again, pretending to be asleep. He felt her steps get close to him. She lifted his head and brought the towel around his mouth and tied it tightly behind his head as she muttered something in Russian.

"Please," Yusef croaked from the kitchen floor. "He is just a boy."

"Then tell us who your operatives are in D.C.," Icy Blue Eyes said.

"I told you, I have no idea what you mean."

"Fine. The hard way then." Jesse heard ruffling and the rattle of small things in plastic. A small plastic item was aggressively set against a counter.

Baronova said something else in Russian.

"I don't really care how the Dowager wants things done right now. Things are kind of fucked right now, haven't you noticed?"

She replied back.

"She will have to wait, then. This is *your* mess I had to come over and clean up, don't you forget. And if that wasn't enough, you need to go talk to Xuannu."

Baronova was quiet. He felt her place one knee in the gap between his legs, close to his groin, and her other foot stepped near his left arm, which was stretched out. She reached down and picked it up. One hand grabbed his wrist and the other was pressed on his tricep. He had seconds before his elbow was snapped.

Jesse bent his left knee and clamped his calf into the pit of his right knee, hooking Baronova's upper right leg in his thighs. He swayed and twisted his hips to the right and brought his right arm across the carpet around his head. Baronova's center of gravity was swept away. Her hand still gripped Jesse's left wrist as she fell over to the right. Jesse used the momentum to swing his right arm up as he twisted his body to the left and around back to the right. The combined momentum swung his body as she fell over Jesse to the floor. Jesse, still being gripped by his left wrist, brought his right fist over and crashed it into Baronova's face at the same time the back of her head crashed into the television set.

She blurted and grabbed her face as blood sprayed out. Jesse scrambled to Yusef's baton. He crawled over to it, grabbed it, and stood up to face Baronova, who was already getting back onto her feet. His head felt heavy and his left shoulder was stiff. Blood streamed down from Baronova's nose and she looked pissed. She reached into her jacket and flicked out her baton, *chk-chk-chk*.

Jesse didn't give her a chance to charge it up. He moved to attack.

"I wouldn't do that if I were you," the man bellowed from the kitchen. He held Yusef in front of him, his knife set against his throat. Jesse saw blood as a large spot, as smudges, and in trailing streaks along Yusef's clothes. His face was battered. A bloodied kitchen mallet lay on the kitchen counter. Yusef stared back at Jesse without fear. "Drop it," the white man ordered.

A loud bash came from the door. A second one with wood splintering. Then a foot crashed the door open. A black man rushed in, brandishing a knife.

"Aron?" Jesse exclaimed with shock.

"Don't you fucking move, Sjöberg," Aron warned with a pointed finger to the kitchen. Then he turned his attention directly in front of him. "We got unfinished business," he said to Anna.

She reached behind her waist with her off-hand and unsheathed a knife. She invited him forward with it.

Jesse turned back to Sjöberg, the man with the icy blue eyes, and gripped his baton with both hands as he began stepping toward him and Yusef. Behind him he heard grunting and shuffling, an occasional crash. "Don't come any closer," Sjöberg said and pressed the knife into Yusef's neck. A trickle of fresh blood flowed.

Yusef's elbow thrust back and his other arm shot up to grab Sjöberg's knife-hand. "Jesse, go! Run!"

He heard Aron yell out in pain behind him. Yusef wrestled with Sjöberg as the white man quickly regained leverage over him. Jesse turned and saw Aron gripping Baronova's knife-hand as she tried to stab it into his chest from behind him. Aron's knife was on the floor and blood streamed from one of his arms. His bloodied right hand tried to stretch out Baronova's other arm away from him, which held the baton crackling with electricity, closer and closer to his face.

"Leave him! Go!" Yusef stammered as he brought both hands against Sjöberg's knife arm, freeing up Sjöberg to start punching Yusef in the kidney.

Jesse took a giant, jumping step back and swung the baton into the back of Baronova's skull. She went partially limp but still stood. Aron freed himself and picked up his knife. Jesse clicked a button on a wired attachment to the hilt of the baton. There was a whir and high-pitched tone. He bashed the baton into Baronova's back. He didn't need to try very hard to keep it there. The electrical charge flowing into her body almost made it stick.

Baronova fell over and her crackling baton hit the soiled carpet, right next to the bottle that Jesse had flung at her before. There was a loud pop and a blue spark. Then the soaked carpet erupted into a giant flame, Baronova lying unconscious right in it. The flame shot like a line across the trail of oiled carpet back to the bar counter and jumped on top of it, creating a small explosion amidst the puddles of liquid Jesse had smashed earlier. The bottles next to the counter exploded, followed by a wash of flame.

Still fighting, Sjöberg and Yusef fell to the floor as Sjöberg freed his knife and brought it down. They disappeared behind the bar counter as flames jumped across the kitchen. Fire caught and spread across the carpet and onto the cheap furniture.

Jesse stepped toward the kitchen but Aron grabbed his arm from behind. "It's too late, man. We gotta go!"

Black smoke was visible and Jesse started coughing uncontrollably. He looked down and saw Baronova's clothes burning and her hair singeing. The smell was terrible. He tried to go for Yusef again but Aron grabbed him tighter amidst more coughing. "We can't be seen here, man. This is the way it is. We gotta go!"

The couch caught fire and now heavy black smoke streamed up and gathered at the ceiling. "'Sef!" Jesse yelled. Tears, both smoke-filled and drenched in anguish, flowed from Jesse's eyes. "'Sef! I'm sorry!"

There was still a struggle happening behind the counter. Legs kicked and thrashed. The refrigerator crashed again and teetered.

"I'm sorry," Jesse's voice broke and whimpered out, crying. Aron pulled him back to the door, but Jesse's free arm was still outstretched to the kitchen. Hungry flames ate the furniture and carpet, filling the apartment with smoke that rushed against the ceiling and raced to find escape. The television continued to blare out reports from protests. Loud bangs and pops from tear gas grenades and flashbangs shot from the television. "'Sefff!" he screamed and coughed. Black smoke pushed out to the hallway and a fire alarm blared into their ears as they struggled against each other to the doorway.

Jesse XXXIII
We Were Playing the Wrong Game

Aron pulled him out of the apartment, coughing. Down the hall a few doors were opening and heads came popping out. Jesse pulled forward back into the apartment. "Wait! My bags." Aron jumped back in with him, both of them ducking low. Jesse set the baton down and put on his backpack.

Opening up Jesse's gym bag, Aron quickly rifled through it. He found some t-shirts and tossed one to Jesse. Aron tore another, wrapping a part around his face and the other around his bloodied arm. "Come on, quick!" he ordered in a muffled voice.

Jesse nodded. He grabbed the baton and collapsed it by slamming it into the ground, then placed it into his gym bag. After zipping it up he painfully brought the strap over his shoulder. Crouching out into the doorway, he tied the shirt over his face and gave one last look into the apartment as he left. The kitchen was out of view and the flames were everywhere.

They made their way through the apartment complex along with the evacuating residents, flashing lights and alarms blaring. Aron constantly looked back. "My car is this way," Aron said as he led Jesse out to the street. He stopped to look behind them. A giant plume of black smoke rolled into the sky.

"Why do you keep doing that?" Distant sirens drew near.

"We gotta make sure we're not being followed. Didn't Yusef teach you anything?" Aron walked a bit more down the crowding sidewalk to a slightly beat-up blue car and slipped a key into the door.

"Nice ride," Jesse monotoned with a sniffle from the passenger side. He rubbed away some watery snot from his nose.

Aron twisted the key and all the doors unlocked with a collective click. "Oh, and does your whip do that?"

"I don't got one." Jesse said, looking down and opening his door.

"Exactly," Aron replied, getting into the car. "Throw your shit in the back and don't complain. I just saved your ass back there."

"Who the fuck are you?" Jesse asked, as he pulled his extra shirt down off his face.

Turning the ignition, hip-hop music blasted from the speakers. Aron pulled down his make-shift mask and reached his bloodied hand over to Jesse. He saw it, then used his mask to wipe the blood. Then he stuck his hand out again. "Aron Franklin," he said. "Ranger. Former and disgraced apprentice to Yusef Abdel, defender of the Republic, sworn enemy of the Apostles."

Jesse shook his hand. "Jesse. Ramirez. I don't understand anything you just fucking said."

Aron put the car in drive and checked over his shoulder before pulling into the street. "That old man didn't teach you shit." He stopped himself and pressed the brakes. "Hold up. You got a phone?"

"Yeh."

"Can I make a call?"

"It doesn't have service. It's not on a network or anything."

"It's chill. Let me see it. I got ways."

Curious, Jesse fetched his phone from his jean pocket and handed it to Aron.

"Unlock it for me?"

Jesse swiped his code and handed it back. Aron took it and started swiping. Jesse sat up and leaned over to see what he was doing.

"Why are you in my settings?"

Aron kept swiping and tapping. "There." The phone made a jingle Jesse had never heard before and the screen went blank. Then he flipped the phone over and opened the casing.

"'Ey. What the fuck?"

With the casing opened, Aron pulled out the memory and SIM cards. He snapped them both in his fingers.

Jesse's eyes went wide. "Bro! What the fuck!"

Aron grabbed a water bottle while he rolled down the window. He stuck his hand out and dropped the broken cards onto the street. Then he took the bottle and poured water on them.

"Bruhhh."

Aron handed the phone back to Jesse. "You haven't realized it yet. You can't go home and hide." Releasing the brake, Aron checked to merge and accelerated onto the street. "Any way we can be tracked, we gonna be tracked. We're dealing with the shadiest, most powerful alliance of organizations in the world. I ain't getting made because you wanna try to get nudes from your hoes."

"Wait. You mean the Apostles?"

Chuckling, Aron confirmed. "Yeah, my man. 'Powerful organizations' and secret societies jog your memory a bit? Guess you're the weakest link, not Yusef." He cleared his throat. "I'm sorry, by the way. That… that was a fucked up way to go."

Jesse lowered his head and then glanced out the window. He remained silent.

"The man went out fighting, though. Took down a few of his mortal enemies with him. Can't ask for a prouder death than that," Aron went on, continuing to drive along the busy street as an ambulance wailed its sirens past them on the other side of the road.

Jesse still remained silent.

"Look," Aron said. "Obviously, Yusef looked out for you. Probably brought you up out of nothing when you didn't have a hope in the world. And helped you become something you never thought possible. Gave you power, and more importantly, purpose."

Still avoiding him, Jesse was turned away to the window and he wiped a tear from his eye.

"But did you ever stop to ask yourself why?"

There was a pause as Aron let Jesse turn this question over in his mind. Jesse sniffled and finally turned to Aron. "Why what?" Jesse asked, almost annoyedly.

"Why you?"

Jesse pressed his memory to the beginning. "I chose him."

Nodding his head with pursed lips, Aron let Jesse's words linger. Then he took his eyes off the road for a brief moment and looked over at Jesse. "Did you, though?"

Jesse remembered the summer heat. He saw Yusef's watch on his wrist glimmer in the sun as he ran down the street. "A perfect target," Jesse repeated. He continued replaying from his memory. *You could not be more correct. But not for the right reason.*

Yusef had sighed. *It is not about the watch.*

And I know about the prison with no windows.

"What the fuck are you talking about? Like you can read me like a book or some shit?"

"Huh?" Aron asked.

Jesse looked out the window and saw a helicopter flying low. "Ghetto birds are out."

Aron squinted. "Yeah. Shit's hit the fan."

Looking at his wrist instinctively, Jesse quickly remembered he sold Jesse's watch. He had wanted to examine underneath, at the squiggly impressments the watch band had made on his skin. Marks it left. A sigil. He had a sigil on him since the first day he met Yusef. "He read me like a book. Because he wrote it." Jesse remembered the first dream that Yusef took him through. Yusef showed him future versions of himself that all catered to Jesse's insecurities and desires: graduating with honors, making his family proud, having Maria dote all over him. He remembered how Yusef let him feel in control by being pushed off the rooftop. "He created these… instincts or desires in me."

"Impulses."

"Yeh," Jesse agreed. "He chose me. But why?" Outside, people on the sidewalks were carrying signs or sticks of sorts. Some wore masks. He saw a few people tagging on walls and windows.

"Now you're asking the right questions, my man."

Jesse was about to go on but stopped himself. "Why are you here? Why did you show up last night? What's… what the fuck is going on with everything? I don't understand."

"Sounds like that's the first time you've actually ever asked that. And actually wanted to know." Aron let the silence sit. He pulled over calmly as police sirens wailed from behind them and then the squad cars raced past them up the street. He continued driving on.

Jesse was quiet again. "Where are you taking me?"

Aron took an onramp to the interstate west. "We gotta go. We can't stay here."

"Why? Baronova and that other guy are toast."

He looked over his shoulder and in the mirrors to merge onto the freeway. "Bruh. The old man really had you in the dark, didn't he?"

"What the fuck you talking about?"

"Nicolas Sjöberg ain't it, man. Anna Baronova was a pawn, like you. Maybe she a knight, at best."

"The fuck you just call me?"

Aron scoffed. "Huh. Sorry, man. You just a pawn. Like I was." He scanned the mirrors again. "Hey, bro. I know you got a lot of questions and all. But I think we're gonna have a lot of time to talk this shit out. But right now, I need you to make sure we don't have a shadow."

Jesse was lost in his thoughts, swept away in questions and loose ends. Assumptions and falsehoods. Emotions tossed back and forth like pebbles caught in the tide, rolling back and forth on the sand. "Huh?"

"A tail, dude. Make sure we're not bein' followed."

Jesse stared at him.

"Psh. Just keep an eye on the cars behind us. All of them. Especially the ones kinda far. Look for anyone on a phone or talking into something."

Jesse rolled his eyes at Aron. "You shitting me? 'Anyone on the phone'? I be watching everyone, then."

"If that's what you gotta do." He drove on speechless for only a little bit until Aron reached over and switched the radio over to public broadcasting. A live report was going out from the protests in D.C. The anchor cut to another correspondent reporting from New York City where protestors were clashing with police.

"We fucked up," Jesse muttered.

Aron nodded.

"What did you mean when you said I was a pawn?"

"Yusef taught you how to play chess, right?"

"Uhh… kinda."

"You never learned it?"

"I mean, he might have shown me a few times."

"You weren't paying attention, were you?"

"That shit was complicated! So many rules!"

Aron shook his head. "He really chose a good one this time."

"What you mean?"

"What was it? His leverage? What did he use to convince you to join him? You needed to help a family member? You got yourself into trouble and he was your last chance?"

Jesse was quiet.

"Don't be embarrassed, man. It's hard times. They happen to everyone."

Jesse pursed his lips and scrunched up his chin.

"That bad, huh? Did you fucking kill someone?"

"No! A girl! It was a girl, alright? I really liked her. A lot."

Aron took a moment. "You're here -- all this shit is happening around us -- because of a *girl*?"

Another report discussed an anonymous source from the Justice Department stating that the new flu virus was genetically engineered out of a Chinese city where the flu allegedly originated.

"Well, I did get in trouble before."

"Yeah, no shit. I bet you did."

Jesse raised an annoyed eyebrow at Aron. "And I did have a family member in trouble after I agreed to train."

"Yeah. But you said it was about a girl."

Nodding slowly, Jesse said, "Yeh."

"So? Did you get her? Did the magic happen?"

Jesse shook his head and looked down at his feet. "Nah."

"Then why you still here?"

Jesse thought. "My abuela was taken. By ICE. I gotta stop all this shit and make things right."

"I'm sorry, man. That's gotta be tough."

"Who-- what side are you on? Were you friends with Yusef or not? Where are we *going*?"

"Years ago, I was Yusef's apprentice. He taught me almost everything I know."

The news went on, now transitioning to a report from the Centers for Disease Control and Prevention, advising everyone to begin wearing masks immediately and to self-isolate in their homes. Aron and Jesse looked at each other. They shrugged.

"But when I really began to understand his value set, and where he was coming from, and what his ultimate goals really were, I asked questions. Hard ones," Aron continued.

The radio broadcast switched to a report coming in from Portland, Oregon.

"I didn't know what his plans were. But even then, I knew something was off. As benevolent as that old man might seem, there's a vendetta in him. Something as old as history. That definitely became clear when he tried to bring Sharonda into the picture. I didn't want any part in their schemes."

"Sharonda? You know her, too?"

"Yeah, man. I mean, not well. But enough to know I didn't want to fuck with her. She's got a hatchet to bury, too. Don't know what, but it's there. In her eyes. In her soul. She's on a mission. And so was Yusef."

"A militia identifying themselves as a chapter of the Proud Boys, a white-nationalist and pro-gun group," the female broadcaster continued, "fired upon a crowd of protestors in downtown, killing nine and wounding at least twenty."

Jesse buried his face in his hands. He wept and yelled, muffled and drowned by his hands and tears and snot and anger and sadness. Jesse took a deep calming inhale, and shuttered. Crying, he repented. "I failed! I fucked it up! I fucked everything up!"

Aron's eyes were wide. "Hey, man. It's chill. It's alright."

"No! It's not fucking alright! I wasted the last six months hung up on this stupid girl. I should have been focused on my training! I was playing fucking games on my phone and looking for memes. I was worried about my stupid rep. I should have been ready! I should have studied and trained harder, and faster. I should have taken these assholes down, and before they came for my Lita!" He broke down into tears again. "And 'Fredo! And Marcy!" he punched the dashboard. "They deserve better. Lita deserves better. Everything I've put her through!" He let out a terrible moan. "I fucking miss her! Where is she? What the fuck is going to happen to her?" Jesse said through tears and a contorted, wet, reddened face. "What if they come for 'Fredo and Marcy?" He was screaming now. "I won't fucking be there!"

"Jesse. You can't take on the world by yourself. No one's that powerful."

"Why the fuck not? I'll do it."

"You're angry. You're upset. You want to help your family. I get it. I want to help my family, my people, too. We need clear heads, though. We gotta figure out what to do next."

Reports continued streaming in from Los Angeles, Dallas, Minneapolis, St. Louis, Miami, Richmond, Montgomery, Albuquerque, Seattle, and on: riots, looting, arrests, shootings. Jesse used the shirt to clean his face. He sighed through a stuffy nose. Outside there were a few more plumes of smoke appearing across the city. Jesse shook his head. "We lost."

Aron shook his head now. "We were playing the wrong game."

Jesse turned off the radio and turned away, bringing up his knees to his chest and twisting his body toward the passenger door.

"Yusef never wanted to prevent this. He wanted to direct it. This -- all of this -- was going to happen, regardless. No. Matter. What." Jesse still sat motionless, save for his sniffles. "He used you, Jesse. I told him about Tilson, and Sjöberg, and Chu Tien, and The Dowager Xi Wang Mu a long time ago. I was the idiot that expected him to help me. If anything, Jesse, this is *my* fault. Not yours. You just got caught up in it."

"I only knew about Tilson," Jesse muttered. "And that was only at the end."

Aron looked over and saw Jesse's eyes were shut and tears welled up in his eyelashes. "No, man. This is just the beginning."

Jesse rubbed his eyes and looked over his shoulder to Aron.

"This civil unrest, civil war shit -- it was always going to happen. It always happens, eventually. But this was designed, decades ago. Engineered to create a slowly building tension and struggle between Americans: Left versus Right, Blue versus Red, Home versus Away, Us versus Them. A slowly draining downward spiral that would weaken our country and distract Americans -- not just from our own problems, but all the other shit outside our borders. An endless tug-of-war that trades the illusion of power between two sides that are heavily influenced by the people playing them against each other."

"But why?"

"Why weaken the strongest and most influential country on Earth? Probably because we have something *they* want. Or we can stop them from getting it. Enter Xi Wang Mu, AKA 'The Dowager': heir to some of China's first emerging international businesses. She single-handedly expanded the reach and influence of her corporations into global tech, banking, and manufacturing empires. Her influence in the Chinese Communist Party is unmatched and her financial power over other political leaders is unreal."

"So what the fuck does she want with America, then?"

"Absolutely nothing. For now. She wants it out of the way. Xi Wang Mu wants American foreign policy to benefit her as much as possible, and Americans distracted from caring. Her eyes are set on expanding her empires across west Asia and the Pacific: to capture Africa's vast resources, and to solidify her influence into Eastern Europe and Oceania. She's working with the Russians, but eventually she'll topple them, too."

Shaking his head and rolling his eyes, Jesse turned back to the window. "I just wanted to do something right for once. I wanted to be proud of myself. And have people look up to me, finally. I didn't want to get involved in any of this complicated shit."

"Jesse. This complicated shit is your fucking world. No matter how much you turn your head or fantasize about who you want to be, that world is still out there. It's not going away. And it's going to catch up with you," Aron said, waiting for a response. But there wasn't one. He let them drive on in silence.

Jesse perked back up when he smelled the sea. He saw the freeway split off into various off ramps and bridges. Huge cruise ships anchored in the harbor. Peaking over buildings and bridges, giant cranes towered in rows at the far end of the shore. "Why are we here?"

Aron took an exit that said "Harbor E - Shipping." The off ramp went in the direction of the cranes. "This is just a stop."

"Aron, I gotta get back to my brother and sister. I was only supposed to be gone for a couple of days. I ain't getting on no boat."

"Jesse, man. You still don't get it." Aron drove them across a very tall bridge that spanned across an inlet. The shipping yard was on the other side. "They came to Yusef's apartment. When I rescued you on the Plane, Baronova was already in your head. The world is coming for you."

"Huh?"

"The Apostles, bro. That's just for starters. Now you got Xi Wang Mu's attention. You fucked up her plans. She didn't want this chaos. Not yet, anyway. Yusef pushed it forward, out of her hands. He tried to break this country so he could reshape it how he wanted. But he's gone now. Who knows what the fuck Sharonda Clarke is up to. She's probably the one out in D.C. that took out Tilson. Xi Wang Mu's just got the President in her pocket now. But, haha, we know that won't do her much good," Aron said, still laughing. "Ahhh, what a clown. Homie can't even control his own tweets."

Jesse thought about Dali's message. Now he was really worried about her. But he decided to play dumb and not reveal that. "I still don't get it. Who is She… wang… moo?"

Aron's joking demeanor went away. "She makes Tilson look like a kid in a sandbox, man. Everything you know about the Apostles? She owns them, bro. They kiss her fucking feet." Aron exited the ramp and made their way to a parking garage.

As Aron reached out to take an entry ticket, Jesse read the prices on a placard. "This long term parking?"

"Yup," Aron said, tossing the ticket on the dash and entering the garage. "So…" he continued, "you can't go back home. They're gonna be waiting for you. They're gonna try to use your family as leverage against you. They're gonna fuck up your life." He drove up the levels and finally found a spot on the top floor, in the sun. "They gonna fuck up yo girl. These people don't tolerate loose ends. They've got too much at stake."

Jesse was quiet again. "They're gonna think I left them. I promised I was coming back."

"You can't tell them a goddamn thing, Jesse. This is bigger than your feelings, your reputation, or even your family. We can't leave any trace behind. We can't give them anything to use against us or to find us. Do *not* contact them. We gotta go. We got to make this right."

Jesse shut his eyes and rested his head against the window.

Aron put the car in park but left the keys in the ignition. "Look. I'm gonna trust you here. You need to trust me, so I'm gonna take the leap first." Jesse waited in silence without looking up. "You stay here. Lock the doors, keep the keys, and don't talk to anyone until I come back. I'm taking some money from my bag in the trunk, and leaving the rest with all my shit here -- with you. I am coming back. Then we are going. Together. You got me?"

Rubbing his bruising shoulder, Jesse nodded.

"A'ight. I'll be back. Fifteen minutes. Twenty, tops." He popped the trunk, took the shirt off of his wrist, and hopped out of the car, closing the door behind him. Jesse watched him through the mirrors as Aron went to the trunk for a minute, then shut it and walked away to the stairs with a jacket on, covering up his cut wrist.

The radio reports kept coming in as politicians were speaking about the wonderful work that Tilson contributed to the country, and the great contributions Erik Peters made to Americans in promoting patriotism and freedom. They spoke out against the protestors and commended the diligent work of the police in putting down the unrest, decrying the protests as downright disrespectful to the life and legacy of Representative Tilson and his surviving family members. Jesse had enough and switched to the first station that wasn't talking about the riots, the rap beef, children in cages, the election, or famines in other countries, and was just playing music.

He considered running. Making his way across cities filled with riots, brutal police, looters, and whoever was hunting him. He imagined, maybe in a day or two, coming through his front door dirty, bruised, and smelly. Marcy and Fredo would run up to him and hug him, and Dominique would look at him from the kitchen, slightly upset but overcome with relief. He'd be back at school and start flirting with other girls to make

Maria jealous.

The song on the radio was over, and the DJ began warning listeners about areas of heavy rioting and looting to avoid. He went on to talk about the kinds of masks that were advisable to get and others that weren't recommended.

There's no escaping this, Jesse thought. *He's right. I can't go back. Everything is fucked. It's my fault, and I have to fix it.* Jesse reached to shut off the radio. As he did, the DJ announced another piece of breaking news. Erik Peters had reportedly been dead for hours before the paramedics arrived on scene, suggesting his assassination happened in the middle of the night.

When he spotted Aron returning, Jesse got out of the car and went for his bags in the back. Aron jogged up a little surprised. "You good, man?"

"Hey. Did you see Yusef on the Plane at all last night?"

Aron responded with a frown. "No. I was staking out Tilson's den in Telluride. I was extra careful since the last time I got caught. That shit sucked. I'll have to tell you all 'bout that long-ass nightmare."

"You sure you couldn't have missed him?"

"No way. I had an extremely good vantage point. I followed when I saw Chi-Yu, that creepy-ass golem with the legs that Chu Tien sends around, take off to the vortex. That's when Ebisu and I attacked Chi-Yu and Baronova."

Jesse's brow furrowed and scrunched.

"You're finally putting it together."

"*He* did it. Yusef bailed on me as soon as he cleared the vortex. He left the Plane and assassinated Peters."

Aron nodded.

"And he just *left* me there. As bait."

"A distraction. He needed Peters' -- and probably Tilson's -- Readers focused on the Plane and not the waking world. He left you there for the taking, like a piece on a chessboard, while he made the big moves. But he must have been sloppy somewhere, 'cause they posted right up on y'all."

"*That's* what he was getting me ready for? All this *fucking* time?" Jesse spat out angrily.

"Where were you supposed to go with him, today?"

"He wouldn't tell me. I think he tried to explain something about

Telluride. He was trying to show me something on the ma--"

"Jesse? You alright?"

His mind went back to Yusef's other hand. He was holding his baton. That was before Baronova and Sjöberg had even broken in.

"You did save my ass back there."

Aron stared back at Jesse with the slightest look of pity.

"I wasn't making it out of that apartment today. If it wasn't those dicks that were going to get me, it was going to be Yusef."

Solemnly, Aron nodded. "You see now, why I didn't trust him?"

"Did he try to take you out, too?"

"No. I don't think so," Aron shrugged. "But I think that was always in him. You know, he's from a different generation, Jesse. And he saw so many sad, fucked up things in his life. He was too caught up with trying to win, to have all the answers and to create a vision he always thought was ideal. Like so many others in his generation, like our leaders and our mentors, they're willing to strengthen us just to use us. But when we become loose ends and put their perfect vision of their world at risk, they toss us away. But this isn't their world, anymore. And they don't have all the answers."

"And they're not always right," Jesse chimed in.

"Yeah. You know that. I'm sorry, Jesse. This is a nutty day, and I'm sorry I gotta break all this to you. Are you good? You alright?"

Jesse winced in pain as he put his backpack on and then his bag. "Yeh. I'll be fine."

Aron popped the trunk and grabbed his bags, then shut it. He kissed his fingers and then pressed them onto his car. "You served me well, Cinderella. You done good."

They raced down the stairs and Aron directed Jesse once they were past Customs, not to say anything to anyone and to pretend he didn't know English. He explained that he had to find the right Customs agent that Aron had infiltrated some time ago as preparation for a quick escape like this, but he needed more persuading, since Aron had not planned to bring Jesse before. He already knew which ship would take workers with no questions asked -- the Chinese ones. The pay was downright disgraceful. But it was pay, a ticket out, and a low profile.

Aron shook the Customs agent's hand when they reached the check-in. Jesse saw cash moved in the handshake. The agent gave a quick look, groped the folded money with his finger, and nodded. "Bon voyage!" he said.

They cleared the checkpoint and made their way across a ramp that went to nearby offices. "Now can you tell me where we're going? What the fuck we're doing?" Jesse hissed as he tugged at one of Aron's sleeves.

Aron stopped and turned toward Jesse. "There's a container ship that needs a few hands. It stops in Honolulu, then Guam, and into Hong Kong."

Jesse shook his head vehemently. "China! Are you fucking kidding me right now?"

Aron looked at him dead in the eyes. "I'm tired of being chased, Jesse. Of researching and tracking and falling into traps. I'm tired of playing their games by their rules. We're not waiting around for them to find us. We're going to take the fight to Xi Wang Mu. We're going to kick her ass. Then we'll return to liberate this shit and take our country back. We'll make it how it always should have been."

Jesse gawked at Aron. He slowly nodded his head with determination. "I still got questions. Lots of them."

"Good. I have answers," Aron replied, "You'll get them." He turned around and continued down the ramp. Jesse trailed behind. "We'll heal. We'll get stronger and keep fighting. And we'll win."

They stepped off the ramp to the office building. A giant container ship with Chinese characters loomed behind it. In the distance behind them beyond the shore, helicopters hovered over the city through plumes of smoke. "Ándale pues," Jesse said. "Let's go to work."

ACKNOWLEDGMENTS

This decade-long endeavor probably would have taken another decade without the dedicated guidance, editing, and feedback from Sarah Patterson. I've never had someone so thoughtfully and delicately examine my work with such an open mind and open heart, while still holding a hefty hammer of constructive criticism. You are amazing and I am indebted to you! Thank you, thank you, thank you!

Mum, thank you. You always have my back and you've always supported me on my quixotic quests, no matter what. Thank you for helping with Cashy and allowing me the small spurts of time to work on this book, or get in a quick workout, or to let me live a little and go to a concert, or -- gods forbid -- the rare date. I honestly don't know what I would do without you. I love you.

Abby, aside from being my biggest cheerleader, you really came in clutch for me at the endgame here. Thanks for always gassing me up and checking in on me, and pulling through on the cover. You're a real one.

Thanks to An for being the world's best co-parent. Raising a young boy isn't the easiest thing to do, but it sure has been easier than I thought because of you. Thanks for allowing me the time and headspace to tilt against my windmills.

Justin and Joanna: La Sierra holds a special place in my heart. Your hospitality is life-saving. From recuperating on your couch to being brought giant cups of coffee while I stared at my laptop screen, or chasing our little boys around the yard and waking up to an amazing breakfast, or trading old war stories about dating to judging each other on our music and TV tastes, I am so grateful for those weekend getaways. I love you guys so much.

My Spanish is embarrassingly terrible, so thank you to Rebecca Griffiths for taking the time to give me pointers and suggestions on the dialogue while your beautiful boys played with my son.

Shoutout to the amazing staff at the Night Owl, Intentional Coffee, The Continental Room, and Bootleggers for tolerating my long periods of brooding in the dark corners of your establishments. Thank you for your encouragement, your table space, and your Wi-Fi.

My students deserve a thank you and an apology. Y'all have been so encouraging and excited for me. True supporters. Some of you served as inspirations for my characters. All of you were my inspiration for this book. Thank you. But I must also acknowledge that you did not get 100% of my headspace, focus, love, and time because of this quest. I hope that what I gave you was enough and that after reading this book series you will understand the weight of this: it's the best lesson I could have prepared. Hopefully, people will still be learning from it long after I'm gone.

My friends and family deserve an apology. I've been a ghost for the last few years. Thank you for still accepting and responding to my messages, phone calls, social media shenanigans, and letters. Well, for those of you that still do, anyway.

Thanks to Jenn Aédo, for lighting a fire under my ass and inspiring me to go all-in. I hadn't fully accepted that I had to put all of myself into this until you showed me your hustle, your drive, and your passion. Thank you for helping me see life as it should be, not as it is.

With love and gratitude,
Andrew

November 25, 2020
La Mancha

Jesse and Dalisay will return in

WHAT SHADOWS MAY DREAM

DALISAY'S TORMENT

By

Andrew S. Banderas

Coming Winter 2021-2022

WWW.SHADOWDREAMBOOK.COM

www.ingramcontent.com/pod-product-compliance
Lightning Source LLC
Chambersburg PA
CBHW071544110726
47908CB00007B/1988

* 9 7 8 1 7 3 6 2 2 4 2 0 5 *